Praise for *As It Is On Earth*
2013 PEN/Hemingway Honorable Mention
for Literary Excellence in Debut Fiction

"One of the deep pleasures in reading Peter Wheelwright's gorgeous debut novel *As It Is On Earth* comes from the dizzying journey through the constellations of his protagonist's life as he attempts to untangle the Gordian knot of his family legacy. His world is messy and contradictory, saturated with desire and utterly intoxicating; it's a place where ideas about science and art and nature and history combust until secrets are laid bare. As in the best of novels, Wheelwright both broke my heart and gave me great faith in acts of forgiveness and in the tenderness of our hearts."
—Lisa Fugard, author of *Skinner's Drift*

"Unlike his character Miryam, whose photographs of absent bridges depict only the supporting embankments that connect two sides of the earth, Peter Wheelwright, in this rich and moving debut, attempts to fill in those ghostly, empty polarities of space and time that we call family history -- and, in the doing, offers up a bit of America's history, as well. Like a great bridge-builder, Wheelwright connects past and present, choices and consequences, hope and despair, fantasy and reality, all the while, like Miryam's sturdy embankments, remaining anchored firmly into the land. A masterful balancing act; a beautiful, unpretentious, elegiac novel."
—Joseph Salvatore, author of *To Assume A Pleasing Shape*

"A novel of guilt and its pointlessness...I can't think of another modern novel that melds as well the WASP experience with that of the native American."
—*The Rural Intelligence*

"With a Yankee tap root breaking through layers of granite guilt and miscegenation, Taylor Thatchers' family tree is a challenging climb. From its branches overlooking New England's old farms and old colleges, author Peter Wheelwright peers compassionately at a world inhabited by young survivors of extinct tribes and inherited griefs. Fascinating and absorbing and forgiving."

—Meryl Streep

"...lovely, meditative, and thoughtful; Wheelwright is fearless with jargon and diction...compulsively readable."

—*The Brooklyn Rail*

"Peter Wheelwright's tale is full of mystery and family transgression, anecdote and the oddest facts imaginable, a tale of despair shot through with unexpected wonder. Wheelwright's oddball cast of dreamer and alcoholic holy men, stargazers and crack mystics, naturalists and sidetracked philosophers, will linger in the readers imagination long after the last page."

—Andrea Barnet, author of *All-Night Party: The Women of Bohemian Greenwich Village and Harlem, 1913-1930*

"With great insight into his fascinating characters and the New England landscape they have inhabited for generations, Peter Wheelwright illuminates the Lives of the WASPS as they reckon with the multicultural world grown up around them. The Thatchers of Maine, their aspirations, longings, triumphs and failures, will live on in the reader's mind long after this novel is closed."

—Heidi Jon Schmidt, author of *The House on Oyster Creek*

"*As It Is On Earth* is wonderful...erudite, well written and entertaining at the same time... a richly grained context of place, time, connectivity with human foibles and a linkage to well-defined segments of humanity's accumulated body of knowledge."

—*Metropolis Magazine*

Praise for *The Door-Man*

"*The Door-Man* is a big, deep, beautiful book that ponders the mysteries of identity and existence—where we're from and what we are, and the hidden forces that bind people together and drive them apart. Peter Wheelwright has written a riveting multi-generational saga that is also a meditation on time itself—what it gives and what it takes, and ultimately, what endures."
—Catherine Chung, author of *Forgotten Country* and *The Tenth Muse*

"Like Richard Powers and Barbara Kingsolver, Peter Matthiessen Wheelwright renders the inextricable connection between natural history and human history in this beautifully layered and richly imagined novel. Wheelwright's perceptive and observant door-man, Kinsolver, is a wonderful repository of comings and goings, past and present. As much philosopher and identity sleuth as valet, he excavates the stories of three generations from their entanglement with the geologic history of upstate New York, thereby offering escape from repetition of an aberrant past. One gets the feeling that Wheelwright knows this territory in his bones!"
—Paula Closson Buck, Author of *Summer on the Cold War Planet*

"A suspenseful reflection on identity and memory, with their unsparing strangeness and dreamlike fragility, *The Door-Man* intimates that while time does not heal all, it does elicit forgiveness. Wheelwright reminds us that, like memory itself, life does not progress steadily without opposition, but occurs in unexpected leaps and bounds, seemingly random and always incomplete. A complex and thoughtful book."
—Susanna Moore, Author of *In the Cut* and *Miss Aluminum-A Memoir*

"Good fiction opens new dimensions and perspectives on our existence, and Peter Wheelwright opens many in *The Door-Man* that will be of particular interest to New Yorkers and New York Staters: the history of Central Park and of the city's water system, the emergence of the first forests 380 million years ago in the now flooded town of Gilboa; the dioramas and specimen cases of the American Museum of Natural History, the sanctum sanctorum of the planet's animal diversity; with visits to the Miccosukie people of the Everglades. All in the course of the gripping three-generation saga of an extended family that includes murder, incest, bastard siblings, and all kinds of other skeletons in the closet. A frothy bouillabaisse of narrative history and imaginative storytelling."

—Alex Shoumatoff, literary journalist, prolific author, and editor of *Dispatchesfromthevanishingworld.com*

"Starting from the political intrigue, science, and mechanics of a massive public works project—the creation of a reservoir for New York City by flooding communities in the Catskills—*The Door-Man* is, at one level, a historical fiction, vibrant with the colors and controversies of the region from the early 20th century, and on this strength alone, it would hold us. But Wheelwright's writing, so rich with detail, winds across generations and brings to life a vast array of characters—from muleskinners and paleontologists to murderers and a door man. We are swept into a swirling plot that is at once suspense story, speculative fiction, romance, and comedy. And it is more than these. Just as blasting the earth in a tiny upstate town reveals a history before history, setting in motion the quest to revive a primeval forest, Wheelwright's novel takes us deep into human motivation and beyond it, to a concept of time that dwarfs us. Like his own award-winning *As It Is On Earth,*

The Door-Man asks each of us to reflect on our place on these American lands and among the people we've variously misunderstood, loved, displaced, or forgotten."

—Derek Furr, author of *Semitones* and *Suite for Three Voices*

"Wheelwright conjures another time and world, a once-here historical intrigue as poignant as memory. Filled with insight, deft detail and wry wit, *The Door-Man* is exactly the novelistic embrace we need in our agitated bewilderment."

—John Reed, author of *Snowball's Chance*

The Door-Man

A Novel

Peter M. Wheelwright

Fomite
Burlington, VT

ISBN: 978-1-953236-47-0
Library of Congress Control Number: 2021945095

Fomite
58 Peru Street
Burlington, VT 05401
www.fomitepress.com

03/15/2022

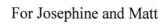

For Josephine and Matt

The Door-Man

You ask whether I shall discuss "man"...I think I shall avoid the whole subject as so surrounded with prejudices, though I fully admit that it is the highest and most interesting problem for the naturalist.

(Charles Darwin to Alfred Wallace; December 22, 1857)

Restoration of *Eospermatopteris* by Winifred Goldring.

The Lineages

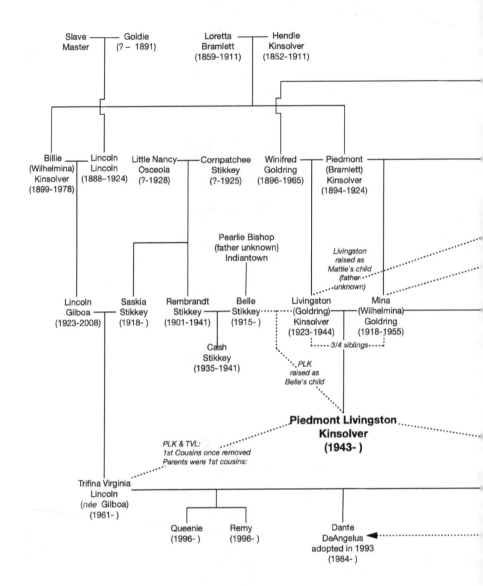

Slave Master ——— Goldie (? – 1891)

Loretta Bramlett (1859-1911) ——— Hendle Kinsolver (1852-1911)

Billie (Wilhelmina) Kinsolver (1899-1978) ——— Lincoln Lincoln (1888–1924)

Little Nancy Osceola (?-1928) ——— Cornpatchee Stikkey (?-1925)

Winifred Goldring (1896-1965) ——— Piedmont (Bramlett) Kinsolver (1894-1924)

Pearlie Bishop (father unknown) Indiantown

Livingston raised as Mattie's child (father unknown)

Lincoln Gilboa (1923-2008) ——— Saskia Stikkey (1918-)

Rembrandt Stikkey (1901-1941) ——— Belle Stikkey (1915-)

Livingston (Goldring) Kinsolver (1923-1944) ——— Mina (Wilhelmina) Goldring (1918-1955)

Cash Stikkey (1935-1941)

····3/4 siblings····

PLK raised as Belle's child

Piedmont Livingston Kinsolver (1943-)

PLK & TVL: 1st Cousins once removed Parents were 1st cousins:

Trifina Virginia Lincoln (née Gilboa) (1961-)

Queenie (1996-)   Remy (1996-)

Dante DeAngelus adopted in 1993 (1984-)

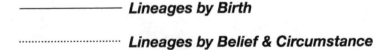

——————— *Lineages by Birth*

················· *Lineages by Belief & Circumstance*

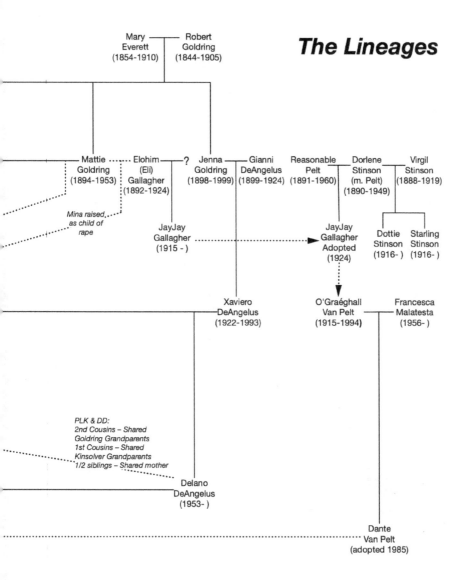

The Lineages

Mary Everett (1854-1910) ——— Robert Goldring (1844-1905)

Mattie Goldring (1894-1953) .... Elohim (Eli) Gallagher (1892-1924) ——— ? ——— Jenna Goldring (1898-1999) ——— Gianni DeAngelus (1899-1924) | Reasonable Pelt (1891-1960) | Dorlene Stinson (m. Pelt) (1890-1949) | Virgil Stinson (1888-1919)

Mina raised, as child of rape

JayJay Gallagher (1915 -) ....▶ JayJay Gallagher Adopted (1924)

Dottie Stinson (1916-)   Starling Stinson (1916-)

Xaviero DeAngelus (1922-1993)   O'Graéghall Van Pelt (1915-1994) ——— Francesca Malatesta (1956-)

PLK & DD:
2nd Cousins – Shared Goldring Grandparents
1st Cousins – Shared Kinsolver Grandparents
1/2 siblings – Shared mother

Delano DeAngelus (1953-)

Dante Van Pelt (adopted 1985)

The Witnesses:
Endurance Fuller
Gust Coykendall
Rev. Daniel Mackey
H. P. Nawn Contracting - Hugh Nawn
BWS Division Engineer Sidney Clapp
BWS Bureau Chief/Miami-Dade Sheriff Darryl Potts
Dexter and Pontrain Twincoat
Waterhouse Hawkins

IT WAS SHORTLY AFTER the peculiar discovery at the Central Park Reservoir that I began dreaming about the men in my family again. About bones.

I have been dreaming about bones in the City's drinking water in one way or another for years, but they were always at the other end of the pipeline, upstate, in the Catskill headwaters near the hamlet of Gilboa. These dream-bones, the more recent ones, feel closer to home.

Last night, another came around. The details change but, as always, the dream was made up of events without order, referring to times without duration, to places without borders,...ghosts, alive again along an impossible horizon.

I don't know how much of it might have once been real, whether one of the family men actually lived it in part, maybe passed it along as a story to the next generation, then on again. Or whether it was just a dream conjured from their dreams, taking its own spectral shape to fit a new purpose, to make its point...this time, to me.

My father's dream? His father's? What does it matter?

I do not remember my father – his stories, his dreams were told to me by my mother. And I never even met *him* – my grandfather. All I know for sure is that I was given his name, as was my father before me, and that he was the first of us on the water. His hand had touched the gold cross on the steeple, the one that had been the surveyor's benchmark – The Cross of Calvary, marking the full water line, the "Taking Line." *That* part, the Taking Line, was not a dream.

I am inclined to tell it as if the three of us were simply one person. It felt that way. A Trinity – Grandfather, Father, and myself, first person plural in one body, our resemblances and dissimilarities congealed over time. I leave it to others to judge which are which.

In the dream's embodied Threeness, *We are...I am...*lying in a boat.

My back is up against the bow, a straw hat pulled down over my face. My eyes are closed as well, putting another layer between the sun and me. It doesn't do much good; the hard white glare is shut out, but the air inside the hat is Florida swamp-shade heat. Stifling; I breathe through pursed lips.

The boat is a three-bench flat bottom johnboat, aluminum, painted army green, one of those beamy open boats that were made in the 1930's to help the boys from the Civilian Conservation Corps get over the low-water crocs and cypress snags in the Glades. The water is the color of weak coffee, the sheetflow brew of tannin, anaerobic peat, and decaying sawgrass. The Catskill Mountains in upstate New York loom in the easterly distance over Florida's Everglades – Place and Time as entangled as I am.

In the dream, despite the rising odors and turbid surface of the swamp, I drop an arm over the gunwale, trailing my hand in the tepid water. The straw hat is now floating away. I watch it drift lightly on the surface toward a low hammock in the distance where Lincoln Gilboa, his daughter Trifina, and Delano DeAngelus are watching the boat, unmoving. The three of them should not be there either.

"Aw, Jesus, Piedmont. Pick up that fucking oar, will you? Fuckin' city boys!"

It's Rembrandt Stikkey, standing up in the stern, leaning on a tall pole. He's feeling irritable, drenched in sweat, annoyed to be poling the boat along by himself. Rem's a "Local Experienced Man" out of Dade

County and often complains that a dollar-a-day from Roosevelt's Civilian Conservation Corps is poor pay for shepherding around soft-hand slicks from up North...even with the Depression going on. Stikkey is calling me out as *Piedmont*, my grandfather...but it was my father, *Livingston*, who was in the CCC under Stikkey's watch.

"Leave him be, Rem. He's looking for the Cross. He's going to save us all, yet. Be patient." It's one of the Goldring women sitting in front of Rembrandt – Winifred, my grandfather's lover. She too is part of Franklin Roosevelt's "Tree Army."

In real life, unlike her two sisters Jenna and Mattie, Winifred was said to look "mannish." But that look of hers was only a matter of style, not flesh. In the dream, she is a lovely woman...and expecting a child.

She sits still, her long skirt spread out mid-boat, wearing a colorful cloth turban and chewing on a long stem of toothache grass like a Seminole matriarch. A Black Powder Frame .45 Colt Peacemaker is tucked into her calico waistband. The waistband holds up her pregnant belly like a sling. From her aspect, one would never know she's an expert on prehistoric life,...the Devonian Period...four hundred million years ago when the first forests appeared on earth, and mankind's ancestors crawled from the shallow seas to be born forevermore on dry land.

"Be patient, Rembrandt," Winifred says again. Her words echo quietly off the water. But it is no longer Winifred who is speaking, it is another woman – my mother...the real one.

I feel a sudden overwhelming sadness, and I slide closer to the edge of the boat. My hand reaches lower into the water. Something is there; I feel it coming. The dark water breaks around my elbow. The hat has returned and sits again over my face. Raising it with our free hand, we peer squint-eyed against the sun over the gunwale. Below the surface, large indistinct shapes swell from the equally indistinct depth; they mingle with the

3

reflected clouds and druidic limbs of bald cypress clawing the hot air overhead. I sense – again, in my Family Threeness – that whatever is there, whatever lies beneath us, it was there before the flooding in 1927 and returns for each of us, each in our own Time.

But it is then, at that seemingly timeless moment, that my grandfather's fingers hook under the arms of the gold cross on the submerged steeple in the town of Gilboa, New York, and my father's fingers hook on the shoulder strap of the bibbed denim overalls, the dead five-year-old boy from Princeton Florida still in them. My fingers, try as they may, elude both grasps.

I awake with clenched fists.

The Third...

Piedmont Livingston Kinsolver III
1993, The St. Urban, New York City
"Speak to the Earth and it shall teach thee..."
(Job 12:8)

KINSOLVER.

That is how I am called.

It does not sound like my name when they greet me. It has an off-hand ring to it, as if we all know that it's not really *me* that is being greeted, rather it is our business together that is being addressed.

Most mean well. I smile and nod. They smile back. I lean away and take hold of the handle. The door swings, the light bounces off the polished brass and refracts through the glass. The reflections from Central Park sweep with it, flickering shards of impressionistic landscapes.

"Thank you, Kinsolver," they say, leaving my name at the door. I retrieve it – my surname – carrying it back in time to the Patriarchs.

I can't blame them; this is how it should be and how I want it; no further address is required. After all, they live here at The St. Urban; I am only a doorman, one of many along Central Park West. No one suspects that it is my considered choice.

Dante, the young boy from the east penthouse calls me "The Door-Man"...pulling apart the compound lexeme; no indefinite article or lowercase for him. It was the boy's downstairs neighbor, Delano DeAngelus, who put the idea in his head. Although DeAngelus has just turned forty and Dante is only nine, they're friends. Del, as he is called, is like a much older half-brother from a father's earlier marriage – a half-brother that actually gives more than a half-shit about their shared blood.

In the beginning, it was a joke between the three of us. "The Door-Man." Sometimes, I will even respond in kind by calling Dante, "The Altar-Boy"...which, in fact, is an accurate moniker for him; particularly most Sundays when he's up the street at The Church of the Immaculate Conception. But lately, there seems to be a more urgent emphasis in Dante's tone. I am not quite sure what is up with this, but neither am I inclined to ask. Not yet at least.

I am good at my job. Door-Man – my very Being coupled with a plane of glass and a set of hinges. I appreciate that in many ways I am interchangeable with the door itself, that it affords me a kind of invisibility, a way to observe comings and goings without being noticed myself.

But it's also what I like to call "The Medieval Thing" – the business of being identified by...well, by your business. Literally – what you *do* on earth rather than how you got there. Mr. Smith?...a metal worker; Thatcher?...a woven straw roofer; Baker?...yes, mincemeat pie. The medieval thing, no soul-sucking scheme of parenting surnames necessary. Even the plants growing on the earth were named for their avocations, for their work on behalf of mankind – The Doctrine of Signatures – curing our bodies, our organs, our bones. Liverwort, eyebright, skullcap, bloodroot...bleeding heart, the earth's bounty ground up in a stone crucible and applied to our flesh and credulous souls. Of course, we were all on God's Watch then. All souls belonged to Him, the only Free Will, His. Faith was Truth, modern Science was centuries away, and Our-Father-Who-Art-In-Heaven had not yet been dismissed as a "gaseous invertebrate" from Ernst Haeckel's laboratory.

When I was a younger man, I was taught quite a few things about life on earth. I am still in the grip of those lessons.

This morning, in the wake of last night's dream, I have taken up my position at the door of the St. Urban – uniform perfectly pressed, eyes forward, hands clasped behind my back, rocking ever so slightly on my feet. Like a pikeman at the portcullis, I face across the avenue into Central Park, surveying my surroundings – to the south, the turrets of the Museum of Natural History, to the east, above the trees, the sawtooth skylights of the Metropolitan Museum of Art...and to the north the great cathedral where young Dante is a server – the Church of the Immaculate Conception. Yes, the Medieval Thing. Perhaps I would have been happier then – before the Earth had revealed its true Nature, and science, art, and religion were not strangers to one another, but rather one and the same, their faint borders indistinct within a holy aesthetic alchemy.

Of course, there is no going back once one understands in the depths of their very being that nothing remains...that since the Beginning, the Earth has been ruptured and folded many times over, along with everything that has attempted to take hold on its fragile surface.

When I look into Central Park, I can't help but see all of this... the Nature of things, the wheeling of the spheres above, the changes of season and light, the landscape's deference to rain and wind, and the modest wildlife that finds a home on its temporary shape-shifting ground. Perhaps that is why I spend as much time as possible tending to the verdant humming of the Park. Tending to the door of the St. Urban behind me is secondary.

7

Today, as is typical of this time of year, the rising sun is shielded by the tall line of old dogwoods, oaks, and lindens standing sentinel along the brownstone wall separating Central Park from the City. Heavy limbs, thick with summer leaves, reach over the wall, mottling the sidewalk with shade. I note the green as I imagine my grandmother Winifred once did – the photosynthetic absorption of chlorophyll swallowing up the colors of the spectrum. All but the green. The sun and the leaves, the sun and the leaves. It begins there; she had known this well – in Ancient Nature – in the aboriginal sunlight, the slow taking up of carbon dioxide and transpiration of water, the release of oxygen molecules. And then,…The Breath of Life – the botanical explosion of forest that filled the atmosphere with air high above the Acadian Orogeny and Pangaea's lonely drift in the Panthalassic Sea. Life in the Garden – the very possibility of science, art, and religion. The very possibility of this City, of this Park,…of this witness.

A sudden tight burst of reflected sunlight fires through the trees, skipping off the surface of the Central Park Reservoir like a smooth stone. I can see only a small silver sliver of the water from my post, only what a brief parting in the leaves allows; it grabs my attention, reminding me that there was a time when Central Park was better known for its position in the space of the city than for its pride of place. It was simply a "central" park, easy to locate…and in its own center – Lake Manahatta – the city's drinking water, a reservoir filled from distant watersheds.

That is yet another history coming to an end. The Reservoir has been decommissioned, the pumps are off, valves shut, and no one is drinking its water any longer. No humans, at least. Still, if history has taught us anything, it is that each ending had its beginning; it's only a matter of how far back one goes to find it.

I shrug off the cool morning air to allow in the sun's slow warming.

Even with my back to the entrance of the St. Urban, I can sense when I'm needed. With a quick turn and smooth slide step, I time the swing of the door to ensure that Francesca Van Pelt does not have to break stride as she leaves the building.

"Au revoir, Kinsolver," Francesca says, sweetly, "Je vais au réservoir."

Francesca is actually Italian, married to a blended Gaelic Dutchman from upstate. She speaks French to remind me that she is a cosmopolitan who has had many doors from many countries opened for her. It is not difficult to imagine why this is so; she is...stately,...attractive to both men and women. She is fit – and makes a point of it – with dark hair and hazel eyes that set a Mediterranean aspect of self-assured noblesse. Today, she is wearing a pair of compression running tights. Black spandex trimmed with orange stripes. Her husband's University colors...Princeton. Colors that I, too, know well, but keep to myself.

"Shall we expect the Signore, as well?" I ask. My address of Mr. Van Pelt comes out sounding as if I am asking about her Italian gigolo. I had meant to say, "the Senator." It is the proper honorific. O'Graéghall Van Pelt is a New York State legislator from District 46, just west of Albany.

I remain expressionless and at Francesca's service, wondering whether she feels comfortable going to the Reservoir alone, given the rumors since the closing – the sightings of unusual wildlife in the water,...and the bones.

"Dear Kinsolver," Francesca shakes her head, smiling at me as if I am a child. She walks sideways past me, raising both arms to tie back her hair. "No, the Senator ran yesterday, remember?...his elevator ride with Mr. DeAngelus?"

"Of course," I respond, lowering my head as if to offer my neck. "How could I forget?"

"One day on, one day off. That's his routine," Francesca says. She pauses with a sweet indulging smile and drops a hand to a cocked hip. "And I won't be alone. I'm meeting someone at The Obelisk…L'aiguille de Cléopâtre."

In my role as the doorman at the St. Urban, I have been well-trained in the task of appearing to see nothing while seeing everything – the play of light and shadow on the sheen of stretched fabric, capturing the shape of Francesca like a second skin. Above her tilted pelvic bone, the small, centered belly button – source of her original being – triangulates with two cosseted nipples, all three embossed on black polymer.

Poor old Van Pelt, I think. *L'aiguille de Cléopâtre*, indeed.

Cleopatra's Needle is the winking misnomer for the granite obelisk from Heliopolis that stands, very erect, behind the Metropolitan Museum. It's the oldest and tallest monument in Central Park. The Senator's wife uses the French term in public, but I happen to know that she uses the English translation in private. Both with her husband and others.

Francesca uncocks her hipbone and turns away. She clocks herself with the traffic along Central Park West, waiting for an opening, then waves the back of a bejeweled hand to me as she lopes with a long easy gait across the street and into the Park.

On second thought, *fuck* Van Pelt. DeAngelus is the one in far more trouble.

It was only recently that Delano DeAngelus learned that we are related, both of us held fast in the grip of the patriarchs, the name-givers. We are cousins – at least on paper we're cousins; by blood we are even closer than that. Like me, he was conceived in the dark, in sins of omission, false histories…and like me, he, too, descends from impounded waters.

I could provide a family tree, one of those genealogical charts with floating names and dates, tied together in a spreading triangle of right angled lines. The dates – birth, marriage, death – appearing to pin each name, each person, to their fixed place in Family Time, and yet, which have an uncanny way of floating free from it altogether. His brother, your fifth cousin-twice removed, her great half-nephew, my grandfather...? Who ever considers or cares that they are one and the same person – the dead, drifting as they do through the different lineages that extend endlessly into the invisible distance of The Family of Man. The dead are always on the move. To another chart, to a different place on another tree, to another family with a different story to tell, or to believe. And the stories are always incomplete, the dead borrowed to fit them as best they can.

Yet, on any given chart, the descent from a selected ancestor downward to the slow horizontal spread of the living at the bottom warns us of what we all share – that we all have been related since the beginning of Time...and our earthly communion is brief. It is as if these family trees mimic the sedimentary layers of death settling on the ocean floor of a primordial sea. The first ancestors, single celled bacteria – cyanoplankton and coralline algae – with its budding life force spent, sinking beneath the surface of the warm Proterozoic water to join others, and others again, on the way down to the vast demersal horizon of dead sponges, invertebrate brachiopods, echinoderms, and mollusk, layers upon layer of calcium carbonate from crushed shells and bacterial silica pressed hard into the sea bottom so that the rest of us, their descendants, would have a foothold on a dry earth.

But that is just the oldest story. As I say, there are always other stories, the more urgent ones that follow whenever men and women couple up without knowing, without looking back at where they came from, or just without giving a damn.

My full name is Piedmont Livingston Kinsolver III.

I say the "Third," but I am actually the first to be called this, to be given this combination of words. I have never seen my birth certificate. It wouldn't make any difference. What matters is that my grandfather was known as Piedmont Kinsolver, and my father, as Livingston Kinsolver. I have their Christian names, I have their blood, and I am the one at the end of their line, the one left to clean up the mess.

Perhaps this sounds harsh, but I say this kindly, with understanding and affectionate resignation. I accept the consequences of deeds of other men at other places in other times. I live content with what I was given. Hindsight is a much too easily acquired skill,...and of not much use.

"Piedmont" was actually not my grandfather's birth name. He simply took it on as a description of his place in the world. It means *"at the foot of the mountains"* – his blessing and his curse. His vocation.

I had no idea that his given name was "Bramlett" – Bramlett Kinsolver – until I was in my early twenties. My mother Belle had never mentioned it, nor did any of the other women who might have known. What I did know is that my grandfather's home had been in Gilboa, New York, a small town along the Schoharie Creek where the free flow of water ran down the streams of mountain slopes. It was at a time and place before the Creek was dammed up, stilled between the stones of mountain walls ("God-damned," as my uncle-cousin Linc likes to say). Where our family home had once been nestled on the east bank of the Schoharie; it now lies beneath its waters. Like my grandfather's lost first name, Linc asks, how does one ever reclaim such a thing?

Most of what I know about the past, about where I came from, was learned in the way most people learn about accidents of nature, how over time, far away, these accidents fit together to form us in the places where we now stand. They're found in the stories of happenings – anecdotes, confessions, histories – unpredictable, unexpected, unsolicited,...discovered. Discovered, most often because they have been written down. Written down and saved, innocently, without anticipating the next accidents, at later times, that will follow on the reading. It is surely a form of natural selection when one truth carries forward, adapting to so many others.

I found my truth during my last year at University…it was a kind of graduation gift, my truth, waiting for me in an old steamer trunk in the attic of the Goldring home, just west of Albany, at Slingerlands. I had been beckoned there by my great-aunt Jenna Goldring DeAngelus.

I had not been to Slingerlands since the funeral of Jenna's oldest sister, Mattie, ten years before. That earlier visit had been memorable,... and confusing. I was too young for it. Mattie was my grandmother on my father Livingston's side...or so I had been told. My mother Belle had stayed behind in Florida for reasons that were unclear to me. She'd sent me up north with friends of the family – Linc Gilboa and his common-law-wife, Saskia Stikkey.

I remember standing at the edge of the open coffin, finding it hard to believe that Mattie Goldring's lifeless flesh could have given birth to anyone, much less to my father Livingston. Of course, having been too young to know my father before he died, birth rites had always been unclear to me. Mattie's only daughter, Wilhelmina, was also absent from the funeral. Unlike my father, she was still alive.

I was told that the reason she'd missed the funeral was because of an unusual heart condition in her newborn son, but I'd heard other talk. Grown-up talk.

"Mina" – as she was called in the family – had taken up with Jenna's son Xaviero before I was born. Their marriage had been frowned upon because they were first cousins, but matters between them seemed worse than that, something unsettled, a family secret. My mother Belle would stiffen at the mention of Mina's name. Others would change the subject. Whatever had happened was not for my ears.

At the funeral service, I was standing next to Jenna's other sister, Winifred, the middle one of the three Goldring women. I had never met this great-aunt and didn't take much notice until she took hold of my hand. I remember her from that time, tall and gentle with big sad eyes, smiling down at me and whispering that families were like rivers, flowing in separate courses toward a shared sea, always to meet again. Always, she said. Her words made little sense to me, and I never saw her again, but ten years later, back again in Slingerlands as a young man, I finally understood what she had meant.

I was sorry that I missed Winifred's funeral, but I was glad that my great-aunt had sent for me shortly after. Jenna was in her mid-sixties – now, the last of the three sisters – and living alone at the family homestead with her ten-year-old grandson, Delano. She wanted me to see what Winifred had left behind; something that had been kept for me, safe up in the attic.

The house where the Goldring girls had been born around the turning of the century had worn itself out through the years. In the attic, the steamer trunks that had belonged to Winifred Goldring, had marked the time as well. There were two, both covered in a fine dust; no one had opened them in years but, clearly, they had once seen plenty of use. Old shipping labels, cracked and puckered with water stains, still held tight between the bentwood staves and frayed leather straps. The Bay of Gaspé, Chickasaw Nation, Havana – places Winifred had traveled for her work – different worlds of climate and color. Places she loved…mostly for what could not be felt or seen on their surfaces. I have come to learn she was like that. Wherever she went, across oceans and deserts, over hard-scrabble mountains or through thick tropical forest, she would search beneath the diverse flora and fauna, beneath their different natures for what was the same – the underlying rock and fossils, forged through the Eons on fractured Supercontinents drifting across the latitudes and longitudes, geological formations indifferent to the fleeting boundaries struck by the map-makers on the earth's surface. Old things, that was what she was drawn to. Very old things.

Her fingerprints – at least, I like to think they were hers – were still visible on the dulled brass clasps when I opened one of the old Saratogas. It contained a large wooden crate about the same dimensions as the trunk itself. The crate looked fairly new, as if it had been made in more recent years to fit inside the old trunk. It had no markings other than a small, embossed metal plate screwed on to one corner. '*The New York State Museum in Albany*' was engraved on it and beneath those words were two more. Latin words. I could not translate the Linnaean binomial at the time, though they have become familiar to me since. Part of my great-aunt's specimen collection, I suspected. There was also a hasp on the crate with a heavy lock on it and no key that I could see anywhere in the trunk. Closing the lid of the Saratoga, I figured that I'd find a way to open the crate inside another time.

It was in the second trunk that I found what I was searching for – her notebooks and letters. Like the dreams they've since triggered, there was no order to them or their contents. They lay in a jumble beneath the top removable tray, as if tossed into the trunk the way one might discard something that had, finally, become useless. Each of the small graphing notebooks was bound in an abraded black leather cover with a number on it. They looked like liturgical psalters, but their gridded pages were filled with science – pencil sketches and notes on ambulacraria, ammonites, crinoids, and other long extinct invertebrates from the Cambrian Explosion that had ushered in the Paleozoic Era more than five million years ago – "The Time of Ancient Life" – long before Creation and the Songs of Israel.

I began sorting the notebooks by their number. There were eight altogether, but one seemed to be missing. Books 1 through 7 were there, as was a Book 9. But number 8, if it had existed, was not in the trunk.

It was in the fifth notebook, as I recall, that I found a letter from *The Board of Water Supply* in New York City glued to a back page. It was from J. Waldo Smith, *BWS* Chief Engineer, sent in 1921 to a Mr. Hugh Nawn of Roxbury, Massachusetts. It authorized Nawn, as the lead contractor, to halt construction of the Schoharie Dam until further notice in order to allow the investigation of a fossil discovery in the Riverside Quarry. The letter had been forwarded to The State Museum in Albany from *BWS* Division Engineer Sidney Clapp who had written in the margin: "We look forward to the arrival of the men." A slash, struck with a green pencil, cut forcefully through the word "men." It seemed like an angry mark, but it was softened by a sketch on the facing page in the notebook where she'd placed the letter. It was drawn in the same green pencil – a tall fern-like plant with curling fronds and splayed trunk like a palm tree – it was her beloved *Eospermatopteris,* The Gilboa Tree. Beneath it she'd written the words: *What love is lost is found in one born of it.* And beneath that, my initials: *PLK, son of my son.*

I dropped the book into my lap and, staring through the eaves of the attic at old memories, I could feel the weight of uncertain years fall from my shoulders.

It was then, at that moment, that I learned who I was; but it was a moment later that I learned how I came to be.

Peeking through a frayed stitch within the floral lining of the trunk's dome-topped lid, I found a letter. It was from 1955 and addressed to Winifred from her niece, Mina.

I had not heard my great-aunt on the attic steps behind me. Jenna was turned slightly, unsteady, with both of her hands gripping the stair rail for support. Ever since the drowning of her daughter-in-law in the Schoharie Reservoir shortly after Delano's birth, she had been suffering from Bell's Palsy. It made her speech difficult, and the left side of her face was lifeless. Whatever was on her mind – Winifred? Mina?...or the letter in my hand – who could say, but her look told me enough. Tears falling on half a face can still make their point.

I will try to find a proper beginning.

* 2 *

The First...

Bramlett "Piedmont" Kinsolver
1917, The Central Park, New York City
*"The waters of the hills meet in gladness,
and the world rejoices in the glory of the Lord..."*
(NY Times Front Page)

IN GLADNESS. THAT WAS how the headlines of the New York Times put it. If nothing else, they got that part dead wrong.

Bramlett Kinsolver was in New York City for the three-day festival in October of 1917 when the Catskill mountain water, drawn from the Ashokan Dam at Olivebridge a hundred miles north, was shot up against gravity out of the Central Park Reservoir and into the city's stormy skyline. Despite the forbidding weather, the city had gone ahead with the Columbus Day weekend event to celebrate its new drinking water. And the people had come; the downtown patricians mingling with the new citizens, particularly, it seemed, the Italians...Cristoforo Colombo was their man, and these recent immigrants, mostly from southern Italy, intended to make the world he "discovered" theirs as well.

On the second day of the festivities, the Reservoir was surrounded, hundreds – man, woman, and child – deep. The NYC Board of Water

Supply had a fountain installed just below the surface west of the South Gatehouse; it was hooked up to tanks of synthetic food coloring – five spouts in five different colors, each representing one of the five Boroughs from the recent confederation of New York City – Manhattan, Brooklyn, Queens, Bronx, and Staten Island. The crowds cheered wildly, watching the plumes of dyed mountain water from the distant Ashokan pool. They couldn't have cared less where the water came from, so long as it was there when they turned on their taps. The colorful spray filled the air over the south basin of "Lake Manahatta," drifted a bit in the breeze across the dividing weir, and then settled on the placid surface of the Reservoir's north basin in a blend of turbid brown foam. That was the last straw for Bramlett Kinsolver. He was still a young man then, twenty-seven, but he would be "Piedmont" Kinsolver forever after. He'd heard it said before: *Piemonte* – "*at the foot of the mountains.*"

It was two days before when "Piedmont" had left his home at the foot of the mountains. As if setting himself to the slow flow of the Catskill water coursing its way by gravity south through the new Aqueduct, Piedmont had – like the water – traveled the two days to get to the City. First by horse, following the Old Susquehanna Turnpike out of Gilboa eastward to Jefferson Heights near the river town of Catskill. Even with his late start, he took his time on this first leg of the trip. The early fall hardwood forests were making their fiery last stand, sending their food stock into rooted ground for winter. He could smell the forest's rhythm in the cool drying air. It was familiar and he wondered for how much longer it would be so.

In Jefferson Heights, he left his mount with an old friend, Samson Lockwood, who ran a livery there, and walked down to the docks in Catskill where he boarded the paddle wheeler *Half-Moon* for the slow trip down the Hudson River to the rail station in Poughkeepsie. He had missed the tide and stood on deck watching the sunset sparkling off the sheets of falling water from the western sidewheel as it pushed against the tidewaters rolling upriver from the Narrows of Lower New York Bay toward Albany.

He missed the Poughkeepsie train as well. The next day, at sunrise, after a benchnight among a group of rowdies – local boys heading off to the 27th Infantry Division for training at Camp Wadsworth in Spartansburg, South Carolina – he finally boarded the NY Central.

It was in Harlem that he disembarked and hitched his ride to Central Park in the sidecar of an Indian Scout Twin Cylinder with Erwin "Cannonball" Baker.

This last leg of his trip probably changed the course of Piedmont's life as much as that godforsaken Dam. Erwin Baker and his motorcycle had just broken a world speed record. While Piedmont had taken two days to cover a hundred and twenty miles, Cannonball hadn't needed much more to cross the entire North-American continent.

Cannonball Baker was another poor young man heading unbeknownst to his death in the Great War. Perhaps he did know something when he sold Piedmont one of his used Scouts in exchange for a leather saddlebag, an original Bowie knife that had come down from Piedmont's mother's family – the Bramlett's of Bandera, Texas – and fifty dollars in cash. For two dollars extra, Cannonball gave him a spare headlight and a horn that Piedmont had to install on the stripped-down motorcycle himself.

And so, Piedmont crossed over into the Age of Mechanical Transportation. Winifred Goldring would later tease him about fueling it with her beloved fossils. Piedmont would laugh, but he would never ride a horse again.

The rest of the Gilboa men, waiting in front of the Reservoir's South Gatehouse with their black rain slickers draped over their arms, were none too happy when Piedmont came wobbling up in backfire smoke through the crowds down Fifth Avenue. He'd missed the meeting with the Board of Water Supply Commissioner the day before, but worse, the fifty-two dollars now in Cannonball's pocket had been town money, raised in Gilboa for the trip's room and board.

Despite the holy call of the NY Times' headlines and the presence of the town's Methodist minister Reverend Daniel Mackey, none of them – Endurance Fuller, Virgil Stinson, Elohim Gallagher, or Gust Coykendall had traveled to New York City to "rejoice in the glory of the Lord." On the contrary, they were hell-bent on saving their "water of the hills"...and their town along with it.

The Catskill Aqueduct Celebration Committee had arranged the construction of a covered stage around all four sides of the South Gatehouse at the edge of the Reservoir so the dignitaries could hover over the water as they watched the fountain bursts. To the Gilboa men, the pavilion looked like something out of the Schoharie County Fair. Painted up in barber pole stripes, the red and white stage was adorned with embroidered swags of blue and gold hanging from the railings – the state colors, flapping in the increasing breeze off the water.

The old Gatehouse stood its ground stoically, its rusticated blocks of weathered gray granite indifferent to being trussed up in the frilly wooden skirt and the men in top hats and black sackcloth promenading around its hem. Centered in the rough stonework above the stage, one block of granite sat more proud than the others. Honed smooth, it held the chiseled date of '1864' marking the last time the City had celebrated here...it also marked the first time the City had taken the water from other places, from other people, and made the water its own.

Arrayed around the Gatehouse at the foot of the stage, a semi-circle of vigilant Metropolitan Police stood shoulder to shoulder. Their side-arms were holstered, their billy clubs were not. It was War Time – the Gatehouse held the five 48" mains that were now the lifeblood arteries of the five Boroughs. And, in a city of reluctantly welcomed immigrants, rumors came easy. Mostly about foreign interest in New York City's newest water supply.

Ignoring the growing wind and darkening clouds, the Mayor of New York, John Purroy Mitchel, was holding forth, waving to the crowds, and clapping his hands to the rhythms of John Phillip Sousa's marching band high-stepping in front of the arc of police, their polished brass instruments gleaming under the pewter sky.

Mayor Mitchel, too, was doomed by the upcoming fight in Europe but, that weekend, he was as lively as could be. Hundreds of children in their school sashes and choir cassocks filled the tree covered lawn between the sloped berm of the old York Hill Receiving Reservoir and the serpentine shoreline of Olmsted and Vaux's "Lake." The children were there to sing after the Mayor's speech – an unfamiliar piece of music called the *"Star-Spangled Banner"* which President Wilson had only recently proclaimed the new Anthem of the United States Military. The children had been practicing the difficult notes and tongue-twisting lyrics for months and at last were ready to show off their accomplishment. Like penned sheep, they jostled one another with excited anticipation under the admonishing eyes of their shepherding choral masters. The Scouts of America – Boys and Girls, another recent national addition – stood at disciplined attention in their uniformed ranks, proudly flanking the other unruly children with a mixture of haughty privilege and envy.

The Mayor shared the dais with the Aqueduct's Chief Engineer, J. Waldo Smith, and the four Commissioners of the Board of Water Supply. Former Mayor George B. McClellan, on leave from the U.S. Army Ordnance Department, and City Comptroller Bird Coler were there as well – the two men who'd had the idea to go into the Catskills for more water, and who'd made the tactics of "eminent domain" their most proficient skill. Pride and power held center stage.

Sousa held up his hand and silenced the music as Mayor Mitchel walked over to the large transmitter looming over the coils of black wire tied off to the stage railing. Throwing his shoulders back and his voice forward to the City, he called out in praise "the pure untainted waters of Genesis and Heaven's natural bounty restoring civilization to its proper health and destiny." His words boomed over the horn loudspeaker, echoing across the water in an odd synchrony with the thunder of the approaching storm. Leaning then into the crowd, he added, conspiratorially, "Of course, it is hard not to believe that the Lord was anything but pleased to have been helped so ably as he was by some of the Visionaries of Gotham. And speaking of one of those visionaries, let me bring forward my fellow Democrat and your former Mayor, George Brinton McClellan, the man who saw our future in a small New York river, many miles away, and *acted* in order that we might enjoy it here, on this most *present* day!...Mayor McClellan!" Mitchel stood off to the side and held an arm out to his predecessor.

Sousa's baton brought forth a short burst from "*See, the Conqu'ring Hero Comes!*" as McClellan walked over and linked arms with Mitchel. He leaned into the transmitter. "Thank you, Mayor Mitchel." McClellan turned and nodded at Mitchel, then pointed out toward the crowd. "But let's not forget the men with picks and shovels, or those who carry the brick hods. As you well know, all of you out there, the course of human events is not altered by the great deeds of history, nor by great men...but, rather, by the small daily actions of the little men."

A roar from the crowd. McClellan, pausing, stood back and swept a hand across the swell. His other hand, he placed, Napoleonic style, in the pocket of his waistcoat. "It was twelve years ago," he continued, "that State Law 724 authorized an additional supply of pure and wholesome water for the City of New York..."

A whoop and cry from down front, "The McClellan Act!...nine-teen-ohhh-fahve! Yessir! Hoorah!...that was *his* little action!" An elderly bare-headed man in the audience did a small jig, pirouetting with his hands on his hips. Laughter and another roar from the crowd.

McClellan raised a quieting hand. "Well, yes, that's quite right...and for the acquisition of lands or interests therein – for the necessary reservoirs, dams. aqueducts, filters and other appurtenances to achieve this great goal. So, we went north, and we built the great Ashokan Reservoir which today holds 123 billion gallons of water,...*our water*! And then, together, we built the great Catskill Aqueduct, to bring it here...today, into our Central Park – ninety-two miles of magnificent engineering through mountains, under rivers, across wide valleys – an engineering feat twice the distance of that little man-made stream called the Panama Canal...and twice its grandeur!" On cue, Sousa directed another short burst of *"Stars and Stripes."*

McClellan paused and grew serious. "But as I speak of the little men, there are others we need to remember as well. Those who have shared with us their farms, their industrious little mills and shops, who have allowed us into their homes and their communities. They too have joined with us in generous sacrifice, joined with us in the Brotherhood of New York men and women everywhere."

This last remark was too much for the Gilboa men.

Elohim "Eli" Gallagher was leaning with his back against the reservoir railing, scowling. His coat was open, and he had his hand on a bone-handled knife sheathed on his belt. He'd already been drinking from a muzzle-loader powder flask, filled with White Dog liquor that he'd brought on the trip. He might just as well have loaded it with real gunpowder, which, as it turned out, had indeed occurred to him back at the Schoharie. "*Brotherhood*, that's a good one," he barked, his voice cracking into a high pitch. "Tell that to the mayor who ain't up there. The dead one. There's your mule's ass." He tried to hitch his boot heel nonchalantly on to the bottom rail, but it slipped, sending him floundering forward. He spit at his footfall.

"Now, take it easy, Eli." Endurance Fuller stepped in front of Elohim Gallagher, and put his hand on the man's chest. "Best keep those thoughts to yourself...and that knife as well; you're too quick with it when you've been tipping." He looked around at the crowd. "There're clubbers everywhere, and some of them won't be in uniform."

Up on the dais, McClellan did not seem to take notice. He was looking at the sky. A slow rain had started falling. Heavy drops, widely spaced, puckering the Reservoir like small pebbles. Umbrellas began blooming from the crowd. Sousa's musicians shuffled out of formation, putting their instruments away. The waiting children choruses huddled.

"But let me finish with the words of our Chief Engineer, J. Waldo Smith, the man whose Promethean skill has parted the waters and bent the earth's will to our own." He cleared his throat, continuing in a solemn ministerial voice. "The work we set out to accomplish has been very largely completed..."

"You lyin' bastard!"

"Eli!...hush up."

"...and practically every difficulty overcome..."

"Pffff,...I wouldn't count them chickens just yet, McClellan."

"Eli...Gallagher!...c'mon, lower your voice."

"...and now, we have one last task. We have prepared for this all these years. Our friends in the Catskill Mountains have offered us one last valley, one last river."

"The Schoharie *Creek* ain't a goddamn river,...least wise, not yours, *friend!*"

There was a stirring among the police guard. Glances exchanged, waiting for orders. A few clubs slapped into the palms of their owners.

"...Some of you will continue on in this last endeavor, some of you will not. But wherever you go, far or near of field, it is my earnest wish that you carry abroad in your new associations the same spirit of truth, of loyalty, of common honesty and of regard and respect for the rights of others that you demonstrated so keenly in these, the great works of the Catskill Aqueduct."

"Mi scusi, dov'è questo fiume? Signori, theese reever, is...Where ees?'

A young immigrant, seemingly just a teenage boy, tapped Piedmont Kinsolver on the shoulder. He was wearing a worn military tunic with padded shoulder rolls and a feathered field cap. He was short, his baby-face unsettled by a ragged scar, recently healed, that ran slant-wise from the hairline on the right side of his forehead, across the bridge of his nose, to his left cheek. He looked up at Piedmont, asking his question with an imploring earnestness,...as if he had misplaced the Schoharie River himself.

Before Piedmont could answer the young man, there was a sudden concussive clap of thunder, lordly and annunciatory. The rain came. Fast, gray wind-strewn sheets, sweeping horizontally over the crowds, scattering all, helter-skelter, from the Park. The Reservoir roared back at the sky from its roiled surface, but Piedmont stood his ground, watching the young Italian turn away and run to re-join his friends. He felt an odd significance, as if something had indeed been announced. And indeed, it had. An unlikely set of paths had crossed.

Piedmont Kinsolver would later remember this moment as the first time that he'd laid eyes on Gianni DeAngelus. The next time would be the following year, when "Johnny of the Angel" came north to Gilboa to cut stone with some other boys from the Italian "Alpini" – the few mountain troops who'd survived the cruel campaigns at the Isonzo River on the Italian Front. Piedmont recognized him by the scar. There were actually two on the young man's face. On the left side of Johnny's forehead, also at the hairline, another slant-wise cut had been started, heading in the opposite direction. This cut had not quite made it to the bridge of his nose. Something,...or someone,...had stopped things before Johnny had been "crossed" out, likely for good; the raised flesh of the scars suggested the cuts had been deep.

In the racket of the storm, it was difficult to hear, but Piedmont suddenly could hear one of the Gilboa men clear enough. Eli Gallagher was laughing wildly and shouting with his arms spread, "And behold I, even I, do bring a flood of waters upon the earth....C'mon, Uncle J. J. let 'em have it!... J. J. Gallagher! Your redemption is at hand!"

Endurance Fuller had grabbed one of Eli's arms and was trying to pull him away from the Reservoir's railing. Piedmont ran to Endurance's aid, and with Mackey, Stinson, and Coykendall on his heels, they hauled Eli rapidly through the crowd toward the shelter of the evergreen trees along the carriage road that ran up the west side of the Park. Olmsted's "Winter Green Carriage Drive" was failing, thinning out, soon to give way to the planting of deciduous trees, but that day the evergreens provided enough shelter for the Gilboans.

"That was poorly considered, Eli. What the b'jesus were you think-ing?!" Piedmont was short of breath, heart pounding and angry. Virgil Stinson and Gust Coykendall paced about with hands on their hips, kick-ing at the ground. Even Reverend Mackey squatting on his haunches, was cursing quietly to himself. Only Endurance Fuller stood still, his arms folded on his chest and his back to the others, staring out at the Park.

Eli Gallagher smirked and awkwardly pulled a pistol from under his coat. It had been tucked into his belt behind his back. He was wild-eyed and challenging, looking back over Piedmont's shoulder toward the Reservoir. The gun was the last straw. Without another word, Piedmont stepped forward, grabbed it away and kicked Gallagher swiftly between the legs. The man fell face first onto Piedmont's chest, then slowly rolled off with a groan on to his side on the ground, cocked up over his groin like a dead man folded into a child's coffin.

"You have to get rid of it." Reverend Mackey stood up, and took hold of Piedmont's arm, raising the hand that held the Bulldog 32. pistol. Beads of rainwater glistened on the black gunmetal like small pearls. All the men could see the initials *"JJG"* scratched into the gun's wooden grip. "They'll know it belonged to Gaynor's assassin," Mackey said, quietly.

Piedmont nodded. "I know..." He looked down at Eli, "and they'll come after him, us along with him."

It had been seven years earlier, during the thick of the work on the Catskill Aqueduct, that Jules James Gallagher, an unemployed munici-pal worker, went to the Hoboken docks and put a bullet in the neck of McClellan's successor, Mayor William J. Gaynor. "J. J.", as the shooter was known, claimed the Mayor had "deprived him of his bread and butter." Gaynor survived the actual shooting and served the city for three more years before finally succumbing to his wound. As for J. J. Gallagher, he was sent to the New Jersey State Lunatic Asylum. His nephew, Eli

Gallagher of Conesville, NY, visited him there every month, until his uncle's death from the Asylum's unusual practice of "focal sepsis psychology." The Asylum doctors, believing that their patient's psychopathic behavior was the result of localized infections of the body, removed most of his teeth, his gall bladder, tonsils, and colon. After they went for his testicles, J. J. Gallagher used his remaining back molars to gnaw through a live electrical wire while standing, free of his guard, in the ward shower.

Eli said his uncle's only regret was that he had shot the wrong Mayor. He had been after McClellan – the Mayor who'd gone after the Catskills and the Gallagher homestead in Conesville near Gilboa.

Endurance Fuller had turned back to the group and was looming over Gallagher.

"And now you think you're going to be the man to get him? Do you, Eli? Him and Mitchel both?" Endurance asked, sardonically.

He spoke with authority, steady and forceful. A big man, bespectacled, with a barrel chest, neck beard, and the hands of a stone mason. But his real authority, at that moment, ran beyond his physical presence – Endurance had been the one to arrange the trip to New York City. He had connections here.

Despite his burly rough-hewn appearance, Endurance Worthington Fuller was as quick and smart as a whip. Known as "Endy" to his friends, he was not only the editor of *The Gilboa Monitor*, a highly respected Catskill newspaper, but he'd won the top medal in fencing during the 1896 Athens Olympics. Most importantly, at least for the matter at hand, he had also been Mayor "Max" McClellan's classmate at Princeton University ten years before the tip of his dueling sword had touched the gold. Most everyone in Gilboa respected "Endy" Fuller; Piedmont looked up to him as a son to a father.

Eli Gallagher slowly sat up and wrapped his arms around his knees, lowering his head in between them. "They were only blowin' smoke," he whimpered, "...wasted our goddam time." He raised his head, turned, and vomited a yellow stream of corn liquor into the tall grass, then unsheathed his knife and began idly jabbing it into the ground between his legs.

"You should've stayed home, Eli, you're too hot-tempered. Bad enough you brought that knife of yours, but the gun...that was way out of line," Piedmont said. He watched Eli twisting his knife blade in the dirt, "And that knife, I know you're good with it, but one day it's going to bring more trouble for you than you bargained for."

Piedmont looked back toward the Reservoir, then added, quietly, "Anyhow, we had to come down here and try; Endy did his best."

Indeed, Endurance Fuller had tried his best. His talents and standing had been sufficient enough for his old classmate to convince Mayor Mitchel, Chief Engineer J. Waldo Smith and Charles N. Chadwick, a seasoned Commissioner of The Board of Water Supply, to take a meeting with him at City Hall. But it did not go well. At the last minute, Mitchel asked that Endurance appear alone, leaving the others "hanging fire" outside the Mayor's Office in Lower Manhattan. The fact that Piedmont had arrived a day late had made no difference at all.

The night before the meeting, Endurance had dined at the Knickerbocker Club with McClellan and Gaston Drake, another Princeton classmate who was headed to Miami-Dade in Florida to start a business in lumber and fern farming. McClellan chose to stay away from Endurance's talk of moving the Schoharie Dam project away from Gilboa – maybe moving it further upstream back to Prattsville where everyone seemed to want it – or maybe shutting down the project altogether. After all, that's what the city's powerful Republican Club wanted; the whole thing was an expensive boondoggle in their eyes, New York City's water supply was topped up, "tanked 'til Judgment Day." Even without the many recent immigrants heading back to Europe for the big fight, they figured the water they already had stored in the Ashokan was endless.

But McClellan was a Democrat, and it was a done deal in his mind. At dinner, he got drunk and avoided the Dam issue, focusing instead on Drake's fern farming scheme, howling with boozy laughter at the thought of Drake becoming "sissified" as a supplier of *Plumosa* ferns to lady flower shops for their "lolly boo-*kays*." Drake, drunk as well, puffed up his chest insisting that he was first and foremost a lumber man. "Them ferns are only a side venture...Florida's thick with em." The two men ended up arm-wrestling over Hors D'age Brandy in the billiards room. Endurance, disappointed, gave in to the old boy antics and acted as referee. Both Drake and McClellan knew they could never best "Endy" in anything "manly." Back at Princeton, they'd learned never to tease him about his white fencing knickers; in a boxing ring, Endy's fists could come at you harder and faster than black Jack Johnson's.

That following morning, McClellan begged off the meeting downtown, citing a conflict of interest and the need to prepare for his speech at the Reservoir. "I feel poorly for Gilboa, Endy, I do, but New York City is too far into it now. They're going to have their water, no use kicking against the prickles, as it were."

It turned out there was no need to be concerned about the prickles. The Mayor and Commissioner Chadwick couldn't have been more pleasant, and Smith couldn't have cared less. The whole affair was nothing more than a courtesy.

Mayor Mitchel wasted the first half of the meeting glad-handing "Brother Endy Fuller," talking about his recent honorary degree from

Princeton where he'd given the Commencement Speech to the young swells who were turning in their sheepskin diplomas for woolen doughboy uniforms. He was planning to enlist as well if the mayoral election the following month did not go his way. "The Flyboys, that's the ticket for me. The Escadrilles. Maybe I'll get Brother McClellan to come along as well...and that other buddy of yours. What's his name?...Drake? Black and Orange Princeton Tigers flying our Sopwith Camels, what do you think?"

Endurance showed his patience, and finally was able to steer things toward the Dam.

He addressed Chadwick about Prattsville. Good lord, it had become a Catskill "boom town" after the news arrived that the State Conservation Commission had approved the city's choice for the Dam site three years before. The town had seen gold in the project, gold not seen since the town's founder Zaddock Pratt had clear-cut the surrounding hemlock forests and shut down his tanneries forty years earlier. Since then, Prattsville had been running on memories and little else. Furthermore, with the shortages that the Great War was sure to bring, the locals were only too happy to move out of the way of the big Dam for some steady work and the cash flow from the hundreds, no, thousands of workers who'd be coming to the Schoharie Valley. And six miles downstream, that was fine with Gilboa; they'd lose a mill or two in the reduced flow, but life essentially would go on as always. However, last year, after the BWS surveyors began setting up their tri-pods along the Manor Kill at the Falls just outside of Rev. Mackey's church, it didn't take much for everyone to realize that Prattsville was going to be bypassed. And sure enough, the City set its new sights on Gilboa. Endurance Fuller had been fighting the decision ever since.

Commissioner Chadwick said there was no turning back to Prattsville. They'd already let out the contract on the Shandaken Tunnel. Work was beginning that month; the dynamite was already on site at the Tunnel headworks set for the middle of the new Reservoir's western edge...north of Prattsville. And that meant the Dam itself could only be even further north; it was in the engineering, there was no choice – Overlook Hill in Prattsville would provide a mezzanine view of both the slow flooding of Gilboa and the hair-pin turn of a northward flowing creek as it flushed into the 18-mile Tunnel running backwards, southward, into the newly completed Ashokan Storage Reservoir. Once in that Ashokan pool, the water no longer belonged to the Hills, it belonged to the City. The Aqueduct was a sixth Borough.

Endurance persisted, showing Chadwick the affidavits that he'd collected from the utility companies. The small power plant that lit up Gilboa was irrelevant, but not the larger plants further on at Colonie and Cohoes. For years, the fast-moving Schoharie had brought its power downstream to the Mohawk River, filling the big river with its water before turning east toward the Hudson for its natural southward run into Lower New York Bay. The utilities feared the reduced flow would put their new 3-phase AC Generators out of business. The locals feared the same. Sure, they'd suffer the loss of ice cut from the creek for their winter kitchens, less water for bathing and cleaning, the fishing camps drying up along with the tourists, but the loss of their power plants, that seemed like the end of times – New York City was greeting the new century with a bright future, while upstate, homes were being rolled back to the dark ages, oil lamps and all.

Chadwick showed Endurance recently signed agreements "*regulating releases of water to protect and enhance the recreational use of the rivers and streams affected by those releases, while ensuring, and without impairing, an adequate supply of water for power production for any municipality.*" He was expecting The Cohoes Power and Light Corporation to come on board by the end of the week.

Finally, Endurance brought up the Lockwood Fossils.

It was a long shot, but it had been on his mind since the night before during McClellan and Drake's arm-wrestling. Ferns...ancient ones, from an ancient forest, *Psaronius erianus*.

Endurance Fuller was not a man of science, but he sensed there may be more at stake than the parochial interests of his small town. The evidence was scant, but sixty-five years earlier in 1862, a local minister named Samuel Lockwood – the grandfather of Piedmont's friend in Jefferson Heights who was now stabling Piedmont's horse in perpetuity – had found what appeared to be a fossilized foot of an elephant. He found it emerging from a sandstone cleft in the Manorkill creek just below his Methodist Church. With the help of his sacristan's two sons, Lockwood hauled it up the hill and stowed it behind the altar out of sight of his congregation. A man of God, he'd heard the talk of Mammoths roaming the continent before The Days of Creation, but he believed in "Noah's Sea" where all the extinctions known to man had surely occurred. For a number of days, the Reverend wrestled with his angels before finally giving in to his curiosity and sending a letter to the state paleontologist in Albany. The response he received changed life on earth for Lockwood after that – forget Creation, forget even the Mammoths, the fossil turned out to be a sandstone cast of a tree stump that had been rooted three-hundred and fifty million years *before* the Mastodons.

The abrupt thrust back in Time was altogether too much for Reverend Lockwood's imagination. He had his sacristy team place the heavy lump of sandstone up on the altar so he could walk around it and study its detail at eye-level – the lithic impressions of wrinkled bark, dead cells embossed between endless patterns of weaving rivulets and tumors on the outer cortex of a tree that had died millions of years ago. Soon the heavy brass altar cross and sacred vessels were on the floor and Lockwood was born again.

34

"Endy" Fuller was a ten-year-old choir boy when he caught the Reverend, half-naked, masturbating before the fossil in a rapturous return to the prelapsarian Garden. At the time, it had spooked him badly, seeing the Reverend with his cassock bunched up above his waist in one hand, and his cock in the other; he was awfully glad when Lockwood left the ministry and Gilboa shortly thereafter. Yet, many years later, when he was a student at Princeton, Endurance visited the state museum in Trenton and discovered that Lockwood's love affair with fossils had taken a healthier turn. Apparently, armed with a late-in-life doctorate from Rutgers in paleo-zoology and a chisel-edge rock hammer, Lockwood had gone on to discover hundreds of new fossils in the cretaceous clays off Raritan Bay in New Jersey. The museum at Trenton had most of them; one was from the Early Jurassic Period, "The Age of Dinosaurs"; it was a marine reptile with the eponymous label, *Plesiosauris lockwoodii*.

Piedmont loved Endurance's story, told it to others often. Fossils meant little to him, but clearly they meant something pretty special if they could make a man's talleywacker as hard as the rocks of ancient life. His own stiff cock among the fossils was still a few years away. Winifred Goldring was coming for him; he did not know that then.

In presenting his case to Commissioner Chadwick and Mayor Mitchel, Endurance Fuller left out Lockwood's passion at the altar, but pointed out how more "elephant feet" had continued showing up throughout Gilboa over the next forty years, in local quarries, road banks, and stream beds feeding the Schoharie. Not only was the State Museum in Albany collecting specimens of the Devonian "tree fern" stumps, but the United States Geological Survey in Washington had put out a call to all forty-eight states to undertake a serious search for fossil plant material in order to help establish, at a national level, Botany as a new paleo-discipline in order to "*bring plant life out of the ladies' garden clubs and flower shops and into the light of the science of Man's origins.*"

Mitchel and Chadwick smiled knowingly at one another. Even Chief Engineer Smith was roused from his leather chair in the corner and began chuckling when Endy read from the USGS call for the new science of Paleo-botany. Endurance gritted his teeth; he knew what they were thinking. They were men, and he knew that wartime was making them feel even more like men. Paleontology was a man's game, particularly Paleozoology – *that* was the manliest game of all – ancient animals – a form of "big game hunting" that took men into the field, where they roughed it in search of signs of creatures that had once walked the earth, nightmarish creatures, the very thought of which would make a woman faint. Many of these men, although edified by Darwin's case for evolutionary descent, still clung to the mastery set forth in Genesis, that Man had been made in His image to have "dominion...over every creeping thing that creepeth upon the earth." And it took a strong constitution to hunt for one's fossilized ancestors while their "descendants" still creeped underfoot, or worse, were hunting you, in turn.

Mitchel deferred to Commissioner Chadwick.

Charles Noyes Chadwick was an old patrician, a *real* Ivy League man, Yale '76, with a handlebar moustache and a scrubbed bald head encircled with neatly trimmed white hair. Better dressed than the other two men, he wore a wing-collared shirt with a bow tie, and his pinstriped lounge coat opened on to a matching single-breasted waistcoat with a silver chained watch pocket. He sat, twirling a silver-knobbed cane between his legs like a bow-drill. Chadwick knew of the Gilboa fossils, vaguely, from his position as a Trustee of the American Museum of Natural History on West 77th Street across from Central Park. But he was a "monied" Trustee and knew even less science than Endurance Fuller. His real interest was on the other side of the Park, opposite the Museum of Natural History, where he was also a Trustee of the Metropolitan Museum of Art.

"Devonian Period, they believe,...yes?" he asked. It was a rhetorical question. "Inconclusive, I gather." He tapped his cane on the floor. "You know, I once visited the town of Devon on the English coast and saw those fossils that gave the Devonian Period its name – odd-looking fish with jointed fins as if getting ready to walk right up on to the beach. What do they call them?...athro...no, arthro, yes, arthropods. Old cockroaches," he joked. Looking up at Endurance, he said, "Gilboa New York seems a bit far afield, don't you think?"

Chadwick was correct about the Geological Period and the index fossils that had given the Period its name, but Endurance quickly realized that Chadwick's understanding of geological strata and drifting continents was even further afield. It seemed unlikely that the Commissioner could ever appreciate the "Gilboa Tree" – even if, indeed, it proved to be Devonian as suspected, even if it marked Life's transition from water to land, from lunged fish – scraping their lobed fins landward out of the littoral shallows – to tetrapods — four-limbed beings dwelling in the first forest on Earth, the first home for Man forevermore.

Endurance was right about Chadwick. Ancient plant life did not interest him, and old forests, only if they were being properly managed by the new US Forest Service so he could hunt the Western "Reserves" with his fellow Trustee and Ivy Leaguer, Teddy Roosevelt.

Rising from his chair, Chadwick beckoned Endurance over to the window, and leaned forward with both hands on the head of his cane. "See there, Mr. Fuller? That's the tallest building in the world. It's Frank Woolworth's, the five-cents man. Frank didn't waste his time looking backwards, he looked to the future...and that building there on Broadway is it. Industry, Commerce and, thanks to men like J. Waldo here..."

Chadwick poked a thumb over his shoulder at Smith, "...Engineering." He turned to face Endurance. "This is a big country, Fuller, we have work to do. A few plant fossils scattered here and there in the rocks of Gilboa can't stand in the way; if they're important, there will be others, elsewhere. You men from Gilboa, you have a great opportunity with this Dam project; why don't we leave the botany to the women." Still holding the head of his cane with one hand, Chadwick reached into his waistcoat with the other and pulled out his pocket watch. The meeting was over.

Days later, Endurance Fuller learned that while he was standing there in Mitchel's office, the State Courthouse in Troy, New York had already been given the go-ahead to issue Public Notice 73 stipulating that all the land parcels in Gilboa were to be acquired by the New York City Board of Water Supply. End Times for the small Catskill town had waited long enough.

"Our work is done here, Daniel," Endy said, quietly. He stood with Piedmont and Reverend Mackey, their boots covered in mud and pine needles within the sheltering circle of Olmsted's dying evergreens. Virgil Stinson and Gust Coykendall were out in the rain, draped in their rubber slickers, walking Eli Gallagher around to sober him up.

"Yes, I've seen enough," Mackey said with resignation. "Let's get our things. We can dry off down at the Terminal." He called out to the others in the rain, "C'mon, boys, we're leaving."

Endurance turned to Piedmont. "You and that machine are on your own; we've barely enough money left for the fare home, nothing to spare. I suspect you'll be as resourceful going back up as you were coming down."

Piedmont smiled sheepishly, uncertain where he was going to find the petrol. Then, looking up, said, "I'll get rid of this, Endy." Piedmont was holding Gallagher's pistol.

Endurance nodded solemnly, "Be sure you do. See you back in Gilboa."

Piedmont buttoned up his slicker and walked into the open field where the other three men stood. He put his hand on Eli Gallagher's shoulder. "You okay, Elohim? I shouldn't have gotten you like that."

Gallagher smiled wanly. "Don't tell her, will you? Don't tell your sister you thumped me in the jewels. Don't want her to think I can't put a smile on her face." His smile turned into an awkward leer. "I'm still hoping she'll find her shine for me." He looked up into the sky, water dripping off his face. He spread his arms, as he had done earlier. "...*and the waters prevailed exceedingly upon the earth; and all the high hills that were under the whole heaven were covered.*"

"It looks that way, Eli," Piedmont said softly. "And I suppose only Noah himself knows where the Taking Line will fall."

Piedmont turned away and began walking up the carriage road toward the Reservoir's North Gatehouse. That was where the Catskill water first surfaced into the City's daylight after its forty-eight hour run in Chief Engineer Smith's long dark tunnel. He figured that was as good a place as any to get rid of the gun.

He was soon alone. The crowds had dispersed, some south toward the sheep's meadow where the last of the summer flock was still grazing, others west to the new subway at Columbus Circle at 59th Street, others had turned east, taking shelter in the concession tents set up around the Vanderbilt Obelisk next to the Metropolitan Museum. The storm, as well, was dispersing and, somewhere along Central Park West, Piedmont could hear singing. School children...*Praise God from Whom all Blessings Flow.*

Arriving at the North Gatehouse, he took the pistol from the pocket of his slicker and checked the cylinder. Two bullets. "What were you going to do next, Eli, you dumb bastard," he muttered to himself. He closed up the cylinder and, taking a deep breath, raised his arm toward the Gatehouse. He shot out the two windows overlooking the Reservoir, then quickly flung the pistol as high and as far as he could toward the water. He did not watch it land. Piedmont was done with the Reservoir. His new motorcycle was on the other side of the Park, unless it had been nicked. Best to keep moving...time to go home.

But one person saw the pistol's landing.

Gianni DeAngelus, the young scarred immigrant whom Piedmont had encountered earlier, was hanging back in the trees. He saw the gun bounce, then gently settle just a few inches below the surface on the concrete weir that split the Reservoir down its middle from the North to the South Gatehouse. That night, under the cover of darkness, his pants rolled up to his knees, "Johnny of the Angel" jumped the Reservoir fence and walked along the weir to retrieve the Gallagher pistol. No one would have imagined then that it was headed back to the ill-fated town of Gilboa.

* **3** *

Bastards...

Delano "of the Angel"
1993, American Museum of Natural History, NYC
"He that sleeps feels not the tooth-ache..."
(William Shakespeare, Cymbeline)

YESTERDAY, I HAD TO call Trifina Lincoln at work...at school, to alert her about Delano DeAngelus. I had a hunch where he had gone after the elevator incident with Francesca's husband. I was right. He'd gone into the Forest. Trifina found him there.

She said that when he raised his head from the forest floor, he had no idea where he was. The compressed flesh on the side of his face had gone numb; the evaporating drool felt like someone else's, and his eye ached. Then he'd remembered. Of course. He'd been there before. Many times... there and not there.

Trifina had watched him pull himself up into a sitting position, slide back, and lean his back against the wall. He'd squinted deep into the woods, one eye closed, wiping at the strands of moss stuck to his damp cheek as his world began to reassemble. She figured he could smell it in the oil paint around him – the double-curve of the Titian sky setting off the flaming distance of drifting sunset clouds. And in the forest – the leaf litter soaked stiff in wallpaper paste; wire-mesh trees hardened with plaster cast bark. The taxidermy of the glandless skunk – *Mephitis mephitis* – black and white fur fixed in preservative, marble eyes peering at Delano from the floor of its plywood den. Nearby, *Castor canadensis*, the great North American Beaver frozen in its aquatic dive beneath rippled plexiglass... The Upholstered Dead.

Trifina stood at the open door, watching him twirl the acrylic moss in his fingers as he stared at his reflection. She could see his reflection as well. Through the dense synthetic underbrush, he looked as if he was emerging from the Heart of Darkness...which, of course, he was.

Yes, he had been there before – The Great Northeastern Oak-Hickory Forest – his refuge at the American Museum of Natural History, the diorama farthest away in The North American Hall, but the one closest to the home where he was born.

Recently, "Del" DeAngelus has been feeling like a passenger in his own body. Ambling into one awkward situation after another, he feels as if he has become an entangled observer, an unwitting go-between, unable to steer himself clear of his body's encounters with the world.

At first, I thought it might be connected to the turn of events at the Reservoir after the Lungfish first appeared in the water by the North Gatehouse. That had been unsettling enough, but when the bones and fossils – Del's area of expertise – began showing up in evolutionary sequence, things became even stranger. Someone was mimicking *The Descent of Man* – or, perhaps, *The Origin of Species*, depending if one counts Life backward rather than forward in Time.

But Del said it wasn't the Reservoir; it was not of the Flesh. Rather, it was as if his "soul" had slipped its biological shell, his "self" come unglued and fallen, Augustine of Hippo tapping him on the shoulder to get his attention and bring him back into the fold: *I have to myself become a vast problem.* He was joking when he quoted Augustine,…but not completely.

Del is no longer a Believer, but for a time he gave it his best shot. He tried, in part, to follow in his father's footsteps, despite the fact that those footsteps had taken Xavi DeAngelus away from his son to follow the call of God in a Benedictine monastery outside Poverty Hill, New York.

I, on the other hand, have never Believed, but for some reason Del now believes in me. Nevertheless, when I suggested they were the same thing, the self and the soul, just suited for different points in time, one for the Here and Now, the other for the Hereafter – the There and Then – he didn't even crack a smile. Maybe it was too close to home… or maybe, too far.

Call Del's condition whatever you like – dissociative identity disorder or a form of angelism gone bad – the bottom line is that he is not fitting very comfortably into himself.

He has felt this way before; as a child when he first learned of his "condition." In this case, it was indeed about the Flesh. His grandmother had told him about it as gently as she could, but a young boy's imagination has its own ears. The news that his guts were reversed inside his skeleton left him with an enduring sense that he had been packaged wrong by God – 'S.I.T.': *Situs inversus totalis* – his heart, lungs, intestines, spleen, liver, gall bladder, the blood vessels, nerves, lymphatics, the works, all transposed within his rib cage and abdomen. Although he was told that his father had had the condition, that one in ten thousand of God's children were born with "S.I.T." and lived perfectly normal lives, Del was not reassured. He had grown up in his grandmother's house without a father or a mother. Furthermore, early in his childhood, his grandmother Jenna had suffered from a stroke that made her look "off-center," asymmetrical in her aspect. For Del, normalcy had always been elusive.

Nevertheless, over the years, Del accepted the idea that his insides were the mirror image of other kids, of other people, and he had made the necessary adjustments. He carried a special identity card to alert the Emergency Medical Technicians that a burst appendix would not be where they would think it was, or where to best place their defibrillator should the need arise. But always having to move a sweet girl's hand to the right side of his chest when she, lovingly, felt for his beating heart, that proved difficult. After a while, he said he just stopped putting himself in that position with sweet girls.

It was his position with *bad* girls, however, that had sent him into the diorama at the Museum.

I missed the beginning and the end, but Trifina got his whole story. This is another thing. Del has become increasingly confessional with Trifina and will share the details of his interior life with her in a way that he does not with me. With her, he is neither sheepish nor evasive when trying to explain his bouts of "angelism." I suppose this is a good thing.

In any event, before heading off to work, Del had shared the elevator with State Senator O'Graéghall Van Pelt. All the way down from the penthouse. Twenty-eight floors. Del had actually been on his way up but thought better of it when the elevator door opened. He'd stood aside to let the Senator in, mumbling something about pushing the wrong button.

Van Pelt has never acknowledged Del; they have never been formally introduced. Had they been, the Senator would have shaken hands as "Gregory" Van Pelt. It is easier to pronounce than "O'Graéghall," unless, of course, one speaks Gaelic, which the Senator often will do when he is drunk,…which is also often.

The two men have, in fact, seen one another on occasion outside of the St. Urban – Van Pelt is a Trustee of the American Museum of Natural History. Last year, Del was called upon to make a presentation to the Trustees and donors at the Annual Fundraiser. His PowerPoint on the preservation of soft tissue and bone in the Museum's mammal collections did not go well – there had been too much detail, too many close-ups of viscera. The audience was still eating. Del was not invited to speak this year.

The two men have another connection – Van Pelt's penthouse apartment.

Del knows it well. Too well, in fact. He knows the marble foyer that he's often crossed in stocking feet, shoes in hand, and the kitchen with its saturated smell of O'Graéghall Van Pelt's basil-laced meat sauce. He knows the back pantry and the way out – the dented brass knob on the service hall door, the door's weight under its thick layers of dark green paint. He knows how to close that door in silence without even a click of the latch. The bedroom...well, that is always noisy. Francesca Van Pelt makes sure of that. She is the part of the Van Pelt apartment that Del knows best of all. Except perhaps for her adopted son Dante, Del is very careful to make sure that when his young friend the "Altar Boy" is there, Del is not.

We are all fond of Dante, but Del most of all. Before his fall from Catholic Grace, Del was the boy's catechist at The Church of the Immaculate Conception; he even arranged for Dante to become an altar server. Now, he seems bent on de-coupling the boy from the altar. Sometimes, when Dante gets out of Middle School at Ignatius Loyola across the street from the Metropolitan Museum of Art, Del will meet him at the edge of the Park. They'll go to the Met to look at the art, or, other times, they'll cross the Great Lawn to the Museum of Natural History for the science. Despite the Jesuit certainty that they have both been exposed to, it has become a game of chance, a coin toss on the grass to determine whether they will discuss the science in art, or the art in science.

I often wonder if Del's misguided affair with Francesca Van Pelt is only on behalf of the boy. I know his heart is not in it. The affair, that is. I think he'd prefer that Francesca loved her husband, and he, her; maybe had their own children, or at least, loved better the one they brought home. But their marriage has been a power arrangement, all too common with Million-Dollar Men. And Dante, brought in for domestic appearances, is caught in the middle. When the Senator found it unseemly that an older catholic bachelor was spending time with his nine-year-old son, Del found another way to stay close to the family.

It has not worked; the closer in Del has gotten, the further away he wished he was…even though it was where he found me.

What are the chances? He had been nosing around Van Pelt's study in his boxer shorts, going through the Senator's bookshelf, and there I was – tucked between a leather-bound volume of *Victorian Erotica* and *The Rules of the Senate of the State of New York* – on page seventy-three of one of Van Pelt's Princeton University Yearbooks: *Piedmont Livingston Kinsolver, Class of '65.*

My appearance is not what it was twenty-eight years ago. The blond hair has gone gray, the rebellious moustache and sideburns are gone. I now wear glasses…and the smile? Well, that is gone as well. Van Pelt would never have made the connection, even if my appearance when I was in school had held. It was a long time ago when we met there; I was one of the hundreds of students protesting his appointment to the University Board of Governors.

"Keep the Damn Women out…and if that fails, perhaps Princeton might offer some new introductory courses for them, courses without the current

pre-professional emphases we reserve for our men. Indeed, the faculty might make a special effort to encourage our women students to generalize and to speculate as there is little point in graduating a group of 'little men.'"

This had been alumnus Van Pelt's public comment as the University of "best men" was considering co-education – the admission of "unnecessary girls." No, he would not remember me from that time. And now? He knows me only by the name he uses at the St. Urban door – "Kinsolver." A fellow alum from Princeton is the last person he'd imagine holding the door's handle for him.

As for Del, he'd found a relative in me....but he also seems to have found more trouble with Van Pelt. It was a good thing that I was in the lobby yesterday morning when their elevator arrived.

Coming down with the Senator, Del had taken a deep breath to calm his beating heart, perhaps it was too deep a breath; he watched Van Pelt out of the corner of his eye. Gray temples groomed and still slick from his morning shower, Van Pelt, despite his seventy plus years and all the boozing, seemed a picture of well-heeled health. He was off for a power walk in the Park and wore a black and orange monographed warm-up jacket with a pair of matching polyester-blend running pants. His outfit was tailored; "Princeton University" was stitched in an arc over his heart.

"The morning constitutional," Van Pelt had said matter-of-factly, his eyes cool and straight ahead. He began rolling his shoulders, stretching his arms behind his back. Then, putting his hands to his hips, he leaned sideways, first to the right, then to the left, then back again. "No better way to start a day than to leave the last one behind, don't you think?"

It was elevator talk, something to fill the air on the way down, no response needed, none desired. But Del said he could not help himself. He could smell Francesca Van Pelt's lavender soap. His assenting grunt fell half-way between a whimper and a moan.

The Senator hummed a few bars of a Corelli *sonata da chiesa,* then stopped and slowly turned, asking, "Have we met?...in the Park? At the Heliopolis Obelisk...Cleopatra's Needle?"

That was it. Del knew it was not a real question. His misplaced heart slammed, once again, in his chest. *Her* song, *her* smell, *her* agonizing coitus reservatus nickname for both his and her cuckold's roused "needle," all crowding in on his confinement within a six-foot square box falling through space. The floors rang by, teasing, and Del's self-absence came on like gangbusters. Ignoring Van Pelt's question, he tilted his head vacantly up and to the side, locking on to the elevator's upper corner – the Cartesian x-y-z pinpoint in space where two of the elevator's walnut walls met the mirrored ceiling – it was his exit point.

The elevator had already taken up the easy rhythm of Van Pelt's warm-up, but Del upped the ante. Mumbling about his own love of exercise, he also began swinging his arms, rolling his shoulders inside the tight fabric of his suit jacket. He reached down with both hands and drew a knee up to his chest, then he went for the other one. That done, he began to jog lightly in place, all the while grinning lopsidedly at his beckoning reflection in the elevator door. Del's synapses were sparking with the speed of light through other worlds in other times. He saw himself and the Senator as fleet Atticans of Ancient Greece – not *of* but *in* the human race – restless at their marble starting blocks, ready to fly under a high Olympian sun at the drop of the Hellenic cords. Like the chiseled marble underfoot – metamorphic limestone congealed by the titanic crush and molten heat of the earth – they too had been built from the antediluvian crystalline chemistry of the Cosmos,...Men of muscle, bone and flesh, flashing their challenge before the Gods, stealing their place at the center of the universe. Del swelled; he had all Life by the balls. But, of course, he was wrong; the only testes in anyone's grip were Senator Van Pelt's.

The Senator had stopped stretching and was crouched, braced over bent knees, knuckles white, clutching the elevator's polished brass handrail in a death grip. The elevator had lost its tempo and was banging with noisy arrhythmic objection against the walls of the shaft.

Del was hauled back from the Athenian hardscrabble.

He groaned in silence, aware that, once again, he had set things into inappropriate motion. He grimaced at the floor numbers flashing above the door, at himself, and at the likelihood that the elevator would now plummet, out of control, to the basement below.

But he was wrong again; it did not. Instead, with a whine of lashing cables and the thud of counter-weights, the elevator cab bounced to an angry stop at the ground floor.

For a moment all was silent. Then, slowly, the doors opened and Van Pelt, shaking his head in disbelief, eyes fixed on Del, edged carefully along the brass rail and out of the cab. He did not go far. Once clear, he paused and looked back again at Del, then re-entered the cab and piston-punched him directly between the eyes. "That's for *this*," he said, "The next one is for my wife, you cocksucker."

It was at that point that I got involved.

The Senator was rearing back for another shot and had barely spit out the word "cocksucker" when I raced across the lobby and pulled him off. Del remained where he was, open-mouthed, blood running from his nose, bobbing gently in the elevator. Eyes wide, he raised a hailing finger as if offering a corrective,... *"Cuntsucker?"* It was all he said. I heard it, but Van Pelt did not. It would have made no difference, *in flagrante delicto,* the damage was done.

I had managed to turn the Senator away from the elevator, but as I ushered him carefully across the polished stone floor toward the door – guiding him along the tracery of cracks that wove through the lyrical

Tuscan grain of Carrara marble – I couldn't help thinking that *she* was everywhere...Francesca Van Pelt, following us toward the door. It was the furnishings, the eclectic tableaus that she'd arranged, with the approval of the Co-Op Board and her husband, the Board Chairman, for the building's large lobby.

I steered Van Pelt deftly past the German Rococo gilt settee that she'd bought at Sotheby's, past the original painting of Jacob van Ruisdael's *Torrent in a Mountainous Landscape* that hung above it. We side-stepped the two Louis XV *fauteuil a la reine* that faced the settee and the hand-painted Swiss console table from the last days of the Austro-Hungarian Empire. As we reached the Iberian lyre-footed sideboard near the door, the Senator banged against it and slammed his palm angrily down on its olivewood surface. For a moment, I worried that the large oval mirror, George III, on the wall above would fall. But it held, along with the two tintype photographs of Frederick Law Olmsted and Calvert Vaux, who remained peering down from their embossed foliate frames of Revere Silver, their gazes fixed like a pair of crossed-swords on the miniature casting of Vanderbilt's Heliopolis Obelisk – Cleopatra's Needle – wobbling on the center of the sideboard like a raised middle finger to the molder of Western Civilization...Yes, I have each of Francesca Van Pelt's furniture pieces memorized. In my position, it is good to know these things. I am often asked; it impresses visitors. And knowing their precise placement also allows me to move quickly when necessary to attend to other business.

In any event, once we were out the door and on to the sidewalk under the awning, I made certain to remain at my most solicitous with his outrage – The Doorman and the Chairman – in full compliance with the symmetry of our positions at the St. Urban. I smoothed his running suit *and* his temper with seasoned skill, marveling that a man his age could still punch another man's face with such precision. Distracting Van Pelt from turning around, I watched, over his shoulder as Del stepped out of the elevator, turn away from the front door, and head to the back hall and the service alley exit. I had a good idea what might be coming next.

It often came like this, a great silent howling yawn that would well up inside Del's reversed organs and burst forth as if to fill a vacuum – *Hypnos*, Sweet Sleep, immortal twin to *Thanatos'* deadly worm. And whenever *Hypnos* came, it was best for him to find safe haven. He took his usual route, in his usual way…into the Forest.

Outside in the alley, he'd marched past the dumpsters, through the wrought iron gate, across the sidewalk to the curb and then, in a pause of traffic, across the street. He jumped the wall into the Park, removed his shoes and began walking quickly, south on the grass, along the wall's inside edge toward the Museum of Natural History. Eight blocks later, he leapt the wall once more, back on to the sidewalk, and, again, crossed the street. Hurdling up the granite steps, under the watchful eyes of Boone, Audubon, Lewis, and Clark, past the mounted Roosevelt with his two attending bronzed savages, he pushed through the revolving doors, waved his shoes at one of the security guards, and disappeared down the stairs to the Hall of Biodiversity. From there, on to the North American Hall. A quick card swipe at the discretely disguised staff door got him out of the Hall and into the operations' corridors; from there down another half-set of stairs into the low-ceiling side alcove where he was able to climb through the small maintenance hatch into the Great Northeastern Oak-Hickory Forest. Once inside, at a dark hidden corner of the painted New England sky, he placed his shoes on the moss, removed and tucked his jacket under his arm, then leaning back against the wall, lowered himself along its surface into an aboriginal squat. Alone, in the hollow drum and musty smell of the diorama, he fell over sideways, asleep.

I pictured him there, as I have at times before, set free at last into a state of boundless Nature,...the great Mystery, everywhere but elusive, not unlike the great words carved into the Museum's marble entablature – *Truth, Knowledge, Vision* – futilely resisting their slow corrosive eroding by the elements, the periodic swerves of time, and the quickening stuff of dreams.

It was actually Trifina's father, Linc Gilboa, one of the Museum security guards, who got to Del first. He'd been on his way to his security station on the fourth floor – Vertebrate Origins – when he saw Del come in, waving his shoes at him.

Trifina said that Linc's head was already inside the hatch when she came speed-walking down the hall. He was whistle rapping at Del's sleep with urgent whispers at the door. "Dee,... Dee! You gotta get up now, Dee. They're gonna be looking for you,...come on boy, get off that moon."

Only Linc calls Del, "Dee." Sometimes it's "DeeDee" – "Delano DeAngelus" has too many twists for his tongue. Linc needs to keep his words simple; he's missing a small chunk of tongue from his younger days in the Civilian Conservation Corps. If he speaks too fast or with too many syllables, his words whistle out of his mouth like a tea kettle.

When Del emerged from the Great Northeastern Oak-Hickory Forest, a scarlet oak leaf, curled at the lobe tips, had followed him out of the diorama and lay on the marble floor. Del reached down, picked it up and absent-mindedly placed it in his jacket pocket.

"We got a call, Del," Trifina had said, almost apologetically. Del nodded. He would have known that it had been me. "Kinsolver?" he asked, anyway, dropping his shoes and wiping at the dust on his coat sleeves. "I'm okay, Trifina," he said. Trifina nodded, then turned to her father and said, "You better get back upstairs, Lincoln. They'll be wondering where you are."

Linc Gilboa gave Del his quick salute and a wink, "Time for the Ant Farm, Dee," he said, sharing an inside staffer joke with him. Trifina watched him march off down the empty corridor, sing-whistling one of his ditties about "Ol' Saint Francis, keepin' watch on all of God's Creatures."

Linc likes to keep things simple and will ham it up at times, but he knows a thing or two. One of which is, indeed, ants. Soldier ants. He knows them from his time in the Corps down in Princeton, Florida and is glad to be rid of them. The last time he saw a living soldier ant, it was one of many dragging the cut flesh of his tongue down into their mound.

Linc's in very good shape for a man in his early seventies,. He still has the lanky long-armed body that served him well when he was pitching in the Negro Leagues. He was good at it, pitching. He shouldn't be working as a security guard, he should be traveling the world, spending down his major league pension. But he played professional baseball at the wrong time, back in back-of-the-bus days. I look up to Linc. Among other reasons, he has in him some of what I have in me. Our shared rootstock. He's also a survivor. A survivor of his generation. He was good enough for the Civilian Conservation Corps, but not for service in the wars that came after when Del and I both "lost" our fathers. But we are as lucky as Trifina that Linc survived – he knows quite a bit about both men – one dead, one gone missing.

After Lincs' lilting tune had climbed the stairs and faded, Del and Trifina were left alone in the maze of echoing basement hallways underlying the great museum. "Sweetheart, you're going to get my father into trouble if you keep this up," Trifina had said. She was being gentle with him, but I noted that. Sweetheart, she'd said.

"09:45; 06.19.93," he'd replied, sheepishly, looking at his watch. "Military time. Your father's right, it's time for the Ant Farm." He put on his shoes, and after a deep breath, he left Trifina alone, and walked back the way he'd come.

The Ant Farm.

"Ant Farm" is the staffers' name for the weaving hallways in the three story basement of the Museum. Up and down, hither and thither, the hallways are alive, echoing with activity – the scientific staff, zoologists, anthropologists, geologists, cosmologists, their researchers, doctoral fellows, curators, and exhibition staffers, docents and the PR folks, mingling with the maintenance crews of carpenters, painters and electricians, as well as Trifina's fellow conservators, the diorama artists and Linc's vast team of uniformed guards sharing breaks with the sleepy custodians. Beneath the great edifice, sprawling across eighteen acres and twenty-five interlinked buildings, the subterranean life of the Museum's work force mimics the micro-faunal activities of the earth's biomantle – burrowing rodents sharing the soil with earthworms and nematodes, fungi, and bacteria, ingesting and releasing the sediment grains of the museum's natural history, constructing and re-constructing its branching network of galleries and chambers, infilling the empty spaces – an endless re-mixing of the death in the planet's supple upper crust, in order that above, on its surface, the Walk of Life can proceed apace. And further up, on the top floor of the Museum, the cycle starts all over again. There, they'd be waiting for Del to show up for work – the ghouls in the bone lab, the de-composers and their bugs, the real detritivores.

Del had told us the week before, that a Dwarf Crocodile, *Osteolaemus tetraspis*, had been brought to the lab from West Africa – Burkina Faso. The carcass had been saved after a gun fight with hide skinners poaching in the UNESCO Biosphere Reserve at Mare aux Hippopotames. Del's hollow-eyed boss, Dr. Winton Conrad, and his fawning assistants in the osteological preparation lab on the seventh floor of the Museum were going for the full skeleton, setting their flesh-eating dermastid beetles on the remains. The lab would be stinking to high heaven by now, even with the new vent hoods hovering over the stainless steel "feasting" tubs.

That was what Del had to look forward to. No wonder his day had started badly, Trifina said when she met me in the park, pleading his case to me. She'd thought about him all afternoon while trying to restore one of the wax-cast fish from the 1935 Andros Coral Reef diorama – a child visiting the Museum had pointed out a large beeswax fin from the Nassau Grouper that had fallen to the sea bottom. That diorama is too old, she said, wistfully, at dinner. More of it would be falling. The reef was doomed.

Trifina Virginia Lincoln (...née Gilboa)
Central Park Reservoir, NYC
"History is direction – but Nature is extension –
everyone gets eaten by a bear..."
(O. Spengler)

"You're worried about him, too. I know." Trifina Lincoln faces me with her arms around my waist, hands clasped behind my back. She is leaning back against the Reservoir railing, looking up at me with her head tilted. "It's about this place, isn't it, Kinsolver? The Reservoir." she asks, "Ever since the Mayor's Report came out...and the Lungfish, the bones."

She is right, but I do not answer her.

We're taking an evening walk along the new cinder path surrounding the Central Park Reservoir. There is still some lingering daylight. Joggers and speed-walkers, eyes set to a vague distance, pass us by like charged-up magnets along the iron railing, counting time in their counter-clockwise turns around the water's perimeter. Over Trifina's shoulder, the city's sky-line is folded over, upside-down, duplicating itself in its reflection at the Reservoir's far edge. An out-of-season Bufflehead dives the surface with a pair of Mergansers, roiling the image of the city. Below us, a Great Blue Heron suddenly rises from the cobblestone revetment and begins crossing the water like an ascending aircraft. Two Eastern Turtles swim out from the cattails and purple loosestrife, a plastic milk carton bobs in their chevron wake.

Mostly, however, the Reservoir water is still. It is not for lack of a breeze; the valves at the South and North Gatehouses have been shut down. Rumor has it that the Reservoir is going to be drained, all one billion gallons of it.

In the recent Mayor's Report – *The Decommissioning of the Central Park Reservoir* – the official word on the shut-down of the valves is that the City no longer needs the water. There is no mention of the Lungfish or the other "Paleolithic" discoveries in the Reservoir, but there is a concern regarding bacterial contamination. Trifina says it's unlikely that the fossilized bones found by the Gatehouse Keeper could contaminate the City's Water Supply – they were from the Jurassic Period. I take her word for it.

Trifina is a scientist "without portfolio" at the Museum. She is on staff as a conservator, sometimes in the Exhibition Department where she does background touch-ups for the dioramas, and sometimes in the Objects Conservation Laboratory where she recomposes once animate life into inanimate object. Her position comes only with a small stipend, part of a work-study Fellowship. If all continues well, next year she will be awarded her doctoral degree from the Museum's Graduate Program in Comparative Paleo-Biology.

Trifina Virginia Lincoln does not use her father's surname, just as Linc does not go by the surname of his father before him, but Trifina is also my cousin. Yes,…like Del, she is a cousin, first cousin once-removed.

The relationship is not documented on paper – too many name changes. And few would believe it, even if it were. She is African-American by way of Florida Indians – Miccosukie – and I am a blue-eyed graying-blond by way of the British Isles. Nevertheless, we do share blood. We are also the offspring of bastards.

Bastardy, like our shifting names, is a family trait. Trifina prefers to use the term "out-of-wedlock" to describe her birth and her father's before her, but Occam's Razor works best for me – "bastard" has the kind of bulls-eye precision that says all that needs saying. I'm a bit Old World like that. I get it from my grandmother.

Besides being bastards and cousins, Trifina and I are occasionally lovers. We have been for a while. The fact of our consanguinity has not mattered; neither of us cares about that. Being "occasional" lovers simply works for us. I am too old and set in my ways to search for anything more, and she is still young, thirty-two, biding her time for something better. She says she finds me reliable, and I suspect loves me in the way women love older men when they have been disappointed by the younger ones. She imagines I have found calm in life's unpredictable storms. Our love-making is gentle, affectionate, and, largely, palliative. We are both grateful for it.

In truth, the reason Trifina imagines me calm in life's predictable storms is that I avoid them whenever possible. The Storms. I find that they most always come with other people. Over the years, I have learned this, and I have learned to leave my closeness to others behind – my friend-ships, my acquaintances and colleagues,...my family. They all now line a distant shore from which I have chosen to drift away. With each gentle surge of the current or sweep of a wave, that shoreline recedes further from view. Perhaps the time will come when it will be forever out of reach, when there will be no getting back, and I will be a solitary speck in a sea surrounded only by an endless empty horizon. Perhaps. But Life will continue on, even mine; it will begin again, as it always does...in water.

Trifina once had a child. It was brief, a boy born when she was in her early twenties. She'd tried to hide the pregnancy, but her mother Saskia could see it clear as day. The two of them were heading down to Saskia's family in Florida for the birth of the child when Trifina's water broke at Port Authority. She passed out in one of the toilet stalls in the women's room and awoke a week later in a maternity ward sweat bed at Roosevelt Hospital. There had been a lethal bacterial infection in her amniotic fluid. She never saw the child, or if she did, she has no memory of it; both were lucky to be alive. The child's father was a white kid, a child himself, he wanted no part of any of it. The baby was given up, disappeared from her life but not her heart. Lost children have a way of doing this...disappearing while never leaving. We rarely speak of her child, but the Altar-Boy, Dante, keeps it in mind; they would have been about the same age among other things. I imagine the Van Pelts chose to adopt their baby because of his white complexion and blue eyes and hadn't expected the tight black curls hugging the sweet African face that has been maturing these past nine years.

Although in our different ways we have found one another, Trifina and I do not live together. She lives with her parents in the small apartment that sits above her mother's flower shop, *Blackwater Ferns & Flowers,* on the north edge of the Park. Cathedral Parkway. I live on the east side of the Park, Carnegie Hill, Fifth Avenue, Museum Mile...in the penthouse. I can see my place of work at the St. Urban from my bedroom window. From my bed, in fact. The St. Urban's copper mansard roof hovers just above the canopy of the Park's trees on the far side of the Reservoir. I have planned it this way, to keep watch on things. The view from the ground and the view from above. Immanence or Transcendence, neither one alone quite captures things for me. I could live anywhere, much further out of sight, as I once did. An outer borough, or a well-heeled suburb, but I now prefer being in the belly of the beast. Museum Mile is like a treacherous gauntlet that I have mastered. I even walk with a different gait on Fifth Avenue – long strides, shoulders back on the East Side, slightly bowed with a slight shuffle on the West Side. Countless times, I have walked, unnoticed, past the men, women, and children for whom I have, at one time or another, opened the door at the St. Urban. Trifina thinks it perverse; I find it oddly thrilling – the thrill of hiding out inside of one's own life.

Trifina and her parents, Linc and Saskia Gilboa, are the only ones who know about my unusual way of *being*, about both my fallen and risen state here in New York City. Trifina wonders why I have not done more with my life, given my education and my...well, "resources." Linc believes it's just another "family trait." In fact, it was Linc who brought me to the city and who got me my job as a doorman. He knew the Superintendent at the St. Urban, Buckles Hanrahan. The Super had owed him one; there was an opening, a deal was struck with the union, and I was "placed," as they say. Linc and I both thought it would be a good fit...for now.

Trifina has reluctantly come to accept my decision to handle the door at the St. Urban. She irons my uniform every few days. I have watched her, shaking her head over the empty coat sleeves, as if trying to understand the man whose arms fill them, the arms that hold her close without asking much in return. Yes, Trifina accepts that my uniform is more or less permanent, that this is the life I have chosen. I am surrounded by men in uniform, she jokes wistfully. Her father just turned seventy-one,... she's rarely seen him out of his.

I tease Linc about his uniform. The Museum of Natural History does not provide them for their security guards, only the specifications. Mine comes with my job. Among those in my new trade, The St. Urban is considered a plum position – the Co-Op Board likes to make sure that their men at the door look smarter than the neighbors'. Still, given our different lines of work, Linc and my uniforms are almost interchangeable. Charcoal gray, white and maroon stripes, polished brass buttons, tight woven gabardine, neatly pressed. Sometimes when I walk down to the Museum to meet Trifina and Linc for lunch, I am reminded of my college days as a member of the Reserved Officer's Training Corps – a couple of officers, Linc and I – one more senior than the other – flanking their young female recruit. Trifina says I outrank her father because I have two stripes with a fleur-de-lis at the end of each of my coat sleeves, while he has only one red stripe. My doorman's cap – Pershing style with 2 rows of braid and matching cord – also lends authority. We both know, however, that Linc outranks me. As with all achievements, rank comes with the passing of time.

Good ol' Linc. He's always been there for me, for the *family*, even though its composition has been vague. His position at the Museum suits him, standing guard on the fourth floor in The Hall of Vertebrate Origins, watching over the wide-eyed crowds jostling one another among the fragile glass cases of their ancestors. The bastard son of Lincoln Lincoln – his double-named father – Lincoln Gilboa has been watching over the vertebrates, living and dead, for years, trying to maintain order on both. It has not been easy. I know he regrets letting my father, Livingston, slip his watch. They had been close friends in the Civilian Conservation Corps, but Livingston had not been as lucky in his uniform. After the CCC, he donned another uniform to fight in World War II – the aftermath that is. It put an end to him. Nineteen Forty-four, the day of my first birthday. The bastard son of "Piedmont" Kinsolver should have been home by then, but he stayed a few days too long. *One* day too long, as always happens when misfortune makes its move.

"I have the graveyard shift tonight." I take Trifina's arm in mine and begin walking with her again along the Reservoir. "Hanrahan put me down for it, said he has something important going on. I can't say no."

"Buckles?" she snorts, "I can only imagine what he's up to. I don't trust him one bit. Linc is sure that he's the one stealing from the Museum's collection." She turns and points at me, "And we both know what was taken and where it is now."

I nod. "Yes, he may be a thief, *the* thief. But he's Van Pelt's thief. As long as the Senator is running the Board at the St. Urban, Buckles is going to be his man. And, as long as he's a Trustee at the Museum, Del's supervisor in the bone lab, Winton Conrad, will be the Senator's man at the Museum. Hanrahan had to have had help with those bones."

Trifina sighs with resignation. We walk without further talk. Perhaps we are thinking the same thing. I put my arm around her, my hand moving along her back. I can feel her spine, the smooth muscles, the rise and swell at her hips. I picture the double dimple on her lower back and draw in her smell, grateful that I have found her...grateful that I might have her for a bit longer. The crunch of cinder and gravel underfoot breaks the hum of the towering city and the wide silence of the water.

Arriving at the South Gatehouse, Trifina stops and turns to face me, squaring us up. "I have to leave you here," she says, looking up into my face, "I'm working tonight, too."

"Let me guess," I say with a smile, "The Origin of the World?"

She smiles back and leans into me, her chest to mine. "You want to come by and watch before your shift? Try your hand?" Her smile breaks into an impish grin.

"Don't be cruel," I laugh. I have watched her before.

As long as I've known Trifina, she's been a member of L'Origine du Monde Guild, a union organization of figure models. Women only. She first began working as a freelance artist's model when she was an undergrad at Parsons School of Design, downtown. At the end of each school day, she'd step out from behind her own easel and shed her clothes in front of it for the first year figure-drawing students in the evening classes. Soon, she had work at a number of the art schools in Manhattan and Brooklyn, and then, after she joined the Guild, she took on the subscription classes at the Art Student's League, The Academy of Fine Arts, and some of the uptown art museums.

The Guild took its name from Gustave Courbet's scandalous painting of a woman's hirsute pudendum – a kind of challenging in-your-face thing that the women of the Guild apparently share with the 19th century painter...*Fuck me, if you dare.*

I recently signed up for one of Trifina's sessions at the National Academy Museum, right next door – "Sketching the Human Form." I did it out of curiosity, but I admit that I was also there to protect my interest. I have no idea what was going through the minds of the men and women drawing Trifina's human form, but it was clear to me, after watching her robe slide down to her feet, that it would be better for me if I didn't return.

Despite being one of the few African-Americans in the Guild, Trifina feels right at home. *L'Origine du Monde*...The Origin of the World...the name means a lot more to her than a demoiselle's birth canal. She's a firm believer in the "Out of Africa Model" – Black Mitochondrial Eve, gathering supplies in the East African Savannah before the big push north, her rarified DNA poised to spread itself across the face of the earth into the cells of modern man – the *Homo Sapiens* juggernaut, knocking all the other hominid species off the Tree of Life like bad fruit.

There are those at work, at the Museum of Natural History, who disagree. Del's boss, Winton Conrad, is one of them. He supports the "Multi-Regional Hypothesis" – *Homo Sapiens* evolving out of an *Erectus* mash-up with other older hominid groups that had never set foot south of the Mediterranean or west of the Urals, Neanderthals included.

Dr. Conrad is an under-nourished lifer at the Museum from Mobile, Alabama. Anyone who happens to be in his company as he passes through the Akeley Hall of African Mammals will hear his claim to have been Carl Akeley's assistant when the great naturalist went off to his death in the Congo back in 1926. The truth is Conrad was only a boy on a cub scout trip who'd been selected to watch the famous 'father-of taxidermy' prepare a specimen for one of the museum's Paleozoic Era exhibits. Whatever he witnessed in Akeley's lab made an impression, and Conrad seems to believe that Akeley couldn't have done it without him.

Conrad's boastfulness is not his only curious fault. Unfortunately, for someone ostensibly interested in the trans-global evolution of species, he hasn't been able to let go of his own roots in the deep South. He refers to Trifina as "The Black Madonna," and her father, "The Missing Link." He thinks he's doing this behind their backs, but often misses who's in the room. Trifina considers Conrad an obtuse maladapted Southern cracker, who should simply stick to his bugs.

Unfortunately, there are others like him with their bad jokes, knee-jerk racism, and thinly veiled misogyny. Sometimes it's about women in science. Not the older women, the ones who have already done battle and survived to scare the shit out of the young male scientists who have come along after. The problem is always placed on the "girls." When Conrad learned that Trifina was in the Guild, he gleefully spread the news throughout the Ant Farm. One of her male colleagues, working on an upcoming exhibition: *First Farmers: The Neolithic Culture of Kerma,* then asked if she might pose breast-feeding a mannequin of a Nubian child for the display on the genetic evolution of lactose tolerance. He was trying to appear serious, all business, but he couldn't help himself, asking if he might check to see how "perky" things were. Even when Trifina warned he could be brought up on charges of sexual harassment, he was undaunted. In a kind of compendium retort pulled from all the Departments in the Museum, he responded, haughtily, "You'd have as much chance of proving that as spotting a quartzite brachiopod on a fruit fly's anal plate hidden in the gut of an extinct Placoderm swimming upstream past a North American Grizzly into a Black Hole."

Trifina could only shake her head in pained disbelief at the childishness and go to lunch.

Sometimes she wonders if its just in the Science, in its objectifying nature. It's like high school over there, she says, hazing in the ninth grade science club, internecine warfare – the paleontologists look down their noses on the anthropologists for their short-sighted, navel-gazing on humankind without fully appreciating either "deep time" or the evolutionary contributions to those very same navels. Even when the anthropologists do look back in Geological Time, *beyond* the very recent appearance of humans to their swamp-dwelling ichthyic grandparents, factions in their own ranks break out in a dust-up over whether human behavior evolves in the same way that boneybrain pans do, or whether we just make up our shenanigans as we go along out of thin air. Then again, the paleontologists aren't much better. Heaven help the poor folks in *Invertebrate* Zoology – insects, arachnids, tongue worms, horseshoe crabs, exoskeletons made of cockroach chitin – ugh, no back bones. These are the kind of creatures that the folks in *Vertebrate* Zoology like to step on.

And so it goes on down the food chain. The Protists and Fungi specialists don't bother to circulate in the Museum's main cafeteria; spore talk stays between them. And the Archae and Bacteria folks? Trifina rarely lays eyes on them; they stick to the climate-controlled yeast tubs on the seventh floor and their own eyes rarely leave the microscopes. It seems that the further creatures drift from Vitruvian Man, either in size, the number of limbs, disposition of body parts, or mode of travel – flit, slither, or crawl – the easier it is to imagine we can do without them.

I think that's why Trifina prefers eating with the Astrophysicists in the new cafeteria at the Rose Planetarium. They're a breed apart. To them, it's either all just stardust, or they're looking for Life on another planet. The Earth?...been there, done that.

This is what happens, I suspect, when one spends too much time in the company of dead matter – when Life becomes "specimen," mortal flesh tanned and stretched on armatures of bones bolted to metal, the Kinship of Man and Beast laid out in glass vitrines and their Habitat embalmed in shellac, resin and rubber latex. Looking into the eyes of another living person is surely a perilous affair, but too much time spent staring into the abysmal depths of the two marbles lodged in the pensive face of *Pan Troglodytes* – the stuffed chimpanzee in the Hall of Primates – is every bit as challenging. Worse still is trying to stare down the impassive gaze of the Inuit 'Eskimo' in the Hall of Human Origins – the tall fellow that looks both at you and through you. It's rough, even if you don't know that the skull is real, pinned to a steel-alloy spine wrapped in sealskin and Caribou hide.

Trifina blames a good deal of it on the mounted statue out front – Theodore Roosevelt – him, and his big-game hunting Ivy League patrician cronies in the Boone and Crockett Club. Once they began underwriting the Museum after its bumpy start in 1887 at the old Menagerie where the current Central Park Zoo maintains a lingering memory, Natural History became a kind of victory dance for those holding pride of place in the Tree of Life's canopy. For Roosevelt, it was a class thing. Class *Mammalia*, to be precise - the Big Animals. They were the ones most worthy of reverent respect because they could teach us about ourselves. Not so much about where we came from, but how to measure our strengths, our capabilities and values, our civility,...our nobility. And in the great wild *Primates*, we could test our nobility most acutely. After all, there's nothing more "noble" than a creature that looks vaguely like a human being yet can tear it apart limb from limb. Except, of course, for the creature with a high-powered scope and .458 Winchester Magnum with a slug that can pierce a charging Silverback's skull and keep traveling right out its asshole to finish off the female running behind.

So, it was decreed. Roosevelt and the other Presbyterian Trustees of the Museum could accept evolution as the Game of Living Things, but only because they believed the Lord had rigged it in their favor. Natural Selection was not just a meandering crap shoot in an indifferent "environment," it had a direction – upward – "guided" by the human-like hand of Providence toward those made in His image. The Trustees could heed the words of Job inscribed on the bronze plaque in the main hall of the museum – *Speak to the Earth and it shall teach thee* – because they had no doubt that when the Earth spoke back, it would confirm Man's "*dominion over every living thing that moveth*" upon it.

Then again, Trifina points out, not *all* of Man. The African gun-bearer who passed up the .458 Winchester Magnum to the President apparently didn't count. Trifina rolls her eyes whenever she looks at Roosevelt's sidekick walking bare-foot, rump-end of the President's horse on the granite plinth in front of the Museum. And as for the Native-American walking on the other side of the horse?...much of his time was spent dodging the same bullets that got the Silverback.

I hear all of Trifina's complaints about the Museum. In fact, I hear everyone's complaints about everything. Doormen usually do; it's part of the job description – complaints and secrets. Pretenses.

At Vaux's Bridge No. 24, just north of the Metropolitan Museum of Art where she will be working, Trifina and I part company. It's early June; the setting sun is still warm. I lean for a moment on the bridge railing and watch Trifina cross the East Drive and disappear into the City. On the bridal path beneath me, a woman and two men are on horses, trotting leisurely by. They are neck in neck, three sorrels pacing easily in the long shade of the evening. I recognize Francesca Van Pelt, posting at her mount's neck, her black suede riding helmet rising and falling with her horse's gait. I can also see by the blankets under the saddles that they're from The Old Dominion Riding Club out of the Claremont Academy Stables on 89th Street.

Old Dominion...the Confederate State of Virginia.

"Virginia" is Trifina's middle name. That was where her grandfather – Linc Gilboa's father – had lived before he went north to work on the Dam. "Lincoln Lincoln" had been his name – Christian and surname alike. Before he'd arrived in the upstate hamlet, he'd never even heard of Gilboa, except as a place in the bible, and he did not live long enough for the naming of his son. Trifina took back her grandfather's surname for herself when she turned twenty-one. As I've said before, scrambling names is another family trait. It's as if we're all trying for the best fit.

4

Patriarchs and Matriarchs…

Lincoln Lincoln
1921, Gilboa, NY
"I can pop my initials right on a mule's behind…"
(George V. Horton)

"CHRIST AW'MIGHTY, DID YOU hear about Mitchel?"

Eli Gallagher leaned on the handle of his shovel and spit again into the open ground at his feet. At the far end of the hole, moist earth flew up and out on to a sloping pile of dirt at the hole's edge. A young boy, six or seven years old, sat on top of the pile picking out small rocks from the dirt balls he'd been making. He was shirtless and shoeless, wearing bib overalls torn at both knees. His pale skin was streaked with brown dirt. He'd been mimicking Eli Gallagher, wadding together his tiny collection of dirt balls with his own spit.

"You mean that Mayor? The one we saw down in the city?" asked a voice from inside the grave. Another shovel of dirt rose up into the cemetery air; Gust Coykendall was doing the digging.

"That's right. That's the one, that big-mouthed mayor that's now got us shoveling this fuckin' dirt. Piedmont got a letter from Endurance Fuller. He said that *ex*-Mayor J.P. Mitchel had enlisted a few years ago and fell right out of one of those bi-planes; landed flat out like rolled dough. They had to scrape him up off the ground with a smoothing plane." Gallagher laughed at his own poor joke. "Army Air Service. He was training somewhere down south; never even made it to the Krauts. Guess he missed the lesson about using a harness. What d'you think there, *Misss-ter Lincoln Lincoln...Lincoln?*"

Gallagher turned, and looked up at the black man in the buckboard behind him, teasing out his name with a derisive roll of his tongue. The boy looked up as well, alerted by the familiar ill-tempered tone in Gallagher's voice.

Lincoln Lincoln sat relaxed, elbows on his knees, hunched comfortably between his shoulders on the spring-seat of the buckboard. His hands loosely held the heavy leather straps to the harnesses of two mules. "Could be, Mister Gal'gher, could be," he said, feigning a deferential grin.

Hearing Lincoln's voice, the mules raised their heads and took a few disjointed steps forward and back, shifting the stack of pine boxes in the back of the wagon. "Teeyo!...t'yo!" Lincoln whispered firmly to his team. He checked the reins with a quick twitch of his wrists, elbows still on his knees. The mules, reassured, settled drowsy-eyed back into place along with the coffins.

Gust kept digging. Gallagher kept leaning on his shovel; he looked at the boy. "JayJay you best get off that mound, lest we bury you right along with it when Gust starts back-filling." Gallagher chuckled to himself, then added, "'Course, not sure your momma would be too put out about it."

Gust groaned theatrically from inside the hole. "That jes' ain't nice, Eli. Not coming from the boy's daddy...Or his uncle, still ain't sure which is which," he said, scratching his head.

"Not your business to know where my pecker's been, Gust. No one's business but mine," Gallagher said, gruffly. He looked up again at Lincoln Lincoln. "Least of all, *his.*"

Gallagher was still trying to provoke the man in the buckboard. It bothered Eli knowing that the only one there he could have a decent conversation with was Lincoln Lincoln. But the Virginian never took his bait, never answered him straight-up, and never seemed to care one way or another when Gallagher talked. He always kept Eli off balance, as if he knew how to twist up a man's thoughts. And today...in front of the boy; that made it worse. Eli gritted his teeth and squeezed the shovel handle hard with both hands, thinking about Lincoln Lincoln's neck.

The muleskinner paid no attention to him, or to the others. His own thoughts were elsewhere. Far away, but still there...in the valley. It was late in the summer. Dry. The time of year when the woods and the high open meadows were usually quiet, poised at the seasons' threshold, green days clinging wearily to the last of their fading hue under a flat blue sky. One would typically be hearing only the whirring rise and fall of chittering cicadas, but not that day, not that year. That year, the lower valley down by the Creek was shrouded in gray dust, and all Lincoln could hear was the dull rumbling drone of machines pushing hard against the Gilboa hills.

Although he was a muleskinner, Lincoln knew a lot about machines, particularly about their engines. He'd even helped Piedmont Kinsolver re-build his Indian Scout twin cylinder. But these machines, these engines at the Schoharie Creek, were not for travel, they were for moving mountains. He had never before seen anything like them in his life. Never. From his seat in the buckboard, he could see down into the valley where the Holt "caterpillar" crawler tractors – their military-issue tank tracks perfected to roll over the trenches of Verdun – were running up the angled slopes and back down with belches of blue smoke, dragging the earth behind their huge blades, depositing it in mounds at the bottom of the widening reservoir-to-be's side banks. Russell Graders, the self-propelled levelers out of the Minnesota farm country, spread apart the mounds of dirt, pushing the big rocks out of the way so the ten-ton Monarch Steamrollers could shatter the smaller ones as they compacted the reservoir bottom. The smooth crush of shale, mudrock, and dark quartzite clay was laid down behind the rollers like an unfurling lithic carpet. Off to the side of the rollers, a disarray of pneumatic hoses ran snake-like from whining strap compressors to men covered in white stone dust wielding the weight of Ingersoll-Rand Jackhammers as they reduced the big rocks to rubble. Two hundred feet or so above the men, up the sweep of a massive wall of concrete, a flat-bed train car on narrow gauge rails ran slowly along the half-mile length of the Dam's crest. Heavy blocks of carved sandstone, three-foot square, were being hoisted at intervals from the cars for their placing on the Dam's finished face – the part of the face that would be visible above the water, above the "Taking Line."

The sandstone was from the Riverside Quarry, just down stream of the Dam's stepped spillway. Lincoln knew his friend Johnny of the Angel would be there – in the Quarry, he and the other stonecutters, the ones from "Il Palazzo Alpini" work camp. That was the camp where the Board of Water Supply had put the most skilled Italian masons, the carvers who could fashion sandstone like Michelangelo Buonarroti. The BWS wanted to make its mark, whatever would be seen of the Gilboa Dam, whatever stood above the water-line, was to be a work of architecture comparable to New York City's great monoliths. It had been Commissioner Charles Noyes Chadwick's idea to use the matching stone and details from the Woolworth Building.

Above the Dam, above the train cars, high over the dust cloud and the mangled valley floor, three steel cables, each nearly a mile long, cut in different directions across the clear air like thin fracture lines in the vault of the Catskill sky. They were strung between steel-trussed towers and seemed to emerge from some unseen distance out of the four compass points, rising and falling with the weight of swaying claw buckets dumping their loads into the concrete mixers on the scaffolding around the Dam – screened sand from the Patchin Pits to the south near Prattsville; crushed stone from the Stevens Mountain Quarry to the east; cement from Conro's Flats off to the west, all of it coming together in the wash of the massive mixers fed by the diverted Schoharie water. One bucket after another, all day, six days a week, Lincoln Lincoln could watch the concrete slurry being hoisted from the mixers to the hopper chutes for their seemingly endless pour into the Dam's vast formwork.

The irony of the diverted Schoharie water was not lost on Lincoln,... nor to the Reverend Daniel Mackey. Mackey had made the point in his sermon a few days before – the doomed Creek was being forced to carry its own Cross to Calvary, to build its own tomb. Millions of tons of concrete to hold back millions of tons of Creek water. And the doomed town of Gilboa, caught in the middle, was following the Stations of the Cross.

Some of the town's buildings had already been torn down, but Mackey's Methodist Church was still there, its spire's gold cross still bright in the sky as if holding out hope for its dwindling congregation. The other remaining buildings were mostly empty, dwarfed like miniature dollhouses at the foot of the looming gray wall that now terminated the town's main street. Many folks had left, but some were staying until the end.

The post office no longer accepted mail; delivery had moved upriver to Prattsville. The shelves at Stinson & Bidwell's General Store carried the essentials, but not much more. Virgil Stinson, the sole proprietor, had "broken from the struggle," died two years before when his rusting Ford pick-up, overloaded with cement bags, fell through the old Manorkill Bridge. The BWS had re-built the bridge with steel, and limited truck loads to 100 bags, but it was too late for Virgil's wife, Dorlene. Besides her twin girls and the BWS settlement – amounting to little more than the lost load of cement – the store was all she had; she was doing the best she could.

The water-starved grist mills and tanneries were also dying off; they now found themselves inside the cofferdam that surrounded the dry work zone – the water they needed was outside. A few sawmills had been moved off their foundations to the re-located flows; cut lumber was needed. The livery stables and blacksmith were kept busy as well, and the Sonoco garage had been expanded by the BWS to help maintain the equipment.

But whatever remained was temporary – even the fully-occupied boarding houses, the Devasego Inn, and the rented homes for the BWS accountants, surveyors, engineers, and construction managers. They were as temporary as the hastily assembled work camps strewn along the valley side hills to house the thousands of immigrant men and their families who had come north out of the city to work on the mammoth wall across the wilderness.

The Masonic Hall of Gilboa kept local spirits as high as possible, but the ranks were thinning. There were those who were fatalistic; the town had always held tenuous ground. Ever since the mid-1800's, after the early farms had clear-cut and exhausted much of the good land and the Susquehanna Turnpike had opened the way to the ripe western Ohio Valley, Gilboa had mostly been a stop-over for folks heading somewhere else. Those who settled the town, who stayed on, for whatever reason – poor finances, fatigue, or simple laziness – argued over the town's name before resolving the matter by randomly opening the Old Testament...*1 Samuel 31*. Now, with some of the locals packing up to leave the Schoharie, King Saul's bad end at the hand of the Philistines on Mount

Gilboa seemed like just deserts. But others saw the Bible differently; they planned to stay "come hell or high water," praying for a King David.

Nevertheless, nobody took it as a good sign when Endurance Fuller closed down *The Gilboa Monitor*, the town's only newspaper, and left for Princeton, Florida, to partner up in the fern business with his old college friend, Gaston Drake. And after that, news only got worse. The Board of Water Supply re-calculated the holding capacity of the Valley and moved the Taking Line forty-seven feet higher. The City wanted the insurance for its swelling citizenry, and the revised surveyor's "line" doomed the last six farms and sixteen additional homes. When folks realized that it also put the gold cross on Lockwood and Mackey's old church steeple just below the surface, they took it as another sign. It was an imaginary line – the "Taking Line" running horizontally around the natural valley, dead level over its rolling irregular hillsides – but it felt as if it was marking a long-past flood coming back. The drowning of men's hearts was done well before the water would even rise.

A muffled boom ruptured the air in the valley, its echo lingering above the steady noise of the machines below. Lincoln's mules started up again, stepping nervously in place. The detonation came from the east, beneath the long ridgeline of Stevens Mountain where the less-skilled southern Italians were working a different quarry, blasting apart the hillside for crushed rock fill and "cyclopean plums" – the large orbs of limestone rubble used to reinforce the Dam's guts. The Alpini men from northern Italy looked down their noses at their countrymen in the Stevens Quarry; Johnny of the Angel worked stone with the delicate precision of his eyes and hands, the southern *paisans* with their aching backs.

It seemed both sad and magnificent to Lincoln. Mountains sculpted over the eroding millennia were gone in a finger snap. Still, it was hard not to admire the power set before him. Then again, he could afford his ambivalence; Gilboa was not his town. "Tee...Yo!" he whispered once again into the ears of his mules.

Gallagher tossed his shovel up next to the boy who was still sitting on the mound with his small arsenal of dirt balls. Climbing down into the hole, Gallagher paced it off, then called out, "Seems big enough, Gust. Go grab another one from the wagon. Maybe *President* Lincoln there can help you this time."

"Can't do it, Mister Gal'gher," Lincoln said, with a wry smile on his face, "...just a skinner, not suppose' to handle the dead." He stayed put in his seat on the buckboard.

"Aww jeezus. Fuck ya," Gallagher cursed.

Gust Coykendall walked to the rear of the wagon and pulled one of the yellow pine boxes to the edge of the buckboard, waiting on Gallagher.

"Fuck ya twice," said Gallagher. He hoisted himself back out of the grave hole, and walked toward the wagon, spitting twice at the feet of Lincoln's mules.

"Fugya, fugya, fugya," giggled the boy as he, too, spit, climbing off the mound and skipping after Gallagher. His poor-shot spittle came out as a long drool, parting the caked dirt down his chin. Wiping at his face, he threw a dirt ball at one of the mules, but his effort twirled him, and the clod hit Gallagher in the back of the knee.

"JayJay, you are a little rat bastard, aw' right," Gallagher muttered, as the boy ran out of harm's way, back behind the dirt mound. "I shoulda left you w/ Dor and the girls. She and them kids ain't even here for the re-burying. And ol' Dorlene, why the hell she has such a shine for you, JayJay...beats me."

Gallagher and Gust slid the loaded coffin to the ground. There was an inscription burned into the yellow pine lid:

"Too bad...Virg, you was some fun to drink with," Gallagher said, wiping the dirt off the back of his pant leg.

For a moment, Gallagher looked solemn and thoughtful. He stared down at the inscription, thinking about the futile visit to New York City with Virgil, Gust and the others four years earlier. He could remember most of the trip, less about the last day during the storm at the Central Park Reservoir. He'd been angry that day, drinking alone and drinking a lot. And he'd lost his pistol, a family heirloom...or maybe one of the men had taken it from him. He just couldn't remember, but he often stewed with his suspicions.

"Was it you, Virg?" Gallagher asked the coffin lid. He scoffed, "Hah, don't matter, you got your own problems now. Bet you never expected your wife Dorlene'd be takin' up with a BWS man in your stead...Reasonable Pelt...where the hell does a man get a name like that...*Reasonable*."

He turned and looked up at Lincoln, "And you up there, you're jes' glued to that seat, ain'tcha, you and your BWS rules...fuckin' *Bullshit Water Supply*."

"Fugya, fugya, fugya," called the boy again, his head appearing, cautiously up from behind the mound, "shit, shit, shit."

Lincoln was well within rights to stay put on the buckboard. The BWS had strict policy for the hired men, even for the negroes from Virginia hired to handle the mule teams. Some of the policies had to do with the new labor unions in the City, others with efficiency, but in the early years of the Dam construction, most had to do with keeping the '*nations*' separated.

It started in the citizenry of the work camps – "Il Palazzo Alpini" for the Riverside Italians, "Little Sicily" for the Stevens Italians; "Colcannon

Heath" and "Boxty Broads" for the large families of Irish machinists and electricians; "Lattimer Fields" for the Slovak miners who'd survived the United Mine Workers massacre in Hazelton, Pennsylvania and escaped to Gilboa with other "bohunks" to handle the explosives; the Orthodox Ukrainians held company in "Three-Barred Cross," proudly working the supply sheds and dispensaries while keeping their camp clear of crypto-Bolsheviks. The Canadian ship-riggers from the Newfoundland fishing industry, hired to cable up the tramways, started out living with the "Harps" but, after a few Catholic brawls over the Celtic Catechism, they were moved away from the Welsh-Irish to "Halifax Wharf."

And then there was "Old Dominion." That was where Lincoln Lincoln and the other Virginia muleskinners and liverymen bunked together – separate, equal to some, but not to others. Particularly not to a local like Eli Gallagher. The fact that Lincoln was educated with light-skin and sparkling blue eyes annoyed Gallagher, but it was the repetition of Lincoln's presidential name that set him off the most...even before Lincoln met Billie Kinsolver, Piedmont's younger sister.

Years before, back in Virginia, Lincoln Lincoln's mother – known only as Queenie – had met the sixteenth President at Appomattox. He'd held her hand and kissed her on the cheek. In front of everyone. Whenever she recalled it, tears would come. After she gave birth to her first and only child, she made certain he'd recall it as well by doubling up on the child's name, first and last alike. Her son wore it well and proudly. He never bothered to explain it to anyone; didn't seem necessary. All he knew about his real father was that he had been white...with blue eyes.

Lincoln was looked up to at "Old Dominion." Even among the darker "African" men. Tall and strong-backed with a handsome smile, he was skilled with his animals, diligent in his work, quick-witted and clear-eyed in his encounters, generous with the younger less experienced skinners and gracious with the seasoned ones. Most everyone at "Old Dominion" followed his lead. And Lincoln's lead took the Virginian wherever and whenever the BWS needed him to haul a load – the quarries, cement works, lumber yards, machine shops, and sometimes to the graveyards. Along with his string of mules and draft horses, he became a familiar face around the Dam works, and soon enough the other men, in the other work camps, came to admire him as well – a few of the women included; Piedmont's sister Billie was one of them.

For the most part, by 1921, the Dam builders in their separate camps got along fine. The concentration of new Americans had been partially diluted by the streams of locals from the Catskill region flowing into their ranks. Most of these men and women from upstate New York were there for the downstate money. The City and its contractors had offered pay for legitimate support services: delivery men, laundry services, cooks and moppers, water-boys and runners, loggers and grubbers. Gust Coykendall and Eli Gallagher worked the graveyards. It was one of the better paid jobs. Not many in Gilboa had the stomach for digging up their kin, either in the two town cemeteries or from the back yard plots in the homes below the Taking Line. Most of the time, there was not much left to deal with – the old coffins were dry-rotted and pretty much empty except for bone dust, threadbare silk ties, faded brass buttons, silver neck pendants, and curled shoe leather. When there were bones, they were often light and easy to heap into the new pine boxes supplied by the BWS for re-burial in the new Gilboa Cemetery, a mile uphill from the Dam. But the fresher burials, some of the young bodies sent home from the War, that was hard duty. Even for Gallagher, who by then had a shoebox full of gold rings and neck pendants.

There were other jobs, too. Offered just to the locals. Piedmont Kinsolver, for one, moved homes.

The Gilboans had been given a choice. They could not keep their land, but if they wanted to keep whatever sat on it, they were free to move it elsewhere. Otherwise, they'd be paid "value," and the buildings – when the time came – would be burned to the ground. Sometimes Lincoln Lincoln would help Piedmont with the "re-locations." His mules did the hauling, despite the BWS policy against freelance work. Piedmont and his crew, including his tough younger sister Billie, would carefully jack up the old wooden structures off their foundations and, setting their capstans, would drag them onto log skids. Lincoln's team would follow Piedmont's motorcycle, slowly pulling the house – often with the owners and their furnishings still inside – along a winding traverse to its new home on higher ground.

Billie soon began sitting up with Lincoln, ostensibly to help guide. She was a sturdy young woman, in her early twenties, a full-fleshed daughter of the Catskill Mountains with their same wild and mysterious beauty. At birth, she had been given the name of "Wilhelmina," but it just didn't fit; "Billie" captured her better, made her feel equal to the boys. She took no teasing, insult or guff from anyone, not even from her older brother, but despite her challenging ways, she was appreciated for her good looks and curious mind. And, of late, she had become curious about Lincoln. They were growing close, right under everyone's noses, including Eli Gallagher's. Gallagher had always felt he had a claim on her, but he was alone on this.

There was a third line of work around Gilboa. Some of the men who were late to the BWS dole, or not on Nawn Contracting Company's payroll, or simply more interested in "side ventures," provided a different kind of support for the Dam – saloonkeepers living off bad gamblers and bad English, night suppliers of bootleg alcohol from the old Hops farms, and downstate slicks trafficking in nighttime women. Far from the crowded bustle of the Lower East Side, the mountains around Gilboa seemed cold and bleak, but cheap entertainment offering a little danger kept the blood hot. Even the locals warmed to it despite their own chilly turn in fortune. Sometimes after a graveyard shift, Coykendall would follow Gallagher to *Shem's FingerBreak*, an abandoned hunting club turned speakeasy up in the hemlock woods behind Conro's Flats. They'd drink home-brewed White Dog, play a bit of cards, and listen to a little bad music from Shem's poorly tuned upright. Gust still lived with his elderly mother and wouldn't stay long, but Eli, despite having his darkening heart set on Billie Kinsolver, took his pleasure with the FingerBreak women whenever and for as long as his drunken state would allow.

The Board of Water Supply had their own police force to oversee or, in the case of the FingerBreak, *overlook* law and order. It was known as The Bureau. Most of the patrolmen were Army Service veterans accustomed to the blood and fury of other nations; they had seen it up close in the War – desperate wild-eyed men on the attack, shrieking into the faces of their enemy in strange tongue. On the wartime Front, things could get out of hand quickly, but when skirmishes broke out in the camps or in the illicit backwoods of Gilboa, the fighting seemed particularly dirty even by the standard of the vets. Fortunately, The Bureau was a mounted force and could run their horses right over any trouble. It was also an advantage that their swinging nightsticks were at the head-height of the fighting men on the ground.

The Chief of The Bureau, Darryl Potts, was a crusty and taciturn former Indian fighter. He'd spent five years on the frontier at Fort Riley in Kansas, and rumor had it that the twelve notches on the cantle of his saddle counted off Sioux scalps. After the Indian Wars, and still in his twenties, he went on to command a fearsome brigade of Roosevelt's Rough Riders through the Cuban jungle at Las Guasimas. He had loyalties; some of his fellow Riders followed him into the BWS Police Bureau. They were the best horsemen on the force and, after Las Guasimas, had no trouble running through the thick woods around Gilboa.

Lincoln Lincoln appreciated Potts for his horse sense. And Potts felt the same way about Lincoln. The mules and draft horses of the skinners shared a paddock with some of the Bureau's quarter horses, and the two men could often be seen leaning on the fence line, arms folded over the top rail, discussing horseflesh. Sometimes, on Sundays, Johnny of the Angel would be there as well, but it was usually just a stop on his way. His English was still poor, and the talk of withers, shanks, fetlocks, and bot flies more often than not would quicken him on his way to the infirmary. It was not that he would be feeling ill; there was a nurse at the infirmary that had recently gotten hold of his heart.

"Johnny of the Angel" (né Gianni DeAngelus)
Riverside Quarry, Gilboa
"Ye Mountains of Gilboa, let there be no dew...nor fields of offering."
(2 Samuel 1:21)

The close friendship between Lincoln Lincoln and Gianni DeAngelus was well-known in the camps, mostly because it seemed so surprising. Worlds apart, and barely able to understand one another when they first met, the two men had bound themselves together over one deeply shared affection: music.

Both men had strong and beautiful singing voices, as good or better than most in the camps had ever heard. And both men could play almost any instrument that kept their voices free for accompaniment. But it was together, when they sang and played with each other, *tenore e basso*, that was the most lovely to hear. Their harmonic fit, as with the fit of their friendship, was seamless.

81

Gianni had some classical music training in Verona before the War, but his range of musical interests was wide, including anything American from Tin Pan Alley to Ragtime. Lincoln, self-trained in rural Virginia, could also sing almost anything – gospel, jazz, cigar-box blues, Cohan musicals and, to most everyone's surprise, European Opera. It was the southerner's operatic singing in a talent-show arranged by the BWS to entertain the camps that first caught the attention of the younger Italian stonemason. The show was held in the Community Hall, known to the workers as "The League of Nations," and Lincoln had surprised the audience by performing Rossini's *La Pietra de paragone*. The crowd had expected a somber spiritual, but Lincoln had gone with a lively libretto. Gianni was in the front row. The two men seemed to hear Rossini the same way and, before Lincoln had finished, DeAngelus was up on stage doing *Giocondo's* call to the muleskinner's *Count Asdrubale*. The plank floors of The League of Nations thundered from the stomping of feet when the two men finished.

Occasionally, Gianni and Lincoln would take their singing to the FingerBreak. Either one could make Shem's run-down pianola sound good, even to those who weren't drunk. Negroes usually weren't allowed in, but any of the black Virginia men that came with Lincoln, or Gianni for that matter, were given a seat. If Gianni DeAngelus ever had a problem with the African race – which seemed unlikely – he'd lost it at the Isonzo River. Lincoln once told him something that Mark Twain had said: *I believe I have no prejudices whatsoever. All I need to know is that a man is a member of the human race. That's bad enough for me.* Gianni liked that. Not so much the humor of it, but its truth – Gianni had the scars to prove it.

Although DeAngelus wouldn't talk much about his time in the Great War, Lincoln figured the soft-spoken young man from Verona had been way too young to serve with the Alpini troops on the Italian Front when they tried to storm the Julian Alps on the Austro-Hungarian side of the Isonzo river. The fight had been a blood bath, but it only got worse when the ammunition ran out during one of the last battles in 1916. The Hungarians and Italians had fought on with one another, first with bayonets and swords, then hand to hand with knives. By the time the last man fell, the soldiers were cutting their enemy up with scrap metal from blown-up tanks or grappling leg-locked in the trenches trying to garrote each other with barbed wire. In addition to having his face cross-cut by a crazed Hungarian officer wielding a razor-edged firing pin from a shattered howitzer, Gianni lost two fingers at the middle knuckle trying to keep from being strangled by the wire. He wasn't much good as a soldier after that; they had been his trigger fingers. The War and Europe was finished for him. He never returned to Verona or anywhere else in Italy, and never looked back either. He crossed the Atlantic with some of the other wounded men of the Alpini and was in New York City when word went out for men who could carve sandstone for the face of the Gilboa Dam. He had come from a family of carvers, and just as he only needed eight fingers for the FingerBreak piano, he needed only eight to render a perfect chamfer joint to chisel-dressed stone. He was *that* good at both things.

Gianni was not big, nor was he particularly strong. Beneath the scar, his face was still soft with shining playful eyes and a young man's marred beauty. In the company of all the roughnecks working the Dam, he might have been an easy target for bullying, but he was given a clear path. It wasn't that the gruesome scar was so disarming, it was the easy open smile that the scar could not seem to cross out, as if his good heart could render invisible the misfortune that he'd suffered.

Gianni DeAngelus also owned a pistol. At first, Lincoln wondered if potential trouble-makers stood down because of that; but he soon realized that no one else knew about the gun. He only saw it once himself. The two of them were alone in the Palazzo Alpini bunkhouse, when Gianni unfurled one of his sock rolls. Inside it was an old Bulldog 32 caliber. Gianni said it didn't belong to him. He told Lincoln the story of the men he'd seen in Central Park four years before, and of the one who'd thrown the gun in the water. At the time, he thought that had been the end of it, finder's keepers. But, shortly after arriving in Gilboa, he realized he had brought the gun home. Now, he was just waiting for the right moment to return it to Piedmont Kinsolver, and to ask him about the initials – '*J J G*' – carved in its handle. "*Bene*, can't even fire it *propriamente*," he'd said with a smile, wiggling a trigger knuckle at Lincoln. That was all he said before stuffing the pistol back into the socks and into the bottom of his duffel. Lincoln didn't press him, and soon forgot all about it.

When they weren't singing, the two men enjoyed each other's company down at the Riverside Quarry. Every few days, Lincoln would be sent there to haul out Gianni's handiwork. The muleskinner would tease the carver during the loadings, feigning alarm as Gianni's precious stones swayed precariously in the rigging above Lincoln's reinforced wagon. It was more often than not just a trick to distract the Italian, so he'd be sure to step into a flop of mule shit. But the teasing was from respect and a fondness for the beatific young man with the "X" etched into his face. It was Lincoln who conferred on Gianni DeAngelus the name he would be best known for: "Johnny of the Angel."

Lincoln was also the one to introduce him to the infirmary nurse that Johnny would go see whenever he could slip free of Darryl Potts' horse paddock. She was a good friend of Billie Kinsolver's named Jenna Goldring, one of three sisters from the town of Slingerlands near Albany.

The Goldring Sisters
Slingerlands, NY

"Field work is dangerous especially for girls in knickers. It's alright for a man to make the trip, but a girl, even armed with a revolver, never."
(John Mason Clarke, NY State Paleontologist)

Like an unexpected breeze that begins softly and grows steadily in strength, the sound of a single-note steam whistle rose up out of the rumbling din and cut through the valley. The shrill alarm wound down, then rose up again as soon as its echo was gone from the hills. Three times, the clarion signaled all work on the Dam to stop. Immediately.

The men in the graveyard stood still at their shovels. Lincoln raised his head and sat up attentively, holding his team firmly in check. Eli looked down at Gust, then toward the sky as if the whistle had written its warning there for them all to read.

"Now, what in God's name..." Gallagher said, "Another dumb bohunk fell into the formwork or got turned into a griddle cake under one of them crawlers? Whadda you think, Gust?...think we need to dig another hole?"

Gust, standing in the bottom of the grave, shrugged, removed a work glove, and began picking at his teeth. The boy had also climbed down into the hole; he sat on the freshly placed pine box, idly tracing the dark wood knots on the coffin lid with his fingers.

"Shit, Gust,..." Gallagher said, "You got less and less to say of consequence every god-damned day. Get JayJay out of there, before I bury you both."

The machines in the Dam site began shutting down, one by one, breaking apart the noise in the valley like an ensemble of different mechanical instruments dropping away in ritardando. Within moments the only sounds Lincoln could hear were the distant calls of men, and the whining groans of heavily loaded buckets of crushed rock swaying on the motionless tram cables. The quiet made his ears ring. Above him, two turkey vultures glided slowly in large vigilant circles over the graveyard, the convection currents pushing each looping orbit of the birds sideways until they disappeared into the silence behind Stevens Mountain.

The stillness, like a withheld breath, lingered only momentarily before being broken by the popping sounds of an approaching vehicle. It was Piedmont's Indian Scout; the motorcycle was racing ahead of a dust cloud up the dirt road toward Lincoln and the others. Piedmont's sidecar was attached, and a tall woman holding on to her broad-brimmed hat sat inside. The men were surprised to see that it was not Piedmont leaning over the handlebars, rather it was his sister Billie Kinsolver, long hair whipping loose in the wind.

As the motorcycle slowed and drew alongside Lincoln's buckboard, Gust Coykendall clamored out of the grave, leaving the boy still sitting on the coffin lid. He stopped at the edge of the hole as Gallagher pushed past him and planted himself between Lincoln and the motorcycle.

"Hello there, Mizz Billie, what're you doing on Piedmont's horse?" he asked. Eli was trying to be funny, but he quickly turned red-faced, flushed by the young woman's lack of response. His smile wilted, and he turned his eyes away.

Billie Kinsolver was wearing a faded pair of her brother's cast-off denim coveralls and one strap hung unbuckled at her waist, her white homespun shirt was two buttons open at the neck. As she leaned over to dismount from her brother's motorcycle, Eli could see she was not wearing a corset or even a camisole. It was typical of her, he thought, confusing his feelings even more. He knew that Lincoln, up in the spring-seat of the wagon, could see even more down Billie's open shirt; his resentment added heat to his already flushed face.

Ignoring Gallagher, the young woman hooked her thumb under the fallen shoulder strap and brought it back into place, her eyes sparkling up at the mule skinner.

"Lincoln, do you know where Johnny of the Angel has got to?" she asked. Gesturing toward the motorcycle, she added, "This here is Jenna Goldring's sister; she's looking for him."

The woman sitting in the sidecar nodded to the men. She was quite tall and thin and did not fit inside the sidecar very well. She sat erect in her seat, stiff and business-like, as if her comfort was second to more important matters. She wore a khaki-colored linen duster and a motoring hat; the duster was open to a cotton shirtwaist skirt buttoned up to a four-in-hand necktie common to women from the city. Older than Billie, but still a young woman, she was not pretty exactly, more like handsome with an attractive mouth slightly upturned at one corner to form a small dimple. Her eyes were gray and steely, set beneath premature strands of white hair running through darker hair tied back below the brim of her hat. From his seat up top, Lincoln could see she was holding what appeared to be a small black church psalter in her lap...and her skirt was cinched at the waist by a gun belt with a holstered sidearm. She returned his look with a steady, unflinching gaze.

As Lincoln began to speak, Eli interrupted him. "Well, don't that beat all. We got us another one. Sister Mattie lits out for New York City, and another one shows up."

Gallagher had regained his composure; he moved closer to the wagon's running board, trying to block Lincoln from dismounting. The muleskinner jumped over Gallagher's shoulder to the ground. "You must be Miss Winifred," Lincoln said, removing his hat.

The woman smiled at Lincoln, "Well, I am indeed." Then, standing and stepping out of the sidecar, she turned to Gallagher and said, "Mattie is the oldest sister."

"And Jenna, our nurse, the younger," said Lincoln, offering Winifred Goldring his hand. "Lincoln Lincoln, ma'am."

"Yes, I know who you are. You're one of the music men, you and Mr. DeAngelus. Jenna has spoken often of you both." Pointing at the child who was now climbing on all fours up out of grave, she asked, "And who is that young fellow?"

Gust Coykendall laughed and started to answer, but Gallagher stopped him with a sharp look. Gust mumbled something at the ground and went back to picking his teeth. The boy skipped up to Gallagher and ducked behind him, peering shyly out at the tall woman with the sidearm.

"That's young JayJay," Billie said, shaking her head, "He never leaves Mr. Gallagher's side. Don't know exactly why, he doesn't get much care."

"Aw, that's not true, Billie. He's my good luck charm. He can't speak too good, but I couldn't do without him, ain't that right JayJay?" Eli turned and put his hand on the boy's shoulder, giving it a rough squeeze.

Billie Kinsolver turned away and looked again at Lincoln. "So?...You know where Johnny of the Angel is, or not?" She put her hands on her hips and stuck out her chin at him with a coy challenging smile. Lincoln knew that smile; he'd seen it more than a few times when she would be sitting close to him in the spring-seat as he hauled Piedmont's houses to their new homes. Nevertheless, Lincoln pretended not to recognize Billie's flirting and addressed the woman in the sidecar instead. "I guess I know why you're here. I was with Johnny when he found 'em. Fooled us all, living things turned to stone like that. Mr. Clapp said you'd be coming. The Angel is likely in Engineer Clapp's office now, along with Mr. Nawn's man. They've been waitin' for you."

Eli released the boy's shoulder and stepped forward. "Someone going to tell me what the hell the President here already seems to know?"

Lincoln winked at Billie, before turning to Eli. "Dinosaurs, Mr. Gal'gher," he said, "That's what. Dinosaurs been roamin' in Gilboa."

"Not quite, Mr. Lincoln," Winifred Goldring said, with a smile, "It was long before the dinosaurs,...millions of years before. What Mr. DeAngelus found are fossils of the trees that gave them the air to breathe when they *did* come along. Petrified stumps from an ancient forest, that's what he found cast in the sandstone...one of the very first forests on earth."

It had been seven days earlier. Lincoln was in the Quarry for a loading when Gianni DeAngelus noticed a dark figure of rock emerging from a split face of the buff-colored sandstone. Then another. Soon, an entire course of sandstone was peppered with the strange looking rocks. They were almost as big as the blocks on Lincoln's wagon, and when Gianni called over the quarry foreman, he was not too happy; good stone for the Dam facing was hard to come by as it was. A number of the rocks had already been pulverized to get to the sandstone before one of the Italian masons pointed out how much they looked like the stumps of the palm trees on the Adriatic Coast. That stopped everyone for a closer look. Soon, one of the BWS engineers, a geologist, was called in to identify the stratum. He didn't know exactly what Gianni had found, but he knew the stone had been cast from life on earth. The Lockwood Fossils, "the elephant feet," had reappeared, hundreds of them.

And this morning, Lincoln knew that the work on the reservoir Dam had been shut down because of the arrival of "the men" from the State Museum in Albany. That was what BWS Division Engineer Sidney Clapp had said: *the men*. Clapp didn't know that Winifred Goldring would be there ahead of them. But Lincoln and a few others did; the camp nurse had told them that her middle sister was on her way.

A mile or so down from the upland cemetery, Division Engineer Sidney Clapp was in the Gilboa Post Office, waiting. There was no mail coming or going in the old clapboard building, not since the BWS took it over for the engineering division the year before. Clapp, tall and lanky, sat on the edge of the former postmaster's desk, his hands clasped behind his head, long legs stretched out before him, talking quietly with Hugh Nawn, the owner of The Nawn Contracting Company. Nawn, too, was a big man, but portly in his wrinkled suit, his pants riding up to his full waist as he sat in Clapp's chair chewing on an unlit cigar. Nawn had won the seven-million-dollar contract to build the Gilboa Dam two years earlier and had come all the way from his offices in Boston to meet with the head engineer. He was there mostly to review progress, but, in light of the fossil discovery, he was anxious to hear Clapp's proposal for the work stoppage. Both men knew that the stoppage would cost Nawn thousands of dollars a day; he had to pay his men, work or no work, and the BWS would have to pay him in return.

"Reasonable, do you have those numbers yet?" Clapp turned and called out to an adjacent room. Inside, a small bespectacled man wearing sleeve garters and a green visor was standing, head down, bent over a desk. He was working a hand-crank calculator with one hand and furiously scribbling numbers on a ruled pad with the other.

"Almost, Mr. Clapp...give me another minute."

Clapp winked at Hugh Nawn, saying in a low voice, "Finest fellow I ever hired...I suppose I couldn't have missed, given his name...*Reasonable*." He shook his head to himself, "Besides being good with numbers, he's the best sanitation engineer I got."

"He the fellow with the bright idea to lock up the privies on the train? The one passing by the Ashokan?" Nawn asked gruffly, his cigar bobbing in his mouth.

Clapp chuckled, "Yes, indeed...and it's helping. The Delaware & Ulster was dumping crap and everything else right on the tracks along the Reservoir. From there it was all washing into the water. 'Putrescible matter,' Reasonable calls it. He and his men have cleaned up compost heaps, outhouses, manure-choked stables, and fields all over this water-shed. Unfortunately, he's made a lot of enemies among the locals, but the water's getting cleaner, drinkable soon enough."

Clapp stood up from the desk and stretched his arms in front of him as he turned to two men sitting by the front door. "But not quite, right, Piedmont?...*almost* drinkable. You folks can appreciate that, give ol' Reasonable and his boys a break, what do you think?"

Piedmont Kinsolver and Gianni DeAngelus were sitting on a bench by the Post Office door. Piedmont nodded and smiled at Clapp, "Yessir, I suppose so." His true thoughts he kept to himself...the Division Engineer had been paying him well for his work; no sense in grousing that water deemed unfit for City folks had been just fine for generations of Catskill families.

Clapp had sent for both men shortly after Nawn had arrived. He needed DeAngelus to show the man from the Museum the stratum in the Quarry where he'd made his find. And he also had a job for Piedmont, a good one for a local fellow who knew his way around.

Sitting on the bench next to Piedmont, Johnny of the Angel was nervous. He had been up at the infirmary, idling with Jenna Goldring, when he was called to Clapp's office; he was supposed to be at the Quarry. He kept his head down, picking at the worn toe of one of his boots.

Piedmont Kinsolver stood up and walked over to the office window. He was also feeling nervous, but he was thinking about his motorcycle.

Staring out through the dust-speckled window, Kinsolver worried that he'd made a mistake sending Billie to fetch Jenna Goldring's sister. Billie could handle the Scout, but she was reckless; she drove it faster than she should. Then again, he thought, maybe it was fitting. Billie's wildness often reminded him of Jenna Goldring's *other* sister, the oldest one, Mattie. Maybe it was Mattie that had been the one to pass that streak on, the wildness. Billie used to follow the older woman around like a hungry puppy.

Piedmont thought of Mattie often. She had been the first in her family to come to Gilboa, seven years earlier in 1914, but she did not stay long. Fresh out of The State Normal School in Albany, Mattie had left Slingerlands to teach the first through sixth grades in the one-room schoolhouse next to the big bend in the Manorkill off Scudderhook Road. She was tall and slender, like all of the Goldring girls, and many thought she was the most attractive of the bunch. She acted as if she was. It was not long after she arrived, that young men were pecking around the schoolhouse like a flock of feeding juncos. And Piedmont was one of them. He had gotten close with her, but only as much as she allowed; she was secretive. Billie Kinsolver was in her teens then and idolized her. Mattie was a big sister to her...and more. Billie's heart may have been the one most broken when Mattie disappeared after her second year at the school. But Billie knew, or at least suspected, why Mattie had left Gilboa. Both she and Piedmont had been surprised when Billie received a letter from New York City. It included a black and white Kodak of Mattie, smiling, eyes wide and happy, cheek to cheek with a baby daughter. The child had been named Wilhelmina, to be called "Mina," for short.

Billie had never liked her own given name – *Wilhelmina* – but she was flattered that the baby had been named after her. Still, she worried it could come with trouble. A few folks in Gilboa thought they knew who the father was – there'd been rumors about a bad thing – but most everyone was wrong,...including Billie.

Jenna said that Mattie had always been the careless one and should never have come to Gilboa on her own, even though, four years later in 1920, it was Jenna, alone herself, who followed her sister's trail to the Schoharie.

Jenna was nothing like her elder sister. More assertive and friendly, Jenna was the tallest of the Goldring girls, and with bigger bones, strong and athletic. She had received a nursing degree from Russell Sage College in Troy with the hope of joining the Army Medical Corps in Europe but, only a few months after graduating, the armistice with Germany was signed at Compiègne, and she signed on instead with The Board of Water Supply to tend to the internationals in the infirmary at the Dam site. She took her work very seriously and demanded the same of others. Not much more than a year after arriving, Jenna was already in charge of the camp's two clinics and was the scourge of any camp doctor who didn't carry his proper weight.

More recently, Jenna had also fallen into a requited love with Johnny of the Angel. Unlike her sister Mattie, she had no trouble declaring her feelings for a man...or a woman. She would not countenance whispering and kept the company of the young stone mason with the scarred face as much as her work at the infirmary would allow. They were an odd couple. She was taller, outspoken, couldn't sing a lick and spoke no Italian, but he was gentle, made her laugh easily, and his scars did not reach down to the tenderness of his lips. He teased her that his discovery in the Quarry was his gift to her after he learned that it was bringing the third Goldring girl to Gilboa; he knew how much Jenna missed her big sisters.

It had been difficult for Winifred – Clapp's "man from the Museum" – to get there. The tight confines of Piedmont's sidecar had been the easy part. When word of the discovery at the Dam site arrived at the State Museum in Albany, Winifred Goldring was hopeful that she'd be sent to Gilboa to verify the find and collect samples. She knew the stratum where they'd been found; it was her Geological Period: Devonian.

Winifred had been at the Museum for six years, attached to what some of her colleagues referred to as "The Garden Club." The Director of the State Museum was a friend of her father's and had reluctantly taken her on to fill an empty niche in the Paleontology Department – Botany – flowers and plants, the ancient ones. She was the first woman on the scientific staff, and a gamble. Two degrees in the sciences from Wellesley College, a master's thesis in geological morphology guided by the Harvard faculty, and a year at Johns Hopkins studying late Silurian and Devonian Period flora looked impressive on a man's resume, but not on a woman's. Science work just wasn't very feminine. Nor, from the point of view of some her colleagues, was she.

The previous year, Winifred had been "promoted" to Assistant to the Assistant State Paleontologist. Her title had no precedent; everyone knew it had been conferred on her simply to keep her quiet. There had been no advancement in either responsibility or pay; she expected that, she knew she was lucky to have the job at all. But she also knew that she was more than an 'assistant.' Anyone who suggested otherwise met with a whiplash tongue and was soon in retreat.

"Fred," as she was called behind her back – even by some of the timorous women who actually were "assistants" – was considered to have a "man's turn of mind." This had originally been meant as a compliment during her schooling in paleontology, but it had taken a sarcastic turn when she took her schooling into the profession. Mastering the physical universe was just that – the work of masters, not mistresses. She had heard it all her young life, in school and elsewhere. The predictive sciences – physics and chemistry where mankind's future was being determined – were not for women. Womankind had no aptitude for the required mathematics and logical inference; cool precision, not easily heated passion, was necessary in the laboratory; rolled-up sleeves, not long skirts and dewy emotions. Even in biological and anatomical research, putrescent organs were unseemly in delicate hands meant for holding children. But it was worse in Winifred's chosen field of science – the science that looked backwards in time to understand the present. Hunting for the origins of life meant rough travel around the earth's lithic sphere in search of rough rock faces and the minute markings of fossils embedded in titanic folds…far beyond civilization, far beyond a woman's safety.

But Winifred Goldring had always had a formidable and fearless mind, and she was insistent when it came to the Gilboa Fossils. She'd heard that Gilboa was a particularly disorderly "civilization" with its roughneck clash of nations, dispirited and dark-minded locals, and the relentless mayhem of machines ripping apart the ground beneath them all. Still, she could take care of herself, as she had always done.

When Winifred came to work and displayed her father's Black Powder Frame Colt .45 to the Director as a means of reassuring him, he felt only embarrassment for her and tried to put her off. "Field work is dangerous, especially for girls in knickers. It's alright for a man to make the trip, but a girl, even armed with a revolver, never." The Director had intended his remark kindly, but he was serious – the men, when they could be spared, would be sent to Gilboa instead. She held her ground, standing over him with folded arms as he sat at his desk. Perhaps it was the way she held the gun, confident and relaxed in one hand, nestled into the crook of her elbow,…or just that he couldn't bear to stare down the steel in her eyes. He finally gave in. It would be unpaid leave; she'd have to make her own way and find her own lodging. That was fine with her, she had a sister in Gilboa, and she felt it was payment enough to get there ahead of the men. Which she did.

Fate is only one way to describe unpredictable things that look predictable after the fact. Endurance Fuller had made this remark to Piedmont Kinsolver on the night before leaving for Princeton, Florida. Both men had been slightly tipsy. They were sad to be parting after all this time, sad about what fate had brought. Fuller had become resigned to the Dam, but the point he was trying to make was larger – that the men and women who find each other against all likely odds, the joy and pain of blind circumstance that follow on their chance encounter, and the subsequent choices that seem to appear from thin air but have the weight of gravity, are what binds one fast and forevermore to their particular life on earth.

Endurance warned the younger man that lives were like that, unfolding slowly, in disjointed moments, mimicking the slow fashioning of the earth itself. Sometimes out of pure accident and coincidence, other times from hard intention, caused and effected, and most often from a mixture of them all, made up in equal part by what occurred and by what did not – the millions of other possibilities, other paths to other places that might have been taken,...to other people.

Piedmont believed Endurance to be right. Looking back, anyone could see that fighting the City had always been a lost cause. Nevertheless, that last night with Endurance, it was far more difficult for him to see that the Dam across the Schoharie had already begun pooling the lives of four families, walling off all the other promising courses that the flow of their lives might have taken.

In Gilboa's last days, what had begun with the men, the name-givers – Kinsolver, Lincoln, and DeAngelus – found its finish in the Goldring women who came to them. It was only much later that it all seemed inevitable, that the families would fall into one another as they did in 1921, three years before "The Great Dying."

5

The Great Dying…

X-Men
1993, Central Park, NYC
"Every day is a fight to save the World…"
(G. Champion)

TODAY, DELANO DEANGELUS HAS joined the X-men for the first time. I am pleased.

For much of the summer, on Sunday afternoons, a group of us have been meeting at the Arthur Ross Pinetum in Central Park to exercise together. We call ourselves the X-men. It's an honorific that comes with a complementary dose of irony; most of us have grown soft and can neither run nor ride bicycles – weak ankles, bad knees, plantar fasciitis, or just plain laziness – low impact sports work best for the X-men.

It was the "Garbage-Man" who suggested Tai chi.

Dennis Fong is a past martial arts master who works for the Department of Sanitation. He's an enforcer, not a hauler. He issues tickets to building owners who violate the sanitation laws – wrong pick-up nights, filthy sidewalks, and the like. The St. Urban is on his route. Tai chi keeps him sane, and he felt it might help the rest of us as well.

It was easy enough to get me on board. Why not, I am drawn to…

well, unconventional pastimes. The others soon followed – Chavez, the "Elevator-Man" who handles the service lift at the St. Urban; Rosenberg, the "Telephone-Man" from Verizon who keeps the St. Urban's dwindling land lines alive; Prickitt, our "Mail-Man" who happens to be a woman but doesn't mind that we call ourselves the X-men instead of the X-*people*. She gets the point; we're all hybrids, part human, part 'thing'…or, better, part 'infrastructure' – unsung superheroes who have undergone a fleshaltering transformation in order to ensure that the City can conduct its ordinary business unimpeded.

Protagoras the sophist got it backwards… *Things* are the measure of all men, not the other way around.

Before settling on the grove of *Pinus virginiana* in The Pinetum, the X-men used to meet at the monuments. It seemed appropriate. More hybrids…inorganic objects linked to once organic flesh. Fong thought the meditative postures of the statues, anchored in their broad pedestals to fixed centers of gravity, might help us with our *taolu*. Furthermore, since there are currently fifty-two statues spread across the Park's eight hundred and fifty acres, it seemed like a nice idea to "push hands" at a different one every week – Alexander Hamilton, Beethoven, Columbus, Shakespeare, Webster…King Jagiello. They are like fossils – men and women turned to stone.

Mostly men, that is.

We were on our sixth week, six statues in, up near 103rd Street, standing in front of the cast figure of Dr. J. Marion Sims – the "father" of American gynecology – when Bev Prickitt finally realized that there were no women on pedestals. Other than three fountain sprites and two versions of Alice in Wonderland, it was all "X-men" and bronzed animals. Even the Bethesda Fountain's *Angel of the Waters,* commemorating the 1842 Croton water system, was a biblical make-believe from the Gospel of John. No more meanders in the Park. The Arthur Ross Pinetum, just south of the Reservoir, keeps everyone closer to home. Me most of all; I can see the water.

The Pinetum's small circular arboretum was donated to Central Park by a wood pulp magnate in memory of the large pine and spruce trees that originally lined Olmsted and Vaux's stately carriage road up the west side of the park. When the last of the "Winter Drive" evergreens died off shortly after the turn of the century, the park authorities decided to replace Olmsted's *Sempervirens* with a stand of deciduous trees along the grand winding allée – less gummy needle sap on the children and less rust-colored tannin in the water bodies. It worked well for the fall colors, but as the season changes, where the thick year-round greenery once broke both the wind and white of winter, the "Drive" is now a bare-limbed and wind-chilled gauntlet for any out-of-towners daring enough to tour the park on a Valentine's Day carriage ride. Wrong trees, wrong place.

On the other hand, the dense memorial cloister of assorted pines in The Pinetum works just fine for the X-men. It's private and shelters our odd slow-time motions as if we are a coven of thawing druids, stoned on the aromatic terpene resin of the hovering conifers.

"I suppose you could call me the 'Camera-Man,'...but it's not exactly a camera. It's a field emission scanning electron microscope."

As he speaks, Delano DeAngelus rotates very slowly on his left foot, while lifting his right leg and bending it at the knee. His right arm is bent at the elbow, crossed in front of his chest, level with the ground; it remains fixed in place as it follows his body around. His left arm, perpendicular to the right one, is stretched out, fingers up, palm away, as if "pushing off" his interlocutor.

"It's called a 'SEM'– scanning electron microscope. It can magnify images up to a half-million times larger with resolution down to two nanometers," he says, staring at the back of his hand, "Plus, it comes with a cathodoluminescence detector, a backscatter electron detector, and energy dispersive x-ray spectrography."

There is a momentary pause. The X-men try but can not hold back; they burst out in raucous laughter.

The spell is broken, the great Qi disrupted – the rhythm and flow of the 'life force' that our small Tai chi group is trying to get in touch with teeters off into the Cosmos.

Del, too, loses his balance, and begins hopping in reeling circles on one foot. In an instant, we have gone from a slow-motion balletic ensemble to a spasmodic sextet of doubled-over whirling dervishes.

"Okay, okay...I'm the Camera-Man." Del looks slightly embarrassed by the outburst, but he is smiling. I am glad to see that Del is joining in the fun.

It was a stretch – my introducing him as the "Camera-Man" – but it was even more of a stretch for Del to try and explain his work with the digital imaging equipment in the osteological preparation lab at the Museum.

It's true that Del doesn't use a conventional camera to capture the strange microscopic formations of biotic material underlying all visible life and death – the morphology of tiny organisms and their even tinier organs, or, smaller still, the bacterial and viral hordes that swarm inside those organs. But when Del's taking pictures, glued to his computer-aided Hitachi S-4700 electron microscope – his eyeballs facing off with the huge back-staring eyeballs of a larval dermastid beetle – it gives new meaning to the idea of the zoom lens. I find it impressive that he has the wherewithal to even click his computer's mouse to capture some of his images. There are forms of life that are best kept out of sight.

Regaining his footing, Del turns to me and, in a low voice, says, "I was afraid you'd be taking us to Cleopatra's Needle." Del is referring to the Heliopolis Obelisk in the Park, not to the nickname that Francesca Van Pelt has conferred on his penis. But I get the connection; Del's concern about where her cuckold might find us in the Park is understandable.

Recently, Del told me that the Senator is also an "X-man." It turns out that 'Cleopatra's Needle' is also the brand name of the Senator's surgically implanted non-inflatable penile insert. He'd had the procedure done a few years ago. Now, with a quick bend of subcutaneous silicone and flexible stainless steel, he apparently can be as hard as...well, steel. The Million Dollar Man – part metal, part man. Francesca told Del that all it did for her was add the willies to her faked orgasms. But she liked the name, and at least Del seems to live up to it for her.

It mystifies me what Francesca sees in her unusual lover. I suppose, on the surface, it's understandable; he's a handsome fellow...when he gives himself permission. The flesh and bone are there, along with the dark Mediterranean hair and eyes that I have seen in photographs of his grandfather in the Riverside Quarry at Gilboa. But where Johnny of the Angel's prominent scar crossed his face, Del carries his in the form of an absence. He is there – somewhere behind that good-looking face, but I doubt Francesca could ever locate his true heart, even if she knew on which side of his chest to look for it.

"Don't worry, you're safe here, Del; this isn't the diorama. The Senator won't find you in *this* forest," I laugh, gently teasing him, "Besides he's more than likely gone upstate to his District." I am lying, hoping to ease Del's concern.

Del nods but continues to look furtively around the Pinetum. He knows that, like me, Senator Van Pelt is a shapeshifter.

Yes, Van Pelt is an 'X-man' in a sense other than his manhood. Like me, he is not who he says he is. We both have identities of convenience. If Del had looked further and deeper in the Van Pelt's collection of Princeton yearbooks, *Princeton Yearbook '38,* he would have found James J. Van Pelt – the young State Senator-to-be along with his correct first name.

The name "O'Graéghall," he took for himself, later – a masked taunt, hidden from and never questioned by the Senator's current constituents in New York District 46.

He can get away with this because The State Legislature in New York State has always had a history of murkiness. Ever since the days of "The Black Horse Calvary" it's been vague in its methods, its backrooms, and its agendas on behalf of the people of New York. Background checks just don't seem worth the effort when elected officials are pulled into power on invisible strings. Van Pelt is no exception. An upstate interloper, he is, in truth, a downstate carpet bagger who spends two days a week in a rented Albany apartment representing New York District 46, and the rest of the time in his penthouse overlooking Central Park, feet up on the terrace railing, drinking Manhattans.

On a map, District 46 runs east from the town of Amsterdam along the Mohawk River to the southern edge of Albany, then down along the western bank of the Hudson River to Poughkeepsie, where it turns west through Ulster County and jabs a sharp corner into the Schoharie Reservoir before returning to box northward back to Amsterdam.

One might imagine, because of the Dutch connection, that his blood relatives would be centered on the town of Amsterdam – but they'd be wrong. There are certainly plenty of Van Pelts there, or "van Pelt" if you're local, but they're not the Senator's *blood* relatives. His relatives are from further up the tributary on the Schoharie side of the District. This is where his faux Celtic Christian name, "O'Graéghall," hits its mark. And it is that possessive preposition – *O'...* – that accounts for the contested jab into the Schoharie Reservoir on the District map.

Most of the Schoharie Reservoir – ninety-five percent of it – belongs to District 51 where a different Senator, "Big Bud" Klosson, holds power. The missing five percent of the Reservoir in District 46 sticks in Big Bud's craw, and he's been fighting O'Graéghall Van Pelt all year over that five percent land-grab. The political wrangling has been unseemly; both Senators are Republicans. Furthermore, they're fighting over territory that, to most people, would seem fairly insignificant – the only constituents in Van Pelt's corner of water are Chain Pickerel, Smallmouth Bass, Black Crappies, Walleyes, and runs of Bluntnose Minnows. And as for the water, it doesn't belong to either of them, man or fish; it belongs to New York City. Nevertheless, the small sharp jog on the map bounding the two Districts is a poke in "Big Bud's" eye.

It came about through re-districting. Upstate, this is usually just a polite term for political punishment, and this was a usual case. It had been Van Pelt's idea, pushed through the state senate in a pay-off alliance with some downstate Democrats. Klosson was being taken to the woodshed for backing the "Coalition of Watershed Towns" in its upcoming lawsuit against New York City. The lawsuit had been in response to the City's Amendment to the Safe Water Drinking Act which, in turn, had been prompted by concerns about the increasing amounts of agricultural and waste run-off from the Catskill hillsides into the watershed aquifers feeding the Reservoir. The City worried that other life forms were being stocked in its drinking water besides the sport fish; in particular, *Giardia lamblia* and *Cryptosporidium parvum* – two nasty parasitical descendants of Precambrian protozoa that wreak havoc on modern mammalian intestinal tracts. When the Board of Water Supply came back upstream with new ordinances to clean up the *terroir* of its "champagne drinking water," Big Bud and thirty Catskill communities circled their wagons.

To many in the communities, the amended Safe Water Drinking Act seemed like 1917 all over again, another eminent domain juggernaut – land acquisitions, buffer zones, easements, being told how-where-and-when to take a crap, costs falling heavy on their own dime. "Willing buyer, willing seller" had not worked out so well seventy-six years earlier, and memories were long. In the upstate reservoirs, stone walls and old foundations still showed up in low water, and submerged property lines, places of the heart, had become stories told with pointed fingers and wistful faces reflected on the surface of the stilled reservoir pools. Property rights would not be relinquished so easily this time. The 'Coalition of Watershed Towns' took the position that if the water wasn't good enough for folks in the City to drink, then they should clean it up at their own front door; they had all the money – build a high-tech water filtration plant and "*tweak the parts-per-million of whatever the hell they find in their taps to their hearts' content.*"

Van Pelt's move against Klosson had not gathered much attention. Few noticed that the re-districting would place a small section of the Schoharie Reservoir's west bank inside his District. Even fewer were aware that the City maintained a small building there – the Shandaken Tunnel Intake Chamber; whatever water was not released northward as overflow at the Gilboa Dam went south through that Intake Tunnel, all the way to Van Pelt's wet-bar at the St. Urban. The Senator had wrangled himself a stake in one of the City's largest reservoirs…at both ends of its pipeline.

Downstate, folks felt certain Van Pelt would use his newly acquired vote on the State Water Board to do the altruistic thing on behalf of more than half the state's population. Upstate, they wondered if he'd gotten too much sun on his penthouse terrace. I believe that Van Pelt's interest in the Reservoir and the Shandaken Tunnel Intake has a different agenda altogether. It's a personal matter, and not just his. My grandmother Winifred Goldring had intimated as much in one of her notebooks. The Shandaken Intake Chamber might be the cenotaph to all of our families.

"Hello there, Kinsolver. Out sporting with these nutcases again, are ya?"

An elderly man walks, with a side leaning gait, into our circle. A small monkey, leashed to a tiny red leather collar with embossed gold studs, sits on his shoulder. It's Waterhouse Hawkins and "Dolores," his white-faced capuchin monkey, *Cebus capucinus*. The man's wide grin leers from beneath an unkempt shock of yellow-white hair that matches the hair of the small animal's face. His smile is not aimed at me, it's aimed at Bev Prickitt, the "Mail-Man." For a moment he stands still, hoping for a response from Bev; there is a hint of a smile, but she pretends to ignore him and continues spinning slowly about her axis. He then turns his sweeping grin over the rest of the us. He raises his elbows, flapping them like a pair of wings, and breaks into a shuffling tap dance.

"You got room for me, fellas...and mademoiselle?" he asks mischievously, jigging his shoulders and doffing an invisible hat to Prickitt. One of his shoes sports a three-inch lift that rhythmically scuffs the ground like the head of a leather sledgehammer. His pet simian, her large round eyes warily locked on our motley crew, rides his bouncing shoulder like a jockey.

Waterhouse works near the Pinetum. His job is maintaining the large screw valves in the North Gatehouse at the Central Park Reservoir. He's also an honorary member of the X-men. We could have called him the "Water-Boy" or the "House-Boy," either name would suffice given his current vocation, but his given name is just too good – *Waterhouse* – downright Middle English, bundling his moniker with his job description.

But I leave his name as it is,...for another reason.

Besides Lincoln and his wife Saskia, Waterhouse Hawkins is the last connection I have to my father, Livingston. They knew one another, fifty plus years ago – Civilian Conservation Corps, Highlands Hammock Camp SP-3 in Sebring, Florida. Lincoln, Waterhouse, and my father enlisted at about the same time. Each of them came from a different part of the country, but they spent time together at the Highlands camp where Saskia's older brother, Rembrandt Stikkey, was the Superintendent. The three young recruits fell in with one another playing baseball there, and afterward, when my father was killed in the War, the other two men remained close.

A few years after Linc came north in the early sixties, Waterhouse Hawkins followed. There had been a few divorces, a bunch of kids gone and settled into their own lives, and not much left in Princeton Florida "for an old ladies' man," as he would put it. He'd been a master plumber working in the Miami-Dade area and, once north, had no trouble finding work with the crews manning the valves at the Central Park Reservoir. Almost twenty years now on the job, he took the news of the Reservoir's decommissioning hard. The City kept him on to watch over the facilities, but now, with the pumps shut down, he and his capuchin monkey work the Gatehouse alone, running off vandals and watching the graffiti grow like lichen on the outer walls. "Could just as well be a chained-up German Shepherd," he complains, "...'cept that wouldn't work for Dolores."

Drawing himself up, Waterhouse walks over to me. He is now looking serious.

"Come by the North Gatehouse when you're done, Kinsolver," he says quietly, "There's been another visitation." He nods toward Del. "Bring along looney of the angel. The Altar-Boy showed up again this morning,...and something else, as well."

Del has not overheard Waterhouse but looks over at me as if he has. I respond to his look with a shrug; more funny business in the water most likely,...but The Altar-Boy?

Saluting the group, Waterhouse ambles out of the circle. "Carry on, men," he says, then, doffing a twirling hand to Prickitt, "and ladies,... there's a world to be saved."

"Another dead fish in the Reservoir?" Prickitt calls out, teasing, "Hey, Mister Darwin, when is this evolution business ever going to stop?"

Waterhouse turns back to her and puffs up professorially, "Well, that would be a matter of Natural Selection, Lady Prickitt," he says, with a wink. On his shoulder, Dolores bares her teeth and gums, eyeing the Mail-Woman like a jealous banshee.

Waterhouse Hawkins does not really understand Natural Selection, how it works, or even what it really means. But it was he who first discovered that "Deep Time" and Darwin's "Origin of Species" was being played out in the waters of the Central Park Reservoir.

It began with the public scare about the *Giardia* and *Cryptosporidium* in the Schoharie and the concern that the offspring of the Precambrian parasites might find their way to the Reservoir in Central Park. A notice had appeared on the Gatehouse door, Del's Hitachi S-4700 microscope camera had been used for verification, results were pending.

Then, there was the sudden infestation of cockroaches, *Periplaneta americana,* hordes of them swarming over Waterhouse's empty bottles of Smoking Loon Blackberry Wine like a second Cambrian invasion: spineless arthropods with chitinous exoskeletons and jointed limbs. Waterhouse calls them waterbugs, but they are not. Unlike their ancestors

– the sea bottom dwelling trilobites – cockroaches prefer dry land and the aerated smell of fermenting fruit.

In hindsight, I was glad the creatures that evolved *between* the amorphous free-floating microbial parasites and the arthropodic cockroaches had not been part of the plan. Those creatures are the stuff of frightful dreams – harpooning hermaphroditic cnidarians 'penis-fencing' with one another for gender rights, single-hole flatworms with mouths doubling as anuses, or the larval sea squirts consuming their own brains to prepare for adulthood as a transparent bag of sea water. All of them working their random way – past the ancient polypifers building coral homes on the foundations of the dead – toward Us.

Nevertheless, whoever had the knowledge and the peculiar idea to re-stage the theory of evolution in the Central Park Reservoir must have figured it was easiest to jump right to a life form that made some sense, something more recognizable, a relative more familiar – like an ancestor with bilateral symmetry and a skeleton. The fish kill proved me right.

It came when the Reservoir valves were shut down and the aerators turned off – small mouth bass, endoskeleton vertebrates, spine-down, belly-up, floating in the oxygen-starved water. Poor Waterhouse was days with a skimming net, double-bagging the rotting descendants of Ordivician Period teleosts in thirty-gallon Hefty Clinchsaks.

As I've said, all of this seemed oddly intentional, but it was only when Waterhouse saw the live Lungfish, *Neoceratodus forsteri*, swimming across the dividing weir in the Reservoir that anyone realized that a countdown to mankind might actually be underway. The Queensland Lungfish could only have been stocked.

At the first sighting, Waterhouse had been badly spooked. The fish was a good three to four feet in length with no discernible tail. It looked more like a scaly mammal – a miniature humpback whale without the

109

flukes. It had a single flap of dorsal fin running up its cartilaginous "back-bone," and instead of front pectoral fins, the Lungfish swam with long fleshy paddle-like appendages as if doing a breaststroke.

Pulling on his hip boots, Waterhouse walked out on the weir between the Reservoir's north and south basins for a closer look. As he scanned the water, he heard a wheezing sound behind him, like a blast from a small bellows. The fish was there, having its closer look at *him*, head out of water, wide mouth open as if taking in the air. Which it was. When the Lungfish loudly inhaled for a second time, Waterhouse went over backwards and nearly drowned in the south basin when his hip boots filled with water.

He called Linc. Linc called me. I called Trifina. She confirmed the identification, noting that the fish had probably been taken from its natural habitat in the Burnett and Mary River System of Eastern Australia. "It's our transitional ancestor," she said, watching the fish's slow sleepy rise to the Reservoir's surface, "Paleontologists call it a living fossil because it looks pretty much the same as a cast from the Devonian Period. The Age of Fishes. It's *transitional* because one of our earlier ray-finned ancestors had developed dual oxygen intakes – gills and lungs. The lungs were a hedge; the swamp waters were receding, and the first forests were beginning to put air into the atmosphere. Schools of Devonian fish had to cross dry land from one drying pool to the next, and distances were increasing. "Back then...," Trifina said, twinkling a smile at Waterhouse, who was still drying off from his spill, "...it wasn't how long you could breathe under the water, it was how long you could breathe above it."

"You see those front fins?" Trifina points at the Lungfish. "It was the ones with the most muscle in their pectorals that evolved the advantage, the ability to pull themselves forward from the fresh-water shallows onto dry land."

"Aqua-man...crawling along like a leg-shot soldier," Linc cracked, poking Waterhouse in the ribs.

"Or mermaids," Waterhouse responded, poking Linc back.

Trifina ignored both men. "And once those rear pelvic fins evolved," she said, "it was just a matter of time before their descendants were lifting themselves off the ground on amphibian hands and feet...tetrapods. It was an important moment in our natural history."

Waterhouse shook his head at the fish. "Either way...there's a crazy fucker out there somewhere, if you ask me," he said quietly. Trifina's lesson on mankind's great chain of being had not explained the kind of man behind the Lungfish swimming in his Reservoir. "Gotta be some *craaazy* fucker's doin' this," he said, again.

For the next two weeks, Waterhouse Hawkins watched the fish whenever the Paleozoic doppelganger surfaced for air. No one else seemed to notice, not the joggers nor the park rangers. Waterhouse began to think of it as a pet. Then, last week, the Lungfish was found dead.

The weather had been hot, no rain. The Reservoir water was down, the top of the weir was above the surface, coated in a crust of dried slick. An algae bloom had appeared in the south basin. The Lungfish had been thriving in the turbid water, but the City ordered Waterhouse and his crew to open the valves to aerate the basin. Apparently, the Lungfish had not evolved enough to crawl up and over the weir into the north basin, and neither its gills nor its lungs could keep it from suffocating in a flushing of chlorine and hexafluorosilicic acid. The city's purified drinking water was just too poisonous.

Trifina and I were there when Waterhouse nudged the dead fish along the weir to the shore, lifted it awkwardly from the water, and tossed it onto the Gatehouse stoop. It hit the stone at our feet like a large pile of wet mud. It was already becoming rank, but it seemed wrong to dispose of it in one of Waterhouse's Clinchsaks. It was time to get Del involved. Perhaps his dermastid beetles at the Museum could, at the very least, save the skeleton.

It was Del who suggested that Waterhouse's 'crazy fucker' might not be done.

"The Great Dying," he said, solemnly looking over the carcass. I figured Del might have two thoughts in mind, and both had to do with our ancestors. I was glad that his explanation referred to those quite a bit further back in time.

The Great Dying was short-hand for the Permian-Triassic Extinction – the bottle-neck that our ancestral species barely squeezed through two hundred and fifty million years ago. Meteors, volcanoes, radical climate shifts, oceanic eruptions, all or some, it's not certain; but whatever it was, the riled-up earth shook off almost ninety percent of the animal kingdom like pond water from a wet dog. Then, with so much bio-diversity gone, it was inevitable that a mono-culture would follow for a bit. And it did – Dinosaurs.

Del had predicted it. He didn't say what form it'd take, but I suspect he had an inkling. Last Sunday, when Waterhouse was walking along the weir hoping to find himself another Lungfish, he found instead a three-foot section of fossilized tailbone from a *Hadrosaurus foulkii* lodged just inside the stone archway at Valve Chamber No. Two.

Waterhouse thought it might be the skeleton of a Lungfish picked clean by the few small-mouth bass remaining from the fish kill, but when Trifina saw it, she recognized the caudal vertebrae of a Late Jurassic Period dinosaur.

There was something even odder about the finding. Trifina had gone down on her haunches to take a closer look at the bone and realized that three of the vertebrae were made of plaster. They were covered with vestiges of shellac. She poked at one of them, and it crumbled to her touch like wet chalk. "This has been restored," she said, "It's from a museum. Look." She pointed at a small embossed metal band at the top of the tailbone. There were initials stamped into it – *AMNH* – and beneath them, the words: *On loan from The State Museum in Albany.*

I decided to take the fossil home. Not to where it belonged, not that home, not yet at least. I wrapped the tailbone in one of the Clinchsaks, carried it across the Park and into the service elevator of my apartment building on Museum Mile. It's now sitting at a west-facing window near the foot of my bed. Each morning during this past week, I have thought to return it to the American Museum of Natural History, but I haven't. Not until I am sure about things. I worry, staring at that fossil, that the extinctions aren't over.

It was Permian-Triassic that brought forth the dinosaurs, but it was the Cretaceous-Tertiary that finished them off, allowing our skittish shrew-like ancestors to live long enough to bulk up and turn evolution in our direction. In paleontological time, these two earth-clearing events had been a hundred million years apart. But we are now in 'crazy-fucker' time at the Reservoir – The Mesozoic Era was over last week, the Cenozoic is about to begin – the big mammals are on their way, Primates in the lead. I figured there'd be more bones in the Reservoir before all this was over. But I had the wrong Reservoir.

After leaving the X-men behind in the Pinetum and making our way to the North Gatehouse, Del, Waterhouse and I are greeted by Linc and Saskia Gilboa, sitting together on the Gatehouse stoop.

I am surprised to see Saskia. On Sundays, she's usually either at her small fern and flower shop on Cathedral Parkway or at the First Corinthian

Baptist Church with the other Florida émigrés from the Glades that came to the city following the Second World War. Both her shop and the church are special to her. The First Corinthian Baptist Church, like Linc and Saskia themselves, is a coupling of African-Americans and displaced Seminole and Miccosukie Indians who found one another in a communion of diaspora. Her shop, *Blackwater Ferns & Flowers*, is an outpost of the church. Each week she festoons the high altar with fronds to "carry back home" many in the congregation. Cabbage Palm and Hand Ferns plucked from the boots of Sabal Palmettos; Southern Wood Ferns from the Live Oak hammocks; and the Plumosa Ferns that tangle in the limestone outcrops of the Glades where Saskia and her brother Rembrandt played as children.

Besides arranging her fern displays, Saskia has been a "Greeter" at the church for nearly thirty years serving the S.M.I.L.E Ministry. Linc says there is no one more suited to this than Saskia – *She's done it for me since the day we met, he says: Serve, Motivate, Inspire, Love & Empower.* I believe him. Saskia has always treated me like a son, despite her quiet disapproval of my relationship with Trifina – she looks away in her thoughts, but sees us in her heart, as if her daughter's affair with me has inevitable roots.

With time, Saskia has softened, her body rounded and slow-moving like other women in their seventies. But she is still lovely, with long gray hair streaked with the last of youthful black, and dark Indian eyes, clear and set deep on high cheek bones. Trifina looks a great deal like her mother and hopes to age like her as well.

"There you are." Saskia smiles sweetly at me and reaches out her arms. I bend to kiss her cheek and she takes my hand in hers, pulling me closer. She is arthritic, but her slightly clawed grip is insistent about something. "We have a guest," she whispers in my ear, nodding her head toward the side of the Gatehouse.

Stepping back to look, I see the Altar-Boy perched on what looks like a round fissured concrete block set in the corner where the reservoir railing meets the brick wall of the Gatehouse. Trifina is with him, on one knee, her hand on the boy's small back. Dante is facing the water, trying to twirl an orange pistol around his index finger like a gunslinger. The plastic squirt gun clatters to the ground.

"Found us a runaway," Linc says, rising from the stoop. He points at the round block under the Altar-Boy. "And *that*, as well."

More surprises. The concrete block changes before my eyes as I recognize the stump from my grandmother's drawings. The boy is sitting on a fossilized stump of The Gilboa Tree.

"Showed up this morning. Both of them," Waterhouse says, drawing near. He picks Dolores up off his shoulder and unclips her leash. The capuchin jumps to the ground, hesitates, and leers at Saskia who is blocking the way to Waterhouse's bottles of Smoking Loon inside the Gatehouse. Without rising from the stoop, Saskia leans sideways; the monkey darts past her through the open door.

"Young Dante was just sitting there when I came in this morning. Sitting on that thing," says Waterhouse. He gives me a quizzical look, then turns to follow Dolores into the Gatehouse.

Trifina stands up and beckons us over. Del hangs back.

"What are you doing here, Dante?" I ask the boy, "Aren't you supposed to be at Mass with your mother?" I have one eye on the boy and another on the fossil.

"I was," he says, defensively, "I was there." He studies the twirl of his plastic pistol, avoiding my gaze.

"He's loaded that thing with Holy Water," Linc says, chuckling, "Took it right out of the font at The Immaculate Conception."

The Altar-Boy is timorous in the surround of adult attention. He jumps off the fossil and skips over to the Reservoir railing. Without speaking, he begins firing streams of sacramental water from his pistol in high arcs over the sloping embankment into the pool of the Reservoir.

"Tell him, Dante, tell him what happened at home," Trifina says gently.

Dante does not respond. He continues firing into the water, watching Del out of the corner of his eye.

Del is holding the edge of the Gatehouse door, holding it away from the wall to see its outer surface. At his head height, a large 'X' has been carved into the door's face, the grooved wood is fresh, pale-yellow and splintered within the dark weathered oak surface. Del raises his hand and traces the crossing with his forefinger, then walks slowly over to boy's side at the edge of the Reservoir. He leans forward with his forearms on the iron railing, hands clasped, watching the arcs of holy spray from Immaculate Conception. Dante looks up at him, imploringly, "I don't want to go back home," he says softly, "Please don't make me...*you* know."

At my side, Linc mutters scripture, "And the devil who had deceived them was thrown into the lake of fire and brimstone where the beast and the false prophet were, and they will be tormented day and night forever and ever."

Before I can speak, before I can ask Linc what the hell is going on, he touches my arm and says, quietly, "You better come inside. Waterhouse has something you should see."

The Gatehouse is unusually tidy, floor swept clean, the four large brass valves controlling the crest gates far below the stone floor are polished bright. No sign of wine bottles. Dolores is up on the sill of the clerestory window, swatting at summer flies. Below her, a worn slat-back swivel office chair sits at an open rolltop desk placed against the granite wall. Both chair and desk have been polished.

"Being inspected, tomorrow," Waterhouse says, looking around the room, as if making a last spot check. "They're inspecting everyone and everything up and down the Aqueduct…ever since this." He picks up a folder from his desk. "It's from the Bureau of Water Resource Management," he says, handing it to me.

The paper in the folder is brief and private, two pages, each stamped with the words: *Draft Report: For BWRM Distribution Only.* I look up at Waterhouse.

He shrugs and waves his hand dismissively in the air. "Someone shouldn't have left it lying around. Go on, read it," he says.

The date on the *Board of Water Resource Management Stakeholder's Report* precedes The Mayor's Report on *The Decommissioning of the Central Park Reservoir* by less than a week. It describes the discovery of bones in the drinking water – Upstate, in the Catskill headwaters near the hamlet of Gilboa. A local welder, working on the filter screens at the Shandaken Tunnel Intake on the west bank of the Schoharie Reservoir had found a human femur with flesh still attached. It had been sucked in and stuck fast to the steel mesh. The following morning, a leak appeared in the sandstone facing on the headwall of the Schoharie Dam near the site of the former Riverside Quarry. Divers found what they believed were more human remains, well-preserved, soft tissue waving in the currents from an eroding fracture in the concrete. The pathologist's report was forthcoming.

"Van Pelt's got an interest in this. He's going back upstate." Linc says, softly, looking over my shoulder at the Report. "That's what his boy says. Says he's leaving tomorrow, taking the family with him. Dante don't wanna go, that's for sure." Waterhouse, at his side, nods in agreement.

"I heard that as well…that he was heading up," I say, turning and looking at Linc, gravely. As for Van Pelt's 'interest in this', I'm still trying figure out how deep it goes.

"And the timing, that's something else. You saw that cut on the door...the mark?" Linc asks.

Before I can answer, we're interrupted by a sudden commotion outside the Gatehouse, loud and angry. I recognize the voice of Francesca Van Pelt. Tossing the Report on to Waterhouse's desk, I rush to the doorway. Around the corner, Francesca, her face hidden beneath large sunglasses, is arguing with Trifina, backing her up against the Reservoir railing. She's wearing a white sleeveless summer dress and matching high-heels. One of her shoes is missing its stiletto. Dante, his upper arm held fast in the angry grip of Francesca, is at her side with his little shoulder hitched up; he winces each time his mother's anger shakes him. Del is nowhere to be seen.

"I promise you; he was here when my father and I arrived," Trifina says, both hands raised defensively in the air. "He's fine; he's safe."

Francesca glares at Trifina, then turns to the boy. "And you!" She shakes Dante again. She has the boy's squirt gun in her other hand and waves it in his face. "Father Anthony saw you filling this from the font! How could you?"

Dante whimpers, looking down at his feet.

Saskia Gilboa has risen from the stoop. She looks at me with alarm, uncertain what to do.

"Mrs. Van Pelt," I call out, walking quickly toward the women. "I was about to take him back to the St. Urban."

Francesca has her back to me but turns quickly at the sound of my voice.

"Kinsolver?" She is momentarily disarmed, calling out my name as a question. I am caught up short by the sight of her face. From beneath her sunglasses, her nose and her upper cheek on the right side are bruised and swollen.

118

Following my gaze, she releases the boy and raises her palm to her face, as if intending to re-adjust her sunglasses. "Don't bother, Kinsolver," she says, quietly. Reaching down, she takes off her good shoe, and snaps off the heel. "We're late. The Senator wants us to go north with him to Albany. We have a lot of packing to do. And homework," she adds, looking at her son. "We'll be taking Dante out of summer school for the week."

Returning the shoe to her foot, she takes the boy again by his hand and begins walking away, shoulders thrown back, stiff and straight. Trifina remains standing with her back to the Reservoir. She folds her arms and watches them leave. Saskia walks to her daughter's side.

"You know, that boy out there, he could be hers," Linc says quietly, looking over at his daughter. "If we're right about Van Pelt, he'd do that... just to get back at it."

Just to get back at it. I turn to the stigmata, to the carved graffiti on the Gatehouse door –the 'X' mark of the DeAngelus family from The Age of Fishes.

"Do you think he's returned?" I ask.

Linc gives me a fatalistic smile. "Xavi? Looks like it. Johnny of the Angel's prodigal son has come out from behind the walls of Heaven." He points at the cast of the Gilboa Tree next to the Reservoir railing. "That's probably why the fossil is here. The past and the present, comin' together. The last time I saw it, it was on its way to the monastery of Mount Savior at Poverty Hill. Jenna had it sent to Xavi; it had been Johnny's....and now we got it here."

Linc's words sank in slowly. I had let Xaviero DeAngelus fade away in family thoughts, just as his monastic life in western New York had promised the same for him. I have never met him. He had shut him-self away from everything and everyone sometime after Del was born. Two hundred miles from Slingerlands; he could have been on another planet. And now he's here; perhaps he, too...*just to get back at it?*

I have always thought of Linc as the only one of my father's genera-tion who could tell the full story, that it was only he who could connect us to the generation that preceded him, to their dying.

Damn Grandfathers. They're supposed to be an easy comfort, sated playfully with long life and harmless tall tales, twinkling eyes still bright in wise wrinkled faces that trace their response to life's good nature. It is hard to picture them otherwise – as young men, young bodies burst-ing with scatter-shot desire, fighting for a life with meaning, with love. They just don't seem to fit. And, yet it is harder still to picture them without the generation that binds them to their grandsons – the missing fathers, the men that would have allowed a young boy to feel the kinship, the slow rhythm of descent, the mirror of themselves within a family. Without that, everything is marked by what is missing. And what little understanding there is, comes from what's also left behind in the sad unbalanced embrace of a mother's broken love.

Maybe if all the families had not scattered – had stayed put, filled the local cemetery – the stories and offspring of the generations might have maintained a confirming proximity; one would always know where they stood relative to others. But this was not the case. After the Dam was finished, the concrete set and the river stilled, everyone went their separate ways, away from Gilboa, other men died, also away from each other. All that was shared in the scattering was the unforgiving silence of gray concrete anchored to the mountains, and the fading rumor about the family men entombed inside it.

I do not know what Xaviero DeAngelus knows, if he knows the history, what happened or who fired the shot; or who fell and where... taking the gun with them. And I wonder if he believes what his son Delano DeAngelus has long believed – that Johnny of the Angel and Eli Gallagher had killed one another before meeting their shared grandson.

"It's been fifty years since I've seen Xavi," Linc says, "Last time was just before he left for Italy at the start of the war; then he went missing over there for five or six years. When he returned, he was changed, I guess. They had a go at it, he and...well, even before *she* died, he was gone again out there to Poverty Hill. Do you think he's here for Dee after all this time?"

I shrug. Linc rarely utters Mina's name in my presence. "Maybe," I say, "but I'll bet that Xavi's looking for a relative in the other direction. I'll bet he's come for Johnny of the Angel. The bones in the Schoharie Reservoir."

As if she has overheard our conversation, Dolores comes running out the Gatehouse and jumps up on the Gilboa Tree fossil, then, from there to the Reservoir railing. The small monkey shrieks at the water and begins slapping the iron railing with her hand. Turning toward the Reservoir, I see Del in the far distance, standing on the barely submerged weir. He has his back to us, and his arms spread. A dark figure, small in the mid-expanse of water, his face to the blue sky and the golden glitter of sunlight strewn at his feet like sparkling jewels as he walks slowly across water.

"Christ almighty...Dee's his father's son alright," says Linc, at my shoulder.

"Loony of the angel," Waterhouse mumbles, shaking his head.

"*Chayahlom ooche,*" whispers Saskia at my other shoulder. Indian words, Miccosukie, her family tongue; words that I've thought about many times in my life.

...the lost son walks.

6

The Scattering...

Fathers
1941, Highlands Hammock Camp SP-3, Sebring, FL
"Boys who 'can take it' will get much out of the CCC..."
(Civilian Conservation Corps Handbook)

"THE MONKEYS THAT YOU saw on the Silver River are neither indigenous nor did they arrive from South America. They're Rhesus Macaques from Africa – catarrhines, *Macaca mulatta* – Old World monkeys. They were let loose on the river by the jungle cruise captain for the tourists."

There was a rustling mid-aisle as a large acetate transparency was removed from the overhead projector and a new film sheet placed. A Capuchin monkey leered from the wall, next to a poster of a shirtless young Civilian Conservation Corps recruit swinging a pickaxe, seemingly at the primate's head.

"This is a New World monkey – *Cebus capucinus* – from South America. It's actually an older genus. Its ancestor rafted from Africa during the Eocene Period, sometime between thirty and forty million years ago. Note the nostrils. They're called platyrrhine, meaning flat or broad nosed."

"Looks like one of them nigger fellas from Myakka," whispered one of the boys in the back, loudly.

"You think she knows what she's talking about?" whispered another.

"Who's listening," whispered a third, "I'm only here for the view."

"Now, boys, let's just keep it down, shall we." The company subaltern, hands clasped behind his back, rocked on his heels, mid-aisle. His voice was stern, but it was the tone of a conspirator. Boys' talk.

The muffled laughter mingled with the boisterous shuffling on the "classroom" benches, the benches that Livingston Kinsolver had only finished hammering together that very morning. He and his cousin, Lincoln Gilboa, had not even been given the time to brush on the linseed oil. The cured wood had been cut and stacked a few years back by the first Civilian Conservation Corps recruits at the camp, Highlands Hammock SP-3. They had been older boys, quite a few of them men, WWI vets who survived the war but then lost their lives trying to save others down at Islamorada in the Keys during the Hurricane of '35.

Normally the Rec Hall at the Highland Hammock Camp would be filled with rank sweat from a day of grubbing out the creeks, but it was a Saturday – a day off, or a school day, depending on one's ambitions – and the smell of the freshly-sanded slash pine planks filled the air. The CCC Education Classes were in full-swing. Some of the boys would be in the automotive or machinery shops down in the maintenance Quonsets, others were learning math or book-keeping at Administrative Headquarters up the small rise near the camp entrance, some were in the Mess, learning how to cook, and others were just playing hooky – sleeping in, or seining for crawdads in the cypress swamp. But, in the Recreation Hall, additional benches had been lined up quickly for the Natural Science Class; it was over-subscribed. The first week, only three boys had shown up, one of whom was Livingston, but word had gone round about the teacher.

Livingston picked at a large splinter on the bench next to his right thigh, digging it out with the eraser end of his pencil. He was irritated by the snickering in the back, but he kept his quiet. He, too, appreciated "the view" of Miss Belle Stikkey, the young science teacher from Indiantown. He didn't want to admit it, not even to himself. He focused on the splinter, wondering whether it was he or cousin Linc – "*one of them nigger boys from Myakka*" – who had missed it during their sanding duties.

The Capuchin Monkey slid off the wall and was replaced by a Chimpanzee. "*Pan Troglodyte*," said Miss Stikkey, "Chimps are apes, not monkeys. Many scientists believe they're our closest cousin among the primates."

Livingston flicked the splinter to the floor and sat up. He tried to study the chimp, but his gaze kept drifting back to Belle. She was the prettiest science teacher he had ever seen; maybe prettier than *any* teacher he'd ever seen. Her dark hair was soft and straight, cut short in a fashion that city girls up north had taken on of late, a kind of bob that swooped at her cheeks; it moved freely whenever she turned away from the wall to address the class, but always fell back into place. She wore a print cotton dress, belted and buttoned in a formal way to the neck, but when she put her hand on her hip and leaned back to get a better look at the images on the wall, the fabric pulled back at her breast. Seeing her stand like that, reminded him of his sister Mina, of her naked body and the way she had sometimes stood...in front of him. Belle was older than his sister, but not much, he guessed. All the recruits knew that the science teacher was married, but that only made her more desirable to Livingston. Dangerous affection was something he seemed to be born to; it shamed him, but it ran in the family.

Livingston looked away, down, and opened his notebook. He put his pencil to paper, and the two women out of his mind; he'd promised Linc that he'd take notes for him. *Our closest cousin among the primates,* he wrote.

It didn't seem fair to Livingston that his cousin, just because...well, he looked like a negro, couldn't attend classes with him. The day before, Linc Gilboa had been welcome enough to make the benches, but at day's end, he was sent back to the Myakka River Camp SP-11 with all the other colored boys. It made for odd sense; Linc's mother, Billie Kinsolver, was as white as the bleached sand that the Myakka water cut through to join up with the Gulf of Mexico.

It had taken awhile for the cousins to find one another. A certain Mr. Endurance Fuller from Princeton, Florida, had had a lot do with it. Everything, in fact.

Livingston's sister Mina, and her mother, Mattie Goldring, had spent some time with Fuller six years before, down on his plantation southwest of Miami. That was in '35. Livingston had to remain in school and didn't make the trip. He was still a boy – even more than he was now – living in the Bronx and attending Christ the King Elementary where Mattie taught third grade. Fiorello La Guardia was mayor, Roosevelt was trying to dig everyone out of the Depression, and young Livingston, just turned thirteen, was still using Goldring as his last name – his mother had been single all his life, and his and Mina's father, dismissed as a "man in my past."

Mattie Goldring and Endurance Fuller had some shared history from up north, and, along with it, a shared affection for Linc Gilboa's mother who managed the cut-foliage end of Fuller's fern business. Ostensibly, Mattie had brought her daughter along to meet the woman who was her namesake, but she was really clearing the way for her boy. Livingston was growing up, asking questions; Mattie wanted to make sure it was the right time for him to meet his father's side of the family.

Linc Gilboa's mother was the *first* "Mina" – Wilhelmina Kinsolver – but everyone knew her as Billie. She had given her son his last name. It did not come from the family, his father's or hers; it was the name of the town where he was conceived, and where his father was buried in an unmarked grave. Billie had her reasons; her brother Piedmont shared a grave with him.

The last time Billie had seen Livingston, he was only a bump under a dress, cinched in by a gun belt. It would be years later that Livingston would learn that it had not been Mattie's dress, nor her gun belt; both, including the fetus, had belonged to Winifred Goldring, and all three had been gifts from Billie's brother, Piedmont.

It was destined to happen eventually, that the women, Mattie Goldring and Billie Kinsolver, would start to put the families back in order. In hindsight, the fact that the Civilian Conservation Corps played such a big part also seemed liked destiny. After all, Roosevelt's "Tree Army" had been saving families since '33, when the first "Hoover Pullmans" left the train stations, scattering unemployed young men across the country to work the land. People were bound to cross paths.

In March of 1933, when FDR first took office, Livingston Goldring was still waiting for his eleventh birthday. The President's pledge – his "new deal for the American people" – was just a jumble of initials that Livingston could neither decipher nor understand – *PWA, HOLC, NRA, CCC, FCA, ECW, TVA, FDIC.* He knew they were government programs meant to help, but they all sounded like private clubs to him – like the *OSIA* over on Bathgate Avenue across from the asphalt playground where he played stickball with the Italian kids. Except he knew what those initials stood for; *The Order of the Sons of Italy of America* was as bad off as everyone else. Worse, if anything.

It was hard for Livingston to be certain which families were on the state relief rolls and which ones were not; he knew that, for some, there was dignity to be maintained. But he had teammates who lived in the playground with their parents, in frayed bell tents out by the chain link fence in deep center field. The rusted chain link out there had been cut for an opening to a makeshift privy surrounded by a wooden stall over one of the storm drains on Bathgate.

It was that following summer in '34, when Livingston discovered that some city folks had gone back to the land altogether, and, in his own way, he would become determined to follow them.

On July 4th, Livingston's older sister Mina took him down to Central Park in Manhattan. It was his very first visit to the park. There was going to be a band and a parade of soldiers, World War I veterans, marching along the East Drive. It was supposed to be family fun, a distraction from hard times, but it turned into a melee with the police from the Central Park Precinct. Some of the soldiers were infiltrators, carrying placards and calling themselves the "Bonus Expeditionary Force." They began chanting, drowning out the music, demanding the bonus pay that had been promised them, compensation for their time abroad.

The World War Adjusted Compensation Act of '24 had called for the pay-out to be delivered in 1945, but the vets wanted it now. They needed it now. Chants turned into shouts, marching turned into pushing and shoving, the music stopped, fists started flying, the police from the 20th Precinct joined the fray, guns were fired, skulls cracked. Mina almost pulled Livingston's arm out of its socket, trying to get them both clear. They ran across the park, heading for the Bronx bound El train on 9th Avenue, but when they rounded the walls of the old Yorkville Reservoir, they found themselves on the edge of a large settlement of families living among the ruins.

A hand-painted wooden sign was propped up against the rubble of one of the stone walls that had once contained the city's water supply – "Welcome to The Greatest City in the World." Lime-spall and broken brick, weathered lumber planks peppered with termite holes, corrugated and soot-blackened sheets of tin, heavy carpets, nub worn and sewn together with rope – the homestead shanties were strewn along a cock-eyed main street of hardened mud as if their property lines had been drawn up by children.

Livingston had seen photographs of the "Hoovervilles," he'd even seen the Movietone newsreels at community night in the auditorium at Christ the King. But those images were always in black and white, ashen, like life and death. What he saw before him now was different. There was a colorful pride here. Children ran free, climbing trees and chasing squirrels, dogs followed the chase or rooted for the rear-yard slops, mothers chatted in doorways, tossing scraps to flocks of pigeons and mourning doves. Everyone was poorly clothed, but they looked clean, and, although their hovels were leaking, their homes had a wealth of dry humor in their addresses – 'The Casino' with its burgundy velvet carpet walkway to the front door; 'Radio City,' a tangle of wires and *Puttin' on the Ritz* crooning from its only window, 'Dunwiddie Manor' even had a mailbox with a make-shift flag up, as if expecting an unlikely delivery. One homeowner had scavenged two fluted Greek columns for a front portico; its pediment read 'The White House,' patriotic smoke from a red-painted stove pipe, curled in white arabesques into a bright blue sky.

Maybe it was because the men were off looking for work, any work, gone into the city to join one of the long lines, hoping their particular spot along it would fall on the right side of whatever was available. It was cheerless outside, out there in the City that surrounded the Park. Lives had been turned inside out. It seemed only natural to do the same with Central Park, start fresh within Olmsted's wilderness – Civilization hewn from the heart of Nature, as it was, rather than the other way around.

When Livingston and his sister reached Summit Rock at the edge of the park, they could see the pockets of men and women gathered in the lower clearings. The distant sounds of the brawling had moved to Fifth Avenue, muffled in the dense canopies of trees; the cooking smoke from the Yorkville encampment drifted lazily in a late afternoon breeze out of the southwest toward the Upper Reservoir.

Mina was out of breath from all the running and the climb to the high point of the Park. She had dressed up for the outing and was wearing her Sunday pumps, two-tone leather with high sling-back heels and open toes.

She cocked a leg across her knee to check the heel on one of her shoes. It was loose.

As she bent over, Livingston saw that her dress was torn. A side seam had opened, exposing the skin beneath the strap of her bra. He turned away, then looked again at the almond-shaped pucker of her open dress, thinking of her scent, how she smelled after taking a bath. He thought of the keyhole back home, how he always wished that she would move further away from the bathroom door so he could see her better. And when she finally did, he was certain she knew he was watching; she had turned to face the door, to face her younger brother full on, hands on her hips, as if extending the offer of the dark triangular wisp between her legs outward to her elbows. At first, he couldn't understand why she stood as she did, and even as it continued she never said a word. He didn't know if it was a secret they shared, or just his alone. His sister was like that. Five years his elder, she was different, hard to understand. Even after she had explained the truth to him about who they were.

"O damn! Dammit to hell!" Mina said. She had felt the breeze on her bare skin and had lifted her arm to inspect the rip. Leaning sideways, she reached across herself and fingered the large tear along the side seam. "Mom's dress," she groaned.

The dress was the dark blue wool twill that her mother had made for her out of material from one of her own discarded dresses. Mattie had followed a pattern that was fashionable with young women who could afford it, adding a white silk ribbon tie and chevron stripes at the neck, and between the shoulder darts, a rear flap with embroidered stars. At seventeen, Mina was out of school for good, and needed to look the part if she was going to help their mother make ends meet. Livingston thought she looked like a sailor but kept it to himself; she had a temper, certainly could swear like a sailor. "Dammit, dammit, dammit!" she cursed, between clenched teeth.

"What's that?" Livingston asked, pointing at the Upper Reservoir. He was trying to distract himself and his sister from her dress, but he was also genuinely curious. It was the largest lake he had ever seen.

"That's the way home," she said, blankly.

Livingston thought she was talking about the buildings beyond, the ones poking above the distant tree line. "No, I mean the water," he said.

"I know what you mean, silly." Mina was softening. "That's where we come from, you and me," she said, smiling mischievously down at him, "We could take off our clothes and swim home."

It was then that Livingston learned about Gilboa and the Catskills, about where the water had come from, and about the mountains and forests as far as an eye could see, about the people who lived there, people who'd never been to the city just as he had never been out of it. And they talked of more that he did not know.

He remembered that day. Not because of the guilt, the confusing feelings he had for Mina, nor because those feelings would soon leave the keyhole and expose themselves in a greater guilt, in his flesh, in her flesh, joining them to one another in a careless and terrible secret. What he remembered of that day in the Park, long before his innocence was lost with his sister, was a vertiginous and suffocating sense of the enormity and otherworldliness of things, as if he realized for the first time that there was far more to the world's surface than he could see, and that it came from deep inside the earth and from high above, beyond the even deeper blue sky.

He remembered sitting on the gray rock that emerged from the grass-covered hill's summit like a shaved tonsure, and he remembered the far and the near. The tops of the trees, spreading away from his sister and himself, surrounding the distant reservoir like a soft quilt of multi-hued green with its mixed fragrance, as if each different shade of green was woven with its own earthy scent; and at his fingers, the feel of the rock where he traced its seams and palmed the soft cushions of moss that had taken hold in its weathered rivulets.

The rock was not the dull lifeless gray of the Bathgate asphalt playground, it was *alive*. The smooth Manhattan Schist with its sparkling veins of minerals coursing along its surface beneath his fingers was the scripture of Past-Time-Still-Unfolding...the doxology he had been taught at Christ the King:

As it was in the beginning, both now, and always...

Years later, he would come to understand the truth of this, the life he had sensed in himself and within Summit Hill – the protoliths, folded and congealed eons before in the Archaen cauldron of the earth's core, then shot to the Paleozoic surface of Gonwanda to cool in the lithosphere, only then to be folded and remade many more millions of years later in the uplift and crush of other metamorphic rock from slow-forming continents. The great faults and fissures, laminated with the frayed veins of elemental minerals – mica, pink feldspar, ribboned quartz and other igneous intrusions – were the recordings of deep time in their very presence, then and there.

But it was not finished, then and there. Also written on the rock's surface was a more recent time, millennial time, clocked in the grinding traces of Cenozoic ice sheets scraping the land raw as it dragged great boulders, rock on rock, across the veining of Summit Rock before retreating and leaving behind the glacial till that buried much of it beneath new and future soils. The clawed grooves in the rock, running northwest to southeast, pointed like compass needles, orienting the space of time, animating what was no longer there.

Then the witnesses. Humankind born of a different chemistry and a different sense of time. They could see the weathering of seasons, of days, the forces of sun, wind and rain that smoothed surfaces and carved valleys. But that was all they could see, as if at the advent of the Holocene, the ruffling world had been *given*, tout court. Its true creation was lost – the quickening scale of earth time from Eons to Eras and Periods, to Epochs – had given way to Years and Days, disappeared into the sheer immensity of what had been, what was, and what might be again.

He had been just a boy on a rock. The briefest hot spark of all. One small beating heart, there, soon gone; but not before feeling in that very heart the subtle urgency in the indifferent, imperceptible, and inexorable drift of continents, the herculean press of tectonic plates into new arrangements, and the surge, like the vast swells of ocean waves, of mountain ranges born on the eroded remains of ancient ones slipping quietly into the seas where the dark abysses widened.

...and to ages of ages. Amen.

Five years later, when Franklin Roosevelt lowered the age to seventeen for enrollees into the Civilian Conservation Corps, Livingston Goldring left the city, from the world where he had been raised, and headed out as Livingston Kinsolver to the country, to the earth where he had been born. In all ways, it was a return home; there was more family waiting for him, and the family he was leaving behind had not been true.

Livingston should never have been allowed to join the CCC that year; he was only sixteen. But, thanks to a bit of swagger and some sloppy paperwork at the local enrollment board where the Dept. of Labor was culling the boys, sixteen years of age proved close enough.

It was Endurance Fuller who arranged to have him assigned to Highlands Hammock Camp SP-3 in Sebring, Florida. Mattie had written to Endurance with the news that Livingston had dropped out of school and was leaving home; there had been some kind of difficulties between him and his sister. But what worried Mattie most was that Livingston's CCC papers said he was being sent to the Boiceville Camp P-53 in upstate New York. Into the Catskills...she worried that was way too close to home.

Endurance understood. He was still well-connected in Washington and pulled some strings. He also knew the Camp Superintendent at Highlands, Rembrandt Stikkey. "Rem" had been his tree foreman on the plantation before joining the Corps as a "Local Experienced Man."

When Livingston's reassignment papers came in, even he was happy about going to Florida. One of the kids Livingston played ball with, Dino Silverio, the second baseman, had an older brother who'd just come home from a camp in Boiceville, New York, scarred by poison ivy and missing two toes from the chisel end of a pickaxe. He said that Boiceville was a "bug camp." He and the other boys spent their days, either grubbing gooseberry plants to root out the Blister Rust that was killing the softwood pines or burning oozing clumps of Gypsy Moth larvae that were chewing up the leaves of the hardwood stands. Once, in a mess hall prank, he'd been force fed larvae, said they tasted like grass dipped in kerosene. The Silverio boy missed having all his toes but figured maybe it had been a fair trade for the ticket out of there. The days had been hard, slow and long.

Livingston wanted to get out of the Bronx and into the country, but, after hearing about Boiceville, he was not looking forward to *that* country. He was relieved when his "troop train" pulled out of Pennsylvania Station heading south, heading somewhere he could never have imagined.

Mattie didn't want to be seen crying at Penn Station and said her good-byes at home, but Mina surprised him at the tracks. She pulled him aside with an urgent grip, telling him that she had not told him everything about Gilboa that summer in Central Park years before. There was more he needed to know about who he was, about who *she* was.

Mattie had sent Mina to the train to tell Livingston what she could not tell him herself, to tell him, then and there, about his real mother, Winifred, and about Piedmont, his father. Mina's news had barely settled its effect on Livingston when she told him about *her* father – "the man from mother's past." He had been from Gilboa and taken advantage of Mattie...a very unkind advantage.

Mina spread her arms wide as if introducing herself to Livingston for the first time. To his surprise, her solemn expression slowly turned into a mischievous grin. Then his "sister" wrapped her arms around his waist and kissed him hard and long on the lips. She was making a point...she was *not* his sister, had never been; they were cousins...and they could love each other however, wherever, and for as long as they wished. But she was shaking, arms too tight, the kiss too desperate.

The CCC train had been strung with freight cars set up as sleepers for the boys, and he lay there in the dark wrestling with his feelings. It was difficult enough thinking that he was leaving Livingston *Goldring* behind on Bathgate and heading south with his real name, south to where he was already known as Livingston *Kinsolver*. Nevertheless, as unsettling as this thought was, he was even more unsettled thinking of Mina's kiss.

He could not let it go throughout much of the night. The sudden change in their family relationship had not changed his belief that they had done wrong, that even mistaken beliefs could not undo actions committed in their name. And now, even cousin-love was troubling, taboo, even illegal in some states. It was nearly dawn when the creaking sound of swaying hammocks lulled him to sleep, and the rumbling of the rails became far off thunder in his dreams.

Two days later, mid-day, just outside of Ocala, Florida, the train slowed and came to a halting stop in a heat thicker than anything Livingston had ever experienced. The boys were unloaded into the blinding sun, blinking, and shielding their eyes before a line of men in military uniforms posted at intervals along the platform. Behind each officer, a group of young men stood at loose attention, smirking, and elbowing each other. Orders were barked, whistles were blown, the boys from the train separated into their companies and, with duffle bags slung on their shoulders, marched down the platform to a convoy of waiting Liberty Trucks idling in the summer heat. The other boys, the smirkers, were marched in the opposite direction toward the train. They began hooting and calling out wise-crack warnings – *You're in the shits now, fellas. Stay clear of Clark Gable, that whistle crazy top kick will twist your shorts up good. Give sweet Miss Cookie a pinch on the bottom for me. Your dipshit dollar-a-day not gonna pay for what you got comin'!*

More whistles, more barking, and the teasing gave way to the sound of shuffle-marching feet. At the rear of the truck transport for Company 144, an officer sporting a thin clipped movie-star moustache and wearing a broad flat-brimmed Stetson held back the canvas flap. He stood next to a hawk-nosed, weather-beaten man with folded arms and a taciturn face framed beneath smooth black hair combed into a gelled pompadour. The man was out of uniform; he looked local; years spent in the Florida sun. But he was the one doing the inspecting, studying each boy closely as they climbed into the back of the truck. Livingston was the last to load. He hitched himself up and took a seat on the hard wooden bench lining the flat bed. The officer handed over his hold on the tarp to his partner and with a nod to him, walked off. The Florida man stood before the open tail gate, still looking the boys over, then said, "That there was Officer Gable, the camp subaltern. You can call me Superintendent Stikkey. I ain't no officer anymore, but you will follow my orders, I can guarantee you that." He slammed the tail gate shut with one hand, then addressing Livingston, said quietly, "You're Kinsolver, I'm bettin'."

"Yessir, I am."

"City boy...Mr. Fuller says to keep you in line. That okay with you?"

"Yessir"

"Then, that's good."

Changing his demeanor, Rembrandt Stikkey broke into a wide friendly grin and turned to the full company. "But, first let's do some sightseeing. I'm gonna show you whips the Flaw'da crocs and mocs." He clicked his teeth, then drew the flap closed.

Before heading south to the Camp in Sebring, the truck went west to Silver Springs. The Superintendent said he liked to take "his new boys" into the Florida swamp-woods, said it helped them to get acquainted, not with each other but with the Florida swamp-woods. None of them could have guessed that they'd be spending their first Florida afternoon drifting down the Silver River in glass-bottom boats at *Colonel Tooey's Jungle Cruise*.

The Colonel – whose "rank" turned out to be his given Christian name – was a friend of Stikkey's. They had served together as boys in the American Expeditionary Forces, buck privates. Private Colonel Tooey had been wounded in the battle of the Argonne Forest and dragged clear by Stikkey. The patch over his lost left eye gave him the look of a buccaneer which worked well for his tour-boat operation.

Rembrandt and Colonel had also worked the clean-up down at Islamorada after the Hurricane of '35 swept through Matacumbe Key. The Argonne had been hard but cleaning up the death on Islamorada had been worse. Many of their old friends from the Expeditionary Forces – out of work men from the "Bonus Army" that Livingston had seen years before in Central Park – had been sent there by Roosevelt to build bridges between the islands of the Keys. Most of them died in that water.

It didn't seem fair. In the Argonne, death made sense; it was always nearby, out in the open. But on Matacumbe Key, it had come out of nowhere, littering the white sand beaches with bloated bodies, still sparkling with silicate and dry sea salt, sun baked eyes gone vacant but still wide open in disbelief.

After that, Colonel Tooey went to fresh water. He set up his operation in the middle of the state as far from the coasts as he could get. He was there, on the Spring River, ready and waiting, when Rembrandt drove in with his enrollees. These visits were welcomed by both men, mostly to affirm that they were not alone with their bad dreams.

Tooey's slow-moving river ran along stands of cypress draped with dry spanish moss, the water's edges lost among the cypress knees and dark back-shore oaks throttled by banyan stranglers. But, in the channel, the water was surprisingly cool and crystal clear. Rembrandt said that was where the river got its name, the underground springs; they even made underwater pictures there. Hollywood. Before joining the CCC, if he could get away, he'd drive up from his home down in Princeton to help Tooey on the film shoots, keeping back the alligators and the crocs brought up from the lower Glades. He and Tooey used their old Springfields for the water moccasins and diamondbacks.

The monkeys were the worst he said, pointing out a macaque squatting on an overhanging limb in the upper story.

"Don't even belong. They brought a few here for that *Tarzan* picture last year, and they got loose. Now, they're cluttering up the oaks throwing shit at everyone. I'd shoot 'em out, but Tooey's making too much money off the gawkers." He shook his head at the boatload of young chins leaning up to the high cypress canopy. "Just don't belong," he said again, wistfully.

That was the first time Livingston ever saw a live monkey. It was also the first time that Livingston caught a glimpse of the brooding in the dark eyes of the Camp Superintendent.

Rembrandt spent that afternoon lecturing the men on just what did belong in Florida. He pointed out the custard apples and scrub willows, the heart-shaped moonvines and the slick trails of tree snails, the river-otters and long-tailed weasels, snowy egrets, white ibises, and swallow-tailed kites, the "chizzle winks" and dragonflies. He spoke of the endless sawgrass and palmettos that would await them further south, the ancient leather ferns and Florida Arrowroot which had been used by the Everglade indians to make "sofkee," and the oak and slash pine hammocks that barely kept the clawed toes of digging armadillos above sea-level.

And there were warnings, too. The Black bears, spike-shelled snappers, and the Florida Panther, all tending to their own business but right ready to turn on them just for crossing paths. When one fellow asked about the Indians, about the Seminoles and Miccosukies who lived there and hunted unseen, Rembrandt just said it was best to stay off that path as well.

After the cruise, before boarding the truck again, Livingston learned that Rembrandt had come from the Everglades, been born there, with family generations back. He was part Indian. The most part. Colonel Tooey quietly suggested that no one, none of the boys, better call him a Seminole to his face.

"Rem's a Miccosukie. Them Upper Creek Indians ain't never been conquered," Tooey winked with his good eye.

They would have days ahead with one another. Livingston Kinsolver and Rembrandt Stikkey. A brief lifetime, in fact. But, on the ride down to Sebring, then, there in the stifling late afternoon cover of oiled canvas and the sweat-smell of anxious young men, Livingston thought only of the departing train he'd left earlier in Ocala, the pressure release of it's brakes, and the silence of those on board who had come to know this place and were taking their memories away with them.

For Livingston, there was no going back. Not to the Bronx, not to the city, not to that world. He was going to plant trees, clear streams, restore eroded earth, and sleep in the embrace of open skies. He pulled at the damp cling of his shirt a few times, fanning his chest, cooling the smooth skin of a CCC man who was, in most ways, still just a boy. Perhaps that was why the trouble was inevitable, that Livingston would find himself so drawn to Rembrandt's wife, Belle Stikkey. He'd not been allowed to be an innocent long enough.

The Superintendent was quite a bit older than his wife. They had been married only a couple of years, but there was already a son, a four-year-old boy. Most figured that the marriage was arranged for Belle's protection, or for the boy's, but, either way, Rembrandt loved his new young wife and the child that may or may not have been his.

Everyone who knew the couple would joke that, despite their age difference, she was the one with the brains, kept Rembrandt on his toes with her book smarts. Unusual, they said, that such a pretty face could have so much learning behind it. Belle had raced through high school and a few stints at the local community college whenever a course on biology or zoology was being offered. She was always at the top of her classes and would have kept going as an older student, but her boy was long out of the sling and growing into a handful; she took the teaching job with the CCC instead. It seemed like a good alternative to just slip to the other side of the same learning.

In truth, Rembrandt was no slouch himself; they were both smart, just in different kinds of way. He liked field work, being out in the woods tracking bird calls; she preferred a laboratory bench where she could study the anatomy of avian vocal cords.

Their home was down in Princeton, Florida, next to Endurance Fuller's plantation where Rembrandt had worked overseeing the fern green houses and groves of tropical fruits and Royal Palm. He had skills in many capacities: horticulture, machine maintenance, carpentry of all kinds, and the disciplining of men. When he was younger, he'd been employed by Gaston Drake, a friend of Fuller's who'd come south in 1918 with an idea to build a business in the slash pine forests on the eastern edge of the Everglades between Homestead and Miami. The business he founded became the Drake Fern & Lumber Company and the town he carved out of the forest clearing became Princeton, Florida, named after the University he had attended up north. Endurance Fuller had been Gaston Drake's classmate and – after he failed to convince another classmate, former New York Mayor George McClellan, to stop the Gilboa Dam – he'd followed Drake down a few years later to try his own hand at fruits and nursery palms. Drake said that he wouldn't have any trouble finding Princeton, Florida; all the municipal buildings were painted in black and orange to match University colors.

But Gaston Drake had never been a good student at Princeton

University, and didn't fare much better in his eponymous town. When bad investments, a poorly treated work force, and too much clear-cutting felled the last of his trees along with his lumber business, he went bankrupt, sold the fern operation to Fuller and returned to New Jersey to live out his glory days. Rembrandt Stikkey took a job re-painting main street, and then crossed over to run Fuller's rotational system of silviculture. Planting things suited him better than slash-and-burn.

Unlike Drake, Endurance Fuller had been generous to the land and to his foreman. A few years later, after the *real* Depression had settled in and forced him to cut-back his operation, he was able to get Rembrandt a position working for the Department of Agriculture in the Civilian Conservation Corps. Rembrandt was hired as a LEM, a "local experienced man," brought on for their local knowledge and expertise. It could be any kind of expertise so long as it helped the out-of-staters adapt, survive, and complete whatever work in the wilds that the CCC had in mind, including building the boys into men. In Rembrandt's case, it was to oversee the reforestation of the slash pines, live oaks, and cypress that Drake and his kind had mowed down for the quick money.

Florida's forests had been suffering badly for years, even before the Depression hit in '29. Drake had not worked alone. There had been way too much unruly land grabbing and land grubbing, particularly around the Everglades and the big lake that fed it – the sweet-water pump in the heart of Florida at Okeechobee. Ever since the last glacier scoured out the limestone flats and retreated back north, the steady seep of water over the southern rim of the shallow Okeechobee spoon had swept through the miles and miles of sawgrass on its way to Bay of Florida where it mingled with the Gulf waters, looped in a hair-pin around the Keys into the Gulf Stream and continued north up the continental coast back toward its glacial headwaters. Beneath the sheet flow, rich black humus had been building in the layers of natural death over the compacted crush of sea-shells for millennia. But the balance of old ways changed for the worse when the railroads and land speculators began cutting through southern Florida with canals, impounding the water from the drained soil for farm-ing, pasturage, and the promise of Florida's good life. The forests were the first to go, razed by bucksaws or turned to standing dead-wood by the sea water pushing in from the coast where Okeechobee's freshwater trib-utaries had once held it back. The cleared desiccated land proved to be a bust; either there was not enough good dirt above the limestone, or it was mineral deficient and susceptible to root-rot. Worse, the denuded pine lands and dry sawgrass were plagued by severe wind-swept fires, umber clouds of acrid smoke drifted from coast to coast, and shrinking aquifers carried increasing loads of salt into municipal water supplies.

The rest of the country, its men and women, had also suffered from its self-inflicted wounds, its killing spree across the face of the land – overcutting, overplanting, overgrazing, and overlooking the fact that life on earth was tender. And they, too, had overlooked how that tenderness could turn on them, suddenly hard and swift; that if there was to be this kind of death, they would suffer its nature the most.

But Florida got lucky. When Congress approved the Emergency Conservation Work Act, mustering its most sorely affected natural resource – the country's young men – into a "civilian conservation corps," more "soil soldiers" came south than to any other part of the country. And the state of Florida was the front line with men like Rembrandt Stikkey, armed with his pick and shovel, in command.

"Kinsolver,...ssssss, Kinsolver."

The camp subaltern, Lieutenant Chick Gable, was leaning over at the end of the bench row, beckoning to Livingston with his finger. "The

Superintendent's outside. He wants some words with you. Let's go," he whispered.

Livingston felt an apprehensive thud in his chest and held tighter to his pencil and note pad. "Now?" he asked.

The lieutenant, standing erect again, nodded.

Kinsolver rose quietly from the bench, sidled past the other men, and followed the subaltern to the front door of the Rec Hall. He turned to look back at Belle. Half of the projected chimpanzee was smeared across the folds of her dress as she stood next to the flat screen, pointing out the chimp's raised index finger. All he heard was the word "human-like" as he stepped outside onto the porch.

Superintendent Stikkey was talking with an elderly barrel-chested man wearing a wrinkled linen suit and smiling under a straw fedora. Livingston guessed right away who it was; he saw the relaxed familiar ease they had toward each other, both men with their hands in their pockets. Like a father and son.

Turning to Kinsolver, Endurance Fuller stepped forward and put out his hand. "I've been looking forward to meeting you, Livingston," he said.

Squinting through his wire-rimmed glasses, Endurance bore in, then, drawing back, drawled, "My God,...don't you look just like him. Your Dad."

Livingston shrugged. He didn't know what to say in response, he'd never even seen a photograph of his father, or if he had, no one had ever told him who it was. But he knew about Endurance Fuller. Christ, he thought, this old man had earned his name. Endurance was well into his eighties, but his grip was strong, eyes clear. He looked like a man in his fifties. To Livingston, just turned seventeen, Endurance Fuller was as impressive as Mattie Goldring had said.

"Let's walk," Endurance said, draping his arm over Kinsolver's shoulder and steering him off the porch. "You let me have him for a bit, will you Rem?" he asked Stikkey.

"That'd be fine." The Superintendent leaned against the porch column and folded his arms. "Thanks again for coming up to get Belle; she's been missing our boy bad," he said.

"Happy to do it. Get to kill two birds with one stone," he said, nodding his head toward Livingston. "I'll see you before we leave."

Endurance had driven up from Princeton in his Zephyr V-12 convertible coupe. He did this on occasion to keep Rembrandt up to speed on things at the plantation, and sometimes he'd drive Belle back home with him. A few months back, thinking to surprise Belle and Rembrandt, he'd brought along their son, Cash. He did this only once. The little boy had been so excited and restless that he had to be strapped down in his seat with the belt from Endurance's pants in order to keep from flying right out into the wind above the open-roofed Zephyr.

More often, little Cash remained in Princeton with friends – a Baptist minister named Frampton Klutterer and his wife, Jilly. They had two boys, an older one, Clipper, who'd been a bit of a rowdy and had recently run off to Miami looking for work; the other one was Frampy Jr., still at home and the same age as Cash, so it worked out nicely. It also allowed Rembrandt and Belle a night alone.

Typically, on the nights before and after her teaching day at the Highlands Camp, Belle would stay with her mother in Indiantown, a few miles from the camp. Rembrandt would be given leave to join her for a conjugal visit. It made his young charges snicker green with envy, not many of them knew that his real purpose was just to get sideways drunk someplace where they couldn't watch.

By day, the Superintendent was present and reliable, but at night came the demons. Livingston learned soon enough they were big ones, and probably more coming. A few weeks back, on his way to the latrine, he'd heard Rembrandt bawling crazy out in the cypress in the early morning hours. He was thrashing about on the ground, wrestling with the Islamorada ghosts in the stench of rotting dead friends who would not leave him be. It had scared the shit out of Livingston right then and there.

On this day, Endurance had arrived at Highlands with Rembrandt's younger sister, Saskia.

Saskia Stikkey was Belle's best friend, and, like Belle, she had witnessed the change in her brother. Both women felt fearful and helpless given how easily he could become someone else. They accepted his drinking as the better part of it, since it seemed to calm his life down when it had gone wild with the haunting. Saskia and Belle increasingly leaned on one another for support, hoping it would all pass.

When Belle would go north to Sebring, Saskia would often stay with the Klutterers to help with her boy. But another part of her heart was often elsewhere – over at Endurance's plantation where Billie Kinsolver lived. Saskia was in love with Billie's son Lincoln Gilboa, and she was pretty sure that at the Myakka CCC Camp near the Gulf of Mexico, his heart was beating for her.

Saskia's skin was darker than her sibling's. At times, in certain light, she looked like she might have more African Maroon than Indian in her. It was said this was not uncommon in "Seminole" families. But it was also unpredictable; there was no telling when the "blood" of an escaped slave would re-appear in the aspect of a Glade indian.

Saskia Stikkey's family were Miccosukie, and, like her brother, she never referred to herself as a "Seminole." That name had been a catch-all, given, unasked, to all the indian "peoples of the peninsula." In truth, not many of these people were actually from the peninsula, and half again were not indian at all. The Florida Indians were just a fractious blend of slowly disappearing Calusas, as doomed as their ancient shell mounds; warring Upper and Lower Creeks who had been driven southeast out of the Mississippi territories; fierce blue-black runaway Ashantis who had paddled north in stolen canoes from the Caribbean plantations, and gentle Gullahs who had beaten the Carolina and Georgia gauntlet in their run south to Florida. These outlaw North-American Indians and West Africans shared little other than the understanding that they were in the way. And that was plenty enough to bind them fast for the centuries to come.

Saskia and Linc Gilboa would laugh, privately to themselves, when people called her a half-breed. No one ever called *him* that. Of course, he'd been warned by his mother, Billie – some blends are more acceptable than others. She'd learned that years before – in the town whose name she'd given to her son – that love is not always color blind.

But Saskia was certain of how she felt. When Endurance offered to take her north to Sebring to visit Rembrandt and Belle, she'd jumped at the chance. He had teased her a bit, telling her that there was going to be a ball game between the Highlands and Myakka camps. Saskia knew what that meant. Linc would be there, pitching for the Myakka team.

"So, how are you liking things here, Livingston?" Endurance asked. He removed his fedora and swept it out toward the campgrounds, then began fanning his face.

"I like it enough, I guess, sir. I like the work,...being outside and all," Livingston answered. He had a lot of questions of his own, but he would let Fuller ask his first.

The flanking rows of one-story barracks stood like soldiers at attention, as the two men strolled through the middle of the compound towards the makeshift ball field at the shaded edge of the cypress. Each barrack was identical to the next, dark stained hand-cut shingle walls supported on squat wooden posts, free of the wide tamped ground that ran clear beneath them all. Shallow gabled roofs with deep overhangs seemed to float above the walls, hovering over a surround of metal mesh screening. The camp had been built for Florida cooling, allowing the nighttime breeze to pass beneath the bunks of sleeping men as it pushed out the daytime swelter caught up in the eaves.

"Well, I can imagine *that*. Things aren't...well, as neatly lined up out there in the hammock woods," Fuller said.

The two men fell into an inadvertent marching step.

"Lined up, yessir,"

Lined up, Livingston thought, like the steel-spring bunks facing each other along the barrack walls inside, and the metal footlockers at the end of the bunks. And the boys, next to them, standing for inspection early in every morning's dawn. There was almost a desperate feel to it, the order-liness of it all, as if it could keep the hammock at bay, keep out its slow creep, the hum and howl of unseen life, and the dark grip of epiphyte stranglers. Like the screen above his bunk, it was meant to keep out the flying insects, but there were always those that could find the crack in the grid to get to the men. Livingston was learning that the rank and file of mankind had always been outnumbered among less orderly living things.

He had not been prepared for the military discipline. In the camp, Livingston belonged to the army, to Lieutenant Gable, to the regimented schedule and to an imperious Company Commanding Officer, whom he never spoke to and whose name he couldn't even pronounce —*Wrezinskavich?* But out in the hammocks, out in the woods away from the camp, Kinsolver belonged to Superintendent Stikkey. Rembrandt could be moody and taciturn, but he welcomed the young men into the place of his ancestors. Out there, men had always moved freely about, unpredictable, on a shifting wet ground beneath a timeless shroud of sun-dappled tangle.

As Endurance and Livingston reached the edge of the compound, the land rose slightly then leveled again onto an open sports field. A group of shirtless men were on the baseball diamond doing drills, taking grounders and shagging fly balls, teasing one another about nothing. Like most of the men at Highlands, they were in good shape, healthy sweat shining on new muscle. Livingston himself had gained almost ten pounds since his arrival to Highlands. The Superintendent had told them all on their first day that hard work would do that – put weight and muscle strength on their bones, particularly on the soft bones of the city boys.

"Oy there, Kinsolver," one of them called out; he had a British accent and walked with a rocking limp. "You playing with us later? Or you going to catch butterflies with the science teacher?...Supe's not gonna like that."

There was laughing and catcalls from the others.

"Maybe he's afraid to face his cousin," someone else called out.

"Or maybe he's afraid of his cousin's *face*," cried another, "I sure would be, if my cousin was a black boy."

"Bugger off, O'Malley. Better *that*, than an Irish idiot," snapped the boy with the limp.

"Fuck you, Hawkins. Gimpy little Brit shoit. Go grab a bucket."

The boys drifted back to their practice.

"It's okay, Waterhouse, ignore them. I do." Livingston raised his hand as if tossing dust at the other ball players, "I'll see you in a bit." He looked down at the ground, feeling slightly ashamed that things had taken place in front of Endurance. "We got a ball game this afternoon against the Myakka Camp," he mumbled, quietly.

Endurance nodded. "I know, I heard." He understood the teasing about Lincoln Gilboa. He'd heard plenty of it ever since taking Billie Kinsolver into his home. "That's why I brought Saskia on this trip. She's looking forward to seeing if you can hit against Linc."

This made Livingston smile. "Yea," he said, "...and that guy, Waterhouse Hawkins, he means well. He's a British kid, been in the States only a few years. He thinks we should be using cricket bats."

"Can't play, tho'," Livingston continued, "one of his legs is shorter than the other. Born that way. He's the coach's assistant. Linc and him are actually pretty good friends. I like him, too...the Water-Boy, we call him."

Endurance smiled reassuringly and gestured toward a trailhead cut into the edge of the surrounding cypress. "Let's get out of the sun," he said, "I've got some things I want to talk with you about."

They walked for a while in silence. The humid air was saturated with the earthy smell of swamp and decay, but, in the humus, there was also the aroma of human excrement. The camp latrine was close by, tucked in the woods off a side trail. Livingston had been on flypaper duty the day before, hanging the traps along the roof trusses above the open shitters. Besides thinking the whole exercise was a waste of time, he was sorry about the butterflies. Gulf Fritillarys, Stikkey called them. Most could beat their way free of the flypaper, but the lime tossed into the crappers to keep down the smell burned their wings. Livingston figured the natural world must have its reasons, but why those butterflies would ever leave the sweet nectar of the Florida Passion Flowers to go gathering whatever it was they were gathering from the damp turds in the latrine was beyond him.

"I see the camp's been planting pine seedlings," Endurance said. "That's good. We need 'em after all the clear-cutting around here."

"Yes sir. When I first got here we were planting more than a hundred a day. Not now tho'. It seemed like every time we'd plant a new forest, an old one gets burnt down. Some of us have been switched to fire duty. My company's mostly been cutting firebreaks and trails so the pumpers can make it into the thicks."

Livingston turned to Endurance. "You know, we built a fire tower with Linc and his group down near Myakka last month. I even got a chance to go to the beaches on the outer keys there, saw the full blown Gulf of Mexico." He paused, then added, "Me and my group did, anyway."

Endurance grunted. "Well, I'm just glad you boys are nearby and getting a chance to know one another after all this time. Your Aunt Billie hoped the day would come. It was hard on her, raising her boy alone. But you and he are family,...and you're all *like* family to me. Your father was as close to a son as I ever got, so I figure that makes you a grandson."

"I guess I should thank you for everything you've done for us," Livingston said, quietly. It was hard for him to express his gratitude to Endurance Fuller, maybe because there was so much more he wanted from him.

There was a quick thrashing in the palmetto near the edge of the swamp. Endurance put his hand up, signaling Livingston to stop. He pointed to a scour of dragged earth across their path leading to a mud slick down a small embankment into the dark shallow water. "It's a gator slide."

"Yeah, I learned that pretty quick when I got here." Livingston said, taking a sidestep away from the palmetto, "Everybody sings on their way to the latrine, some yodelers too, anything to warn them off."

Endurance laughed. "Well, before you fellas put in all these trails, these alligators had a clear swim to the coast, now they have to drag themselves from water hole to water hole,...just like our amphibian ancestors.

"'Course, don't suggest that to Rembrandt...the bit about our ancestors, anyway. He doesn't believe in Mister Darwin's evolution."

Livingston looked up in surprise. "How could that be, with Mrs. Stikkey and all? He doesn't *seem* like he believes in God." Livingston immediately regretted saying what he did, jumping like that to bible talk. It was no business of his, whatever the Superintendent believed.

"It's not church belief. Rem believes the Baptists have it just as wrong as Mister Darwin. For him, it's Indian belief. Tricksters behind all there is, ever was, or ever will be." Endurance chuckled lightly to himself, remembering himself as an altar boy and the late Reverend Samuel Lockwood, the Methodist minister he'd caught with his holy cock in his hand before the Altar of the Gilboa Fossil, "And miss Belle? She can't get him to think otherwise. Stopped trying, long ago."

They grew silent again.

"You know, I met your mother a few times," Endurance became serious, "I was gone from Gilboa when she first arrived there, but I returned the day before the big flood. That was the first time, and I could see that they loved each other, your father and mother." He paused and looked over at Livingston, waiting on him, giving him a chance to reveal himself. To Endurance, it was time.

"Yessir," Livingston said, staring hard into the cypress, "It kind of surprised me to learn about her, about them both. She'd always been just Aunt Winifred to me; didn't come around much, too busy with her research at the Museum up north. Fossils and such. Our *ancestors*, as she called 'em. Mom,...Mattie made excuses." Looking down, Livingston scuffed the dirt with his boot. "Seems like too much time's passed anyway. I don't believe I care all that much, now."

Livingston tried to sound as gruff as he could. He was tempted to say that he didn't believe in evolution either. Not if life came to this, the randomness of nature's choices, the unpredictable lines of descent – who would live, and in what form – maybe the Indian Tricksters were on to something everyone else had missed. But he had accepted, in his heart, whether he liked it or not, that he was his real mother's son. And although the guilt remained, he had been relieved by the space it offered between himself and Mina, knowing, as he now did, that she had never been his sister.

"Billie says your mother is something special. And you know something else? Miss Belle actually met her once. She was just a young girl, visiting some family up north near Albany. I arranged for one of her cousins to take Belle to see Winifred's work on the Gilboa Forest Diorama. Belle never forgot that day; she always had unusual interests; now she reads all of your mother's scientific papers. Your aunt Billie would have them sent to her; Billie couldn't understand them herself, but she knew that Belle could. Not a lot of women in your mother's field; paleontology has always been a man's sport. Especially back when she started, when your father met her. She had to make some hard choices, Winifred did."

"Yessir, but that doesn't make 'em right, tho'," Livingston muttered.

"That may be," Endurance said, nodding his head, "...but finding one's place in the world can be a difficult thing. Most settle in just fine, but others get drawn right out of it – by things beyond their control, by a calling I suppose. And I suppose some losses are more hurtful than others." He put his hand on Livingston's shoulder. "Mattie did the best she could with what your mother asked of her. It was a bad business all around. She'd lost your father; she wasn't going to lose everything else." Endurance paused, then said, "There's something more I need to say. It's Wilhelmina. Your sister."

"Mina?" Livingston felt a turn in his stomach, the shame, fearing that Endurance Fuller knew what Livingston hoped no one would ever know.

"She's run off with your cousin, Xavi DeAngelus. They're on their way here."

Livingston was thunderstruck. "To Florida? Where?" he asked.

"To the Plantation. They seem to have eloped, neither Mattie nor Jenna could stop them. Did you know anything about this...that she was having an affair with her cousin?"

Livingston could barely shake his head. Not *that* cousin, at least, he thought to himself. "No, I didn't think she'd ever even met him. We never saw that side of the family, it seemed like things weren't always cordial between my aunts."

"Yes, well, after all these years, your aunts are certainly talking to each other now. They're not too happy about it," Endurance said, "It's not legal in most states, marrying a first cousin."

"Charles Darwin married his first cousin," Livingston said. He was feeling defensive. He had lost his virginity to Mina when she was his "sister." *That* was bad enough, even if she had known that they were actually cousins all along; in fact, somehow that made it worse, knowing that she'd played along, excited by something that was shameful to him. He wondered if they had been marked by what was different, or the same, in their blood, something tying them together, even as it seemed to rip the family further apart.

"Hmm, that so? Darwin again. Where'd you learn that?"

"The science teacher," Livingston said., "...Miss Stikkey."

Before he could continue, Livingston heard Endurance's name being called out. It came from behind, a woman's voice, urgent and desperate. Turning around, he saw Belle Stikkey running, sobbing, stumbling toward them from around a bend in the trail. Her cries were mingling with the distant shouting of men and the slow rise of the camp bugler's call-to-arms.

"He's gone. My baby's gone. They've taken him," she cried, "They've taken Cash!"

Waterhouse Hawkins, eyes wide and scared, was at her side, running off-kilter, trying to keep her, and himself, from falling.

"We gotta go, Kinsolver. Now!" Waterhouse yelled, "The Company's been ordered to Princeton. There's been a kidnapping."

7

The Gathering…

Mothers
1941, Princeton, FL
*"The experience of one's life is his alone,
the experience of one's death belongs to others"*
(Endurance Fuller)

A LOCAL MISFORTUNE BECOMES a national tragedy not simply because no one expected its arrival, but because everyone, everywhere, feels as if it came knocking on their own front door. Even before Livingston Kinsolver had arrived in Princeton, the kidnapping of Cash Stikkey from the Klutterer home in Princeton, Florida, had been front page news.

The five-year-old had been dressed in his red and white striped pajamas and tucked into bed by Jilly Klutterer, in whose care he had been placed. Jilly's own son, Frampton Jr. had already fallen asleep in the bed next to Cash. She'd read to her charge for a bit, then left him asleep curled up with his threadbare stuffed alligator. Rembrandt Stikkey had given "Skeegie," as the alligator was called, to his son two Christmases before. Normally, the boy would have been put to bed by his aunt Saskia while his mother Belle and Rembrandt were away, but she'd gone north with Endurance Fuller to see the CCC boys. And now, holding tight to her distraught sister-in-law, Saskia had returned to Princeton with them.

The young men from Highlands Hammock Camp SP-3 were only a small part of the manhunt that had swelled by the hour in the days after the kidnapping. After the Lindbergh case nine years earlier, stealing children from their beds had become a national horror. More than two dozen high profile abductions had taken place across the country in the ensuing years, most with bad endings; ransoms paid for a dead or forever-missing child in return. Nevertheless, the Princeton crime seemed particularly alarming.

The small town of Princeton, Florida, founded and then abandoned by Gaston Drake, had never flourished; it wasn't even on most maps. Endurance Fuller's modest fern and palm operation was the largest commercial farm in the area, but it was surrounded by small truck farms surviving on the tomatoes, squash and pole beans that took over the raw red dirt left behind from Drake's clear-cutting for pine lumber. The town center was a general store with two gas pumps out front, Frampton Klutterer's Baptist Church, and a double-duty post office and cafe. Most serious business was conducted either in Homestead for the necessities, or Miami for the luxuries. All in all, Princeton was not the kind of community that would render much of a profit to a kidnapper. Something worse than ransom money seemed to be going on. Cash Stikkey had been targeted, taken from his bed while young Frampton Klutterer Jr., three feet away in the same room, was left behind, safe and sound. Few would say it out loud, but most believed that the kidnapping was a neighborhood affair.

The bedroom on the second floor of the Klutterer's home was above the kitchen. A screen door off the pantry had been cut in the early morning hours, rusty dirt boot prints left behind on the back stairs up. A ransom note was attached to the screen door handle with a rubber band;

ten thousand dollars was the cost for the return of Rembrandt and Belle Stikkey's son. Anyone who might have seen Rembrandt's last bank statement from the Homestead Credit Union would know that ten thousand dollars matched his savings almost to the dollar. But anyone who'd spent time with Rembrandt that June morning in 1941, would never have known what he was feeling. The fearfulness in their own imaginations was not mirrored in the cool determined aspect of the CCC Superintendent.

"Men, this here is Darryl Potts, the Dade County Sheriff. Some of you know of him. And not just you local fellows." Rembrandt Stikkey stood next to the sheriff as he introduced him to the dozen boys from Highlands. The boys all carried machetes, Sheriff Potts wore a sidearm, Rembrandt's Springfield rifle stood on its stock, leaning against the bumper of Potts' squad car.

The light of the early morning sun was still splintering through the palm fronds at the edge of the Glades where the group, one of many, had gathered on Piney Alley. The road had never seen traffic like this; a hundred or more cars and trucks were parked in an endless teetering line along the sloping culvert between the thick foliage of the Everglades and the red dirt of the Alley, freshly tamped by oil spray to keep its dust down. Every fifty yards, small groups of men stood idly by, some sprawled out on the vehicles, others squatting on the road drawing idle patterns in the poisoned ground of the roadbed.

At the rear of the Highlands group, Linc Gilboa stood next to his cousin Livingston Kinsolver, shielding his eyes from the low sun. He had been allowed to leave the Myakka Camp and join the search; Linc had family in Princeton, and everyone in the town was looking worriedly to their own. It had helped that Linc's mother was a white woman.

Linc nudged Livingston with his elbow, nodding his head toward Sheriff Potts. "He's from up north where our folks lived," he whispered,

"Leastwise, he was there when they died. Ma told me he was a horse-man,...shared that with my Pa, she says."

Livingston looked the elderly sheriff over, trying to picture him as a man on horseback, as a younger man in the Catskill woods. Potts looked to be as old as Endurance Fuller, in his seventies, maybe eighties. He moved slowly with a large belly that hung over the top of his gun belt. His aspect was weary, his face aged and sun-wrinkled, centered by a snow-white handlebar mustache. He held a wide-brimmed Stetson in his hand. The trace of the hat's headband was marked on his forehead by a damp circle of smooth white skin under thinning hair that seemed to have rarely seen the Florida sun.

"How'd he get down here? Down to Florida?" asked Livingston.

"Ma said he left Gilboa around the same time as her. She said he was always a proud man and felt he failed in his duty to figure out the killings up there. She didn't know where he went or thought much about it until one day he appeared at Mr. Fuller's plantation with his badge and a real joy at seeing her again. Not sure if he followed her down on account of his friendship with my Pa, but he was sure glad that she was doing alright. He seemed tickled to see me as well. *'Well Ms. Billie, the boy's all grow'd up to look like his Pa, alright,'* he said." Linc clicked his tongue and shook his head, looking over at Rembrandt Stikkey. "And now he's got *this* to take care of...Christ Aw'mighty."

Livingston tapped his fingers on the handle of the machete that he had tucked into his belt, wondering whether or not Potts would think that, in aspect, *he* was his father's son as well.

"You all stand ready to go," Rembrandt called out, "The Sheriff and I need to speak a moment. Waterhouse, go fetch the water canteens for 'em." Rembrandt and Sheriff Potts turned their backs to the boys and leaned over the hood of Potts's patrol car, studying a worn map checkered with marked-up plots of the search sectors. Waterhouse Hawkins gave a serious but unacknowledged salute to the Superintendent's back and hurried off down the road with his rapid limping gait. His unmatched legs were keeping him out of the rough terrain of hammocks and eroded limestone hiding in the sharp sawgrass, but he'd begged to come even if only to handle the water wagon for everyone.

Looking down the road as Hawkins wove his way through the government agents, Livingston and Linc could not imagine how Sheriff Potts was going to deal with all the G-men who had come into his jurisdiction. Or, more importantly, how Rembrandt would deal with them. The Superintendent clearly respected Potts, but he was not taking orders from outsiders. It was *his* son, not Lindberg's or any of the others gone missing; he was going to do whatever it took.

In hindsight, no one was surprised that J. Edgar Hoover had taken over the manhunt. The FBI needed a win after a series of botched investigations. Funding was drying up in Washington, Roosevelt was not helping, and Hoover figured he could brush past a bunch of Florida 'Crackers' to take center-stage. Four days after the boy's disappearance, a few hundred 'Government men' were mobilized to scour the territory surrounding Princeton. The FBI's Miami office worked with Sheriff Potts initially, helping Rembrandt arrange for the ransom, marking the bills he'd withdrawn from his savings, and walking him through the drop-off requested in the note. But Rembrandt had demanded that he drive out alone with the money, convinced that things would turn out well if he just did as the kidnapper's poorly written note said:

> *Put 500 $5 100 $20 500 $10 and 10 $50,*
> *total $10,000 in a shoe box and follow route.*
> *Leave Princeton midnight, go east. Take first oil*
> *road on left just past the negro shacks. At Moody*

Drive turn toward Homestead. When you reach
Piney Alley, look for a stack of three oil drums a
near mile in. Put the box behind them. Notify any
officer, give serial number of any bill, fail to burn
this note and you won't never see him again. Your
boy, that is. He's okay, wants to go home, real bad.
Do this right, he'll be returned to you.

There was reason for hope, Rembrandt kept telling Belle. He kept reminding her about the boy's coveralls. Whoever had taken their son had also taken a pair of his new OshKosh bib coveralls as well. Why would anyone do that unless they planned on caring for the child, too. But after the ransom money was stowed in the palmettos behind the empty oil drums, and Rembrandt had driven back to his home, the only thing returned to him was silence. Two days passed without word or sign of the child before Hoover himself flew into Miami and took personal command of the investigation.

This morning on Piney Alley marked the tenth day that Livingston and the CCC boys had been in Princeton. The Highlands crew had been bivouacked in a "spike" camp on Endurance Fuller's plantation at the edge of a copse of Live Oaks, a short distance from the main house. Livingston could see the house from his tent and kept the flaps open at night so he could see the lights through the netting around his cot. His tent mates complained about inviting in the snakes and armadillos, or worse, a Florida Panther, but Livingston was insistent.

His cousin Linc slept down at the house, mostly because he was not allowed to bunk in with the Highlands boys, but also because his mother Billie lived there as well. There was the expected muttering, not to Linc's face, nor to Livingston's, but it was there in the irritable heat and frustration of the empty searches…*"Mama's Boy in the Big House."* Livingston let it go; the days had been hard on everyone; long, hot, and fruitless hours out on the hammocks; torn up khaki-issue and shirts drenched in sweat from the humidity and blood from insect bites and sawgrass cuts; twisted ankles and rattlers lunging at their boots. And where was the boy?!

Livingston was doing his best to keep his head about him, but it was not easy. His physical discomfort during the days was a welcome distraction from the confusing feelings that would well up in his chest at night whenever he allowed them his attention.

His attraction to Belle Stikkey up at the Highlands Camp made him feel shame in light of the horror she was enduring, but those feelings were now getting tangled up in the lights of Endurance Fuller's house.

He was eager to meet Linc's mother Billie, his father's sister. He'd heard the stories of Billie's wild ways as a young woman. But, most of all, Livingston wanted to see Billie's namesake – his 'sister' Mina. *Her* wild ways still haunted him, and he knew that if she wasn't down there at the house already, she soon would be.

Mina had been the *first*.

Like the Paleolithic carving of the zaftig Venus of Willendorf that he'd seen in one of his 'mother' Mattie's National Geographic's, Mina was the girl-woman-Eve against whom all others were measured. His sister, cousin, angel, lover...apple bearer. Her breast, hips, the curves, hair, her embrace and her smell.

Livingston had once passed close enough to Belle Stikkey to take that last measure – the smell, *her* smell, the one that had conjured the same illicit feelings he'd had for Mina, but without the guilt and shame...or, at least, less of it.

Belle had touched hard Livingston's conflicted heart. But that touch had been at Highlands, *this* was Princeton – a different world where love now laid claim only to a heart sick over a lost child. To Livingston, Mina's imminent presence in Princeton seemed pitiless and mocking, clouding his thoughts with memories that he was trying to forget.

Back at the Highlands camp, ten days earlier, when he had been walking with Endurance Fuller, he had tried to defend Charles Darwin's marriage to his first cousin, but it was mostly meant to defend his own behavior. Now Mina was coming to him again, this time with Xaviero DeAngelus, another first cousin whom he'd never met and who had appeared out of nowhere with his wedding band on Mina's finger.

If they were there, in Princeton, at the house, Livingston had yet to see them. Lying in his cot the night before the kidnapped child was found, Livingston saw only the dark image of his youth and felt the aches in his tired body as lashes to a deserving penitent.

Xaviero DeAngelus and Wilhelmina (Mina) Goldring
1941, Princeton, FL
"*The soul, which is spirit, can not dwell in dust;*
it is carried along to dwell in the blood."
(St. Augustine)

When Billie Kinsolver received the letter from Mattie Goldring's daughter Mina, telling her that she was coming to Florida and that she had married a boy studying for the priesthood, she was surprised. Not about the visit, nor because Catholic priests were supposed to be celibate – after all, Mina had said he was only in his second year at the Dunwoodie Seminary in Yonkers and had not yet "discerned" the Call – no,...Billie's surprise was that the boy was Xaviero DeAngelus. It was a name that she had not heard in years, but the boy – she well knew who he was. And he would be a man now by her calculation, like her own son. These days, in the gathering clouds of war, she worried that nineteen years was already a long life lived.

Billie had grown more serious, quieter and more reserved since her time back in Gilboa. Her youthful black hair now held hints of gray and was cut short for the heat. But she was still strong and forceful in appearance, sought after by local single men in Princeton who thought they could meet her challenge,...and by some men not so single. She had a lover in Miami, a Cuban fellow named Modesto Martinez who played a bandurria in a *Son cubano* band out of South Beach. It was a private affair that she kept away from Princeton. She'd borrow Endurance's Zephyr and be gone a day or two. Endurance never asked; she was too important to him. Besides being his last tie to Piedmont and the town of Gilboa, she kept his plantation books, negotiated sales, and oversaw the seasonal labor and local truck farmers in need of extra work.

Mina's letter to Billie was a reminder of what did not need reminding.

Billie and Xaviero's mother Jenna Goldring had been pregnant together; one out of, and one in, wedlock. But shortly after her husband went missing in 1924, Jenna Goldring left Gilboa with their child and returned to the family homestead in Slingerlands. She had not been married long enough to Gianni 'Johnny of the Angel' DeAngelus for most friends and family there to meet her husband. But her son was a treasure. Everyone would remark on his sweet disposition despite being somewhat mystified by the boy's name. Most assumed it had to do with the Catholic faith of the boy's dead father since Jenna had never been the religious type. But those left behind in Gilboa understood that the name 'Xaviero' was not in remembrance of the Spanish Jesuit, Saint Francis Xavier, but rather was meant to sanctify forever the 'X' across Gianni DeAngelus's face.

Over the years, Billie lost touch with Jenna, but she had heard things. Jenna had never remarried and had become fiercely protective of her son. She called him "Xavi," and was as honest as she could be with the boy when it came to explaining the past. Unlike her sisters Mattie and Winifred who, for their different reasons, withheld the truth of their respective child's conception, Jenna did her best to explain all that she knew about Xavi's birth, his family, and Gilboa.

Jenna's openness, her need to confront the difficult truths that she and her sisters had faced caused friction with Mattie and Winifred. A respectful but firm estrangement developed, hardened by her older sisters having exacted a difficult promise from Jenna. Two secrets were to be kept – the secrets of Mattie's two children. The Goldring sisters would not speak about the real father of Mattie's daughter Mina, nor about the father of "Living Stone" whom Winifred placed, at his birth, in Mattie's care.

Jenna kept these secrets from her son Xavi. He only learned the truth about his two cousins after he fell in love with one of them. His own generation's dishonesty was still in the making.

Xavi Goldring DeAngelus had grown up as a gentle and thoughtful young man. He was tall for his age, good-looking and good-natured, but not particularly outgoing; he preferred books and the company of his own thoughts. He attended the Normal School in Albany where he once heard his aunt Winifred lecture on the Gilboa Fossils and Crinoid Casts from the Helderberg Escarpment. He was impressed by her, but paleontology, or science for that matter, did not hold his interest. He liked paintings. In fact, it was the art books in the library that held his attention best. Less the folios of modern paintings than those filled with what one of his teachers referred to as "transcendental imagery." Religious Art captured his imagination and quickened his heart. He became obsessed with the history of western sacred art, its roots in animism, idolatry, and from the Quattrocento on – the fearsome awe of what could not be known but only represented – the martyr's blessed agony bathed in Mantegna's bleeding vermillion, God's firmament bursting forth in Titian's blue light or Tintoretto's gray storms, the mystic's rapture emerging from the cryptic depths of Caravaggio's chiaroscuro. The more sublime the expression, the more Xavi felt drawn to something deep inside himself...a calling. But it was not to become a scholar in *front* of the paintings, rather it was his desire to enter into them, to pass through the surface of tempera and oil, through the wood and canvas to embrace what it was that lay behind them. To bear witness. When Xavi chose to enter St. Joseph's Seminary two hours south in Yonkers New York, Jenna was disappointed; she did not want him to enter the priesthood. But she was not surprised. One of the Seminary's degree programs seemed to have been written for her son – *Studies in Art and Religion with an interdisciplinary focus on the theological, cultural, and spiritual meanings expressed by, and experienced through, visual, plastic, liturgical, and ritual arts. The program aims to further nurture the aesthetic, moral, spiritual, and creative life.*

Jenna was uncertain whether Xavi was drawn to find meaning in God or in Art.

"Cave paintings, mother," he'd said with a playful smile, "Invisible God in visible Art...Pleistocene cave paintings, over and over again, world without end."

Xavi was only in his first semester of his diaconate when he met his cousin Wilhelmina. Four years his senior, Mina Goldring had left her mother's home on Bathgate Avenue and taken a secretarial job in the office of the Rector of St. Joseph's. She had been raised a Catholic and, like her brother Livingston, had attended school at Christ the King in the Bronx. In her job interview, she was able to talk convincingly about the Society of the Priests of Saint-Sulpice who oversaw the work of the Seminary – despite having long since left her faith behind. She was also good at reading men. During their discussion about Sulpitius the Pious, the Rector's seriousness of purpose could not mask his transparent attraction. He displayed the same awkward attention that she had experienced among many of the Catholic Fathers during her high school years, men stumbling over their lack of practice with women and the confounding thrill of its forbidden nature. The Reverend Monsignor was elated when she agreed to be in his office five days a week.

Xavi and Mina found each other by chance. Their mothers were rarely in touch and unaware of the proximity of their children. It was the 'Goldring' on the nameplate sitting at the front edge of Mina's desk outside the Rector's office that caught Xavi's attention. It was his middle name from his mother's family. He would study it from his chair across the room, wondering, while he waited for his weekly audience with the Rector. Mina noticed the lanky young boy's attention, and teasingly drew him out. She was as surprised as he was when he showed her his school identity card, more so when they realized how their shared name also connected them by blood.

The Seminary at Dunwoodie would seem to have been a difficult and unlikely place in which to fall in love. But, despite his younger age and quiet nature, Xavi was an alluring wonder to Mina. A boy from another world. His utter lack of guile, his passion for the unknown, and his determination to live an authentic life wherever it might lead him. There was no flirting, no coyness nor innuendo, but there was a glint, a spark. His was a clear-eyed offer to her, to a depth of sentiment and meaning. His offer washed over Mina in a way that she had never experienced and gave her hope that a life with him might lead her away from the lack of direction in her own. By the end of the year of their meeting, she had come to love him. Or, better said, she had come to love him...in her way. It was the best she could offer in return, as she tried to ignore the bad things she'd done while also knowing that to keep them from him risked breaking his gift.

Jenna and Mattie Goldring had only recently become aware of their children's encounter when the first cousins took leave from the Seminary and, by-passing the Pre-Cana, eloped on the Seaboard Air Line Railway to Florida. It had been Mina's idea; just before boarding the Silver Meteor, she dropped off a letter to her namesake, Billie Kinsolver, telling her of her good fortune and announcing their plans to visit Princeton.

Mina had included a photo in her letter to Billie, a strip of pictures of the happy couple glowing in one of the new photo booths at Penn Station. Billie had shifted in her chair toward the light in order to study it more closely. Her eyes weren't what they'd been back in her days at Gilboa, but they could still make out the memories. She smiled wanly at the young man in the photograph, remembering his father. Xavi looked a lot like Johnny of the Angel, and she imagined how his father's cross-cut scar would have fallen on the son's face. And Mina? There, too, stood a memory. She remembered seeing the first photograph of Mina as a newborn child in Mattie Goldring's arms; it had been sent to her twenty three years earlier, along with its mystery.

Mattie Goldring had been the reckless Goldring sister. It was a sweet-hearted recklessness – the kind that deserves to survive its innocent impetuous risks. But sweet-hearted recklessness only needs to lose one reckless gamble to lose them all, and Mattie had charmed too many in Gilboa, including young Billie.

They had had one night, swimming in the Manorkill, skinny-dipping after a lively evening at the FingerBreak. Both were slightly drunk, and Billie could still remember the moonlight on Mattie's breasts, and the kissing, the giggling and laughter that went soft, then to silence as

Mattie began showing the young girl how to love another woman. And Billie remembered Eli Gallagher, appearing out of nowhere, watching them from the bank. Mattie had told her to run, to get away.

That was where Billie's memory ended; she had gotten away, and it left her with an aching regret – she should have stayed with Mattie. Billie was young and not to be blamed, but it still wounded her, thinking of Mattie standing in the water up to her knees with her legs slightly apart and hands on her hips, as if challenging Gallagher. Not to come to her, but to be a *real* man and walk away. Everyone knew Gallagher well enough to know that he was not one to be challenged, particularly by a woman.

The sweet-hearted and the dark-hearted.

Billie Kinsolver, sitting there in Endurance Fuller's house, miles and years away from Gilboa, worried that Mina, born less than a year after that night on the Manorkill, was both her mother and father's daughter.

*　　*

The Highlands subaltern, Chick Gable, drove the Willys-Overland jeep slowly through the throngs of men on Piney Alley. Company Commander Frank Wrezinskavich sat next to him, as they approached the boys from Highlands Hammock. The sun had topped the palms and the thick air was already roiling off the oiled road with the day's heat and humidity. Sheriff Darryl Potts had moved up the road to the G-men, and Superintendent Rembrandt Stikkey was waiting for the Commander's inspection; following CCC protocol kept his mind clear of the dread that had been following him for days.

Commander Wrezinskavich stepped from the jeep and saluted Rembrandt as the boys snapped into formation. Wrezinskavich was in full uniform; it was neatly pressed, but large swags of sweat-rings darkened the khaki beneath his arms as he walked the line inspecting his men.

"Bring him home, boys. Bring him home today," Wrezinskavich said, quietly. At the end of the line, he stopped in front of Linc Gilboa and turned to look back at the subaltern. Chick Gable, still gripping the steering wheel, shrugged his shoulders. Livingston, standing next to his cousin, held his breath.

"He's out of Myakka, Commander, but he's a local boy. Knows the Glades as well as anyone," Rembrandt said quietly, moving to Wrezinskavich's side.

The Commander removed his Pershing cap and wiped his brow with his shirt sleeve. "Ok, then, Supe, whatever you need, whatever you think'll get the job done. We're all praying for you."

Behind the boys, along the edge of the road, the sound of brush hacking and the low murmur of men's voices rose up from behind the palmettos. The sharp fronds of Saw and Cabbage Palms began falling to the ground as an opening cleared and two men appeared, each swinging a machete and carrying a canvas haversack strapped with a GI-shovel on his back. Climbing up out of the culvert to the road, they slung their packs to the ground and, ignoring the Commander, nodded their greeting at Rembrandt. Livingston could see that they were Indians, probably Miccosukie scouts, friends, maybe family, of Rembrandt's.

Rembrandt acknowledged the two scouts. "Sip, Charlie,...we good?"

"Chayahlom...ooche," one of the Indians answered solemnly.

Rembrandt put his hand on the man's shoulder and smiled at him wearily, then turned to the boys, "Men, strap tight those gauntlets. We're going in."

Livingston leaned over to Linc and whispered, "What'd he say to the Supe?...the Indian?"

"It's Miccosukie...it means *the lost son walks*."

There were not many that day who would have believed the

Miccosukie scout, including the Indian himself. If that boy was out there, hidden out of sight, the heat alone would likely have killed him days before.

Back in town, Reverend Klutterer was holding vigilance with Belle Stikkey. His own wife Jilly was inconsolable with guilt and taken to bed with fainting spells and night terrors. When the Klutterer's older son Clipper returned from Miami to help look after his younger brother, matters only worsened for the family.

Clipper was known as "Preacher Boy." Some thought it was a nod to the father, but others felt it captured his tendency to spout off on matters that he knew little about. Clipper had returned to Princeton with a pocketful of money. He said he was holding down a steady job, working for the city on the new Dixie Highway down to Key West, said they'd given him time off to come back home to be with his family and help. But Clipper was quickly begging off the searches, to babysit he'd claim, but he was loud in his opinions about how and where the searches should be conducted, cocksure as always. At night, with both parents at home, he'd set on the stoop of the general store, drinking beer, and bragging about the women that he'd had over on the east coast. Most of the locals were used to him and also used to not paying him too much mind; he'd always been an embarrassment to the Reverend and his wife, even though, despite all, they remained caring and patient with their oldest son. Nevertheless, word of the son's behavior soon found its way to Sheriff Potts.

Hoover's men didn't put much stock in Potts' suspicions, they were focused on the negro shacks that had been mentioned in the ransom note. The theory among the FBI agents, shared by Hoover, was that a white perpetrator, or perpetrators, had abducted little Cash and brought on one or more black co-conspirators to keep him hidden down in the "quarters." But Potts believed they were giving too much credit to the white "Crackers," and he kept 'Preacher Boy' Klutterer in his sights. He suspected that there had never been a highway job in Miami, and he was right.

It came out later that Rembrandt Stikkey's discussion with Sheriff Potts on Piney Alley had been about a run-down hunting camp in the Glades where young Klutterer and some friends had run an 800-gallon submarine-still during the last days of Prohibition. Rembrandt sent out the two Miccosukies in the dark of night. They returned with what was left of Skeegie, Cash Stikkey's stuffed alligator. It had been in the swamp, hooked onto one of the camp pilings; the handpuppet's mouth was covered with leeches and its last remaining green threads plucked free by mosquitofish and scrub jays.

After Commander Wrezinskavich left Piney Alley, and Waterhouse Hawkins had returned with a dozen slings of full canteens for the boys, the two indian scouts picked up their haversacks, and the Highlands company led by Rembrandt, followed them into the cut. In the distance up and down Piney Alley, Waterhouse watched the other groups of men, also twelve to a team, dropping off both sides of the road into the culverts and disappearing into the scrubby understory of the Everglades. As the last of his friends disappeared into the palmettos, he hitched his trousers and called out, "I gotta feeling, fellas...I really do." It was the best Waterhouse could offer, masking his frustration at having to remain behind. He slapped, irritatedly, at his crippled leg, and began shuffling up the empty red dirt road back to the water wagon. Overhead, a vigilant short-tailed hawk wove in and out of a slow wheel of Black Vultures, watching the spreading trails of the men and the small prey dislodged in their approach and wake.

Livingston soon lost sight of the Indians but followed the clang of steel on steel from their machetes. "They're giving the crocs a warning," Linc said to Livingston, pointing with his machete into the bush, "And any other critter that has a mind to jump us. Beating those blades together is a hell of a racket in the ears of God's creatures way out here."

Livingston tightened his grip on his own machete, wondering if all the scouts were doing was driving 'critters' their way. Raising his face to the sky, he yelled out as loud as he could, "Number four here, number *four*!"

At Rembrandt's order, the boys had been paired off and given a number before fanning out into the thickets. They were told to weave their search in the direction of the ringing steel but, from time to time, to call out their number so others would know where their neighboring pair was tracking. It was also important to keep everyone accounted for. The ground under foot was mean, tricky, not meant for a human being's footfall; either boggy with sinkholes and large tufted mounds of whipping sawgrass that could cut right though their denim, or hard uneven rock of sharp puckered limestone that broke ankles and tore at boot soles. Livingston shared Linc's concern about the crocodiles and other of "God's large creatures," but it was the smaller ones, the ones you couldn't see before it was too late, that worried him most. Snappers and water snakes in the wet ground, and scorpions or Brown Recluse spiders hiding in the eroded limestone pockets. Rembrandt had warned them all that this part of the earth was unforgiving, and, secretly, he had been praying with Belle that their son had found safer ground...but, in the dark and private depths of his thoughts, he was praying that, at least, little Cash never suffered, that he had died quick.

It was in a small canal shadowed by a large pitch pine that Cash Stikkey was found. The canal was one of the many man-made cuts into the Glades intended to get hold of its groundwater and send it elsewhere, but its banks had become overgrown with muhly grass and Florida bluestem, making it hard to see. Linc caught hold of Livingston's arm just before his cousin stepped off the edge. Neither the diversion nor its dark standing water was particularly deep, but both men walked a few steps back, turned, then took running leaps to clear the canal. Livingston was in mid-air when he caught sight of the boy at the base of the tree, curled up and twisted at the waist, staring up from a strangely roiled eye socket. Poor Linc landed on the boy's arm, jamming it, along with the sucking sound of his boot, into the muck.

"Sweet Jesus!" Linc cried out, swinging his arms and body awkwardly around to avoid any more of the corpse. He fell hard on his back, slamming his head against the pine and knocking himself out cold.

Livingston landed cleanly on the far bank a few feet away, stunned, his breath choked by fright and the surge of adrenalin. Half the boy's body was still submerged in the canal, and the twist at his waist looked as if the child had been trying to clear his mouth from the brown water, but the bloated flesh and the tiny swarm of blowflies laying maggot eggs in the boy's eye socket suggested that the body had been dumped there and lay now as it had fallen, days before. Little Cash was wearing the bib coveralls that had been taken during the kidnapping and the OshKosh straps over his shoulders had already begun to congeal with the moldering flesh.

"Number four! Number four! Help! Oh God, Help! He's here! Oh God, Oh God,... *NUMBER FOUR!*" Livingston was half-howling, bawling, reaching out, down toward the boy, then stopping, then reaching out again, holding back, fearing to touch the body, and sickened at the thought of it. Turning away, he began retching with great dry heaves at the tamped ground beneath the pitch pine, only then did he realize that

173

Lincoln Gilboa, still lying at the base of the tree, was unconscious, blood pouring from his mouth and fire ants covering his neck and lower jaw. Linc's eyes were closed, and his head was propped up on a large mound as if he'd passed out on a hard pillow. Hundreds of fire ants had been roused from where Linc's fall had torn open the sloping side of their colony, most had swarmed to the blood at his mouth.

Slapping off the ants with one hand and pulling Linc free of the mound with the other, Livingston managed to rouse his cousin. Linc gave out a bleary yelp and put his hand to his face, "My tongue, I bit my tongue, bit it off. Can't feel it, no more," he slurred, flexing his jaw and spitting blood from his open mouth. The tip of his tongue was indeed gone, maybe a quarter inch worth, clean cut, straight across where it had once been.

Livingston, having cleared Linc's face, continued swatting the remaining ants off his back, but from the corner of his eye, he was still fixed on the dead body down in the canal, "We gotta do something, Linc. We can't just leave him down there in the water." Stepping away from Lincoln and climbing down to the edge of the canal, Livingston leaned over and took hold of a shoulder strap on the boy's coveralls. He tried to pull him free of the water, up the bank, but the strap peeled away more flesh and quickly broke off in his hand. The child's body slowly rolled over again and slid deeper into the water just as Rembrandt Stikkey and three Highland boys came running up from around the pine.

"Get Gilboa into the water, Kinsolver," Rembrandt yelled. He had an exhausted frown on his face, "They'll get off him right quick." The Superintendent and the others could not see the body in the canal and had figured that Livingston's calls for help had to do with the insects on Lincoln Gilboa. Rembrandt leaned with irritation into Livingston's face, wondering why he was just standing there staring back at him with a dumb look, then brushed him aside to get to Linc. "C'mon boys, give me a hand," he said.

"Wait, wait," Linc slurred in quiet protest. He was still dazed and tried rising to his feet, raising an arm to fend off the others. "He's here,... he's in the water," he mumbled feebly. Linc fell back again and the last thing he saw, or at least thought he saw, before passing out for a second time, was the quarter inch of his tongue being hoisted on the backs of a few retreating fire ants who quickly disappeared with it into their mound.

When Rembrandt finally saw his son's body, he froze up and went silent. The boys with him stepped abruptly back, sucking the air in through their teeth and back out with muttered gasps, reaching out for one another as if to help or be helped with what lay twisted at their feet.

"Get him out of the way, Kinsolver," Rembrandt said slowly, quietly, "Get Gilboa up off the bank." He did not take his eyes of his son, as Livingston and another boy carried Lincoln to clear ground. Then, as if awoken from a trance, Rembrandt dropped to his knees and hung his head from his slumped shoulders. He sobbed softly, briefly, before raising his face to the sky and, emitting a loud otherworldly moan, began crawling into the water to his child.

At that moment, it had been bad enough for Livingston to see the death on the child's face, but it was forever worse seeing Rembrandt's desperate and impossible search for life. With the water at his waist, Rembrandt wiped the blowflies from his son's eye and cradling the boy in his arms began performing mouth-to-mouth resuscitation on him. It shook everyone badly because the child's bloodless face, had been badly poked by mud mullets, and his mouth was so water-rotted that Rembrandt ended up mangling the soft gray flesh, right down to the child's jawbone.

Whatever had turned in the mind of Rembrandt Stikkey in those moments, it would not turn back. Later that day, after the child was brought out and taken to the morgue, the Superintendent walked back to the canal, sat down beneath the pine, and put the Springfield to his own jaw. No one witnessed it, those nearby saw only the frightened rise of birds from the rifle's report. But, for Livingston, it was the beginning of a haunting that he could never shake; he could accept the slow decomposition of a man buried in hard ground, there was a natural calling to it. Not so with water. All life on earth may surely have risen there – in water – but it is no place to die.

The double-burial was a Miccosukie affair held in Little Blackwater Sound near Rembrandt's place of birth. No coffins, no urns filled with ashes, just two ruined bodies placed under palmetto fronds down a five-foot hole dug out of a shaded clearing on a small cypress island. Two tree seedlings – a pond-apple and a hackberry – were brought to the graveside for planting in the soil that would cover the bodies. It was Indian tradition - father and son were dead, but the land was alive; the bodies' would supply the nutrients and foundation on which the trees would grow; and the trees, in turn, would provide food, firewood and medicine for those who, one day, would go as bodies to soil as well.

Besides Company Commander Wrezinskavich, Livingston was the only member of the Highlands Hammock crew to bear witness. Wrezinskavich had felt it best that the subaltern get the other boys back to camp as soon as possible, get them back to their duties and ordered lives where they could work off the tragedy. Initially, when Livingston heard they were all being shipped back to Highland Hammocks Camp SP-3 he was upset and angry, telling Waterhouse he had no intention of returning. They were striking camp on the Fuller Plantation and Waterhouse was doing his best to dissuade him from 'going over the hill' when Chick Gable came over and told Livingston he would be staying with the Commander. The subaltern gave him train fare for his return north to Sebring whenever his family affairs in Princeton were finished.

At the burial for father and son, Livingston stood with his aunt Billie Kinsolver and Endurance Fuller. On the other side of the open grave, Belle Stikkey was stone-faced, expressionless, as if hollowed out of all that had filled her with life. She seemed indifferent to the heaving shoulders of her sister-in-law Saskia Stikkey, who stood weeping at her side. Lincoln Gilboa, his face still bruised and swollen, stood on the other side of Saskia with his arm around her waist as she leaned into him for comfort. Behind them were the two Miccosukie men who'd led the last search, and other Stikkey cousins, men and women, each silently mouthing an incantation to the bodies in the hole.

Livingston watched Belle, wondering what would become of her, what her life would be without Rembrandt and her son. And he wondered about what happens to a family when it's snuffed out so surely, never given a chance to be buried with a proper time's memory of their years together. He thought of something that Rembrandt had shared up at Highlands about the Indians – the Miccosukie Law of Seven Generations. He'd said it was their belief that the fullest and wisest life is achieved when lived at the center of seven generations – to have experienced a parent, grandparent, and great-grandparent on one side of time, and a child, grandchild, and great-grandchild on the other. Such a symmetry, the *axis mundi* of a family's past and future, typically gathers up more than a century of Time, and, as it endlessly passes down like a baton from one generation to the next, it gathers up *all* of Time.

But his thoughts for Belle soon were disjointed, confused by the presence, over her shoulder, of Mina Goldring, standing in a near distance at the exposed edge of the clearing.

Livingston had not expected to see them; not there, at least. On the trip down to Little Blackwater Sound for the burial, Endurance had told him of Mina's and Xaviero's arrival on the East Coast Railway spur line out of Miami; he'd sent a driver to bring them out to the house to wait until the funeral was over...but there she was...there, in Little Blackwater, fanning the damp heat from her face with a man's straw hat. Xavi DeAngelus stood beside her, bareheaded in the Florida sun.

Averting his eyes from Belle and his sister, Livingston looked down into the hole at the two white shrouds tracing the bodies' outlines. Small clumps of brown peat had already fallen from the earthen walls of the grave, speckling the clean white sheets like drops of dark rain before a downpour. Despite himself, he could not help imagining Rembrandt and Belle under these same sheets, or when they might have tossed them to the floor as they made love. And he felt ashamed by the coupling of his desire and his sadness. He thought of Lincoln Gilboa's wounding in the dirt of the Everglades, the insolence of its timing and its indifference to the foulest of wounds – a lifeless child. And he thought of Princeton, desperately trying to shake off its nightmare amidst the mockery of Gaston Drake's overweening pride in the municipality's festive orange and black decor. Livingston was struck not so much by the incongruity, but by the randomness of it all. It seemed to him that God, or Fate, or whatever it was that put events in motion on the face of the earth, had put before him pairs of irreconcilable things, each serving to undermine the place, the significance, of the other. There seemed to be a cruelty to it. And now, Mina and Belle...together, as if his sister-cousin was there to remind him that his affections came in troubling forms and that lost innocence always followed.

So be it, Livingston thought. The innocence of his affection for Belle had been put to death with death, yes, that was true, but Rembrandt's suicide was both a taking and an offering – Livingston knew that if Mina would ever let him free, he would go to Belle...if she would have him.

Livingston looked up and met the eyes of the man standing in the distance with his sister. Xavi DeAngelus nodded at his cousin and made the sign of the cross over his shirt. The shirt was sweat-drenched and buttoned to his neck, white, like the shrouds in the ground. Livingston nodded back. Amen.

As the last shovel of earth was placed on the mound, the surround of mourners drifted apart, talking quietly as they headed to the cars parked beyond the clearing. A few of the Miccosukie men and women disappeared into the scrub forest, leaving Belle, Saskia and Linc alone graveside. Billie and Endurance lagged behind as Livingston walked to his cousins. Although he did his best to draw himself up, to appear strong and grown-up in front of his sister, he was exhausted, still weary from the bad images in his head and the nights of spare sleep. Mina opened her arms to him. "Livingston, I've missed you. I'm so sorry," she said.

Livingston put his hands in his pockets and leaned in to kiss Mina's cheek, but she gripped him and pulled him into her embrace. She began to rock him gently, stroking his head like she used to when he was younger. Livingston kept his hands in his pockets, closing them into fists to help him fight back the tears. For a moment it was just the two of them, then Xavi stepped forward and closed the circle. He was taller than both and easily wrapped his long arms around them, clasping his fingers in a full embrace. "Deus absconditus," he said softly, "His Grace is hidden, but it is there in the signature of all things, vengeances and mercies."

Uncomfortable in the intimacy of the gesture from the cousin he had never met, Livingston awkwardly broke free of the circle. He also felt annoyed by Xavi's invocation of a Catholic god intruding on the Miccosukie Indian burial.

Xavi smiled at him, sympathetically and wistful, as if he understood what Livingston was thinking. "Here as anywhere, we are all mystics in our Faiths."

"Livingston, this is Xaviero...Xavi," Mina put her hand on Xavi's elbow as she looked at her brother-cousin, "He's...family."

Livingston nodded to his cousin. Xavi was three or four inches taller than he was and had the Goldring face, lean and angular with high cheek-bones and cool gray eyes, clear and focused. The two boys were close in age, but Livingston thought his cousin seemed a lot older. The expression on Xavi's face was gracious and calming; an attentive steadiness that seemed genuine, offered without conditions. Livingston felt his irritation and weariness slowly ebb away.

Endurance and Billie approached them. Before they drew up close, Mina quickly whispered in Livingston's ear, "Mother will be happy to hear that I've seen you, Livingston. And I have something I need to tell you." She turned and greeted Billie Kinsolver, embracing her, then, smiling at Endurance, said, "Mattie sends her love and thanks you for keeping your eye on him...for everything you have done for us."

"Yes,...well, he's done fine on his own. And, done a fine thing, too. A hard thing." Endurance looked solemnly at Livingston, then turned to face Xaviero DeAngelus, "And this is Jenna and Gianni's boy, I believe," he said, reaching out to shake Xavi's hand.

"Yes, sir," Xavi said, "I've heard a lot about you, Mr. Fuller."

"Well, young fellow, it's a surprise to see you here, but you're welcome. I met your father. A few times." He looked at Billie, as if sharing with her the distant memory, then, turning back to the boy, said, "Didn't know him well, but he was quite a man, from all accounts. And quite a singer."

"Thank you, sir, I've often heard this." Xavi straightened his shoulders, gathering himself. "I know we have come at a bad time. We won't stay long. Mina wanted so much to see you all and say goodbye before we leave for..."

He was interrupted by Billie Kinsolver. "But you'll stay with us tonight, yes?" Billie asked. She put her arm around Mina who was looking furtively at Livingston, nervously tucking a strand of blond hair behind her ear. "We'll hear all of your news then. Endurance will take you to the house. I'll be along shortly; I need to help with things here."

As Billie began walking back toward the grave site, Livingston saw that his Company Commander had joined Linc, Saskia and Belle Stikkey next to the mound. Wrezinskavich had hold of Belle's hand in both of his and was speaking softly to her. Livingston was reminded of the calling of his heart and the sense that he should leave it unheeded.

"I have to report to my Commander," he said to Mina, "I'm supposed to return to Sebring. Not sure when. I don't know if I'll be able to see you again."

"You will, I'm sure of it," she said quietly, under her breath. Taking Xavi's arm, she walked towards the few remaining parked cars. Endurance Fuller was there waiting next to his Zephyr. Calling back over her shoulder, Mina said in a clear voice, "Mr. Fuller is right. You *have* done a fine thing."

That afternoon, Livingston was awarded a Certificate for Valor for the 'fine thing' he had done. There was no ceremony, only a piece of paper signed by President Roosevelt and given to him by Commander Wrezinskavich along with six months pay and his release from the Civilian Conservation Corps.

Lincoln Gilboa had stood by as his cousin received the honor; there was no Certificate for him – Linc's award was an additional week in

Princeton to allow his tongue to heal before his mandatory return to the Myakka Camp.

"It's not fair, Linc," Livingston said later, "You deserve it more than me."

They were sitting around Endurance Fuller's table at dinner, Billie at the far end opposite Endurance at the head, Linc and Livingston facing Xavi and Mina. Billie sighed, "Let it be, Livingston. Nothing to be done. At least, we have both of you for a bit."

Livingston looked down and forked at his plate. "I figure I could stay around here, maybe help with the plantation?" He paused, then added, "Or maybe help Belle with her house before she goes, things that the Supe used to do for her." As soon as he said it, Livingston felt his face flush. If anyone at the table noticed, they kept silent.

"Saskia believes Belle will go north to her folks in Indiantown," Linc said, gingerly lisping out his words over the stitches in his tongue, "Can't imagine what would keep her here now; everything bein' a reminder and all."

Endurance pushed his chair back noisily from the table, announcing a change of subject. He retrieved a cigar from the breast pocket of his linen jacket. "Happy to have you here as long as you want, Livingston. We'll be needing the help."

As Endurance lit his Cuban Esmerelda, Billie stood up and waved away the plume of blue smoke. "I'm sorry I let Modesto talk me into bringing those dreadful things for you." She began clearing the table.

"Tell me," Endurance asked, "how long have the two of you been married?"

Mina looked at Xavi, sheepishly, then lowered her head. He shifted in his chair and cleared his throat. "We are not married, sir," he said, "I feel badly that we have given that impression. We love each other, but, for the moment I'm still officially in the Seminary...I have my vows."

"It's my fault," Mina said, "I never actually *told* Aunt Billie we had married, but I knew everyone would assume...and then I just thought it would make it easier for us to travel together."

A silence enveloped the couple; the two had been sleeping together under Fuller's roof. Linc and Saskia exchanged furtive knowing looks, but Livingston was the least surprised. It was like her, he thought, like Mina, living outside of the rules, capricious and determined. He was relieved that she was going abroad. It felt to him that the farther away Mina went, married or not, the better it would be. For both of them. He wondered what Xavi knew. Whether he would forgive her if she ever told him.

"Well,...it's your business, I suppose." Endurance said, shaking his head as if trying to catch up with the world and all of its changes. He held his cigar off to the side of the table as Billie cleared his plate.

"Have you told Livingston your plans yet, Mina?" Billie asked.

Mina looked over at Xavi and placed her hand on his, then leaning slightly forward at the table toward Livingston, said, "We're leaving for Italy next week. Xavi managed to book passage on a Liberty Ship under the protection of Vatican City. He has some work there. For his studies. We hope to get to Verona as well to see Xavi's father's family while the country is still safe."

The table fell silent once again, all eyes on Xavi.

As if rising to a challenge, he straightened up in his chair and clasped his hands in his lap. "*Listen to your father who gave you life...*," he said with a shrug,

"*And he who fathers a wise son will be glad in him...*Proverbs 23, I understand," Endurance said, forcefully, "but good lord, man, what are you two thinking?" He blew a stream of smoke at the ceiling in exasperation. "You of all people should know what a godless place Europe is becoming, and now that Mussolini has made his pact with that scoundrel

Hitler, the most godless creature of them all, matters are only getting worse. The devil has just come through Princeton, but over there, Satan has a front row seat. Italy is no place to be right now."

"We'll be with one of Xavi's professor's from Dunwoodie; he's waiting for us in Rome with some of the students from the Seminary," Mina said. "They're hoping to arrange for the protection of some of the Catholic artworks in the north." She turned to Xavi. "Or at least document them in case the fighting comes into the country," she said with less assurance.

"We won't be there long," Xavi said, "and we'll have the escort of the Palatine Guards. Pope Pius is maintaining the Vatican's neutrality; it's being respected."

"So far," Endurance said, gruffly. "But Verona? That's way too close to the border. Palatine Guards or no." He tamped out his Esmerelda in his empty coffee cup.

Billie frowned at Endurance and reached across Xavi for his dinner plate. Standing next to him, she was no taller than he was in his seat. She kissed him on his cheek. "Well, I'm just happy to have all the families here under one roof, even if for such a short time. Your mothers would be pleased as well."

She wanted to say their names – Mattie, Jenna, and Winifred – the three Goldring mothers whose children sat at her table, but she did not; there were too many ghosts among them – the fathers. There was also something else. Mina's aspect. Ever since seeing Mina and Livingston standing together, she'd been struck by how much they looked alike, how much they *both* looked like her brother, Piedmont. She couldn't shake a difficult thought out of her head.

"I think it sounds exciting, an adventure," Saskia said. Then, as if deferring to Endurance's warning, added, "as long as you're sure to be safe. Where will you go exactly?"

"We'll be fine, I'm certain of it," Mina said, eager to share the details of the trip. "From Rome we go to Florence and then through Venice. We're both so excited to see the paintings. Finally! And Xavi is going to write a book about Heaven on Earth." She elbowed Xavi, playfully. "Or is it on Earthly Heaven...Heavenly Earth?"

"Neither...and both," Xavi said, with a somewhat forced laugh. He was embarrassed. "Only about the *pictures* of Heaven and Earth, the representations, how they were depicted by the painters."

"Oh...and how's that?" Endurance asked, as if still challenging the young man for more of his foolishness.

"The relationship between faith and art. Great art doesn't represent the visible, but what is invisible in what is visible. The choice of colors, the light and atmosphere, their density and structure...things of that nature are everything. And the differences in their renderings is the difference in the quest that faith undertakes, the different paths it chooses, as it searches for what is beneath the surface of things."

Linc had his arm slung over the back of Saskia's chair with a bemused expression on his face. He nudged Saskia and crooked his mouth, then winced at the pain of his healing tongue.

"You'd best keep quiet, Linc," she whispered to him.

Billie Kinsolver watched the boy from the kitchen door, the young man at her table. *The surface of things.* She thought of Winifred and her buried fossils; of Johnny of the Angel and his carved stones pulled up from beneath the earth; of her brother – *At the foot of the Mountains*; and of Lincoln Lincoln clasping himself to her in the crawl space beneath the dance floor of the FingerBreak. Beneath the surface of things.

"And how do *you* see the differences, Xaviero? Gods have always come in many forms," Endurance asked.

"What do I see? I'm not yet sure, I guess." For a moment, Xavi appeared thoughtful and uncertain. Then, he leaned in his chair toward the question. "But I believe it's through the images we draw, or paint, or build, or hear in a poem – the aesthetic moments, perhaps even the *beatific* moments, that all Art offers us. It's like seeing a familiar tree, one that we have seen many times before, but suddenly as if for the first time. It's a Law of Nature that each of us sees the same thing very differently – *what* we see, as opposed to *how* we see it – so, too, an image offers itself to everyone, but the aesthetic moment offers itself only to those who see within it what the mystics call the *Signature of All Things*."

"The signature of all things, hmmm," Endurance folded his arms across his broad chest, "Yes, well...not sure what you mean exactly, but I suppose its a reasonable way to describe the unknowable...Not very scientific, but perhaps reasonable."

"Heaven, Eternity, Mystery, the Sublime, it comes by many names... but *Reason* is certainly not one of them. Science and reason can tell us where to look, but Art tells us how to find it, how to recognize it," Xavi said, emphatically. Then, suddenly fearing he'd been disrespectful to Mr. Fuller, he bowed his head, deferentially, and added, "I only mean that we...that *I'm* as unknowing as anyone." He sat back in his chair. "As one of my professors said to me, each of us must go inside himself to find the world. I have faith that Art helps."

Billie stepped forward into the conversation. "Livingston's mother made beautiful drawings," she said. She looked over at Livingston. "Winifred, I mean. Can I call her that now, Livingston? Your mother? Would that be alright?"

"Yes, ma'am," Livingston said, flatly. He looked down, flushed, and dis-comfited by his spoken acknowledgment. It had been unspoken too long.

Billie walked to his side and put her hand on his shoulder. "It was surprising how good she was, given that science, not art, was everything in the world to her. The watercolors. You should see the one of Winifred's tree; it's quite famous now. It's in the museum in Albany, New York." She looked over at Endurance, "The Gilboa Tree," she said, with a wistful smile. "Next to the diorama."

"The diorama, yes. As a matter of fact," Endurance announced, as if cued by Billie, "I've just received a letter from Winifred. She's asked us to send her more palm fronds and ferns from the plantation for the diorama. We've been doing it for years, keeping the exhibit fresh, celebrating her big discovery."

"That's right," Billie continued, "It's a replica of the forest where her ancient trees grew. She used the actual quarried stone, put in a small running waterfall with mosses and sculpted replicas of the trees and other vegetation. Winifred painted some of the background herself. She uses the palm fronds for the tree canopies and the ferns for the ground plants, says they're the closest living leaves to those of the Gilboa Forest. I've heard it's very life-like."

"We saw a diorama in New York," Mina said, "At the Museum of Natural History in the Akeley Hall of African Mammals. It was brand new and very realistic. But it was also kind of strange; as if you're actually there among the animals...but not. It made me dizzy, standing at the glass window." She turned to Xavi. "Real and unreal at the same time...like your Art, your paintings."

"Tomorrow, we'll bundle some Royal Palm fronds for shipping," Endurance said, "You can take them to the station, Livingston. Winifred will be happy to know that they were sent by your hand." He stood up, patted his ample belly, then straightened his vest with a quick tug. One of his buttons broke free. It fell to the floor, rolling before wobbling to a halt at Livingston's feet.

Livingston leaned down to retrieve it. "I'll take that," said Billie, with her hand out, still at his side, "It's my fault anyway. I've been overfeeding him for years."

Early the following morning, Billie Kinsolver took the Zephyr and drove Xavi and Mina to the train. Livingston and Linc followed along in one of the plantation's Plymouth PT50 pickup trucks. The truck was loaded with citrus for delivery to the produce shipping office at the station. It also carried a carefully packed box of Southern Wood and Plumosa Ferns along with a dozen large Sabal Palmetto and Royal Palm fronds. The box was addressed to the State Museum in Albany, care of the State Paleontologist, Winifred Goldring.

They were about a mile from the plantation when Linc, trying to block the morning sun, lowered the driver's side visor. A creased black and white photograph fell from it, fluttering face-up onto the seat between them. It was a picture of Belle Stikkey and her boy Cash taken a few years back.

"Christ,...we're in Rembrandt's truck," Linc said, picking up the photograph. He studied it for a moment then handed it to Livingston.

Livingston barely looked at it before placing it into his shirt pocket. "I'll return it to her," he said. He would do this, he thought, when the time was right, even if he had to follow her back to Indiantown.

The Flagler Flyer was at the station when they arrived, waiting on the spur line track of the East Coast Railway for its return trip to Miami. The Flyer had been named after Henry Flagler, another of Gaston Drake's University cronies, He'd financed the spur track in order to serve the Princeton logging plantations and a few of the smaller truck farms, but ever since the collapse of Drake's businesses, the Flyer's schedule had been unreliable. But that morning, it had arrived early with extra cars to clear the town of the last of the G-men and search volunteers.

After helping Linc unload the crates of oranges and delivering Winifred's foliage to the shipping office, Livingston joined Mina and Xavi at the tracks. Billie had already said her good-byes and stood off by her car with Linc, giving the Goldring cousins their own time together.

"Write to me, Livingston," Mina whispered in his ear as she kissed him goodbye. "I know I have not been a good sister,...or even a good cousin to you, but I love you and always will. Xavi is a new kind of man for me. He is gentle and reliable. He's helped me to believe in God, or Grace...whatever it is that might forgive the things I've done. He doesn't know." She paused and pulled back, looking deeply into Livingston's eyes, then kissed him on the cheek. "He doesn't know any of it." she said, "He doesn't know that I am the child of a rape."

She took hold of both of his hands, squeezing them gently, and spoke more clearly for Xavi to hear. "It can be a new life for me in Italy, and I will be careful with it. And you, you too must be careful. I know, I can see your feeling for Mrs. Stikkey, even without Lincoln having told me. But be careful, she is not who she was. There may be nothing left in her heart after what she has endured."

Livingston felt his face burn. The photograph in his pocket above his own heart, seemed to burn as well. "I'll be careful, I promise," he replied. Avoiding any further talk of Belle, he turned to Xavi. "Maybe I'll visit Verona sometime. Come see your pictures."

The Flyer whistle blew twice, and a cloud of steam raced along the tracks beneath the tender coal-car.

"Time to go, you two," Billie called from the Zephyr. Linc, leaning against the truck, gave a playful farewell bow.

As Mina climbed up into the train, Xavi DeAngelus stood aside and reached into the satchel he was carrying. He retrieved a small book and, jumping back down to the platform, handed it to Livingston. "A gift. *The Confessions*." he said, "Saint Augustine. With pictures."

Livingston was taken aback. "Thank you," he stuttered, "I..."

"Do you remember the nuns reading this to us at Christ the King?" Mina called over Xavi's shoulder.

"Sure, but I don't remember anything about pictures."

"It's a bit beat up," Xavi said, as the train lurched into slow motion. He climbed aboard again. "But it's had meaning for me...I added the pictures myself."

Livingston waved goodbye with the book in his hand as the two disappeared inside. Then, stepping back from the moving train, he began flipping through the pages. Small prints of religious paintings had been taped along the outer edge of several dog-eared pages. The pictures could be folded out to read the Bishop of Hippo's words some of which had been underlined. Inside the front cover, under the frontispiece, Xavi had written his own words: *All life comes out of Eternity into Time and again out of Time into Eternity. We see this in the Signature of all Things.*

And beneath that: *For my cousin - 'Livingstone.'*

The pages of 'The Confessions' fluttered in the air as the Flyer rolled past him. "Living Stone," Livingston whispered to himself. He was remembering Belle Stikkey's presentations on evolution at the Highlands Camp, and how excited she'd been when he told her he was the son of Winifred Goldring. As a young girl on a family trip north, Belle had actually met her – the first woman in the country, or the world for that matter, to hold the office of President of the U.S. Paleontological Society. Winifred had been a hero to Belle, a woman who had pushed back against all expectations to rise to the top of a man's field.

And, at that moment, Livingston had felt Belle's pride as well, despite

Winifred's choice of her work in science over motherhood, her choice to dedicate herself to the ancient life within the lithic Earth's womb rather than the new life within her own. There was even a new comfort, knowing that although his mother had placed him with her sister Mattie, it was she, and only she, who could have given him his name – *Living Stone*.

Billie Kinsolver watched her nephew from the Zephyr. She, too, was thinking of his family. But more so of his father, Piedmont...and of Mina. She had wondered about it at the dinner table the night before, but she was sure about it now. Eli Gallagher's rape of Mattie Goldring had been real, no one doubted that. But Mina had not been born of it. Billie felt certain. She would talk to Endurance before saying anything to Livingston about his more than half-sister.

In the days after the Stikkey deaths, after Linc's tongue had healed and the Goldring cousins parted from each other, the town of Princeton tried valiantly to find itself again. But like an ocean storm that passes then holds stubbornly, tauntingly, at a far horizon, the kidnapping loomed darkly in everyone's mind. It had come out that indeed the kidnapping had been the work of one of their own. Clipper Klutterer, hoping to avoid the Federal Lindbergh Law with its mandate of life imprisonment for kidnapping, wouldn't come clean with the G-men; instead, figuring on a lighter sentence he confessed to Florida State Sheriff Darryl Potts. It was the last bit of bad judgment 'Preacher Boy' would ever display. Florida's "Little Lindbergh Law" was even tougher – it called for the death penalty. Clipper sat out his last day on earth far from Princeton, strapped into Old Sparky at the Raiford Penitentiary in North Florida. Reverend Klutterer and his wife attended the execution, then took their remaining son and left Princeton for Neah Bay, a small quiet town out on the tip of the Olympic Peninsula in Washington State; no greater continental distance could be found to take them further from the tragedy at their backs.

Endurance Fuller knew that life could never be the same. He also knew that notoriety always finds a name and, after the deadly events during that summer of '41, the name "Princeton" would have a very bad ring to it. Pressure came down from the Ivy League University in New Jersey. Its President, Harold Dodds, put in a call to a member of his Board of Trustees. It proved unnecessary. Endurance, as the leading citizen of Princeton University's municipal namesake, had anticipated the President's call to him and, like a Reformation iconoclast, had already begun whitewashing Gaston Drake's dreamtown from top to bottom. Only the fire department was allowed to keep the colors, orange and black, as a reminder of hellfire's smoldering coals.

Nevertheless, like a horizontal gene transfer in one's DNA, Princeton – the town and the University – had leapt across time and place into the Kinsolver/Goldring family, entwining itself about the town of Gilboa. The harm that would follow Mina and Livingston after learning the truth of Billie's suspicions in Princeton had its roots in Gilboa. And the cruelty of being set free from one lie, only to discover the truth hidden in another would be passed on, in turn, to the next generation – to their son in his last year at Princeton University.

* **8** *

The Two Princetons...

Prodigal Sons
1993, New York City
*"He's a real Nowhere Man, sitting in his Nowhere Land, Making all his
nowhere plans..."*
(The Beatles)

ALTHOUGH I HAVE DECIDED – or perhaps my history has decided for me
– that my days here are numbered, I am back at my post at the St. Urban,
attentive as I must be to the outside world, but deep inside my thoughts
about my own. The traffic on Central Park West is steady, but I don't hear
it over the traffic in my head. I am feeling the noisy sadness that greeted
me this morning. More on that later.

I take a certain solace in learning that Del has left the St. Urban for
the Museum bone lab, unscathed. In fact, other than the shut-ins, most
of the residents of the St. Urban have left for their day – the high-powered working couples, parents with nannies and au pairs hovering over
their children at play in the park, secretive singles, secretive lovers,
widows and widowers. And like a changing tide, the swell of residents
has been replaced by those who work or care for them. Apartments are
being cleaned, groceries delivered and unpacked, food prepared, toddlers

watched, medicines given, sheets changed, mattresses flipped. As they pass through my door – the domestics – some give a knowing nod, others are indifferent, guarded, shielding themselves from any intrusion into the proprietary vastness of their own private lives.

When I first arrived for the morning shift, Buckles Hanrahan was hosing down the sidewalk, sleeves rolled up and wearing a pair of Wellingtons. It was supposed to be my job. I was late, he was annoyed. Someone had chalked a large black and yellow yin yang symbol in front the St. Urban door. Probably meant for me and the X-men. Tai chi can appear pretty spooky, even threatening, if you're not sure what you're looking at.

"Ars Celare Artem," I'd said, impassively, watching Hanrahan's brawny shamrock-tattooed arms wrangle the pooling swirls of yellow and black water over the curb into the street.

"Fuck you," Hanrahan had replied, assuming that I was smart-mouthing him. In part, he was right. He does not know Latin, and we have never liked one another. I ignore him.

My Latin comes from Trifina. *Ars Celare Artem'* – Art to conceal Art – is the motto that she and her fellow *trompe l'oeil* painters who work the "tie-ins" of the dioramas at the Museum ascribe to. The tie-ins are the painted coves where the curved wall meets the floor, where the illusion of deep space gives way to the more proximate illusion of middle ground and to the shellacked foreground of earth beneath the "upholstered specimens" behind the glass. Even the glass contributes to the diorama's effect, the viewing window tilted imperceptibly forward to ensure that the viewer does not see his or her own image reflected in the Mirror of Nature.

Private lives, indeed. There is an art to them, to live as if things are not what they are, knowing that the sight of one's *self* in the eyes of others is hidden.

Still, I've known there would be an accounting, an unmasking, sooner or later.

And it had also come from Trifina, earlier this morning,...now the traffic in my head.

"How long are you going to keep this up?" she had asked. Trifina was lying on her side staring at me, her head on the pillow, one hand by her chin and a bare shoulder free of the bed sheets.

"I don't know," I answered quietly, staring at the ceiling. A streak of early morning sunlight, yellow-white, moved across it, slowly bending at an upper corner of the room.

"I mean what good is it going to do you or any of us for that matter?"

"I don't know that either, Trif."

"He would have expected more from you. I can't believe that Endurance Fuller would have done what he did for you just so you could hide out this way."

"Perhaps not, but it doesn't matter, now."

Trifina tossed the bed covers to the side and got out of bed. She walked to the window and folded her arms. Her strong dark back and bare buttocks, the fossil bone from the gatehouse valve intake, the greenery of the park trees and distant waters of the Reservoir with its caustic reflections fell together in the frame of the large window like a surrealist painting. Capturing something both animistic and familiar, earth and world.

Watching Trifina, I stirred, thinking again of holding her close after we awoke that morning. The feral urgency in the clenching muscles of our buttocks – trying desperately to lock soft flesh together against the resistant check of bone, the hard pubis that keeps lovers from truly falling into one another as desire most desires.

But it had been different this morning. The urgency. It came with the clenching, desperately, to hold on to what was ending.

"Come back to bed, Trif," I called softly, as if to prove to myself what I sensed was true – that she would not come back. Not now...or ever again.

She shook her head slowly, looking down at the re-constructed fossil. She touched one of the plaster vertebrates, then looked over her shoulder at me. There was sadness in her eyes. She pointed at the bedside table where my doorman's cap lay upside down with one of Winifred's notebooks propped inside. "I can't do this any longer, Kinsolver," she said, "I won't; it will only end badly. All of it."

I knew what she was saying. It didn't matter whether she was referring to our current affair, or to our past. The return of Xaviero DeAngelus, the appearance of the Gilboa Fern Tree fossil at the Reservoir, and the beating of Francesca Van Pelt, had quickened things; a circle, as one is so often warned, was closing. Trifina, like Del, can only see its partial outline – the arc where she is concerned. The rest of the circumference is mine alone to complete. Then again, given the two Princetons, a closing ellipse with two centers might be more accurate.

Trifina and I did not speak further. We dressed separately and Trifina left. I had held the door for her, but she would not let me kiss her goodbye. I stood alone, feeling exposed and ridiculous in my uniform, and I knew that my days at the St. Urban must draw to a close.

Trifina was right. I have carried one of my grandmother's graphing notebooks for its magic, its magic to stream time unbroken, to guide me home. If my suspicions about Van Pelt are right, I will soon serve notice and go north to Slingerlands for the lost boy.

I re-entered the bedroom and retrieved the small black book from the bedside table. I opened it – as I have done countless times – to the charcoal drawing of the Gilboa Tree. Its tall oddly curving trunk is topped with what appear to be palm fronds, similar to the ones that Saskia Gilboa carries in her shop on Cathedral Parkway. *Roystonea regia.* Smudged over the years with charcoal fingerprints in the margins, the drawing was my grandmother's best guess at the living form of the original Devonian Period 'fern tree.' I say guess, because only fossilized stumps had ever been found at the Dam site – no associated branches, branchlets, leaves or seeds had been conclusively discovered. But the stumps looked familiar. The bottom of each was splayed like an elephant's foot and surrounded with roots of rope-like tendrils found in the common palm tree.

Although after her death, Winifred Goldring would be proven wrong about the Gilboa Tree's genus, her taxonomy had a certain Family truth to it. The arborescent canopy in her drawing had been modeled from Royal Palm fronds sent to her from a plantation in Princeton, Florida. They had been sent by my father, Livingston Kinsolver.

As I've said before, I never knew him, my father, or of his short life before and after the CCC. In truth, I almost didn't make it through the bottleneck his death made in our line of descent. Eight months after he left for good, I arrived, for better or worse. It was actually on my first birthday that my father made his departure permanent. It was 1944. The Allied powers had just agreed on what would become the German Instrument of Surrender. He was heading home and was killed in a jeep roll-over on his way to the airport. Death days and Birth days...we were able to share *that* at least. Linc would never say, but Saskia intimated that my father had died well before that day. Maybe even flipped the jeep himself, beating both Roosevelt and Hitler to the afterlife. Going home is not as easy for some.

Perhaps that is something else we share. Ever since my withdrawal from Princeton University after my awakening in the Slingerland's attic,

I have never returned to Princeton Florida. Not once. Learning who my true mother was, I knew I would never find her at home in Florida.

I hadn't been a bad student at the University, just not very motivated, distracted, drifting in and out of classes, earth sciences mostly – environmental biology, plants and animals. I even had a lackluster minor in paleontology. But I was just going through the motions. There always seemed to be trouble at home and, somehow, I always felt at the center of it. In Slingerlands, I learned that I was indeed caught in the middle of something. Like the Gilboa Tree, I had been mislabeled, given an identity of appearances.

I understood from my studies that the Descent of Man was littered with bastards, that "incest and bastardy" was the default outcome in sexual selection before the ascent of men and their conventions. I also understood kin selection: sacrificing oneself for a relative over a non-relative to ensure the reproductive success of the gene pool in its battle with Nature. But I was not prepared for both at once – the selection of sex *between* kin. Of course, on reflection, it seems obvious that love for one's relatives and love *with* them would have been of a piece back in Deep Time. How else could our species have gotten started when the numbers were so limited? Adam and Eve was a cover-up. But even if I had understood this fact of Early Life, it might not have made much difference. Learning that my father Livingston had slept with his sister Mina was just more bad news at another bad time. That I was their offspring, well, I needed some time to find a way to live with that.

My discovery helped me understand why I never could see myself in Belle's eyes. To her, I was Cash...the lost boy. Belle did her best raising me; dutiful is the best way to describe it, cut from the promise of a second husband, soon dead like the first. But over the years, even the sight of Cash had begun to dim when she looked at me. More of her time was spent in bed, and more of my time was spent fending for myself and making excuses for her. By the third grade, I was preparing my own breakfast and school lunches, walking to school and back home, alone. When my 'mother' could rouse herself, she would be affectionate, and I would be hopeful; but it was an increasingly distracted affection. She began spending more and more time over in Indiantown. Sometimes she'd bring me along, most often not. And, often, I could see the guilt in her eyes.

The year of my seventh grade, I was sent away to a small boarding school in Homestead. After that, north for college, rarely returning home; I'd learned the benefit of keeping distances.

Then, by the time I dropped out of the University, our uneven days were over.

Belle, in her way, had also dropped out, gone over to both the Lord and a liquor bottle in a vagrant Indian ministry. I'm not sure which of us fell further, but I fell fairly far. I'd always been independent, no choice, but even the few friends I had at the two Princetons were left wondering where I'd gone.

As a college student, I'd joined the Reserved Officer Training Corps. Not sure what I had in mind. I suppose it was an ill-conceived nod to my father, trying to connect somehow to a rarely mentioned white cross on a lost grave on the other side of the world. But after dropping out, I hid my ROTC eligibility and enlisted in the war as a foot soldier. It was 1965 and I *wanted* to go to Viet Nam; I wanted what it offered – a clean slate, wiped free of present and past things.

I never made it to Southeast Asia...not even close. Instead, because of my schooling in the earth sciences, the military sent me to the Proving Ground in Aberdeen, Maryland to work on chemical weapons – Herbicides. It was the tail-end of "Operation Ranch Hand," the rainbow sprays of chemical compounds shot from the nozzle guns of UC-123 Provider Transports to clear out the upland forest canopies and dry up the lowland rice paddies. The Aberdeen Proving Ground was where the lethal effects on the plants and people were tested, and where the 55-gallon drums were stockpiled, each marked with an innocent stripe of color and a name right out of a bad television show – Agent Blue, Agent White, Agent Orange. That was Operation Ranch Hand, a bunch of bumbling secret agents making a mess of things; the Vietnamese adapted but that stuff soured the stunned earth of Southeast Asia for years.

I did my job. I had learned the biology of plant life well enough to know the kinds of things that could kill it. Defoliating the ambushing cover of enemy forest or choking enemy food supplies made sense in wartime…if you believed in the wartime. Or, if you didn't believe in anything at all. And that was my state of affairs. Loss of belief.

After serving my time in the military, I continued living my life as a rumor. It helped that I had the financial means. I kept this hidden as well.

I lived many places, never for too long; got close to only a few people, also never for too long. If I have a child out there, one or more, I wouldn't know of them. I was not a likeable fellow.

I worked sporadically, tried different lines of work, on whims mostly – shrimping in the Gulf out of Seadrift, Texas with some Vietnamese refugees. Then, after there was trouble with the local Texas fishermen and the Ku Klux Klan, it was off to Lake Superior and the Park Service in the Apostle Islands, managing RV camp sites in the summer and tagging North Wisconsin black bears in the winter. From there, I went south and west again, worked as a prison guard in the California State Prison system at Norco. Three long grim years. When Linc Gilboa found me through the Trustees at the Bank of New York, I was living up in Cordova, Alaska, running a chair lift at the ski area on Mt. Eyak.

As I say, I had the financial means to live wherever and however I wished. The money for it had come unexpectedly. Endurance Fuller had set up a trust for me after my father's death in 1944. It was meant to get me through Princeton University, but there had been plenty to spare thanks to my share of his plantation in Princeton Florida.

There had been a few stipulations; not binding exactly, but part of a codicil to his Will. Endurance had never married, never had children of his own, nevertheless from his early years in Gilboa until his death in Florida, he had never forgotten the man who had been like a son to him – my grandfather, Piedmont Kinsolver. I was left with a charge:

> *...furthermore, said monies set aside here shall be divided per stirpes to any additional surviving issue – presently unknown – of Bramlett "Piedmont" Kinsolver, late of Gilboa New York, and/or to the person (or persons, per capita) who in the judgment of the Trustees at Bank of New York is (or are) deemed to have determined the true place and means of the death of Bramlett "Piedmont" Kinsolver. Furthermore, should the remains of Bramlett "Piedmont" Kinsolver be found, said monies shall also be used for a legal and proper burial in a location to be determined by his closest living issue.*

I have only a vague memory of Fuller – being cradled as a young child up into his broad chest, his white beard, the smell of camphor, tobacco, and citrus. When I went off to University, he was long dead, but the money he left behind had been intended to save my life, not his. He'd even pulled the strings from his grave to have me admitted to his alma mater at Princeton; Endurance Fuller was a man who had that kind of reach. Me? I was on my way to being just a disappointment. That is, until Linc caught up with me.

Lincoln Gilboa knew where to find me because he, too, had been a part of Fuller's Will. And he had been there in Princeton, Florida, with his young common-law wife, Saskia Stikkey, holding me in his arms, when Belle Stikkey – Saskia's former sister-in-law – learned of my father's death in Europe. Most folks had been happy that Livingston Kinsolver had so quickly proposed to Belle before leaving for the war; she'd always been fond of him and had found solace in their brief few weeks together after the loss of Cash and the death of Rembrandt. But his death was just more of the same for her. At least, there was the boy, they said, a boy born of their union...me. Linc knew otherwise. Livingston's promise to Belle of marriage and family had been true, but his ill-fated stop at Bathgate Avenue on his way to the war had given it the lie. Besides Belle and Saskia, Linc was the only one there who knew whose child it was he was holding.

Up north, on Bathgate Avenue, Mina Goldring also knew, and her child was the least she could offer Belle to restore something of her brother's promise.

*　　*

Hanrahan coils the hose and disappears with it into the service alley. The street in front of the St. Urban is still damp, drying and sparkling in the sun light. It is now the quiet time of day, the urban lull that falls in the late mornings after the sidewalks empty. The vague traces of the graffiti at my feet signals a reminder that it is the time of the X-men. Chavez, Prickett, Fong, Rosenberg, others. I greet them as they come by my door – elevator, mail, television, garbage, telephone – each of them linked to an object of need or desire, the simple things without which all hell so easily breaks loose. I wonder what Hanrahan will make of me uncoupling myself from the door of the St. Urban.

Turning my back to the building, I look into the park. The trees rising above the brownstone wall across the street are full and familiar. Over the seasons, I have come to like thinking we are studying one another, as if we are alive in similar ways, my point of view across Central Park West no more consequential than theirs. I know each one. They are a jostling screen of immigrants and natives, many still alive from Olmsted's time, some from my grandfather's, some from my father's, some from mine. The Kwanzan cherry tree that blooms each spring in memory of its ancestral mountainside home in Sekiyama. Nearby, *Prunus serotina*, the rough-barked indigenous black cherry, crotchety with wispy nests of tent caterpillars, looks down on the demure foreigner. Overshadowing both, *Ulmus*, a hybrid Chinese Elm, free of the Dutch disease that had emptied the park of its odic American cousin. Norway Maples, Great Britain's London Plane, Spanish and Turkey Oaks, Scotch and Austrian Pines, Himalayan Whitebark Birches, Cedars of Lebanon. They are all here. And the natives? They are as "foreign" as these trees – their place in time and space mere adaptations to temperate air, the drift of continents, and the uprootings of passing men.

Beneath the trees, an elderly man is leaning on the brownstone wall at the inside edge of the Park. I first caught sight of him when Bev Prickett was sorting the mail in the lobby. She pointed him out, suggesting that I was being spied upon. She was only teasing, but I am not so sure she was wrong. He has not left his position. His head of white hair rests on his hands, his arms folded along the top of the wall, watching. On the sidewalk, passers-by ignore him, and he, they. I am quite certain he is watching me.

As our eyes lock, he raises his hand in the air in greeting.

Before I can respond, we are separated by a large black SUV that pulls up between us in front of the St. Urban awning. It is one of those over-sized vehicles with mysterious dark-tinted glass that conveys men and women of power throughout the city. It idles for a moment at the curb like a hulking guardian beast.

I approach to open the car door, but as I reach for the handle the rear window is rolled down and Senator Van Pelt stops me.

"I'm not getting out, Kinsolver. I'm on my way to Albany. Find Mr. Hanrahan and ask him to come here, then ring the apartment and let my wife know I'm waiting for them."

Bending down to peer in the window, I look past the Senator and see that he is accompanied in the back seat by Winton Conrad, Del's boss and the director of the Museum's osteological lab. Conrad looks straight ahead, avoiding my glance, but he appears nervous. He picks at his hand, using his thumb and index finger like a pair of laboratory forceps. Beyond Conrad, out the opposite window, I can see that the man across the street has disappeared.

"*Now*, Kinsolver!...I'm late!" The Senator punctuates his dismissal by abruptly rolling up the car window in my face. I am left staring at a tinted reflection. For a moment, I do not move. The hat, the uniform, the vacancy in my aspect...the anger, the shame. My mirrored face vibrates as the Senator raps his knuckles loudly on the glass from inside the car.

I enter the building to ring the Senator's penthouse apartment. As I wait, watching the door, I catch sight of Buckles Hanrahan emerging from the service alley. He is carrying a wooden crate about the size of a small coffin in his brawny arms. He leans back against its weight and walks toward the car slightly crouched, cradling it to his chest, as if it contained a sleeping child. A bad thought crosses my mind. The Senator remains in the car as the trunk door pops open. Conrad jumps out and joins Hanrahan. They confer briefly. Conrad gestures toward the crate, as if he does not believe it will fit. But it does. Under Conrad's careful watch, Hanrahan gently loads it into the rear of the vehicle.

Turning back to the lobby console, I ring the penthouse again. There is no answer. No sign of life. Something feels wrong, but as I go back outside to let the Senator know that his wife and child are not at home, his car is gone. Looking south down Central Park West, I watch it turn east into the Park at 81st street.

"They ain't here. I told him so." Hanrahan is leaning against the brickwork wall just outside the service alley with his arms folded across his chest.

"Where are they?" I ask, "Where's the boy? Where's Dante?"

Hanrahan shakes his head, "Not talking, Kinsolver. Something fucked up is going on; I'm just keeping my head down, doing what I'm told. You'd be doin' yourself a favor to keep your nose out of it, as well." He turns away, heading for the service alley.

"What was in the crate, Hanrahan?" I call after him. He does not answer.

"You're Van Pelt's men, aren't you Hanrahan. You and Winton Conrad," I call more loudly. Without looking back, he raises a tattooed arm and responds with his middle finger.

"The Reservoir! The fossils!" I shout.

This stops him. He lets out a dark laugh, still giving me his back. "You dumb fuck. Look to your own; look to DeAngelus, he knows where the boy is, he's the crazy one. And Conrad's doing him a favor if you ask me. The Senator, too." The squeal of the heavy wrought iron gate follows his last comment into the alley darkness. "There's your fuckin' *arse kala-rum artum.*"

I return to the door, worried by what he means about Del and Dante, and by what else he seems to know. He and Conrad have surely been doing some of Van Pelt's dirty work; there is little doubt. Promises had to have been made, monies exchanged, opportunities offered... something.

For a moment, I consider my options, the timing. I have to find them.

I walk quickly to the curb, waiting for a hole in the traffic. As a break comes, a yellow cab pulls up in front of me, the driver assuming that I am hailing a taxi for the St. Urban. I wave him on, dodging his rear bumper as I run across Central Park West. I cannot hear exactly what Hanrahan is yelling, but his tone is clear. I do not acknowledge him. There will be no going back.

Turning into the park at 86th street, I am surprised to see that the man who was at the brownstone wall has reappeared. He is a bit behind me on the Bridal Path, but walks at a quicker pace than mine, closing our distance.

Despite feeling the need to find Del, to find the boy, Dante, I sense something about the man. Continuing south past the Pinetum, I veer off the path and climb the stone steps up the south slope of Summit Rock. At the bald crevassed gray crown, I wait.

Reaching the base of the hill, the man stops and looks up at me, then begins climbing the stone steps. He climbs slowly, with effort. But he is smiling and looks down at his footfalls as if admiring the steps that have been carved directly into the Manhattan Schist bedrock. Stone shapers, I think to myself, a family of stone shapers.

Drawing up to the summit, the man pauses and studies me for a moment. He is winded, his pale gray eyes glinting with moisture. I brace myself. He opens his arms to me as if I am a child being called forward, then reaches out and takes one of my hands in both of his. "Piedmont Livingston Kinsolver...*figlio di* Princeton, Florida," he says.

It is him.

Xaviero DeAngelus is tall, thin, slightly stooped. He is pale with a vaguely blue-gray tint to his smooth face set beneath a shock of thick white hair. He is dressed in a black tab-collar shirt with round cloth buttons. It hangs untucked over a pair of green khaki trousers that landscapers or park employees typically wear. The shirt is wrinkled, well-worn, but two missing buttons reveal a clean white undershirt; sprigs of matching white hair fan up out of the undershirt collar to his thick sun-beaten neck. A small olive-drab canvas military bag hangs off his shoulder. His hands are rough, but gentle around mine. I wonder if he has been working his father's trade at Mount Savior, whether he might have learned it during his missing war years in Italy, perhaps in Verona where Johnny of the Angel, in another life, would have been buried in a properly marked grave.

Releasing his gentle grip, he cups his hands as if offering me a gift of a small wounded bird. There is dry paint within the creases of his palms.

"It is time that we meet. I have known of you for some time," he says. Xavi peers deeply into my eyes, as if searching for me among his memories. He does not introduce himself. It is as if he knows that I know who he is, that our history is evident to one another, and that a family tie does not need re-tying.

"Xaviero DeAngelus," I say, matter of factly, then ask, "Why are you here? Why have you come after all this time?"

He tilts his head with a gentle but knowing smile. "Come, sit with me," he says, motioning to the low stone bench that curves around the summit. He sits and looks out into the park, taking a deep breath as if catching his wind. "I am here for my family," he says, solemnly.

"Delano...your son," I say, carefully. I suspect that Xavi knows that his son is also my half-brother, that we are bound by the same woman who often came to Summit Rock with my father.

"Yes...Mina's son," Xavi says, softly."

"Have you come then from Slingerlands?"

He nods.

"Then you're here also for your father?"

"That too. My poor old mother Jenna believes they have found him...*Gianni DeAngelus,* Johnny of the Angel." He pauses, "...and your grandfather as well."

"Yes,...I've heard this."

Xavier waits to see if I will be more forthcoming. I will not be.

"I have been gone a long time," he says, "Jenna raised the boy well. And she has forgiven me...*Il figliol prodigo,* the prodigal son who wandered off to God." He lowers his head. "Mina?...it is far too late for her forgiveness.

"If I'd never left for the war, we would not be here, you and I." He turns and waves his hand as if to swat away the existential aspect of his remark, knowing that I would not be anywhere...unborn.

"What I mean is," he says, "War takes apart lives in so many ways. If I'd not joined the Resistance, if I'd not been trapped and captured..." He looks again into the park, serious and thoughtful. "And if I'd not stayed on after it was all over to help my father's family."

He stares in silence at his past for a moment, then says, "Of course, it is *he* who should never have left. My father. Gianni DeAngelus, the finest *scalpellino* in Verona. I was born in the home of my mother, and I have lived in the home of my father...the family of Angel's. Pffff..." he snorts, "Who knows where I will end up."

Shrugging to himself, Xaviero lifts the strap of his canvas bag off his shoulder and places the bag on the bench between us. I catch a glimpse of the black lettering imprinted on the canvas, perhaps the name of the soldier who had once carried the bag into battle; parts of the letters are worn away, others faded and difficult to make out in the folds of the canvas.

"And you?" he says, turning to me, "You, too, have been gone and come back. I have been hearing of you. You, in your uniform. Like a soldier, *carbinieri*. But, no, you are a man at a door," He shakes his head. "I did not understand at first." He raises a finger, waggling it at me, "Ahhh, but she did, my mother, your great-aunt Jenna. You are the gatekeeper... *Charon*. And now is *your* time."

My prodigal uncle reminds me that past troubles must wait for present ones.

"Xaviero, do you know where Delano is? Have you seen him...your son?"

Xaviero shakes his head again. "Not yet. But he knows I am here."

He points toward the Metropolitan Museum of Art on the far side of the park, then turning, he points to the Museum of Natural History behind us. "Do you see these great buildings?" he asks, "And that one, as well," he adds, gesturing toward the crenellated spire of the Church of the Immaculate Conception looming above the tree line to the north. He chuckles to himself, "Yes, even *that* one.

"The grand institutions, places of Art and Science....and Religion, all of them, built on the blocks of carved stone. Like this here." He runs his palm along the stone bench. "And those." He points to the gray weather-worn steps ascending the hill toward us on Summit Rock. "The philosophers speak of material and form – *materia e fiorma* – that a man can shape matter into the form he chooses, but that is only style. And, like a wisp of smoke...style is but a brief moment in time." He pauses, then again raises his finger to me. "The great stones of the earth are carved by those who know better, little men, who learn by the feel of it in their hands, against their muscles and their tools, that all things, all of time – the questions and answers – are locked inside of stone."

I wonder if Xaviero is teasing me, knowing that Del and Dante are often easily found in any one of the three places he has mentioned.

"And you," he continues, "...you have his name. 'Living stone'...the name your grandmother gave to your father."

I am unsettled by this invocation and turn away, thinking now of Winifred. The great arc of the stone bench curves down the slope of Summit Rock on either side of us as if we are its center point. It reaches out to embrace the park below with its open arms, gathering in the Great Lawn and its surround of sylvan cultivars like a set piece, a tableau of fixed landscape. I wonder, as I often do, if I am so much like her.

I can not help but see – in this tableau of "designed" Nature – that things are in constant change with the wild wheeling of the sky; that the city behind me, the St. Urban, and the hard surfaces of Xaviero's "grand institutions," clad in their stylized slabs and blocks of different stone, are just as mutable, only temporarily masking earlier and wilder natures over which Summit Rock once commanded a sweeping view of a vast unnamed ocean pounding at the basalt palisades of a roiled continent.

I imagine this is Winifred's gift to me – to sense only the brute earth from which our worlds are made. The Metropolitan Museum's felsic granite facade forged in the melting heat of Archaen igneous rock; the Natural History Museum's Jurassic sandstone shaped by the titanic crush of sedimentary mineral and rock. And even the ancient death polished upon the older Devonian limestone of the Church of the Immaculate Conception, sparkling with the compressed skeletal fragments of ancient marine organisms. This is Nature without a plan, and it is like one's imagination – anything can happen there.

Drawing himself up, Xavi stretches his legs out before him, and crosses them at his ankles. He now seems restless as well and pulls at his sleeves as if suddenly chilled, clasping his hands together in his lap.

I watch his index fingers rocking idly back and forth, as if tapping out his next thought. On the sleeve of his shirt, the cloth on a small round button at the cuff is frayed. There are actually two buttons, the other also badly frayed, revealing their shiny black plastic nubbin beneath. The exposed nubbins look like licorice jelly-beans...or Del's dermastid beetles. I see now that Xaviero is wearing an old Clerical, its collar trimmed off.

"Have you left Mount Savior," I ask cautiously, "For good?"

"Ah, Poverty Hill. Yes, it is done...I am no longer there," he shakes his head with a resigned smile and sighs, "Xaviero DeAngelus, a Sulpician turned Benedictine with a Jesuit name and an Augustinian leaning,...now the apostate.

"You know, I was one of the first to settle at Mount Savior," Xaviero continues, "We were only a few. We built a home, a cloister, a hall for our food, rooms to sleep, a sanctuary for communion and prayer. At first, we farmed; we lived simply from the farming. Other Benedictines and Augustinians, they came to join us, to help with the land and with our devotions. Soon the outsiders came, visitors. They were curious and initially passed on. But then, some wished to stay among us. Only for short times. They felt the peacefulness, the air was clear, quiet, and to them we were like beneficent apparitions, Fantasmi Santi...Holy Ghosts...mirrors of their self-reflections. We built a place for them to stay apart from our cloister, below Poverty Hill where they could still see and hear the sound of the bell tower." He chuckles to himself and looks down at his calloused and paint-stained hands. "And me, Xaviero DeAngelus, I was able to follow my gifts more and more – the gifts I'd been given – to make paintings and carve stone, and to sing...gifts from our Father to my father, and then to me. I have had a good life...for a bad man. And now my time has finally come, as they say."

"What do you mean by that?" I ask, feeling the need to draw him out further, to understand him better.

Xaviero smiles wistfully, but with a hint of mischief. He looks into the park.

"When Time allows itself to be possessed – to become *my* Time – *well* then, there is a finitude to it," he says. "Time is easily grasped when beckoned by the Angel of Death."

He pauses, staring into the distance. "I once believed it was *His* work...*Signatura Rerum* – the Doctrine of Signatures – but, I no longer have this belief." He looks up at me again and asks, "Do you know of this...the 'signature of all things'?"

"Well, I...yes, something of it," I answer. I know it only too well – the medieval thing. The 'signature of all things' is in one of my grandmother's notebooks. The Monk and the Scientist conjoined in a belief in the same but different things – the *what* versus the *how* one sees the Creation in front of them.

"There is a man at Poverty Hill who cultivates worts," Xaviero says, "Just as was done by the scholastics and mystics of the 12th and 13th centuries. For medicinal purposes. Feverwort, Sleepwort, Bladderwort and so on; plants whose names were given for the relief they offered the body. Some even resembled the part of the human anatomy which it could cure – eyebright, skullcap, bloodwort...It was believed to be God's signature in Nature."

Xavi places his hand on his chest.

"I once told this monk at Poverty Hill that Heartwort would do me no good. God's signature for me is Bleeding Heart – *Lamprocapnos spectabilis* – a lovely flower but one that cannot cure me," he says. "Indeed, I should not have lived as long as I have, however it is only now that my backwards heart has chosen to die."

Xavi pats his chest again and chuckles to himself. "At the monastery, they would joke that my heart sits at the right hand of God, not at the left, at the sinister side, *sulla sinistra,* as with most men of Original Sin. It was a fine joke, but it hid its truth. I was not exalted; this heart was bad from birth. Even now, if I wished for a new one, a transplant; it would not be possible,...nor do I deserve one."

I understand now. Xaviero's hand is on the wrong side of his chest, where his beating heart should *not* be. *Dextrocardia, Situs inversus* – the gift he bequeathed to his son Delano, born with his heart on the wrong side of his body with vascular arteries and veins that would make a donor with a normal heart of no use, the wrong fit.

For a moment we share a silence.

"Why did you turn away from Delano...your son?" I ask, quietly.

I know the answer but need to hear it...from him. Most people count the days since Mina's drowning in the Schoharie as the days of Xaviero's vows at Mount Savior but, in the letter that I found in the Slingerlands attic, she had written that he'd left for Poverty Hill well before when he learned the truth of her first son's birth...of my birth.

For a brief moment, Xaviero's aspect flattens and seems to turn inward, distant...then it softens to a resigned smile. "Ah, yes..." he says, "the old question, with old answers written so many different ways and times in my memory that I can no longer make sense of them. Perhaps Saint Augustine was right that mankind was born to be a vast problem to itself...*And men go abroad to admire the heights of mountains, the mighty waves of the sea, the broad tides of rivers, the compass of the ocean, and the circuits of the stars, yet pass over the mystery of themselves without a thought.*"

Xaviero turns and reaches for his canvas bag. "I have something for you." He holds out the satchel to me. "This was your father's messenger bag during the war. It is difficult to read his name, but it is there." Xaviero points out the black markings in the canvas. I am able to re-form the missing and incomplete letters into the name – *Kinsolver.*

Opening the satchel, he pulls out a worn paper-back book, its cover laced with distressed creases. A purple ribbon tied around the book holds frayed and water-stained pages from falling out. Handing it to me, he says, "I gave it to your father many years ago, when I left Princeton, Florida. He returned it to me when we met again in Italy shortly before his death. Now, I am returning it to you."

"*The Confessions of Saint Augustine?*"

"Yes, but it's a special printing." Xaviero smiles at me. "You don't have to be a Believer. Your father wasn't, but he kept it nonetheless...and added to it. I didn't know exactly why he wanted me to have it back. He was troubled by something that had happened back home but would not say what it was. Only that he hoped to be forgiven...he did not speak of you. And forgiveness, pfffft....it is elusive; from whence it should come and upon whom it is best conferred is simply a choice one makes at a point in time. Despite my calling, I have never believed in Augustine's Original Sin, and blame, like memory itself, is time-bound...we are all at fault."

Sitting back, Xaviero slaps his thighs and rises from the bench. "But enough,...perhaps one day you will take my confession, as I once took your father's, but now we must go find Lincoln Gilboa."

For a moment I remain on the bench, flipping through the worn pages of *The Confessions*. A number of pages have illustrations taped to them, sketched images of well-known religious paintings. I wonder about my father's "confession?" What he said, and what he didn't say. Confessional?...or simply a resigned description of events beyond his control, acts of those who brought him, along their way, into the world, just as I must also include his acts in my confession. Not our sins, just simple guileless acts. Happenstances leading to misfortune.

I know that we are all marked by the events in the chain of descent as surely as we are by the 'blood' in our bodies. But when I think of my father, barely in his twenties, and his generation of survivors, Linc and Xaviero DeAngelus, I wonder which is worse – to die young, or to live as a witness to young death.

I think again of Del and the boy. Overhead, a flock of gulls wing noisily northward over the trees. One by one, their wings steady and take them into a descending glide. They disappear from view, but I see them in a turn of mind, settling together, wings tucked quietly to their sides, in the Reservoir, waiting.

Leaving Summit Rock, Xaviero DeAngelus and I walk north across the park to *Blackwater Ferns & Flowers*, Saskia Gilboa's small flower shop on Cathedral Parkway.

When we arrive, the shop is closed but I can see Saskia and Linc inside. They're cutting flowers and arranging them with fern bouquets for the weekend service at The First Corinthian Baptist Church.

Linc looks up and walks over to unlock the door for us. He is wary and fixes on Xaviero.

Shortly after re-appearing from the missing years in Italy, Xavi had disappeared again inside the monastery at Poverty Hill, never communi-cating, avoiding family...avoiding his son. I know that Linc would want to protect Del...regardless of whatever he'd done with Dante.

Nevertheless, Saskia welcomes Xavi with a warm embrace, and it is not long before Linc is disarmed by the lapsed Brother of Mount Savior. The two men begin falling right into one another as only men do when they're relieved of a shared memory's burden – the loss of a person who had been dear to them. For Linc, back in Princeton, Florida, it had been my father, Livingston; for Xaviero, it had been my mother, Mina.

We gather around Saskia's cutting table in folding chairs that Linc dutifully arranges for us. Saskia sorts away the last of the bouquets inside the large floral refrigerator behind the counter of the shop and comes over to sit next to me. We sit opposite Linc and Xavi, as I listen to them talk about my parents as if I was not there, hearing them share – or correct for one another – their recollections of the events that took place a half century ago...the year; the dinner at Endurance Fuller's plantation; who was there and what had been discussed. There was agreement on one important point – Livingston and Mina had been the center of attention.

Saskia had also been at the Princeton plantation that evening in 1941, and it is with affection and without judgment, that she whispers softly in my ear how much I have always looked like *both* of them.

Talk of their memories reminded me of something written in one of my grandmother's notebooks. She was describing the *'Laws of Original Horizontality and Superposition'*, laws that anyone interested in geology, paleo-biological succession, or simply life-on-earth, lives by:

> *Whether once carried by water, breeze or beast,*
> *material sediments settle in horizontal laminae,*
> *one upon the other, in a natural order through*
> *Time, compressed into beds of rock by the weight*
> *of ages, new upon old. But do not be fooled – the*
> *strata are endlessly on the move. They are like*
> *the layers of our memories, thrust out of order by*
> *the wondrous events of the earth's unpredictable*
> *heart. And we all must build our home from*
> *memory's unstable architecture, knowing that*
> *more than likely, we will never leave the house.*

My grandmother lived the truth of it. She never left her home. Between the opaque symmetry that framed her life – the dark unknowable space that precedes one's birth and then follows upon one's death – Winifred, except for her brief time in Gilboa, lived and died in Slingerlands, in the house where she was born. And when she died there

in 1965, she left with her thoughts and memories equally unknowable...
to anyone but her.

I accept this – the absolute privacy of her mind – but it has been
difficult. The contents of her notebooks can be 'interpreted' but never
'known.' Indeed, considering the billions of interior lives unknowable
to anyone other than the one who lives it, 'not knowing' is one of the
more exhausting traits of our species. The catholic cleric and poet John
Donne was mistaken...every man *is* an island; Donne was simply fooled
by the archipelago.

"Boys were older back then," Saskia says, "Head strong teenagers. Girls,
too. But those poor boys. Times weren't like today, they had to become
men much sooner than their parents wanted. Providing for their families
during the Depression, then the war and all the dying."

"And some of those boys became parents sooner then they wanted...
that, too," Linc leans back in his chair, folding his arms. "I 'member Mr.
Fuller in those days, lecturing us boys. He'd say, when it's just you, and
you're free to move about on the breeze, the thought of death don't seem
so bad...then you think of someone in your care, someone dear to you,
and suddenly death looms up and scares the hell right out of you." He
shakes his head and clicks his tongue, drumming his fingers on his bicep,
"We certainly learned that lesson.

"Course, it's all gone now. The plantation, the house. Hurricane
Andrew took it all, just last year. Even Mr. Fuller's grave got washed into the
waterway, his bones are probably still tangled somewhere in the Mangrove
Preserve if not already gone to sea in the gullet of some manatee."

"Lincoln...please," Saskia frowns at Linc.

"I mean...well, hell, Sass, he was part Miccosukie anyway...at least in
spirit. Earth to earth," Linc lowers his head, looking down at his folded

arms and clicking at his tongue like he always does when she calls him out. Saskia had likely reminded him of her brother, Rembrandt. "Still, it's a shame," he says, "We grew up there. I'm just glad that my mother didn't witness it."

"What ever became of Billie Kinsolver?" Xavi asks.

"Miss Billie left Princeton, moved to Cuba with Modesto Martinez, her musician beau from Miami. It was shortly after your father died," Saskia adds, turning to me. She pauses for a moment, then looking back at Xavi, says, "She never married him, never would marry anyone, not even Linc's father; it was just who she was. Winifred and Jenna had an uncle there, in Cuba, he was running a large research plantation for one of the American universities up north. Harvard, I think. It was just outside of Cienfuegos. It's still there, *El Jardín Botánico de Soledad*. They had just glorious tropical fruit trees, sugar cane...and orchids, the most beautiful orchids you can imagine. Billie would send me plants from time to time. She worked there until Fidel Castro took it over. After that, they moved to a town near Havana. Cojimar, where that famous writer lived...what was his name, Linc?"

Linc looks thoughtful for a moment, then opens his mouth to answer, but Saskia has already moved on. "Oh, it's not important. We visited once, but with Linc playing ball so much and then the Cuban revolution, it was hard getting there."

Saskia pushes herself up stiffly from the table and walks behind the shop counter. Bending down to retrieve something from a shelf beneath, she sighs and says, "Billie had been there once before. She'd gone there... with Winifred early in 1923." Straightening her back with one hand, she holds up a packet of photographs with the other, and looks at me, "That was for the *birth* of your father."

Walking out from from behind the counter, she draws out a small black and white Kodak print and hands it to me.

I have seen it before; I have seen them all, all the pictures that Billie Kinsolver left for Linc and Saskia after she died. I look down at the two women in the photo, standing slightly apart within a lush tropical landscape at the foot of a thickly forested mountain side. The women are separated by a large black igneous rock. The new-born child is held in Winifred's arms, but she is looking away, down at a large lizard perched on the rock outcropping. A tooth-spined Ground Iguana is meeting her gaze. Billie is watching the child. Winifred has named him 'Living Stone.' I imagine she is also thinking of her own child growing inside her, of her lover Lincoln Lincoln and the full life that awaited their family. Thoughts far from the swerve, the unexpected, the grim smirk that the future bestows on the present. Lincoln Lincoln would be buried the following year with Livingstons' father Piedmont...'at-the-foot-of-the-mountain.'

Xaviero turns to Linc, "Mina never mentioned Cuba? Did she know?"

Linc shakes his head. "I don't believe Livingston even knew. If he did, it didn't matter to him, not with everything else that came 'round."

Saskia sits again at the table. She places the stack of photographs in her lap, face down. "Billie brought him back to the States and gave him to Mattie Goldring. It had been arranged. He would grow up in the city with her, no one was to know. And little Mina, may she rest in peace..." Saskia makes the sign of the cross over her heart. "...she was too young to fully understand the arrival of her new brother."

"Did Billie ever return again to Gilboa?" Xavi asks.

Saskia nods and flips again through the stack of pictures in her lap. "Yes, she did. Once." She pulls out another picture and hands it to Xavi. "1944. She and Mr. Fuller brought Livingston's ashes to Gilboa. They were given to Mattie who'd come north as well. Mattie gave them to

Winifred." Saskia sighs and sweeps her hand across the table, clearing away invisible cuttings. "Mr. Fuller took that picture. They were all there, all three of the sisters, putting flowers on the water." Her eyes tear up, and she looks at me, almost fearfully. "You were there, too. Do you know this?"

Xavi hands me the photograph. I don't look at it, but rather reach out with my other hand and place it on Saskia's. "I've seen the photograph, Sass...the women standing on the Gilboa Dam. I knew it was me a long time ago."

Saskia looks sadly down at our two hands. "So long ago, you were Belle and Livingston's little boy then...Belle put you in our care to meet your...to meet...everyone."

Linc clears his throat and nods his head, thoughtfully "You was always in their care, back then," he says, "My mother Billie's,...then Saskia's."

"I know Linc," I say, softly, squeezing Saskia's hand.

How could I forget. Endurance had supported Belle and my life in both Princeton and Indiantown, but it was Saskia who always made sure I was safe when Belle began to drift away. Saskia held the secret and the responsibility of Mina's gift to Belle. Just as Billie had held the secret of Winifred's gift to Mattie – our fates, my father's and mine. It seems so long ago and such a disjointed part of the past – a false past, given the truth of it, like ill-fitting Russian dolls poorly nested inside a family of others.

I imagine how different my life would have been if Livingston had stayed. He had been a brief but real comfort to Belle after the loss of young Cash; I want to believe they could have been happy. Belle would not have started drinking as she did, and the three of us would have grown up as a proper family. Then again, I would still be Mina's son.

There is more to Saskia's story. She need not tell it. Not now, not here.

We all know it. Gilboa and Princeton are places that we think with...our shared *Umwelt*.

Mina had been there at the Dam as well. In Gilboa. Perhaps holding me in her arms, cooing at "Belle's baby," as she imagined a second chance with Xaviero, should he ever return. Forgiveness had been his Calling. Perhaps she was imagining that Xaviero – somewhere in Italy, hiding somewhere behind enemy lines as Endurance Fuller had feared three years earlier – might find a way to accept that the child in her arms was hers but not his. Or perhaps, she was just staring into the water of the Reservoir, imagining the submerged town, sensing that a time might come when she would join the men there, including her own undeclared father. The holy cross on the steeple of Reverend Daniel Mackey's church would have decayed by then, its gold leaf flaked off and settled on the reservoir bottom, leaving behind punk wood riddled with microbes and the feeding of minnows.

That day in '44 at the edge of the Dam had been the coming together of many secrets. Mothers, lovers, husbands, sons, daughters, and grand-children, some absent, more present, all woven together in a biological arabesque. Family Time.

Linc turns to Xaviero. His voice is somber, slow and precise. "They were also looking for the boy. There was a rumor that he'd taken your father's gun. 'Course, it never belonged to Johnny of the Angel. The ini-tials on the handle came from the boy's family...the Gallaghers. That gun had been killing men for generations."

Xavi sits back in his chair and folds his arms. "When I left for Poverty Hill, Jenna wrote to me and said she didn't believe the gun went into the water. Now she says she knows where it is. It has to do with her sister's exhibition in Albany, something about the prehistoric fish in the Gilboa Forest Diorama. An old woman's dream?..." He shrugs his shoulders. "Maybe, but she says it has always been right under her nose."

221

I rise from the table, trying to disguise my surprise. My mind races to Slingerlands, to the attic of the Goldring house and back again to Buckles Hanrahan and Winton Conrad at the St. Urban – my worst fear or best hope is in the crate they placed in Senator Van Pelt's car.

I walk over to the storefront window, wagging the photograph of the Goldring women at my hip as if the picture is too hot. Outside, the traffic along Cathedral Parkway is heavy, and I imagine the smell of exhaust, the fossil fuel, but it is the air of Saskia's shop that overwhelms me, moist with its smell of plants pulled alive from the ground and bundled with others like familiar strangers, cut stems mixing with flower blossoms and aromatic leaves. I try to pick apart the scents, to home in on a particular flower or leaf smell – narcissi, lilacs, old roses,...or lilies, buddleia, geraniums, quinces mixing with junipers...rosemary, eucalyptus leaves?... lavenders, or myrtle? It is pointless. Saskia can do this, but it is a wild floral jungle to me...a Devonian jungle. I imagine swarms of giant dragonflies, hopped up on runaway oxygen levels, cruising the pre-historic canopy with wing spans the size of frigate birds. The dead Lungfish, rotting with its secret in the shallows below.

Winifred Goldring's diorama at the State Museum in Albany in 1927 had a symmetry to it – marking men's' deaths and Man's birth. And it marked a rhythm counted off on the earth's clock. Where the Shandaken Intake Chamber now stands on the shoreline of the Schoharie Reservoir, a Devonian Forest had once stood overlooking the Great Albany Sea. Winifred's simulation of the Forest at the State Museum had been a *trompe l'oeil* sensation – a painted perspectival jungle, thick with moss and swamp mist rising into the orange heat of a fiery Devonian sky, as wildly imagined as the foreground of sculpted trees with canopies of acrylic-sealed Florida palm ferns and small hide-tanned amphibians from Cuba snuffling among epiphytic roots.

The diorama had celebrated the discovery of the Gilboa Forest Fossils, but it was the Lungfish mounted inside at the edge of the diorama that told the full story. Humanity's *Umwelt* – four-hundred million years ago, where and when gills became lungs, fins became feet, and man's fate, having emerged from the Albany Sea into the air of the Gilboa Trees, would become forevermore one of looking back at from whence he came...before it was too late.

"They're dedicating the re-constructed diorama at the State Museum in Albany next week. Winifred's Gilboa Forest," I say, turning back to the others, "They're saying it will be just like the original...but it won't be."

"What do you mean?" Linc asks.

"Del told me that the team working on the details at the Museum has been making private presentations to Senator Van Pelt."

"Conrad's team?" Linc asks.

"Yes, Del's boss, Winton Conrad. He's been keeping it quiet, but it has to do with the Report that Waterhouse showed us in the Gatehouse the other day."

"The bones in the Reservoir." Linc clicks his tongue again and stares down at the table.

As I turn back to the window, Saskia emits a soft groan. It is a recognizable sound, beyond language but clear to everyone there. If that report is correct about the Shandaken Intake Chamber at the Schoharie – about the bodies, the bones – then the Gilboa Forest diorama is going to be a headstone once again.

Saskia stands and walks to my side at the window. She places her arm around my waist but does not speak. Rain has begun to fall. Cathedral Parkway has darkened but shimmers in the water's light. Streaks of wind-blown rain run down the storefront window. Along the windowsill at knee-level, Saskia has created a moss garden with various flower and stone groupings set within an undulating surface of close-cropped green hues of baby-tooth, fern, and spoon mosses.

My thoughts turn to Van Pelt's missing son. Dante is a part of this. I feel it.

"We need to find Delano," I say quietly, "Dante is missing. I'm afraid either that something bad or something foolish has happened."

Saskia squeezes my waist gently. "Delano is with our daughter. She and Dante both. They're in Slingerlands by now. I think they're waiting for you."

My shoulders slump, I sigh, knowingly. Of course, my fight with Trifina that morning. She knew I'd have to quit the St. Urban and go after the lost boy. One, or the other,...or both.

As the streaks of rainwater on the storefront window stream past Saskia's window garden, I gently pull a fallen sprout of moss from between a crevice in a small stone.

...Lost boys; I hope to find them all.

* 9 *

Creation…

The Age of Fishes
1922, Gilboa, NY
"Nature opens her eyes in humankind and notices that she is there."
(F. W. J. Schelling)

JENNA GOLDRING MARRIED GIANNI De Angelus on the first day of the new year, 1922. It had been unseasonably warm in the Catskills with no snow on the ground. The excavation for the Dam had continued up to the December holidays, mostly to the west in the thawed mud at the Shandaken Tunnel Intake. But, to the south, the stone cutters had been mostly idle due to the fossil discovery in the quarry stratum they'd been working. This had worked out well for Jenna and Johnny of the Angel; their son Gianni Xaviero DeAngelus was born premature seven and a half months later. They called him Xavi.

That same month, late in July, at the edge of a stand of pig-nut hickory and rock oaks on a high open promontory overlooking the Schoharie valley, Winifred Goldring lay on her back, her eyes closed to the summer sky.

Piedmont Kinsolver was staring at her, staring at the damp strands of dark hair, falling untended across her face onto the homespun blanket;

the flush of skin, mottled pink above her naked breast; her breathing, counted off in the rise and fall of her pale belly, and the light green moss, freshly gathered from the ground nearby, that she had placed between her legs to absorb their lovemaking.

Propped up on his elbow next to her, Piedmont was naked as well. He reached across her hips with his free hand to touch the moss, gently cupping the dense cluster of tiny emerald fronds mingling with the soft curls of black hair. Winifred, her bare feet crossed at the ankles, wiggled her toes in response, signaling to the valley below her body-memory of the man she had fallen in love with. Across the valley, the dusky outline of the mountains etched the lower surround of the sky's blue dome. Silent witnesses to all of nature's passions.

"The Mohawk women used mosses for many things, not just...this." She looked down at his hand on the moss between her legs. "During their 'moon time' as well. Fresh moss would take up their blood as easily as their men's sperm," she laughed, wiggling her toes again. "And they'd use it to scrub a baby's bottom at the edge of a stream, along with their bowls."

Winifred reached down and pinched a tuft of the moss in her fingers. "*Dicranum Scoparium*." She turned her head toward Piedmont. "Look at these...all of these tender shoots are female; did you know that? Whenever they need a male to reproduce...they simply *make* one. From their own spores."

Piedmont rolled over onto his back and clasped his hands under his head. "Immaculate Conception?" he teased, looking up at the sky.

"Not quite, Piedmont. Better, heaven on *earth*...Nature needs no outside help. And the female of many species does just fine without males around."

"Well, then tell me how this works, Win', you're making me feel a bit defensive," he laughed.

226

"Whether or not the male of the species even *exists* lies entirely within the power of the females of *Dicranum*. During their reproductive cycles, certain spores, like seeds, fall among the female leaves, but they have no gender and remain that way, sexless, until the time to propagate arrives. It can be triggered in lots of ways; the female will suddenly release a spray of hormones that settles on to one of the lucky spores – and, in a burst of chemistry, it becomes male." Winifred took Piedmont's hand and placed it on her left breast. "Genesis misled us. For many species in Nature, Adam is formed from *Eve's* rib. Life on earth seems natural, but it has no *nature*...all things can be, and could have been, otherwise."

She looked at Piedmont, watching for his reaction, looking to see if he understands her in the way that she wants him to.

Piedmont raised his eyebrows and grinned, shaking his head in wonderment. "I guess so. It still strikes me as a kind of Immaculate Conception, just as crazy, maybe more so. But I'll believe whatever you say, whatever you tell me, and love you more with each rock you turn over for me." He turned on to his side and kissed her, lingering over her lips' returning touch.

Raising up, he smiled down at at her. "Like your fossils, your *Gilboa* Tree, the first woods...the forest that was here before all of *this*." He swept his hand outward to the Catskill woods surrounding the wounded Schoharie valley, then patted the soft ground beneath their shared blanket. "I only know this earth as the place where I live, simple as that, not much more. I never learned much science, your science, or any science for that matter. I figured that for something that's supposed to help us better understand our place on earth, our purpose here and all that, it often seems to confuse things. But you, you're different. The things you've learned, the things you believe, the things you've discovered. I feel them. Understanding is one thing, but feeling is something else." Piedmont smiled. "And I feel that you are surely the sweetest surprise of all."

"And you, as well," she said, softly, taking his hand again to her breast, her heart, her rib. "It doesn't scare you, like it does other men – the unpredictability, how small we are, how we are here because of these little green sprigs." Winifred held up the moss in her free hand. "... offspring of the odd little Devonian lycopods from millions and millions of years ago that put the air in the sky for us to breathe, for us to *be*. For you and me to be here." She paused, still looking up at him, then said. "I love that you are happy under the stars without asking what they are made of, Piedmont...I do."

They both laid back on the blanket again, silent, their shoulders touching. Piedmont imagined that their thoughts, too, were touching one another in the quiet of two selves loving the other knowingly.

But Winifred's thoughts had slipped away, stumbling over a small uncertainty that unsettled her, a question she needed to ask. "Did you come here with Mattie, Piedmont?"

Piedmont lay still for a moment, then slowly sat up, wrapping his arms around his knees. The sharp point of her question about her sister made him feel his nakedness, and hers, as if suddenly exposed in The Garden. He looked away, across the high meadow into the valley, watching the slow circling hunt of a red-tailed hawk in the currents below. The raptor seemed to be waiting on his response.

"Not here, Win'. Never here," he answered finally, "And I know what you're wondering." Piedmont looked down at her. "I'm sure she's not mine. Not the little girl." Piedmont tried to sound certain of his answer, but he knew that it could be untrue; and if it were untrue, he'd be lying to Winifred. He promised himself that it would be the first and only time. Ever.

"Wilhelmina. You can say her name,...she was named after your sister."

Piedmont nods. "Mina....I know. Billie adored Mattie, and Mattie, well...she loved her too." He left off, not wanting to remember that Mattie had loved them both – both him and his sister – and in a similar way, with her same intense heat. His affair with Mattie had been brief. She had been too much for him, too urgent and too distant at the same time, as if when she clasped him she was always looking over his shoulder for something else, something that could better handle her fire...anything. Love had not taken hold for either of them.

"Billie is certain it was at the Manorkill. Eli Gallagher. Mattie just won't say," Piedmont said, looking up again at the hawk, wishing it could fly off with some of his memories.

Winifred slid closer to Piedmont and reached between his stomach and drawn-up knees, encircling his waist with her arms, as if to bring him back to her. "I know; it's the way she is. I'm sorry, Piedmont, I know better than to ask you such a question. But something surely happened to her here in Gilboa. Something bad. She'll never say who or what it was, how it happened. But it took a man,...and likely a man worse than most."

Piedmont softened, grateful that she is holding fast to him, grateful that he found the right sister. "Oh, Win', there's so much I don't understand. About past times, past creatures, about exploding stars or why the sun does what it does. Christ, I don't even know what makes men do what they do. All I know is what I know. That's good enough for me. I *thought* I had feelings for Mattie, but I *know* that I love you."

Winifred gently squeezed Piedmont and kissed his naked hip. "And I love a man who can love a woman joyously, knowing that there's little rhyme or reason to what we do, that we are loving one another on earth's indifferent surface. I love a man who accepts that our galaxy is not at the center of anything, that our sun has no privileged place in the swirls of the Milky Way, and that this planet, this *place*…this *life*, is the most unfathomable of all. I love *you*, a man gentle but ready for anything that dares show its face to him…even all of that."

As with Jenna Goldring and Johnny of the Angel, it had happened fast. The same inscrutable circumstances that fashion the universe and the endless unpredictable coupling of men and women had found Winifred Goldring and Piedmont Kinsolver.

There had been a sizing-up at their initial meeting earlier that year when Billie delivered Winifred to Division Engineer Sidney Clapp's office. Piedmont, more concerned for his motorcycle than its passenger, had gone outside to greet his sister's arrival. Relieved to find everyone and everything intact, he offered his hand to Winifred to help her from the side-car. She pretended not to notice. Instead, she stood up from her seat, pulled up her long skirt and stepped out showing a length of bare leg. At the same moment, her pistol slipped from her cinched waistband and fell to the dirt. Piedmont was surprised by both her lack of modesty and the Powder Frame Colt .45 lying at her foot.

"The safety's on," Winifred said, dropping the hem of her skirt and leaning down to retrieve the gun. Righting herself, she offered Piedmont her hand in greeting, looking hard into his eyes to see if Jenna had been right.

Billie nudged her brother with an elbow. Roused from his bewilderment, Piedmont shook his head, took her hand, and smiled sheepishly.

"Been looking forward to meeting you, ma'am," he said, "I know both your sisters; they speak highly of you." Piedmont took notice of the comfortable fit of Winifred's hand in his. "I'm more than happy to show you around."

Releasing Winifred's hand, Piedmont continued, "I'll do my best to keep up with you. Mister Nawn here lent me that book by Charles Darwin, *The Origin of Species*. And I read your paper, as well...on Devonian sea scorpions...from the State Museum Report. I won't say I understood every bit of it, but I'm a pretty decent learner."

Winifred raised her eyebrows, now being the one surprised. "*Eurypterus remipes.*" she said with a smile, "...devilish things, those sea scorpions." She, too, had noticed the fit of their hands.

Standing at the door, Hugh Nawn glimpsed over at Clapp. The two men shared looks of approval. Gianni DeAngelus, watching from the window, sensed a distinct warming in his friend.

Piedmont's official duty was to transport Winifred from the small house that her sister Jenna shared with a few other clinic nurses to the quarry or anywhere else she needed to go. The house, on an old Hops Farm bought out by the BWS, was close by to the infirmary, but a long walking distance to Riverside Quarry. Hugh Nawn placed one of his contracting company's Model T Runabout pickups at Piedmont's disposal, figuring the small truck could carry Winifred to her fossils, and her fossils to wherever need be. But after her ride with Billie, Winifred preferred the side-car of Piedmont's motorcycle. She enjoyed the open air, feeling the speed, the wind in her face and her body so close to the ground. Her sister Jenna had also piqued her interest in the man who, she said, preferred to be at its handlebars. She'd put it simply: *"He's honest, a reliable man of the earth. He can look a woman in the eye without having anything in mind other than a true interest in hearing what she has to say."*

At Shem's FingerBreak, back up in the woods, it had not taken long for the teasing about Piedmont's assignment from Clapp to begin. Smart move on the engineer's part, it was said, enlisting a good-looking local man to escort the lady from the Albany museum. Keep her distracted, get her out of everyone's hair. *"Coddling a woman down in the rocks of the Dam quarry is a job for a man with soft hands,"* they teased, *"we'll jes' twiddle our tougher thumbs for a bit."*

But the teasing had an edge to it, sharpened by enforced idleness and the vexed confusion about the work stoppages. Why a woman in a skirt, armed only with a black graphing notebook, a horse-hair paint brush, and a tiny rock hammer had taken over the entire quarry was head-scratching. Teeth-gnashing for many. On her second day there, Piedmont had driven Winifred down into the quarry. Some of the Little Sicily roughnecks who worked the rubble stone in the Stevens quarry were there as well, loitering around the works. They sat about on the massive limestone facing blocks pretending to be interested as Winifred went about her work, but their soft snickering soon became a chorus of cat-calls whenever she bent over to inspect another section of stratified rock. Piedmont tried to silence the men, but he couldn't speak Sicilian and they just shrugged their shoulders, pretending not to understand, toying with him. He couldn't push it, there were too many of them. He thought about getting Darryl Potts and the Bureau involved, but he knew the BWS police had enough on their hands keeping things calm up in the camps. He was about to suggest that Winifred come back the next morning – give him some time to sort things out – when a dozen of the bigger men from Il Palazzo Alpini showed up. They were led by Gianni DeAngelus. For several minutes, there was a tense exchange, chest to chest, with arms waving, men spitting at one another's feet in the stone dust, and a high-pitched blend of northern and southern Italian insults, but, soon enough, Winifred and Piedmont were left alone in the solitude and silent shadow of the looming concrete Dam.

Sidney Clapp, sitting at his desk in the Engineering Division Office, had been unaware of the fracas. He was drumming his pencil, still wondering who the hell this woman was and why the men from the State Museum had arrived late to Gilboa only to turn around and leave early.

Indeed, Winifred's colleagues from Albany, two men from the Paleontology Department had finally arrived in Gilboa a week after Winifred. And, indeed, they had not stayed long. One of them, Dr. Rudolph Ruedemann, was a fastidious German émigré who had mentored Winifred at the Museum. He'd often found her behavior perplexing, couldn't understand why she was always making a fuss with the others in the Department, particularly the scientists, the men,...but he admired her intelligence and precision and fully expected what he found upon his arrival – she had already tagged, organized, and filled her notebook with detailed drawings of many of the fossils. What he had *not* expected was that she'd also convinced Engineer Clapp and Hugh Nawn into giving her a few additional weeks in the quarry.

On their first day together, Winifred had led Ruedemann and his young assistant, a heavy-set staffer named Charlie Toland, into the quarry. Toland was not a field man; his wide girth usually kept him at a desk or in the lab, but he was there to take notes and excited to be included on the visit to Gilboa. At one point, while Winifred and Ruedemann were down on their haunches inspecting a stratum in the rock face, Toland spotted some small carvings set higher up on one of the large limestone blocks. Apparently, in their boredom, some of Johnny of the Angel's Italians had been shaping discarded stone just for the fun of it, challenging each other by carving outlandish lithic penises and large-breasted figurines. The 'statuettes' had been left behind, scattered about in a loose display on top of the block.

"The Venus of Willendorf!" the young Toland exclaimed excitedly. He hoisted his weight onto the block and reached down for one of the statuettes, not noticing that the block was cantilevered off another. The block tilted over with his weight, the carvings slid to the ground, and he went over backwards, breaking both wrists in the fall.

Jenna Goldring set both of Toland's arms in the camp infirmary and gave him an earful about upsetting her sister's work. Winifred said he'd been lucky to have fallen free of the half-ton block; she didn't need to spell it out, everyone got the picture – he'd have been crushed for sure, his substantial gut splayed like a tanned hide across the quarry floor. Ruedemann stood sheepishly by during the scolding. The next morning, he took Toland back to Albany, leaving Gilboa to the Goldring women. He reported to Director Clarke at the State Museum that the fossils were in good hands.

And Winifred, herself, was also in good hands.

She'd recognized quickly that her sister had been right about Bramlett "Piedmont" Kinsolver. He *was* a sweet surprise. Almost without her noticing, their days became filled more and more with time spent together, with less and less time spent in the quarry. They were easy and natural in one another's company. Piedmont was interested and helpful to her with her work, she was grateful and teased him kindly about his..."*mon cher chauffeur.*"

He showed her the mountains, she explained them to him. He taught her how to handle her pistol to shoot the Colt straight, she showed him how to handle a charcoal pencil to draw the curves of nature. He would lean into her notebook to practice his sketching; she would lean into his shoulder to watch and take in his scent. Soon enough, they were lying together beneath the stars in the swelling of their feelings for one another. He would point out the constellations for her, and she, in turn, would touch each starlight in the night sky as if to pin, within her own account of the expanding Universe, the chemistry of stardust from which all hearts had been made.

It was at the end of Winifred's third week there, that the work on the Dam started again. Clapp and Nawn struck a deal with the State Museum to cordon off a section of Riverside as well as another site, slightly upland, near the diverted Manorkill Creek. Hugh Nawn was pleased with the settlement, but, in truth, he had taken an interest in the fossils. He liked thinking that the very spot where he was standing – somewhere back in time – was not at *Latitude: 42-23'55" N* and *Longitude 074-26'46"* in the cool Catskill Mountains, but rather he was standing on the same landmass, albeit with a different surface, 20 degrees south of the earth's equator in a tropical swamp at the steamy shoreline of the great Catskill Sea, unrecognizable reptilians preying upon wingless insects at his feet, and the canopy of *"Gilboa Fern Trees"* shading the hot Devonian sun from off his back. Part of the settlement came with his own fossilized stump that he had sent back to his office in Roxbury.

At the upland site that was now also cordoned off, there had been a second discovery. It was at the spot on the Manorkill where Virgil Stinson had died. It seemed that no one had noticed that the gouged swath down the creek bank – caused by the bridge collapse and end-over-end roll of Stinson's truck – had unearthed the cast stumps of yet another ancient forest. Piedmont had been responsible for this new find; by then, he'd acquired an eye for the stumps. Winifred was thrilled because they were from a different time period than Riverside. It was still Devonian, but this forest had been buried during a much later cataclysmic event that had once roiled the shores of the Catskill Sea. Hundreds of millions of years ago, but many thousand years later than Riverside. To Piedmont, that seemed like an awful long time between the two forests, but Winifred laughed and snapped her finger up at the sky to keep the earth's clock in perspective for him.

Having to mingle with the endless trails of workers and the noise from the construction was an unpleasant distraction for Winifred, and the dust, in particular, made her work difficult. At the Manorkill site, she found what she believed to be fossilized seeds from the Gilboa Trees. It was yet another exciting find, confirming the Gilboa Tree's genus, but dusting tiny fossils for the minute markings of pyrite absorbed with clouds of concrete and rock "flour" was a wearying challenge.

From time to time, Winifred would return to Albany to review her work with the Director. Piedmont would drive her the twenty miles up to the M & S Dinky in Middleburg where the spur train would connect her to the main Delaware & Hudson line for the run east to the State Capital. He missed her each time she went away, fearing that one day her work would be finished, and she might not return.

But this afternoon, she had returned, and she was back with news. High up in their favorite hidden glade, cosseted in the dappled shadows of the hemlocks, Winifred was very excited and had loved him with a particularly sweet urgency.

"I still can't believe that it's happening, Piedmont. Tomorrow, the Governor and Mayor Hylan *here* in Gilboa. I'm nervous, but I'm ready for them." Winifred was now dressed and standing next to the Indian Scout, smoothing her skirt. Out of the west, hard gray clouds had appeared above the mountains and roused Piedmont and Winifred with the warning of a summer storm.

"The Reverend Daniel Mackey is ready as well, Win'. I hope the *other* visitors don't mind meeting at the church," Piedmont laughed, lacing up his boots. He stood and rolled up the blanket, tucking it under his arm as he walked to the motorcycle.

"I think it's only appropriate that the Reverend is simply keeping the faith of his predecessor," Winifred said with a teasing smile.

"You mean crazy Samuel Lockwood?...Well, I suppose so, but it's not exactly the faith the Reverend has in mind. He may have a genuine interest in geology and your fossils, but he still believes in a different sort of creation than the one you and your guests believe in."

"Well, it doesn't really matter. As long as everyone works together, there may still be a chance for Gilboa...and the fossils."

Piedmont shrugged his shoulders and looked up at the darkening sky. "A pretty slim one, I'd say. A lot of City money has been spent on building that Dam. Can't see them stopping the reservoir now. We tried it once when the chances were better." He sighed, then added, "Well, it's nice at least getting a visit from Mr. Fuller, even though I don't think he holds out much hope that it will go any better than it did before."

"I think he's a lovely man, Piedmont. I'm glad he's here as well."

"Endurance. Yes...he's the best. Maybe, one day, we can get to Florida and see that fern plantation in Princeton he set up with Mr. Drake." Piedmont winked at Winifred; both men had surprised her earlier. Fuller had brought her a gift bouquet of Cabbage Palm Ferns; the fronds matched those of the Gilboa Tree. She didn't know that Piedmont had been sending Fuller sketches.

"First things first. If Dr. Berry and the men from *die Gesellschaft* make their case along with Reverend Mackey, we'll have plenty more to do right here in Gilboa. But, at the moment you'd better get us back down ahead of this rain." Winifred put on her broad-brimmed touring hat and stepped into the side-car. Piedmont straddled the Indian Scout and jumped the starter lever; the Scout popped and roared to life, masking the rumble of distant thunder.

"I don't know, Win'," Piedmont yelled, throttling the engine. "Lot of fellas here lost something in the Great War. Scientists or not, a bunch of German paleontologists wouldn't be the first ones on a Gilboa guest list. They may be your allies now, but the Reverend has his hands full."

Winifred held her hat in place as the motorcycle traversed its way down the high mountain meadow in long back and forth sweeps. They were only half-way down when the rain began in earnest, dampening the riven trail of Wild Rye and Black-eyed Susan that followed their weaving descent toward the last hope of Gilboa.

Piedmont's doubts were understandable. The re-discovery of Reverend Lockwood's 1862 Devonian rapture had brought together an odd alliance between the last-standing locals of Gilboa and the international scientific community. The Reverend Daniel Mackey, the most recent of Lockwood's' successors at the First Methodist Church, spoke for the town, while a delegation of men backed by the American Museum of Natural History in New York City spoke for Science.

Mackey had been with Endurance Fuller and Piedmont on the failed mission to New York, five years earlier, but the swarms of paleontologists who'd flocked to see the remnants of the first known forest on earth had emboldened him again. He convinced Endurance Fuller to come north, knowing that it would help galvanize the community to see the former *Gilboa Monitor* editor. Endurance Fuller also knew the Mayor of New York City, John F. Hylan, from their youth; Hylan was a Catskill man, born in the nearby town of Hunter. Fuller and Mackey were curious to see just how much city life had changed him.

The AMNH group was led by Edward Berry, a highly respected plant paleontologist from Johns Hopkins. He was accompanied by two other paleo-botanists, both from Germany, who were experts on an extinct group of woody spore-bearing plants. Winifred had studied with Berry after graduate school and considered him "very human...for a scientist." He had an international reputation, and Winifred was hoping to get his support for the significance of the find. The *Gilboa Fern Tree* had been a first witness to life's most momentous turn – the moment when a breath of air had rustled the tree's pinnated canopy and amphibious creatures, like the ancient Lungfish, had climbed from the water to forage in its leaf litter and nest in its tendril roots. It was her paper, entitled "The Upper Devonian Forest of Seed Ferns in Eastern New York," that roused Berry. He had been impressed by the illustrations, a few of them proudly drawn by Piedmont Kinsolver.

Berry and the Germans had taken up rooms in the Devasego Inn, and that evening a convocation was held in the church to prepare notes for the following day's meeting with Governor Miller, Mayor Hylan and Thaddeus Merriman, who, earlier that year, had succeeded J. Waldo Smith as Chief Engineer for The Board of Water Supply.

In hindsight, the lashing winds and rains of the mountain storm that had set in with full fury that night might have been read as an omen that Reverend Mackey had joined an angry Lord to their side. But most of the men and women in the Methodist Church had simply braced themselves against the severe weather, trudged through the quickening mud, and packed the pews to hear what the men sitting at the alter on either side of Mackey had to say. The Reverend, looking out from his seat at the "congregation," had not seen such numbers in his church since the early years when the Dam was only a troubling rumor. It was not lost on him that it was Science and not Religion that was now filling his church.

239

Although the presence of the half-built Dam, the revived hope for the town's future, and the strange fossils imprinted with the lived-traces of a seemingly irrelevant past, were on everyone's minds, thoughts in the church nave varied widely. Everyone seemed to have their agenda. The Gilboans simply wanted their home back; they'd even accept the unfinished colossus, allow it to weather away or blow it apart themselves if need be.

Gianni DeAngelus, sitting with Jenna Goldring and their new baby, wanted to support Piedmont and Jenna's sister, but he was worried about what would become of him and his young family, without his work on the Dam. Jenna knew his mind and cradled Xaviero close.

Lincoln Lincoln, the only Negro begrudgingly allowed into the church, sat off in a side aisle at the rear of the church, a defiant Billie Kinsolver at his side. He was with the Gilboans, but only because it would allow him to get the hell away from the town, return to Virginia, and take Billie with him. He knew she would go with him; they'd already been circling the idea.

Eli Gallagher showed up as well. He'd come into the church after most were seated, reeking of alcohol. Brushing hard past Lincoln Lincoln, he walked unsteadily down the aisle and lurched to a stop at the pew where Dorlene Stinson was sitting two seats in. She had her twin girls, Dottie and Starling, with her on her far side, and the boy – Gallagher's boy, JayJay – was between them, cleaned up and whispering mischievously into one girl's ear then into the other's. All three were giggling. On the aisle side of Dorlene, sitting beneath Eli's drunken gaze, sat the BWS Chief Sanitation Engineer, Reasonable Pelt. He was holding Dorlene Stinson's hand.

"Well, if ain't the BWS's own shit-poker," cackled Gallagher. He raised his head and sniffed theatrically at the church ceiling, "Yep, I can smell it on you, must have been a busy day." He leaned in on Dot, "You like that smell, do you, Dor'?"

Reasonable put out his arm onto Gallagher's chest to fend him off, as Dorlene waved her hand in front of her face to clear the air of Gallagher's reek. "Eli, you're drunk,...again!" she said, "Please, leave us be."

Gallagher paused, then reached past her and poked the boy a few times with a drunken finger. "You can take this one home with you as well...he's no use to me." Leaning like that, with Reasonable's hand on his chest, Gallagher rolled sideways onto the shoulders of the people in the forward pew. They pushed him off, and he worked his way back out into the aisle. Walking unsteadily to the back of the church, he raised the back of his hand with his middle finger held high above his head.

JayJay turned in his seat and watched Gallagher with a look both hurt and confused. He had once wanted to be closer to the man he'd been told was his father, but the closer he tried to get to Eli, the farther away the man drifted. Even at his young age, JayJay could sense that his father's life was going downhill. These days, Gallagher was caring little for much. More time drinking at Shem's, less time working. Billie Kinsolver had been lost to him, the whores weren't. And the Dam, well he liked the thought of a high place where he could throw down on the black mule-skinner. *One day*, he'd begun thinking to himself.

Sidney Clapp, sitting in a back pew with Hugh Nawn and some of the other BWS men, watched Gallagher leave; but his thoughts on the Dam were of a different order. He was listening to the storm, grimacing with each clap of thunder. It had been hot and dry for weeks. The diverted river had split into water-starved streams and the desiccated ground around the large cofferdam protecting the construction had begun to shrink and crack apart. Clapp was cursing himself for not having the engineers run a closer inspection. It made matters worse that his new boss, Thaddeus Merriman, was arriving in the morning.

Up at the altar, Reverend Mackey introduced the paleontologists. At

Dr. Berry's invitation, Winifred Goldring sat with the men, but she had not been invited to speak. The Reverend was concerned about her reception among a number of the locals. She had lashed out at a few of the men in attendance who had been rude to her, either questioning her work, her credentials, or what was going on under her skirt. When she began wearing jodhpurs in the quarry, some had made the mistake of suggesting she acted too big for her britches. Other local folks could see that this woman might have discovered a way to save their town, but, when it came to negotiating with the City, that was something else altogether. Although it was almost two years on the books, the 19th Amendment had not yet made it to the Schoharie Valley. Women might be allowed to cast a ballot, but men would be the ones counting them...to most in the church that just seemed natural.

The discussion in Mackey's church began cordially with members of the audience rising to ask Dr. Berry questions or to express their beliefs about the best way to argue the town's position. Berry had done his best to put the fossil discovery in simple terms, knowing that his audience would have difficulty with the terminology, but it became increasingly evident that the discussion was really not a discussion at all. Although the Gilboans and Berry's team from the American Museum of Natural History had joined forces against the City in one last ditch effort to stop the Dam, their positions could not add much to one another. The language with which they argued their positions bore a resemblance but described two different worlds. The Gilboans spoke of saving the town, the men from the Museum spoke of saving the valley. Save our future, save our past; Christ's Laws of Compassion, Steno's Law of Original Horizontality; The Lord's Breath in the labors of the overturned field, Oxygen Expiration and Photosynthesis in the earth's untouched forest canopies. The Families of Gilboa vs. the Family of Man...*Our* time vs. Deep Time.

The Germans, Dieter Krausel and Karl Weyland, used an easel with large drawings to explain just how the Devonian fossils had come to be. Dr. Krausel took the floor, and to the relief of Winifred and a few others in the congregation – for different reasons – Krausel's English was surprisingly clear and good.

"The forest had grown in the swamps at the foot of the Eastern Acadian Mountains that bordered the Great Catskill Sea. North America and Europe were still connected with one another, and the earth's friction with the moon had slowed the earth's orbit to four-hundred days around the sun." Krausel circled one of his fingers around the fist of his other hand, as if he needed to show everyone what he was telling them.

"The Invertebrates were dominant at the time. The Phylum Arthropoda..."

"Ain't got no backbone!" yelled Gallagher, standing with his arms open and puffing out his chest, "Insects. Even I know that." He turned and looked over where Lincoln Lincoln and Billie were sitting, as if his remark had been meant to threaten him while impressing her.

"Yes, that is right, no vertebrate bones," Krausel responded. He signaled with a nod at his fellow German.

Standing at the easel, Karl Weyland flipped over the top sheet to another illustration and tapped it with a wooden pointer. He did not speak.

"*Mein* partner does not *spreche* English as well as I do," Krausel said with a smile and a wink at the audience.

"So, you can see here, on this map, that where you sit today was many degrees below the Equator back then. The climate was very hot, the sun was everywhere."

Krausel raised a finger again to the audience, "And, before the forest could close the bright sky with its canopy, a series of great floods came. A meter high, maybe more, of sand and debris washed out of the Catskill

Sea." He indicates the metric height with his outstretched hand. "Each time, the forest was overrun by flood waters and locked into the mud. Then the waters would recede, and the forest would begin again. Over millions of years, covered and revealed again, back and forth...buried and exhumed by flood."

Behind and above Krausel, lightening flickered across the stained glass rosette of Saint Francis and his flock of wild creatures. It was followed by rolling waves of thunder; wind-driven peals of rain rattled the aisle windows. Turning serious, Krausel folded his arms and, after the thunder passed, said, "The Gilboa Forest is a story of the fragile but determined nature of life-in-the-making. We must protect this discovery for our work...Your town, it belongs to science now."

Reverend Mackey was unsettled.

He looked around at the audience, fearing that the German's presentation might be making matters worse. Besides conjuring the Great War with his German-inflected English, Krausel's proprietary claim – in the name of Science – to the town and the ground where they were sitting could be seen as just another land grab. And sure enough, amid a polite but tentative sprinkling of applause, there was also jeering. Eli Gallagher, with nothing in mind other than the bellicose haze of his intoxication, heckled the two paleo-botanists the loudest.

Endurance Fuller sat in a front pew with Piedmont, shaking his head. Little had changed in the town's thinking. He'd hoped that the visitors could explain the significance of the Quarry discovery in a way that might help Gilboa see their future differently. Dieter Krausel's point was to remind everyone that things come and go, that they always have, including life on Earth. Even if the fossilized forest stumps could stop the Dam, Fuller knew the life of the town would never be the same. There would continue to be diggings that Gilboa would have to stand aside for. The excavations would be of a different order – excavations for the knowledge of the past, rather than the expediency of the future, for the sake of the world, not a thirsty metropolis. Fuller had seen the clear-cutting of the woods in Florida, the change to the land...it was happening throughout the country. If learning about the first forests on earth could save the last forests on earth, Gilboa must bow to that.

Reverend Mackey stood up from his chair and climbed the steps to the raised pulpit. He had prepared for this moment, uncertain if the need for it would arise. In his judgment, it had.

Hugh Nawn elbowed Sidney Clapp. "Sermon time, Sid," he whispered from the corner of his mouth. Winifred looked furtively at Piedmont, "*Le rapprochement,*" she mouthed silently to him. Fuller, next to Piedmont, folded his arms as if gathering up his patience for what might be a long night. He knew what was coming.

Looking out at the assembled Gilboans, Mackey placed his hands on the worn oak rails, then bowed his head. For a moment he was silent, as if searching the heavens for a way to begin. He looked up again and spoke.

"All Truth is One," he said, solemnly. Raising a single index finger high above his head, he repeated himself, "*One*....How can it be otherwise? Two things, both true, cannot contradict one another. All true science and all true religion rely on this fundamental premise. The scientists' picture of the earth history is fully in accord with Genesis. The six days of God's creative work are but the six great geological eons and eras that men speak of in the language of science.

"But a *day*, you might ask. Is not a day...*one* day?...I say to you, look closer at your Bible, remember Psalm 90: *For a thousand ages in Thy sight are like an evening gone.*

"The first day, then, we shall call the Hadean Eon, out of scattered matter cold as dust, *And God said let there be light*. But it was not sunlight, rather it was the *energy* locked up in each tiny dust particle, whose visible manifestation were the drifting nebulous clouds of the cosmos.

"The second Eon-day is the Archaen, when *God made the Firmament and divided the waters which were under the Firmament*. Here He forms the shape of our atmosphere and the heavens beyond; below are the waters covering the planet in roiling seas.

The third Eon-day is the Proterozoic which ends in the Precambrian era – *And God said let the waters be gathered in one place and let the dry land appear*. The earth is now pulled toward its center by gravity, and land rises out of the cooling oceans. Primitive plant life, low to the ground, begins spreading from the waters up on to the land, reproducing and flourishing, capable of making its own food and of being food. This is the first sparking of life, the most momentous event in geological history *and* in the Book of Genesis. Both witnesses, men of God and men of Science, agree that the Precambrian is the chief division point in Creation. All Truth is One.

"And so, what of the *fourth* day? Here begin the three great fossil-bearing Eras and the blooming of all plants and creatures great and small. The first is the Paleozoic, and this era-day is what has brought us together tonight, in this church of God, to speak with these men from the museum.

"If the third day offered the *spark* of life, it is this – the fourth day of the Paleozoic Era – which offers the *breath* of Life. It was then that the Lord said: *Let there be lights in the firmament of the heaven* and the sun shone down on earth from a clearing sky. The new forests grew, our own *Gilboa Trees*, opened their limbs and leaves to the firmament, as if in gratitude for God's Grace. But it also opened its arms to clasp its hands with the shining sun in an exchange of goodness. For what is light without a surface to cast itself upon and without a living witness to its display. This was the gift of the forests, and in return, came the sun's call to life's creatures that a world awaited them in the luminance of blessed oxygen.

"And the creatures do come forward. On the fifth day, the Mesozoic Era, middle life. *God created the great sea-monsters, and every living creature that creepeth, wherewith the waters swarmed, after its kind, and every winged fowl after its kind.* The reptilian hordes overspread the land, the great sea monsters – the whales; not fish, but heralding the warm-blooded mammals, lastly, the dinosaurs and their avian descendants like our own Myrtle Warblers and Red-Tails, the harriers in the hills above the Manorkill.

"It is in the Cenozoic Era, on the last day of work, the sixth, that modern life, as we know it, begins. It is when we ourselves arrive in the Garden. Placed there by God's *offering* hand in his image, if you are a Believer...or, by his *guiding* hand as the descendants of the warm-blooded, land-born, furry quadrupeds who supplanted the reptile cohorts. It doesn't matter.

"And yet, we were not awake. We were as other beasts of the wild, living without thinking, feeling without understanding, desiring without knowing. Do you doubt this?"

Silence from the pulpit. Silence from those listening. Even the storm outside seemed to lift and quell to make room for Reverend Mackey's answer: "The awakening, *our* awakening, arrives on the last day, the seventh...*And God blessed the seventh day, and hallowed it; because that in it He rested from all His work...and breathed into man's nostrils the breath of life, and man, formed from the dust of the ground, became a living soul.*

"Regardless of your faith, or your belief in the soul, there is agreement among scientists and men of the cloth that we – *mankind* – are the first born on earth capable of pondering what has come before us, and what, thereof, we can become. But are we *truly* awake to this? Are we *rested*? Or is it still the seventh day? Sixty million years into the Cenozoic Era, is it simply nightfall?" Mackey leaned out to the pews and shook his head as if in disbelief. "What a sacred duty! What fearsome knowledge we have!...What a blessed burden we carry!" He paused again, then added quietly, "*And a river went out of Eden to water the garden; and from thence it was parted...*Perhaps these men can help us restore our river, restore our Garden here in Gilboa."

Piedmont looked at Winifred to gauge her reaction. He was not sure how much of Mackey's sermon made sense, or how many in the pews could follow it, even if it did make sense, but he had noticed the omission. The "men" would restore the Schoharie. Winifred, sitting at the end of the row had straightened in her seat. She looked at Piedmont with an expression of tired resignation, realizing that her efforts would once again be relegated to a supporting role.

The Reverend Daniel Mackey stepped down from the pulpit as Dr. Edward Berry rose from his chair. The two men stood together and began to outline their plan for the morning's meeting with Governor Miller, Mayor Hylan and BWS Commissioner. However, before they had gotten very far, there was a disruption in the back of the church.

This time, it was not Eli Gallagher. The doors had burst open, as if by a strong wind, and Bureau Chief Darryl Potts along with three of his deputies were walking briskly down the center aisle. The men were shrouded in drenched oilskins and scanning the pews. Chief Potts stopped in front of Sidney Clapp. They locked eyes, and the engineer's stomach knotted. Potts nodded his head.

"The cofferdam has broke, Mister Clapp. We got one hell of a mess on our hands," Potts said. His tone was even, not alarmed exactly, but there was force to it. "There's men down there."

10

The Safekeeping...

Mina Goldring
1955, Schoharie Reservoir
"Human nature is like water. It takes the shape of its container..." (W. Stevens)

REASONABLE PELT HAD BEEN fishing with his step-daughter Dottie Stinson near the opposite shore when he witnessed the woman's slow awkward walk into the Reservoir by the Shandaken Intake. The fully-dressed woman was leaning back, cradling a large rock in her arms. It was partially swaddled in her blouse, and, at first, Reasonable thought she was carrying a small child. It was a Sunday. Later, he would wonder if the Lord had brought the woman before him so that he would be the one to bear witness. He'd always seemed to cleave to death more than most.

Earlier that morning, after Dottie helped him push the boat into the water, Reasonable had made sure to row to where the cofferdam had been, or at least where he imagined it had been. It was now a ruin, thirty-three years under the water; seven dead men had been recovered back then, including the poor young paleontology intern from Germany who'd been found clasped to another man, neither with their trousers on.

Reasonable, working for the Board of Water Supply, had been there that night when the walls protecting the works had given way; he'd been part of the salvaging. And he had been around two years later when rumors had it that the Reservoir had taken the others. Their deaths chilled him even more whenever he surveyed the great wall of concrete, as if the men who might be buried inside it were holding back the water themselves with a mysterious power found only in the Afterlife.

Dottie had vague childhood memories of all of these deaths as stories, but her thoughts about the woman's suicide lay elsewhere; thoughts similar to her step-father's, but elsewhere. Just as Reasonable had wondered if the woman was meant for him, she suspected the drowning woman was meant for her.

Dottie had only recently moved back to the area. Her step-father was getting on and showing signs of senility. He was still alert enough to see the humor and irony that his name brought to his condition, but he'd repeat his self-effacing jokes about having become "*Un*Reasonable" way too many times a day. Dottie did not mind his repetitiveness; she'd always loved the sound of his laughter, and it was fresh with each of his stale quips. But he needed care; his eyesight was poor, and he lived alone.

Dottie's mother Dorlene had died a few years before and was now buried up at the new cemetery next to her first husband, Virgil Stinson. Virgil had been an early casualty of the Dam and one of the first to be placed in the re-located uphill cemetery back in 1921. From their resting places, Dorlene and Virgil now had the best view in the valley. Reasonable had the plot reserved on his wife's other side, and he was waiting his turn. Dorlene Stinson had loved him as much as her first husband, mostly for his sheltering affections toward her and Virgil's two girls, but also for his care with the young boy that she and Reasonable had adopted as their own.

Dottie's twin sister Starling lived in California now; too far away and too tied down with a young family of her own to help with Reasonable.

God only knew where her adopted brother JayJay had gone to. He'd turned sullen after joining their family, no longer the lively boy he'd been before. He went away to school in the eighth grade and got into a good college, but his returns home became rarer and rarer. And then he broke all contact, took off with no forwarding address. To this day, Dottie wondered whose name he took with him, figuring that adopted kids get to take their pick.

The safekeeping of her step-father had fallen naturally to Dottie. She'd never married and had been living fairly close by, two and half hours west in Pine City, New York. She had a job there working as an accountant in the business office of a Benedictine Monastery on Poverty Hill. When her step-father began to decline, she made an arrangement with the Friars. They were understanding and agreed to have her drive back twice a month to reconcile the Mount Savior books.

The day after Mina Goldring's body was retrieved from the Reservoir, Dottie had been scheduled to return to Poverty Hill. Instead, she received a call from Father Xavi, a young Friar who often helped her in the office. He suggested she take some time for herself given the unsettling circumstances. She was surprised that he was already aware of the young woman's death.

She learned later that, of course, Father Xavi would be one of the first to hear.

In the obituary, the Albany Times Union placed Mina's survivors as her mother-in-law Jenna Goldring of Slingerlands, a young son Delano DeAngelus from a previous marriage, and an aunt, Winifred Goldring, a local celebrity who had been the first woman to hold the position of State Paleontologist of New York, now retired, also of Slingerlands.

Despite his mother's entreaties, Father Xavi DeAngelus, would not leave Mount Savior to attend the funeral. Not even on behalf of his son. The *other* boy still loomed too large – the other child born nine years earlier, the other son not mentioned among Mina's survivors.

*   *

The morning of her "last day as a sentient being" – and, indeed, that was how she thought of her decision – Mina Goldring posted a letter to her aunt Winifred, care of the State Museum in Albany. Although her aunt was now retired and living in the family homestead in Slingerlands, Mina knew that the museum would forward the letter in an official envelope, ensuring that no one other than Winifred would read its contents.

Earlier, before sunrise, she'd said goodbye to her two-year-old son Delano who was still in the Albany Hospital being monitored for a minor heart condition, *Dextrocardia with situs inversus*. She was certain that he would be fine without her, that having his heart on the wrong side of his body would not harm him, as it had not harmed his father. Nevertheless, as she kissed the sleeping boy's forehead, she could not escape the thought that having a heart where it shouldn't be had brought her to this day. His father's heart had not been a forgiving one; it had not been a heart that transcended corporeal location.

Her viaticum complete, Mina put her back to the rising sun and drove to the Schoharie Reservoir.

It was early spring, and she first drove northwest to the mouth of the Schoharie Creek, then followed it, as if beating against its northerly flow, southward through the Catskills toward the Reservoir. She passed through its valleys, in and out of the mountains' dark shade, through the slowly warming green bursts of new foliage. It was the start of fishing season, and at times, she could see small figures standing in the stream of the shallow creek. They were too far away for their rods and tackle to be seen and appeared other worldly, unmoving, staring at the flow as if in a ritualistic trance, listening to the water's message.

252

After an hour of driving, she turned east, then north again at a fork in the road and crossed the creek to its eastern shore. The headwall of the Schoharie Reservoir Dam appeared out of the mountain slope as if the foreground of concealing trees was being drawn back for her like a curtain. Up ahead, off to the side of the road, there was a large sign and a visitor's turnoff. The sign was billboard-sized and covered with maps and photographs. The words "*Welcome to the Schoharie Reservoir and the Famous Gilboa Fossils,*" printed in bright colorful letters, arched across the top of the sign like a celestial rainbow. In front of it, on the ground, a half dozen fossilized stumps were arrayed like gray picnic stools at the edge of the gravel parking area.

Reading the sign, Mina allowed herself a weary smile. There was no mention of the lost town. Time, she thought, always seems to have a convenient way of cleaning up after itself.

She was alone, no other cars, no other people. She turned off the ignition. Through her windshield, she could see a photograph on the display of a tall woman, standing with her hand on a rock face. The black and white photograph was framed under weathered plexiglass, but it was clear enough for Mina to recognize the smiling woman wearing jodhpurs and a broad-brimmed hat.

She thought again of the letter she had sent that morning to Winifred. Like the earth's core, her aunt seemed to be at the molten center of everything. Mina sat back in her seat and closed her eyes, remembering why this was so.

It was fourteen years prior, in 1941 – the day before Xavi DeAngelus and Mina Goldring were to board the Liberty Ship *Amerigo Vespucci* – that the news from Pearl Harbor reached the two of them at their small hotel near

253

Times Square. They'd left Endurance Fuller's plantation in Princeton with his warning about the troubles abroad. But Fuller had only been half right – the devil indeed had a front row seat across the Atlantic, but neither Fuller nor anyone else suspected he was in the wings of the Pacific as well.

It had been a tearful night, charged with the desperate emotions that an upheaved world and fear of ending times brings to a couple's bed. They began to make love for the first time. But Xavi was awkward and shy, unable to perform. Instead, they clung to one another as if needing to keep hold of the difficult decision that had been made – Mina would not be going with him to Italy.

The following morning, Xaviero rose at dawn and slipped out of their hotel room. Mina pretended to be asleep. They'd agreed not to prolong their leave from one another; it would be unlike either one of them to linger over the inevitable. But a few moments after the door closed, she quickly rose and went to the window to watch him on the street below. It was warm, wet and foggy, one of those December mornings that doesn't know its own season. Xavi did not look up to where he hoped she would be standing.

After dressing, Mina went downstairs to the lobby with her bag. A small group had gathered there around a radio; Franklin Delano Roosevelt was speaking to the nation. "...*with confidence in our armed forces, with the unbounding determination of our people, we will gain the inevitable triumph – so help us God.*" They listened in silence, strangers to one another with their own reasons to be in that hotel, on that day, at that time; but they were bound together now. Men would be dying – loved ones; war was holding out its cruel offer.

As she left the hotel, Mina thought again of watching Xavi from her window, watching him slowly walk away and fade into the morning mist. Even then, she had imagined his ghost.

Perhaps Mina felt she no longer had anything to lose, or that time was running out. Yes, men would be dying now, but only to join those who were long dead. She'd told Xavi that she was going to return to her mother on Bathgate Avenue, but she did not do that. Instead, she walked east from Times Square to Grand Central Station and bought a ticket to Albany, New York in search of the truth about her father.

Winifred Goldring was in a meeting and had directed her secretary to have her niece wait in her office at the State Museum in Albany.

Given her aunt's position at the Museum, Mina had imagined Winifred's office would be quite formal, but the modest-sized room looked more like a cluttered storeroom than the headquarters of the New York State Paleontologist. Nevertheless, it was clean and, to the trained eye, well-organized. Numerous shelves held books on paleontology, geology and botany, similar books were stacked in open labeled cases. Four large oak tables held metal trays with various specimens of fossilized rock and plant material. Most of the specimens had no identifying tags, but Mina had heard over the years that her aunt had no more need for tags than one would require to identify their own children from their desktop photographs.

In the corner beneath a window, a petrified tree stump sat partially hidden by one of the heavy table legs. It was about two feet high, fissured on its sides but smooth across its top as if sawed from the full tree. On its clean-cut surface, caught in the light from the window, a small hammer, a chisel, and bits of broken stone were arrayed as if in a tableau. It was the first time that Mina saw what she'd also heard about much of her life – The Gilboa Fern Tree.

On the window ledge above the fossil, two small books with dog-eared covers caught Mina's eye. One was a black graphing notebook. It was small, but wedged within, as if a bookmark, was another smaller book – *"Vindication of the Rights of Woman" by Mary Wollstonecraft.* Making sure to hold its bookmarked place, Mina removed it from the notebook and began leafing through its underlined pages just as her aunt entered the room.

"I'm sorry to have made you wait, my dear," Winifred Goldring said. She tossed a sheaf of papers on to her desk and opened her arms to her niece.

"Look at you," she exclaimed with a smile, "A young woman. How sweet of you to come see me after all these years." She gently hugged Mina, then stood back for another look, placing her hands on her hips.

Winifred was in her early fifties, younger than her sister Mattie, but Mina thought she looked older than her mother. Her pale skin carried more wrinkles than her age should have allowed, and her long hair was completely gray. She had tied it up in a loose fraying bun that was now surrounded by a frizzled aura of wild strands. Her dress, also somewhat wrinkled, was unbuttoned at the neck and matched her hair color as if coordinated in a kind of unkempt formality. Nevertheless, she had a presence, Mina thought to herself; she seemed to belong in some earthy way among the dusky lithic specimens scattered about in that office.

Noticing the book in Mina's hand, Winifred flicked her wrist at it and tossed her head to the side as if dismissing its importance. "Ah, Wollstonecraft...she's both dated and ahead of her time; I carry it about like an old habit."

Mina quickly returned the book to its place in the notebook. She suddenly felt embarrassed as if she had thoughtlessly intruded. She worried that her whole trip to Albany was misplaced. It was not so much the violated privacy of her aunt's books; it was the small gold band that she'd noticed on her unmarried aunt's wedding finger.

Winifred walked over to her office door and opened it for Mina. "Come, walk with me," she said, "I want to show you something here in the Museum. It's just down the hall." Winifred took her niece's arm in hers.

The second floor corridor was mostly empty of visitors and its marble floor echoed with their footfalls off the high ornate ceiling. At the far end, Mina saw what appeared to be an extremely large window, almost floor to ceiling, looking out upon a wild landscape. As they drew closer, she realized the trees beyond were not from a Northeastern forest. They were palm trees, or something like palm trees, and the space beyond the glass was inside the museum. She recalled her trip with Xavi to the Museum of Natural History, the diorama in the Hall of African Mammals.

"*The Gilboa Forest!*" she exclaimed, slipping from her aunt's arm, "Your diorama that we've all heard so much about." She rushed forward to the glass. "And the ferns!"

"That's right. They're from Mr. Fuller's plantation in Princeton." Winifred pointed to the canopy of the small fern-like trees hovering behind the strata of rocks closest to the display's window. "Do you see how they blend into the painted forest on the rear wall? One can barely see where the forest begins and ends. The artist was a French man, Monsieur Henri Marchand. I did some of the outline drawings, but it was Marchand and his son who came here from the Museum of Natural History in New York to paint the *trompe l'oeil*. They, so understandably and skillfully, depicted the character of the forest with its heavy moist atmosphere, that its both a wonderful scientific production and a beautiful piece of art.

"And, of course, the rocks; they're real. They were brought over from Gilboa, along with the fossils. You can see the horizons of sandstone where the Catskill Sea flooded the forest and covered its decay with sediment. Deep past, recent past, and the present; they're all here behind this glass."

"What kind of creature is that?" Mina asked, pointing at the large amphibian, half-in and half-out of the plexiglass water at the front of the diorama. The taxidermic mount was leaning upward from the mossy ground on odd-looking lobed fins with its hindquarters still in the water, glazed eyes staring through the diorama glass at the two women.

"*Neoceratodus forsteri*...an Australian Lungfish that was donated to the museum. The modern species has changed very little from its Devonian ancestor who would have lived in the Gilboa Forest before the flood. It's a lovely example of animal life's transition to land from water."

"It looks so life-like, the eyes..." Mina said, "as if it's watching *us* rather than the other way around."

"The mirror of nature," Winifred said, quietly, "Its ancestor is our ancestor as well; perhaps it's looking to remind us of that."

Winifred smiled wistfully and folded her arms, studying, as she so often had, her re-creation of the Devonian forest. There were many things that the Lungfish reminded her of.

It had been fifteen years since the opening of the celebrated Gilboa Forest Diorama at the State Museum in Albany. Winifred had been on staff at the Museum since 1914, working her way slowly up through the men there who blocked her path – some, intentionally; all in deference to tradition and convention. She'd been underpaid in comparison, her opinions patronized or begrudged, and, even with her success at Gilboa, rarely welcomed into the field among the "He-Men." That she was not married, nor seem inclined to be, only made matters more difficult, a source of prurient banter in the men's cloak room.

Fortunately, there was one man who supported her. Ever since she had revealed her Colt .45 Peacemaker in his office, Director John Mason Clarke had worried that she might be too smart for her own good, but he appreciated her skills and kept her on. Nevertheless, after her request to take a leave from the Museum in 1923 to recover from what she called nervous exhaustion, Clarke blamed himself for allowing her so much time alone at the Gilboa site, particularly given the deaths inside the destroyed cofferdam and the subsequent flooding of the fossil floor. He'd also heard talk of an affair with a local man. When she asked for leave, he was quick to agree, glad that she would be with family and far away from Gilboa.

Her plan was to rest and recover at The Botanical Garden in Soledad, Cuba. The research plantation of tropical flora in Soledad was sponsored by Harvard University and run by her uncle there. Family and flora would surely cheer her up; even Clarke believed that all women, without exception, are cheered by flowers; it was in their nature.

When Winifred returned the following year, he was not so sure. She had lost a good deal of weight, too much he thought. And she was more quiet, taciturn, and distant. When Clarke offered her the opportunity to oversee the design and construction of the Gilboa Forest Diorama, celebrating the state's greatest fossil discovery, he thought she would be overjoyed. She was grateful, but unexpectedly subdued in her response.

At first, her work on the Diorama was lackluster, as if her thoughts were elsewhere. Her sketches neither satisfied nor inspired her. It was only after spending a week in New York City that things changed. Clarke sent her there to meet Carl Akeley, the well-known explorer and taxidermist at the Museum of Natural History. Akeley was the one who introduced her to the painter Henri Marchand.

Akeley had just returned from Africa but knew of the Gilboa fossils. It was his idea that she use the actual rocks from the site, and he even offered her a taxidermic mount of a Lungfish from the museum's collection. He'd taken her to the basement to see the mount in storage. "It'll need some dusting off," he'd laughed, stroking the Devonian fish's head, "but look at the muscle on those remarkable lobe fins. I think it might work perfectly in your exhibit, crawling out of the Catskill Sea onto the dry land of your Forest."

Winifred agreed, but it was Marchand's suggestion that she could use actual Palm fronds and Plumosa ferns for the pinnate leaves of her ancient trees that helped her to see what was before her own eyes.

Her majestic "arborescent seed fern," *Eospermatopteris,* was taxonomically somewhere between the ground cover of spore-bearing ferns and the tall seed-bearing trees. And, like the Lungfish, the Gilboa Tree was transitional. They were destined to meet one another – the Lungfish and the Fern Tree – one from water to land, the other from land to sky to make the air for developing lungs.

It was a birthing. Winifred understood this now, viscerally, in her own body, a child's breath, free of amniotic water. And she knew exactly where she would get the ferns for the exhibit.

She went to work with renewed vigor and determination. When the diorama opened the following year, Endurance Fuller had not been able to come north and see what Gaston Drake's old plantation had wrought. But each year, as the diorama foliage began to fade within its imperceptible coat of resin, a new set of fronds would arrive from Princeton, Florida. First, by Fuller's hand, then by Billie Kinsolver's, and, most recently,...by her son Livingston.

"I was fortunate to have the Director's support to make this diorama. He lived long enough to see it, but not long enough to see me take over his position at the Museum." She laughed lightly to herself, "I believe he would have approved."

Winifred took Mina's arm again. "Tell me how is your mother?" she asked, changing the subject.

"I think she's well enough, Aunt Winifred," Mina said, "She gets tired from her teaching and her students. I do worry about her sometimes."

Mina waited for her aunt to ask about Livingston, anxious about her own questions, ones that she still was not sure how to ask.

But Winifred's question came as a statement.

"I understand your brother Livingston has enlisted," she said, off-handedly. She let go of her niece and leaned forward to wipe at a small speck on the glass with the sleeve of her dress.

Mina was taken aback. "What? No, I don't think so...I just left him in Florida. How did you hear this?"

"Mr. Fuller rang me up this morning," Winifred said, turning to her in surprise, "I assumed you knew. Livingston is on his way to say good-bye to Mattie." She paused, watching the news sink into her niece.

"I...I didn't know. No one told me," Mina said hesitantly. She was feeling as if the timing of things had suddenly sped up, overtaking her plans once again.

Winifred, too, seemed unsettled. "It's nice that you have come here, Mina," she said, seriously. "I'm happy to see you, I really am, but perhaps you should go home and see your brother. I'm sure he'd want to have his family near."

Mina nodded.

"Yes, of course," she said, flatly. She looked down at her aunt's hand. Winifred was working the small gold ring on her index finger, rotating it back and forth.

Mina looked back at the diorama, but her gaze shifted from what was behind the glass to her aunt's aspect reflected upon it. She searched for Livingston's face in hers, then spoke.

"Living Stone," she said quietly, "I know that he is not my brother... and that he's not Mattie's son."

For a long moment, Winifred was silent, then without turning or changing her expression, said, "Your mother has told you, I imagine."

"Yes, when Livingston was leaving for Florida with the other CCC boys."

"What else did she tell you?"

"Only that his father was Billie Kinsolver's brother. And that he went missing or died somewhere in Gilboa."

"Piedmont,...his name was Piedmont," Winifred said, staring into the diorama as if speaking to herself and everything that had taken the place of her child. "Our son was born the year before I began my work on *The Gilboa Forest*. The year before Piedmont disappeared."

An elevator door opened at the end of the hallway. A group of school children spilled out and ran over to the diorama. They began pressing themselves against the glass, giggling with delight at the Lungfish.

Winifred lifted her shoulders and straightened up as if not to allow her body to wilt with the memory of 1924 or to show the pain of it to the children.

"Everything is there," Winifred said quietly, pointing down at the Lungfish. "The story of all of our families. There, for the safekeeping."

*   *

Mina opened her eyes and looked out from the car once again at the roadside fossils. They seemed so haphazard and uncared for. If there was anything precious about them, one would have found it hard to believe.

Even her aunt's diorama was gone now; dismantled the year before during a renovation of the State Museum. Placed in storage, *The Gilboa Forest* had had its moment in the sun, an international destination for paleontologists. But other discoveries, scientific papers and Paleozoic

Period theories about Devonian life and strata had eclipsed Winifred Goldring's. She had supported them all; it was the way science was supposed to work. Nevertheless, when *The Gilboa Forest* was taken apart, she retired from the museum and returned to Slingerlands.

A few months later, she traveled to her uncle's plantation in Soledad Cuba for a last visit. Livingston Kinsolver's ashes, which had been given to her in 1944, went with her. Winifred had had her son there at birth and would leave him there at death, painfully aware that she had missed everything in between.

Mina thought again of Winifred's words about the Lungfish: *"The story of all of our families... There, for the safekeeping."* She remembered thinking at the time that her aunt was speaking of evolution and the Family of Man. But Winifred had gone on to explain that she had arranged for Carl Akeley to place a few precious personal items between the pleural ribs of the fish, just in front of it posterior dorsal fin. Winifred had sealed the items inside a small leather-bound box and watched him work. A ten-year-old Alabama cub scout on a field trip to the Museum had been there in Akeley's lab as well. She had regretted the boy's presence, but Akeley, assuming the contents were scientific, had gotten a kick out of showing young Winton Conrad how to hide a time capsule inside a taxidermy for posterity.

Mina smiled grimly at the memory, thinking that 'posterity' is always relative – both in time, and in person – w*ho* gets to see it and *when* they get to see it seemed to her as haphazard as the display of fossils out her car window.

At the dismantling of *The Gilboa Forest*, the Lungfish had gone missing. Only a few knew where it had ended up, and even fewer had seen what had been retrieved from the small, opened suture in the fish.

Mina knew that the letter she had mailed that morning before driving to the Reservoir, the letter to Winifred about her grandson, Piedmont Livingston Kinsolver, would fill in what had been left out of ... *'the story of all of our families.'*

But, the letter would not change this day, or all those years before.

Mina had obeyed Winifred and returned home to see Livingston before he left for the war. She knew, by then, that he was indeed her brother. Not a full brother, but more than a half-brother. And their child, conceived there on Bathgate Avenue during a last self-destructive night, would be passed off, just as Livingston himself had been.

When Mina discovered she was pregnant, she blamed the others, telling herself that Livingston had stayed too long and Xaviero had stayed *away* too long. But there was little comfort in it. She knew it was non-sense. Still, she could not explain her actions to herself other than to fall back on the belief that she'd held all of her life – that she had been marked as a child of rape.

The Rape. It had steered the course of her life as if she was never meant to be in the world. Born from inhumanity, brute craving and violence. She had struggled with this, wondering who would ever truly want such a child? Even when she learned the truth that Piedmont Kinsolver had been her real father, her mother's rape had already done its damage.

It had happened. And Mina had been there, a fetus forming inside Mattie's body. She grew up feeling the transgression in her imagi-nation, vicariously...her mother's uterus pushed to the ground by Eli Gallagher and pressed upon by the repeated viciousness of an unwanted man's groin.

What could she have expected from Xavi when he reappeared from five silent years at the end of the war? Even after they had re-kindled their affections, even after Delano was born, she should have known there would be no forgiveness. Hope against hope would not suffice. Livingston was long dead, and the little boy she'd had by him had been kept secret from Xaviero, hidden away in Florida with Belle Stikkey. It was the pattern in the family. Hers worse than most.

And on this day in 1955, Xavi was in Poverty Hill...and she was tired.

Starting up her car once again, Mina thought for the last time about her mother and their life on Bathgate Avenue with Livingston. Mattie had passed away earlier in the year and Mina had not attended the funeral. Another pointless act of shame that had no explanation.

She drove out of the parking lot to the fisherman's gate a quarter mile down the road. She had planned to stop there but saw that, further on, the security gate to the Shandaken Intake Tunnel Chamber was open. She continued on through the security gate, stopping where the dirt road ran closest to the water just short of the large arched sluiceway at the water's edge. She parked and opened her trunk. Looking around, she could see only one boat in the water, too far away to recognize the occupants. She reached into her trunk for the large block of sandstone and cradling it in the haunch of one arm, began tearing at a roll of military duct tape in her other hand with her teeth. She lashed the stone to her arm with rounds of the tape until her arm was no longer visible nor was much of the stone. Then turning, she walked slowly into the water with her eyes closed, leaning away from the weight in her arms. She had left her shoes on, and the cool water soaked quickly through her stockings as it rose around her. Her dress billowed onto the surface, then was tugged below the waterline as its hem rose to her shoulders. She slipped forward, her footing losing its hold on the steepening incline.

She opened her eyes as she went under. She saw her father, Piedmont, as she imagined him. And her last thought was that her search was over, and that this too was the family pattern...to end, like him – *at the foot of the mountain.*

Slowly, her mouth, then her throat, and, at last, her lungs filled with the water of Schoharie Creek.

* 11 *

The Lost Boys...

Jenna Goldring
1993, Slingerlands NY
*"We are here because one odd group of fishes had a peculiar fin anatomy
that could transform into legs for terrestrial creatures... We may yearn for a
'higher answer'– but none exists."*
(S. J. Gould)

IS IT A KIDNAPPING even if the child goes willingly? Even if the child is
being protected from far worse at home, even if the child is loved more
deeply by his captor? And what of the child who is given away? Is that
too a form of kidnapping? Doesn't the harm still lie in the act, the ransom
paid with the gains of a mother's freedom from responsibility? For either
child, the yearning for a return can easily become a second skin.

I believe that Delano DeAngelus has become convinced that Dante
Van Pelt is Trifina Lincoln's lost boy.

It has been a long time coming. As I've said before, Del's misguided
affair with Francesca Van Pelt was on behalf of the boy. He is unlikely to
admit it but, odds are, even Francesca understands this to be the case.

The same evening that Francesca had complained to Del about the
Faustian bargain she'd made that required her to lay on her back for
"Cleopatra's Needle," she had teetered drunkenly into her husband's

study and flung open a drawer in his desk, dumping its contents onto the floor. There were a number of manila folders. One of them contained Dante's adoption papers. "In case you ever need them," she had slurred, tossing the folder like a Frisbee at Del. The papers did not identify the father or mother, but they offered a means of finding out, if one were ever inclined to go looking.

Del gave the folder to Trifina. She gave it to me without looking at it. *You know about such things,* she'd said, *...you're the Doorman, you tell me.* Trifina believes that I am haunted by lost boys. She is right about this. After all, I am a ghost, a lost boy myself.

Although I had initially been more concerned about the whereabouts of young Dante, it is the other "lost boy" that now preoccupies me most.

JayJay has been found – the boy who had stood next to his father back in 1924, both of them arch-backed like a mismatched pair of and-irons, pissing on one of the Gilboa Tree fossils. Winifred Goldring had been witness, pushed aside, where she watched them smash the fossil into skipping stones. The boy had been scared but did what he was told by his father. Young JayJay Gallagher, nine years of age, watched his stones skitter-jump along the surface of the filling Reservoir, then watched their slow descent in the clear water as they rocked back and forth like feathers downward to join the drowning foundations of Gilboa at the Reservoir bottom.

The account had been in one of my grandmother's notebooks. Number nine, the one I keep close...the one with the drawing of a Lungfish swimming, just above sea bottom, through the lemniscate diagram of the infinity symbol. Above the sketch, she'd written that "...*the boy's father, Eli Gallagher, had died after the trouble at The FingerBreak, and in the years that have followed, the boy has disappeared.*"

And now he has reappeared. Just where he has always been. Among us...in the St. Urban penthouse. The return of Xaviero DeAngelus has confirmed it for me.

Before we left Saskia's flower shop, Xavi recounted how he had learned of Senator O'Graéghall Van Pelt's true identity. It came initially from his bookkeeper at Poverty Hill, an elderly woman named Dottie Stinson. She'd grown up in Gilboa and knew the stories of all the families. She had a sister living in California and a brother whom she'd lost touch with when they were still young. The boy had been adopted during the second marriage of her mother. He'd been a difficult child; remote and hard to control; left home in his teens. When Xavi learned that Dottie's step-father was a city man named Reasonable Pelt, he began to wonder.

It was Xavi's mother, my ninety-three-year-old great-aunt Jenna Goldring DeAngelus – an upstate constituent of Senator Van Pelt's – that solved the "*O'Graéghall*" riddle, the anagram that had been before everyone's eyes. If words direct the course of actions, it is the arrangement of the letters within them that gives them their force. Jenna had indeed found the lost boy "*O'Gallagher*" from Gilboa.

And when she recognized him, she did what any woman might do... she wrote to the wife.

I'm certain that Francesca Van Pelt had no idea that Slingerlands was in her husband's upstate district, and even less idea that her cuckolded husband represented Del's grandmother. It must have upset the Senator a great deal when his wife confronted him. I have little doubt that the bruises on Francesca's face came from the hands of Van Pelt. But it is not just that he has been found, that his true identity has been revealed; it is worse than that.

He is after the Lungfish.

I'd originally assumed that the figure in my grandmother's note-book of the Lungfish weaving through the loops of the infinity symbol along a primordial sea floor was a paleontological reference to our place in Deep Time, our openness to adaptation within an infinite but unpredictable future. But when I turned the notebook sideways, a second reading became possible. The Lungfish now swims verti-cally through the symbol for the number eight – 8 – the number of Winifred's missing notebook.

It had been my worst fear that the boy Dante had been inside the coffin-like crate that Buckles Hanrahan and Winton Conrad placed in the trunk of Van Pelt's car. But now I believe the taxidermic bones of Waterhouse's *Neoceratodus forsteri* are inside that crate. More bones, more upholstered dead heading upstate for the resurrection of Winifred Goldring's diorama and re-burial of whatever Van Pelt fears most. We will see which of us gets to the original Lungfish first.

But I mustn't get ahead of myself; it has only been a few days since the reunion at *Blackwater Flowers and Ferns* and much has happened.

Xaviero DeAngelus had his second heart attack standing at the edge of the Harlem Meer in Central Park. He'd been staying with Linc and Saskia on Cathedral Parkway and left the apartment to watch the chil-dren fishing for bluegills and bass along the water's edge. Like all the water in Central Park, the Meer is upstate water and can be turned on or off as easily as Hanrahan's sidewalk hose at the St. Urban. The kids don't know this, nor would they care; they're more interested in figuring out how to get around catch-and-release for a fish fry at home. But Xavi knows well the ground where the water comes from. Witnesses said he went down on one knee and then slowly rolled over, face first, into the shallows. Luckily, someone got to him quickly and administered CPR.

Linc and Saskia are with him now at Mount Sinai. He won't last long there. But I'm hoping long enough to see his son again.

Del and Trifina have been in touch. They and Dante are indeed with my great-aunt Jenna in Slingerlands. They think they're protecting the child, but I'm not sure from what or from whom exactly. There has been no APB put out about the missing boy. No one seems to be coming after him. The St. Urban penthouse is strangely quiet, the Senator is still away in Albany and there is no sign of Francesca van Pelt.

And Hanrahan is not talking. Not to me, at least. I am no longer his man at the door.

All hell had broken out after I'd abandoned my post at The St. Urban and found Xaviero in the park. There was a robbery in the lobby...the van Ruisdael painting and the Revere Silver frames holding the Olmsted and Vaux tintypes were stolen, taken right off the walls. The thieves left the brass Heliopolis Obelisk behind. It was jammed in the hinge side of the St. Urban door, apparently to hold the front door open while the *Torrent in a Mountainous Landscape* was carried off. Bev Prickett had been walking down Central Park West pushing her mail cart and witnessed the large painting being placed in the back of a beat-up cargo van without plates. She could not see much of them from behind, but she thought, from the shape of things, it had been a man and a woman.

Either way, I fired myself before Buckles Hanrahan had the chance. I had Chavez let me in through the service gate, cleared out my locker, dropped my keys on Hanrahan's desk, then decided to walk through the lobby on my way out. The palimpsests of the van Ruisdael and the tintypes looked ghostly on the walls, like accomplices to my own impending absence. A new door man was already in place. He mistook me for a resident and lowered his head in deference as he opened the front door. In a nod to the Imp of the Perverse, I couldn't resist crossing the invisible line of protocol and discretion with a little rumor mongering between staff and tenant and said, "Hold your head up high, man, and tell your boss, that son of a bitch Hanrahan, to stop screwing the Senator's wife." The poor fellow looked like a deer in headlights. I saluted him and walked away from the St. Urban feeling good.

But soon enough, I was feeling bad again. As I walked across Central Park heading home to my empty penthouse on Museum Mile, I began thinking again about Del's relationship with Francesca; how pointless it had seemed. It was good that he was with Trifina now...the two of them together in Slingerlands. My pace slowed as if the weight of this thought was causing me to drag my feet. *Together,...in Slingerlands.*

I stopped at the edge of the Pinetum, suddenly feeling more alone than I am accustomed to. In my delinquent travels, I have never had a problem of this sort before. But now, it feels that I might have ventured too far from the world,...or had somehow been the one left behind, rather than the one leaving behind others. My solitude and invisibility as the Door-Man had worked for me so long as I was...well, in the midst of company. Safely encased in a clear self-protective shell, I had found a fair enough contentment and sociability in being present while absent, seeing but not being seen, hearing others' thoughts but not speaking my own.

The Pinetum was empty. In my imagination, it was not. The X-men were arrayed like another set of ghosts in a circle for our Sunday Tai chi. They too were dispiriting. The names that I'd conferred on them had been in the guise of solidarity, of community and shared fellowship, but it too was just another way for me to keep others at a distance, to keep them as abstract variables without fixed definition or function other than allowing me to share in their concreteness...a vicarious life, mine.

I sought comfort from the *Angel of the Waters.*

Turning off my homeward route, away from the Reservoir, I headed south across the Great Lawn, past Belvedere Castle and into the Ramble. In the woodlands, I passed the couples – lovers nestled in the small clearings, at the edges of the secret coves, in the folded crags of the Gill, all of them off-path but not quite hidden from mine...they were like fingers wagging at me for all that I have missed.

I crossed the Bow Bridge along the north edge of The Lake, where I could see the *Angel of the Waters* on the far shore, her bronze wings widespread as she touched down on the fall of water from the tiered fountain. Beneath her feet, the four cherubim were veiled and encircled by the blended sheets of Croton and Catskill water – *Health, Purity, Temperance* and *Peace*. And below them, *The Pool of Bethesda*.

Like one of John the Apostle's invalids of Jerusalem, I was drawn to the "stirred waters" of the pool for healing. But I do not believe in such things. Any healing that is meant for me does not lie at the Bethesda Fountain. It will be far away, at the water's source; and yet, I'm no longer certain that I believe in that either.

The plaza around the pool was crowded with tourists, many languages weaving in and out of one another as they knelt like penitents, aiming their cameras heavenward to capture the Angel, hovering above the heads of their family and friends posed at the pool's edge.

I felt a quiet presence at my side.

"She was a lesbian. Did you know that, Kinsolver?"

Francesca Van Pelt had drawn up next to me. Still wearing her sunglasses, she was looking upward at *The Angel of the Waters*, whose bronzed face was fixed downward toward us, returning Francesca's gaze as if having overheard her.

"The artist, I mean," Francesca said, "Emma Stebbins. She was the first woman commissioned for a such an important work of art in New

York City and an open lesbian in a closed world. It was a scandal when the city fathers learned that her lover had been the model for the angel."

By acquired habit, I straightened up and fell back into my other self, back into my protective shell, more startled by Francesca's appearance than her remark. I almost didn't recognize her. She'd cut her hair very short, ignoring the graying roots, and was dressed in a rumpled plaid shirt and baggy khaki trousers. Her stiletto heels had been replaced by a a pair of worn-out leather flats. She turned toward me and removed her sunglasses as if to remind me of what I'd seen at the North Gate House days before. The faded gray-blue crescent cupping her right eye now matched her iris. She looked tired and defeated, a different woman altogether.

"I followed you here, Kinsolver," she said, "I know who you are."

I did not like the tone of her voice.

"Piedmont Livingston Kinsolver. I know about your family. And about the others as well. I know that Delano's father is in the hospital being watched over by Lincoln Gilboa, one of the security guards at the Museum...and I know about your apartment on 5th Avenue. *Your* penthouse."

Francesca paused, without taking her eyes off me. "The Senator knows as well," she said, solemnly.

"Jenna DeAngelus?" I asked, "...Del's grandmother?" It was a question that already had its answer. My protective shell was being shattered.

Francesca nodded. "He wants something from your family."

"You know where your boy is, then," I said.

"Yes. But that's not who he's after. He doesn't care about Dante. He never has. It was my fault for bringing the child into our home in the first place."

Francesca began to cry. "I've left him, this time for good. I'm leaving the country and going back home. The Senator never had custody of

274

Dante and always preferred it that way. The adoption was my idea, mine alone...and I am an unfit mother, Kinsolver."

"Francesca, I..."

Francesca raised a hand and stops me. "I took him out of school. We packed for him...Delano and Ms. Lincoln were with me. I thought he'd be safe with them while the custody papers are being filed...and happier with them. He's *always* been happier with them."

She looked at me imploringly. "I don't understand any of this. Why is the Senator after your family? What does he want?"

I reached out gently and embraced Francesca. She wiped at her tears and buried her head in my chest. "His history," I said, softly.

Notebook number eight, I thought to myself,...*and whatever else Carl Akeley placed within the taxidermy that is waiting for both of us in the attic at Slingerlands.*

*   *

Both Saint Augustine and Charles Darwin saw mankind as emerging from molten fires. The Hell of Original Sin or The Hadean Eon. Augustine's faith in God's Grace offered an escape from Hell, but Darwin offers mankind no choice but to bring Hell with us. It is the dark side of evolution – the physical pain that comes with evolving nerve integration, the anxiety wrought by the emergence of consciousness, and the knowledge that the complex collapse of our multicellular life ends only in our death. Although "descent" plays a justificatory role for both Augustine and Darwin, the true Fall of mankind seems to be upward. In the matter of O'Graéghall Van Pelt's "ascension," as with all things, time will decide.

I know now that Delano is Waterhouse Hawkins's *"Crazy Fucker"* – the Lungfish in the Reservoir's north basin, the mark of DeAngelus on the Gatehouse door, and the fossil of the Gilboa Tree beside it, they are all his doing. In the dark of night. While Trifina and I slept. To get my attention.

Van Pelt is on to us, and Del is worried about the Altar-Boy. As he should be. If Del and I have learned anything in our odd lives as unwitting brothers, it is that the sins of the parents are visited upon the children. But Dante can be saved. If sins course through blood and biology, Dante is already somewhat spared; on the other hand, if sins are conferred by proximity, that is something else. Delano is not taking chances either way.

My decision to address the wrongs of two generations ago will be costly; I don't know how it will all end, nor do I know that 'wrongs' is the correct word for the behavior of innocents or for the provocations of unpredictable circumstances. Events are time-bound and can not possibly control their duration. I am afflicted by the difficulty of letting go of the past when it remains so present.

The trip to Slingerlands thirty years ago set me on this course. My meanderings to Seadrift Texas, the Apostle Islands, the prison system at Norco, and Mt. Eyak – they were diversions interrupted by Lincoln Gilboa's tracking of me. He had Endurance Fuller's Last Will and Testament in hand, but it only served to remind me that my inheritance was more complex. I knew too much and could not seem to spend it down.

My post at the St. Urban and my outpost in the penthouse on Museum Mile brought me closer and closer to what feels inevitable. It is as if, like a child, I have been gingerly nudging along a strange creature to see what it might do, to see if it might show itself more clearly.

Perhaps that was all it was for Van Pelt as well in 1924, a nine-year-old boy nudging along his own strange creature; maybe a heavy gun listing awkwardly in his small hand as he wondered what might happen with a few more tentative nudges. Who knows?

What I do know is that my dreams must end one way or another. He and I will meet over the eighth notebook and settle matters once and for all.

And so, I'm driving north.

To Slingerlands. In a rented car. Alone. Meandering. Now with purpose.

I meander partially to stall what lies ahead, but mostly to follow the course of the water.

It is fitting that I began my trek at the Fountain, the *Angel* blessing the city's original water supply from the Croton hills 120 years ago. After doing my best to reassure Francesca that I would protect Dante, I went to the North Gate House at the Reservoir to find Waterhouse. There was no time to waste, no time to explain the details to Linc, or to Xavi...even if he was able to hear, even if he was still with us.

Waterhouse's Capuchin was outside the gatehouse, sitting on the DeAngelus family fossil as if waiting for me. Dolores' leash was tied to the closed door, Del's carved 'X' darkening in the sun but still visible on its surface. I knocked, calling for Waterhouse. He made me wait before opening the door. Bev was with him, still wearing her post office summer shorts, but her shoes were off. Despite the urgency I felt, I had to smile. Love was still possible in the ruins.

I was brief, letting him know that I knew where the Lungfish was – both his dead one and the one that I'd missed in the attic of the Goldring house thirty years earlier.

"Most importantly," I said, bearing in on Waterhouse, "tell Linc I know where the notebook is. Number eight, the missing one from Winifred Goldring's trunk. It was there all along; I'm going to Slingerlands to get it."

"Wahoo, Kinsolver. And you get Loony of the Angel and that boy with him as well," Waterhouse cheered, "Your daddy would've been proud of you."

Leaving the Central Park Reservoir, I rented the car and continued on, following the cast-iron mains, distribution pipes and masonry water tunnels running beneath me. First, to Jerome Park in the Bronx, where the Catskill, Delaware and Croton waters meet, then out of the borough to Hillview in Yonkers and the larger Kensico Reservoir at Valhalla. I drove slowly, like a tourist...or someone taking a last long look. The brownstone retention walls of the smaller distributing reservoirs were Mayan ziggurats, their gatehouses sitting on their tops like small temples.

From Kensico, I continued north to the Muscoot, the Amawalk, and Titicus pools, all of whose names, in the amnesia of Time, were taken from the Native-Americans fed by the streams of the lower hills before both were removed to make way for the reservoir pools.

I turned southwest to the gorge below the New Croton Reservoir Spillway where the mountain water not needed by the city returns to its original destination in the Hudson River, and onward, like all waters since the beginning of gravity's pull, to the sea.

As I turned north again, paralleling the Hudson, I imagined what the river might have looked like before the Catskill watershed was altered,... the river that my grandfather would have seen on his return trip on the paddle-wheeler *Half-Moon*, back in 1917. He'd brought Cannonball's motorcycle on board, eager to run it through the Gilboa hills. The other men from Gilboa would have been with him – young Endy Fuller, the Reverend Mackey, the doomed Stinson and Gust Coykendall. Gallagher, too; he would have been with Piedmont as well, neither of them imagining what lay ahead for them or their offspring, not imagining what is true for both the mean-spirited and the magnanimous – the bastards will get you in the end.

I passed through Poughkeepsie close to the train station where Piedmont had slept on his way to the city, and then crossed over the river on the Rip Van Winkle Bridge to the town of Catskill where Piedmont had stabled his horse for good with his friend Samson Lockwood. Lockwood had been the grandson of the Methodist minister from Gilboa who'd first discovered the fossils and had his faith shattered not by the amnesia of Time,...but by its retribution.

Once on the Hudson's west bank, I drove southward to the vast Ashokan Reservoir, the oldest and deepest pool of drinking water owned by the city. The Reservoir is downstream from the outlet of Shandaken Tunnel and the layers of chilled thermoclines in its depths are like the sedimentary layers of past lives upstream at the Tunnel – the fruitless spores and seeds of the Catskill mountains sinking into the still water above the ruins of Gilboa. And below the ruins, the bones of dead men long-settled on the remains of an ancient forest floor. Each layer on its way downward to the heat of the earth's mantle.

I turn north to Slingerlands...caught in these layers, caught in a snag within the river of Time whose flow no longer carries me along, nor breaks around me...Time flows through me.

Jenna Goldring DeAngelus does not hear me coming in the driveway. She is on the porch, sitting on a worn divan rocker, flanked by two of the Gilboa stumps set like side tables at the rocker. A stack of magazines sits on one of them, and a bottle of Jack Daniels sits with a half-full highball glass on the other. Jenna's head of gray hair is down on her chest, and she appears to be asleep. I climb the porch steps, but before I speak her name, she lifts her head and breaks into a smile of recognition. It is her half-face smile, the one etched in my memory from my last visit to Slingerlands thirty some years ago.

"Well, here you are at last," she says, reaching for her walker by the edge of the divan. She rises slowly and carefully. Then, thin shoulders hitched, she leans her bird-like weight into the walker and says with a slight slur, "They've come and gone, Kinsolver. They had the police with 'em, but they couldn't get past me." She says this with defiance and pride, but her knuckles are white-tight on the walker handles.

Turning her head to the front door behind her, Jenna calls out, "Your doorman is here, boys," She winks her good eye in my direction. "I'm not too old to know about search warrants."

Dante bursts through the screen door on the porch, a big smile on his face. "The Door-Man is here, the Door-Man is here," he exclaims, excitedly.

"Indeed, I am, Altar-Boy," I drop to a knee and Dante throws his arms around my neck.

"And he's still in uniform, I see." Trifina and Del have followed the boy onto the porch, and Trifina stands with her arms folded, looking down at me with mild disapproval.

"I'm on my lunch break," I say, trying to disarm her. I know her disapproval has a longer dimension to it than seeing me in my uniform here in Slingerlands. But I am wearing my grays for both the Altar-Boy and Van Pelt. I want to be certain that no mistake will be made recognizing me.

"I'm glad they didn't see you arrive," Del says, "They just left, moments ago." Del is wearing a kitchen apron and drying his hands with it. "We were in the back when the cars came in. Two of them. One was a state trooper, the other was a black sedan with government plates. We couldn't see who was inside, but you can guess. The officer asked about stolen property from the Museum. Gran blocked the door, wouldn't let them in."

"I know my rights," Jenna says, arching her back. "And, besides, they weren't going to climb over this to get through me." She lifts the walker and bangs it on the porch floor a few times for emphasis. Her bottle of Jack Daniels wobbles on the Gilboa Tree stump. At ninety plus years, Jenna Goldring DeAngelus – an old woman with Bell's Palsy and a slight drinking problem – is still watching over the generations.

"They'll return soon enough, and they'll have the necessary papers to search the house," I say, stepping off the porch and looking up at the small rose window nestled under the peak of the house roof. One of the panes in the rosette is broken. There will be wasps in the attic; but there will be a lot worse than that if I don't get there first.

"I don't want to go back home," Dante says softly. He looks at me with uncertainty. "Please don't make me." These are the same words the Altar-Boy used back at the Reservoir weeks before.

I step back onto the porch to reassure him.

"I'm not here to take you back, Dante, I promise. And I don't think those men were here for you either."

Trifina walks over and takes Dante's hand. "Sweetheart, come with me. Let's finish up with the dinosaurs." As she passes Del, Trifina reaches out with her free hand and runs it down his arm. It is an affectionate gesture, likely meant for me as much as him.

"He's attached to Winifred's collection," Jenna says. She tucks the Jack Daniels into her armpit and turns her walker to follow them inside. "She had those toy dinosaurs as a little girl and kept collecting them right up until the day she died. Delano's father liked playing with them as well when he was a boy."

As soon as Jenna is out of earshot, I turn to Del. "You know that he's dying," I say, quietly, "Your father."

Del nods, "I saw him before we left."

"Did he tell you who I am?" I ask.

Del shook his head. "He didn't have to. I always thought you looked more like Mina, than I do. At least, in the photographs that I've seen of her."

"I never knew her, Del. I was about Dante's age, living in Florida when she died. You had two years with her, I had two weeks, probably less."

Del walks over and sits on the stump. He leans forward with his forearms on his knees. The kitchen apron swags between his legs. I see for the first time that he is barefoot. On each foot, the toenails of his feet have been painted in different earth colors; I do not ask about them; I can guess by looking at the fossil between his feet. The cast of its outer cortex has been painted to match living bark. Dark browns and gray on its surface with ocher and flesh-colored paint lacing through its fissures.

Del follows my glance. "We had a painting day with Dante," he says, looking down with a smile. He begins drumming his fingers on the fossil, watching the accompanying rhythmic tap of his painted toes.

I lean against one of the porch columns and fold my arms. Del seems more relaxed and settled than I have ever seen him. It is as if he has found a way out of his absences by finding a family with Trifina and Dante. He has taken watch over the boy; she is watching over him.

"Is he her child, "I ask, "...the Altar-Boy?"

Del looks up, but his gaze seems to pass right through me. His expression reminds me of his angelism, but it is different, as if he is looking at a point in time and place that will provide him the best answer.

"It doesn't matter, Del. It's not important. I know it is what Francesca wants. For all of you. For all of us."

Del's gaze comes back to me. "When did you learn who your mother was?" he asks.

"Quite awhile ago...right here. You wouldn't remember, you were too young, and I was just someone passing through; your grandmother wanted it that way. It wasn't about Mina; it was about the older generation. She wanted me to see what Winifred had left behind."

"*Neoceratodus forsteri*," Del says, "...the original one."

"That's right. The Senator is not after Dante, he's after what's up there in the attic. You've known this all along, haven't you, Del?"

Del's gaze drifts away again. "I saw Carl Akeley's notes about the Gilboa Forest Diorama," he says, "The taxidermy. All this time, he wasn't just telling tall tales; Conrad *had* been there."

"I know...a lucky cub scout with an interest in natural history, I know. Have you found it yet? The Lungfish?" I ask.

Del ignores my question. "And Van Pelt was adopted...just like Dante. The son of Elohim 'Eli' Gallagher, hiding in plain sight." He turns and looks at me. "Just like you."

"Del, is the door unlocked?" I ask, quietly, "...the door to the attic?"

Del shakes his head and stands up. He lifts the apron he is wearing and reaches into his pocket. He takes out a large brass skeleton key and hands it to me.

"I know who Van Pelt is," he says, "I've known for a while. But Lincoln and Trifina have convinced me that that is enough. What he *did*, whatever it was, cannot be undone." He points up toward the porch ceiling. "Dante says you're the Door-Man. Open it, if you have to. Trifina and I are leaving in the morning. We're taking Jenna to see my father."

"Ok, then," I say, heading into the house. The key is heavy in my hand. I can smell the faint odor of worn brass emanating from its darkened patina. I think of Del's dying father, Xaviero of the Angel. He had called me *Charon*, the Ferry-Man...shepherding my own lost soul across the Schoharie.

I am surprised to see that the attic is unchanged. It has been almost thirty years since I first unlocked the small arched door off the third-floor landing and climbed the steep stairs into the eaves of the old house. Winifred's trunks are where I last saw them. Even the fan of swept dust and the scratch on the floor where I'd pulled the last trunk around to get at its clasps is still visible within the more settled layers of the attic's undisturbed years. Jenna said she had long since given up trying to climb the stairs and only vaguely recalled helping her sister slide the heavy trunks up through the tight stairwell.

The wooden crate is also where I last saw it – inside the first Saratoga that I'd opened back in 1965. I lift the crate out onto the attic floor and inspect the lock on the crate's hasp as if, in my absence, time itself might have found its key. It has not.

I've brought up a hammer and rusty chisel that I found in Jenna's garage, but I feel reluctant to do what is necessary. Winifred's chest is like a reliquary and to defile it seems a sacrilege; but it is also the dread of discovery that holds me back. Perhaps Del and the others are right. We have done enough...I have done enough.

No.

I grab the hammer and place the chisel. With three fast and hard strokes, I send the hasp and lock skittering across the attic floor and open the crate.

Even knowing what I would find inside I am still startled, flesh eye to marble eye with Winifred's Lungfish. It's propped up on its lobed fore fins with its head raised, staring at me dozily, as if roused from sleep. It is in the same position that it held in the Diorama. The dry air of the attic has desiccated the once smooth flesh of its skin, and I am fearful that the nearly five foot long mount will come apart as I lift it free of the crate. Life-like in its upholstered death, it is surprisingly light in my arms, a mummy without the canopic jar for the entrails. The mount remains intact, even as I finger the seam running between its ventral pelvic fins. I press into the seam like a physician probing an ailing patient's soft tissue, probing for what does not belong.

Just below where the pleural ribs begin to recede and give way to the large posterior dorsal fin, I trace the outline of Akeley's leather box hidden within the ribs' cotton filler. It has weight to it; Akeley had been clever to insert it just above the large rear fin where its weight would help to keep the mount from tipping forward on to its broad odd-looking mandible.

I feel the strangeness of nested things – boxes within mounts, mounts within crates, crates within trunks, trunks within attics. They are like the nested stories we tell ourselves even as we are trying to find our places within them.

The eighth notebook, a braided lock of hair, and a small handgun are in the box. I place them on the attic floor among the cotton batting that has fallen from the Lungfish. The gun and lock of hair are unexpected, but I feel certain the notebook will explain their presence.

It does...

* 12 *

The Troubling of Waters…

The Innocents
1924, Gilboa and Albany NY
*"From time to time an angel of the Lord would come down and stir up
the waters. The first one into the pool after each such disturbance would be
cured of whatever disease he had."*
(The Gospel According to John)

"GOOD LUCK IN THE Olympics today, Lincoln. You should run easily over most in the chariot race, but some of the local men have brought in teams with a thoroughbred or two slipped in; don't know what you're up against with them."

Sheriff Darryl Potts leaned over and spat down at the ground, but his spittle caught the bottom rail of the BWS corral fence instead. He scuffed the spit off the rail with his boot and stood back from the fence re-adjusting his shoulder holster.

"Their drafts and mounts grew up here; maybe yours have gotten used to the cold," Potts went on, "Hell, I'm going to Florida soon as this Dam is finished…maybe sooner, now that the Shandaken Tunnel is running water. I'm done with these hills; only Kansas blizzards are worse than these winters…and I ain't getting any younger neither."

Potts had gained some weight over the past few years and had started wearing suspenders on his pants. This had taken some getting used to since they could interfere with the shoulder strap of his pistol's holster, making it more difficult to draw quickly if necessary. He'd practiced behind the Bureau's make-shift jail, but worried a time might come, as it had in the old days. The violence at Fort Riley and, later, at Las Guasimas had never left him.

Inside the corral, Lincoln Lincoln was shirtless, sweating in the heat as he led one of his mules to a hitching post. Two other mules dozed sleepily at the post.

"Got my three best, Sheriff," he said, "...the trinity, Old Dominion will be jes' fine."

"Then you got those Hungarians or Austrians...wherever they're from," Potts said, "I heard some grew up with those fancy Lipizzaner stallions. Guess we'll see what they can do in the Olympics with a few gray john mules."

Lincoln smiled and leaned into the mule's ear, whispering something to the animal.

Potts laughed. "What're you telling that creature, Lincoln? I know he understands English...probably could speak back to you, if it had half a mind."

"Jes' a little secret we share...jes' a little secret." Lincoln patted the mule's neck and walked toward the corral gate, wiping at the dirt-caked sweat on his arms and chest.

The first "International Olympics" at the BWS Gilboa encampment took place the year of the flooded cofferdam. Seven men had drowned, each from one of the different camp "nations"– "Harps, Colcannon Heath, Lattimer Fields, Three Barred Cross, Halifax Wharf, and a close friend of Johnny of the Angel from "Il Palazzo Alpini." The seventh body retrieved was a young German intern who'd been assisting the visiting paleontologists from Berlin. It had been a mystery why he'd been down in the cofferdam at night. There'd been gossip, but most were just feeling the pain of what seemed like an international incident.

With work on the Dam stopped once again, Sidney Clapp came up with an idea to both distract and engage the camps. The BWS International Olympics pitted the camp nations against one another in friendly competition – organized fisticuffs, ball games, track and field scrambles, wrestling, target shooting; and even some locally inspired events – timber splitting, concrete weight throws, and hand-over-hand suspension cable sprints. But it was the 'Chariot Races' that drew the biggest crowds. There was a lot of betting, odds set up at the FingerBreak. But most came just to watch the draft mules, three to a team with heavy leather harnesses strapped to buckboards festooned as roman chariots, lurching around the leveled half-mile track on the old Hops field below Jenna and Gianni's house.

Lincoln Lincoln and his three-mule team from "Old Dominion" had taken the gold both years – a polished Saint-Gaudens double-eagle twenty dollar gold coin presented by Hugh Nawn. It didn't bother Lincoln that he had to give the coin back at the end of the Olympics for some paper scrip good at the canteen or company store; he was in it for the pride. This year, he was going for the Trifecta.

"Well, look who's coming," Potts said, turning from the fence rail, "It's Nanny of the Angel. Nurse Jenna sure has your friend on short reins."

Lincoln stepped out of the corral and closed the gate behind him. He had a big smile on his face as he watched Johnny of the Angel carefully steering a double high-wheeled pram toward the two men. Johnny's two-year-old son Xavi was on his knees in one of the pram beds, holding on to the sides of the pram, wide-eyed as it rocked back and forth over the rutted and hooved ground.

As Johnny drew close, a smaller and younger child could be seen lying on its back in the other pram bed. The child was too young to be recognized by gender, but the three men knew that the baby was Lincoln and Billie Kinsolver's boy. Unlike his pram sidekick, Linc Jr. seemed unhappy about the ride and was wailing, snot-nosed at the sky.

Lincoln reached in and lifted his son out of the pram, rocking him gently in one arm as he picked the mucus from the child's nose with his free hand. Linc Junior sniffled into silence and nestled into Lincoln's damp chest. Within moments he was asleep.

"You got the touch, Lincoln," Potts laughed, "...you got the touch." The sheriff pulled up on his suspenders, then patted his belly. "I better get going, see how they're doing over at the Shandaken. I'll see you at the track." As he passed the pram, he nodded to Johnny of the Angel and tousled Xavi's hair. "You still got that gun I've been hearing about, DeAngelus?"

Johnny looked taken aback, but before he could answer, Potts raised a hand to stop him. "I don't want to know; you just keep it out of sight so it don't fall into the wrong hands. I've got enough trouble with some of the toughies trying to sneak off with the BWS firearms after the pistol shoots. That's one Olympic event that was one hell of a bad idea."

As he walked off, Potts flexed his shoulders a few times as if to feel the reassuring weight of his own firearm holstered at his arm pit.

"Best you keep quiet on this, Johnny, least 'till we find it," Lincoln said, "Probably a mistake letting the boy see it."

Johnny of the Angel nodded, "You are right. I just did not know he was there. At the window, when I take out the pistol...I should not have left it there, left it behind."

"He's like that; always underfoot, popping up in folk's business unexpected like. JayJay shouldn't have been up at the camps." Lincoln looked down at the child in his arms, "Guess he's just trying to figure out who he is, wherever it takes him."

Johnny of the Angel shook his head in disagreement. "I think that boy is bad, un ragazzino subdolo,...like his father." Looking down at his own boy, he fingered one of the scar lines on his face and said quietly, "That man Gallagher keeps coming, Lincoln. Ever since you and Miss Billie. And now with your bambino. He not finished with you, I think."

Lincoln nodded solemnly, gently put his sleeping child back into the pram. He knew Johnny was right.

*   *

Eli Gallagher had made no secret of his anger that Billie Kinsolver was lost to him forever. He'd never been able to let her go, not in his mind. Even after she'd returned from Cuba with the Goldring woman, he thought the time away might make her see things differently, see him differently. While she was gone, he'd tried hard to straighten up, stop his drinking and whoring up in the Flats. He even got Piedmont to let him join the house-moving crew, hoping Billie's brother would come around and finally put in a good word. Piedmont gave him the work, glad enough that Eli was finding a way to be useful, but at the same time, Piedmont knew what was what with the man; he didn't really expect Eli to last long on the straight and narrow. Billie's baby twisted him up and around all over again.

No one other than Lincoln, Gianni and Jenna knew that Billie had a baby coming. Piedmont thought his sister was just getting lazy and gaining weight. She'd been distant with him after her trip with Winifred. But he'd not been too focused on it since Winifred had withdrawn from him as well.

He should have known.

It had been an unusual few years in Gilboa. Perhaps it was the stress, the feeling of End Times, that was driving couples to at least secure their place in a new generation. It began with the birth of Jenna and Johnny's son shortly after their marriage. That marriage had been expected for a while; no one had been carrying a shotgun. But, after that, unwed mothers and their newborns began filling Jenna's infirmary. The wailing, reverberating off the curved corrugated iron of the Nissen Hut housing the other patients, got so bad that the BWS had to requisition another Hut from the motor pool for a maternity ward. Jenna got some additional help, but still barely had time to breastfeed Xaviero.

Then it was Winifred and Piedmont's turn.

Winifred learned that she was carrying a week after the collapse of the cofferdam. Much of her work and equipment had been lost in the flood. The quarry floor where the lithic traces of the Devonian Forest had been carefully mapped sat under a foot of mud and debris. Clapp and Nawn were sympathetic, but their attention was on designing a better cofferdam, not shoveling muck in the interest of scientific research. Winifred was called back to Albany and re-assigned by Director Clarke to other projects until – and if – the Gilboa site could be re-opened.

Piedmont Kinsolver was uncertain if it was Winifred's pregnancy or her anguish over losing the forest floor for another 400 million years that began to feed her depression and distance from him. The distance was emotional and physical. For much of the late fall in 1922 and early spring of the following year she was away, traveling first to the newly discovered Ordovician echinoderm fossils in the Bromide Formation of Oklahoma's Arbuckle mountains, then north to map Devonian jumping bristletail fossils in Canada's Bay of Gaspé.

But she was unhappy. Her letters to Piedmont became briefer and less often. By March, she was suffering from nervous exhaustion. She'd been hiding her pregnancy from Clarke, but he could see she was not herself. With his blessing, she took a leave from the Museum and went to stay with her sister Mattie in New York. Piedmont believed it was there and then that the die was cast.

When Winifred wrote to tell him that she was considering aborting the fetus, he didn't believe her or, at least, didn't want to. He was still feeling ashamed of his recklessness both with her and Mattie; it was likely not the first time he'd found himself becoming a father. Nevertheless, he'd planned to do right by this one. When he learned of her plans to travel to her uncle's botanical plantation in Soledad, Cuba, he understood that it was not to be. Abortions were legal in Cuba. He offered to go with her, but she put him off, saying it was women's business. Instead, Winifred asked Billie to accompany her. It had been Mattie's idea – Billie Kinsolver was already a keeper of secrets, and Mattie already a keeper of one of Piedmont's children.

On their return from Cuba a few months later, Winifred and Billie separated at the port of Miami. Winifred boarded the Flagler Flyer to stay with Endurance Fuller in Princeton, and Billie continued north on the Seaboard Air Line train to New York with her baby nephew; Mattie Goldring met them at Grand Central Station. The boy's name was Livingston and Mattie's house on Bathgate Avenue in the Bronx would be the only home he would ever know.

What had truly been in Winifred's mind about the change in her body was a mystery to everyone but her. But Billie was only mildly surprised when she realized that Winifred had chosen to have the baby and give it up rather than terminate the pregnancy. Either way, Billie understood that Winifred could not be a mother, not now; she had come too far with her research, too invested in the significance of her fieldwork for future generations. The earth's young life was just beginning to be understood, and she had fought too hard to have her voice heard in the company of the men. The young life in her own body would be raised close by where he'd be in good hands, family hands – in the company of women.

It had been a difficult decision. Nevertheless, Winifred felt that, as a woman, it was her duty to *women*. She well understood that many would see only the irony; the neglecting of her sex – *The Venus of Willendorf*, woman as mother.

But she'd felt alone. There were so few other women who'd been able to follow her calling, and the scant numbers were spread far apart across the sciences. And there were so many others, frustrated by the conventions of society, the inventions of civilized life. Young curious women who had craned their necks to see past the limitations on them, imagining other ways to be in the world, other lives they might be able to lead, only to be frustrated by the opportunities afforded only to the men around them. And Men had let down Mankind. Life's origins had not set a value within the species. It had been the male taxonomists who had settled on the Latin genus *Homo* rather than *Femina*. Winifred felt that their world had overlooked the earth, and she would commit herself to its true nature.

And so, she returned to the Museum with a new mission – to teach the order of things to young women. Arriving back in Albany, she presented Clarke with two ideas. The first was to establish a science program for the teenage girls of The State Normal School using the museum exhibitions as a teaching tool. The second was the creation of the Gilboa Forest Diorama as its first lesson.

*   *

Lincoln walked slowly back to the fence line and picked up his shirt that was hanging on a post at the corral gate. Wiping the sweat from his chest and arms with it, he said, "Miss Winifred's come back, 'that so?"

Johnny nodded. "Si, yesterday morning, but she gone again. Got me hammering her stones. They go back with her. The fossils."

"She see Piedmont?" Lincoln asked, pulling on his shirt.

Johnny shook his head. "She come and go. She no care for the Olympics. Jenna think she return tomorrow after the crowd is leaving and maybe she gonna tell him the truth, but I don't think so. Jenna's still sorry for telling me too, says we got to stay out of it. Not our business to know. She means it."

"Good lord, pity the man," Lincoln said. He was looking down at the two boys in the pram and wondering what Piedmont would make of the surprise of his own son.

"And all we all did is make more of 'em," he said, wistfully, "...Boys; not a baby girl in the bunch."

Two of Lincoln's Virginians, Dexter Twincoat and his brother Pontrain, sauntered into the corral area carrying heavy leather harnesses and straps. "Hi-yo, Lincoln Lincoln," one of them called out, "The Lawd gonna be on on our side today? Git us that gold coin again?"

Lincoln laughed, "You best ask him, Dexter...that mule's risen to his name every time before, don't know why he'd stop now."

"You jes' keep sayin' your prayers, Dexter," Pontrain said brusquely, pushing past his brother to the corral gate. "But right now, the holy trinity's waitin' on you."

Johnny of the Angel shook his head and began rocking the pram back and forth. Xaviero had begun whimpering. "I know how much you like horse flesh, Lincoln, but naming those three like that...it's a sacrilege."

"I told you before, Angel, they're mules and hinnys, not horses. Jack donkeys and mares, jennys and stallions, different species of God's creatures crossbred to show off the Lord's miracles. They weren't on the Ark, but here they stand today."

Lincoln winked at Dexter. "You and Pontrain get the three mules ready. I'll meet you at the Flat's when the races are setting. Right now, me and Johnny are going to work on some music for tonight at the FingerBreak, gonna teach him a new version of *The Camptown Races*." Lincoln looked down in the pram and adjusted the blanket on his son who had joined Xaviero in fussing. "That is, if young Linc and Johnny's boy here will allow."

Sheriff Potts rode his horse down the western slope of Pine Mountain onto the service road to the Shandaken Tunnel Intake Chamber at the edge of the mountain's excavated foothill. The Chamber was almost finished although Schoharie water had already begun running into its southbound tunnel toward the Ashokan. A final concrete pour for a deep-set tieback block to help buttress the main wall of the Intake was coming very early the next morning, and the formwork was fully set with the lugged steel rebars tied in place at intervals.

The wooden forms had been set and staked hard against a vertical cut in Pine Mountain as if the mountain's foothill had been run through a table saw. The service road had also been carved into the hill, on a horizontal blade, its reservoir edge flush with the top of the formwork to allow Hugh Nawn's new Barrymore concrete mixers close enough to empty their loads.

This was not a road for the idle traveler, Potts thought to himself. He walked his horse slowly, peering down into the formwork to see just how far the concrete would fall before reaching the footing. All he could see was a distance disappearing into darkness, even with the high sun overhead.

Arriving at the Chamber's gatehouse, Potts dismounted, tied his horse to an oak sapling and walked over to join Thaddeus Merriman, Sidney Clapp, and Reasonable Pelt on the Chamber's stone terrace. The three men from the Board of Water Supply were looking across the valley's basin, shielding their eyes from the low morning sun. Smoke was rising out of what would soon be the reservoir's east bank.

"Good morning, Potts," said Clapp, turning to the sheriff. "You know Reasonable, of course, but I'm not sure you've been properly introduced to Chief Engineer Merriman."

Merriman tucked a clipboard under his arm and shook hands with the sheriff. The two men eyed one another, both knowing full well the job that Chief of The Bureau, Potts, had been asked to do.

"They're still down there, Mr. Potts. We can't be having this, now that we've got the water running," Merriman said, solemnly, "These folks need to accept what can not be undone."

"It's still Mister Gallagher and a few others. He's got that poor boy with him as well," Reasonable said, "Mrs. Stinson tried to talk to him. At least to let the boy out of there before things got any more out of hand."

"Burn 'em out or flood 'em out...some just don't see the difference, I guess. Not much of a choice," Potts said, looking down at the fresh water flowing underfoot into the chamber's headwall below the terrace. "I hoped it wouldn't come to this." The weight of his shoulder holster hung heavy under his coat.

Across the excavated basin, along the bottom of the east bank, the abandoned town of Gilboa looked small and desolate. Most of the main street buildings, with the exception of Mackey's church, were already running down. None had been painted in years, some of the roofs had caved, side walls were leaning against one another across property lines. Others lay in charred heaps, the smoke still rising from them, thanks to the 'back burners' and the new policy of the Board of Water Supply.

It had been seven years since the work on the Dam had begun. Plenty of time, Potts thought, for people to get used to things. But pockets of resistance kept showing up. There had even been rumors of outsiders, agitators against 'The City' coming north, anarchists like the ones who'd bombed Wall Street a few years before. The camps were made uneasy with talk of Bolsheviks and rabble-rousing Internationalists.

Potts knew that the holdouts in the town were mostly local. They'd squat in homes that weren't even their own, believing that The Bureau couldn't or wouldn't force them out physically. It was Merriman who authorized what he called 'fire control technicians,' under Potts' command, to keep tabs on the resistors. If any of the squatters stepped out of the house, even for a few minutes, to go to the privy or to pick up food left by friends, the 'back burners' would sweep in and light it up. Can't live in the ashes, Merriman would say. Potts and a few of his best deputies in The Bureau didn't like the practice, but he had to agree with Merriman on one thing. You need to accept what can not be undone.

At a second-floor window in the old Stinson & Bidwell General Store, Elohim Gallagher chewed on a twist of beef jerky and watched the BWS men standing on the Shandaken Tunnel Intake Chamber's terrace on the other side of the basin. It had only been a few days since the first of the Schoharie's rising waters had been turned into the recently completed tunnel, drilled for eighteen miles through the southern mountains to the main holding reservoir at Ashokan. The temporary diversion dam that had been built to shunt the creek's flow to the tunnel was not quite finished but it was already doing its work. *Killing two birds with one stone*, Merriman had reasoned to his staff – supplying the first of Schoharie water to the City and providing dry ground for the final placement of the big Dam's low-level outlet into its stepped spillway.

The diversion had been placed just to the north of the Intake Chamber's cast iron sluice gates housed within its inlet structure. The inlet structure itself had been housed – or disguised as some locals saw it – within what looked like one of the grand manor homes from the Prattsville days. The building, backed up against Pine Mountain, was a hodgepodge of styles concocted by the BWS engineering staff. A three-winged Federalist stone-ender with Georgian windows and huge rusticated Romanesque arches set within its center volume.

Gallagher shook his head thinking about it. *Six hundred million gallons of water lost each day into that tunnel...and for what, and for whom. Sure as hell not me, nor anyone else who grow'd up in this valley. And those rat bastards, they done the city men's bidding...Lincoln Lincoln, DeAngelus, and the rest. Christ, DeAngelus and the other wops even cut the stone for that piece of shit building just sitting over there, laughing back at our town, nothing living inside it but fancy machines.*

Gallagher tore off another piece of jerky, snarling at the window. He heard JayJay coming up stairs.

"Pa, I wanna see the race,...kin I?" the boy asked, stopping at the door. He was hesitant to enter the room and bother Gallagher; he'd learned it was always best to keep a bit of distance between himself and the temper of the man whom folks had said was his father.

"Not gonna happen, JayJay," Gallagher said over his shoulder, "I need you right here. Besides, those colored boys just gonna win again. Ain't nobody 'round here can stop 'em." Gallagher turned toward the boy. "And you call me 'Pa' one more time, I'm liable to whip you on the head with this." He pulled a small pistol from his waistband and waved it at JayJay. "Nobody knows who your Pa is."

"I did what you told me,...I got that gun," JayJay said, quietly, holding back tears. "Mister DeAngelus didn't see me. I did good, didn't I?"

Gallagher looked down at the Bulldog .32 in his hand and fingered the initials carved in the handle – *JJG*. "Weren't ever his anyway," he said.

Elohim Gallagher had hidden his surprise from the boy when JayJay handed him the pistol that he'd stolen from Il Palazzo Alpini. He wasn't surprised at what the boy had done. After all, he'd been the one to send him up to the camps to steal it after the boy told him he'd seen a small firearm there. What knocked Gallagher back on his heels was his realization that the gun had once been his – a family heirloom that had been tossed into the Central Park Reservoir seven years earlier. If it had been underwater all those years, one would never have known it. The gunmetal was polished bright and the wood of the handle still hard as hickory. And the dark initials as legible as when he'd first seen the gun as a boy. How the hell had it ended up with DeAngelus?

He'd always wondered about Johnny of the Angel, the scars on the face of the young Italian,...he felt he'd seen them before. The Bulldog .32 was a reminder. During the Columbus Day celebration in Central Park back in 1917, he'd been too drunk to remember much, but he had not forgotten that the gun had been there with him. When JayJay returned from his errand and placed it in his hand more memories came along with it. One was of a young Italian soldier with the rain running down in rivulets between the raised scars across his face.

"Tell you what, JayJay," Gallagher said, "C'mon over here." He put down the gun and, reaching into his pocket, pulled out a deck of cards. "Let's us play some. This gun's making me feel a little frisky."

JayJay's face fell. He knew what Gallagher meant, but he was afraid to turn and run.

It had started a few months back when Gallagher came home one night from the FingerBreak. He was drunk as usual, but he'd managed to win a deck of cards in a poker game. He roused JayJay from his bed and began showing him the silver tint photos of naked women printed on each card in the deck – different bodies, different poses, and different well-dressed men being serviced...in different suits – Spades, Hearts, Clubs and Diamonds. As JayJay was drowsily looking at the cards, Gallagher pulled out his cock and made JayJay take a hold of it, said he was going to teach him about men and women. After a few minutes, moving about, Gallagher gave out a strange groan and fell back, asleep on JayJay's bed. His hand was still gripped on top of JayJay's, and both of their hands were wet and smelling bad.

"Ah, never mind,...another time." Gallagher winked at the boy. He put the deck away and picked up the gun. Pointing the .32 out the window, he turned cold again. "Maybe you ought'a go watch them boys and their mules," he said, "I think I got some other business to tend to up at the FingerBreak."

JayJay turned and ran down the stairs, passing Gust Coykendall who lay dozing on top of the empty store counter. Gallagher heard the store door slam and turned back to the window watching the small boy skip-jump down what little was left of Gilboa's Main Street. He figured the BWS men across the creek were watching as well. *Fuck 'em*, he thought to himself as he stood up and tucked his uncle's gun back into his waistband. All morning he'd been wondering if that gun had come back to him for a reason – maybe it was telling him to finish what he'd tried to start. If he no longer could stop the men who'd allowed the damming of his valley, maybe he could put down a few who'd done the work.

"Wake your ass up, Gust," Gallagher yelled at Coykendall as he came downstairs, "You gotta pay attention. Hell's fire's comin' for you soon enough, but don't let the backburners do the devil's work for him. I'm going up to the FingerBreak."

Gust sat up and swung his legs over the edge of the counter, shaking himself awake. "That JayJay I heard rompin' his way out of here?" he asked, with a loud yawn, "You lettin' him go to the races?"

"Don't matter where he's off to. You just keep an eye on Virgil's store. It's the least we can do now that his wife is off prancin' with that citified clerk from the BWS."

"Aw, Reasonable's not so bad, and Dorlene's got those two girls to raise by herself. Christ, I bet the way them girls shine for JayJay, they'd take him off your hands in a heartbeat."

Gallagher sent a middle finger over his shoulder at Gust and walked out the door. Wincing at the slam of the door for the second time, Gust lay back down on the store counter. He had two thoughts in mind – one was to fix that damn door; the other was to try and fix Eli.

Gust often wondered if it was all that grave digging that had soured Eli so. Even he'd had some pretty bad and wild dreams while they were clearing out the cemetery at the foot of the Dam. But they'd finished the last of that work over a year ago, Gust was sleeping just fine now. And that black fellow, Lincoln Lincoln, he never seemed to mind hauling those coffins.

Gust worried that that was the real problem...the black fellow. Him and Billie Kinsolver. It had been hard enough that Eli had never been able to make headway with that girl's affections, but her taking up with Lincoln Lincoln must have stung him good. And then, mixing the races like that with a little baby, well, that was some bad business. Even to Gust.

Nevertheless, a man has just got to accept his lot and stop making others pay for it.

Gust wasn't the smartest of men; hell, Eli had reminded him of that countless times. But he could see that his friend had become a worse bully than ever. Gust could forgive the stealing at the graveyard, the whoring at the FingerBreak, and even the bragging about screwing the Goldring girl at the Manorkill. But even a slow-witted fellow like himself can only be pushed so far.

Gust's thinking had riled him up too much for napping. He sat up again and pushed himself off the counter. "Sorry, Virgil Bidwell Stinson," he said out loud, addressing the ghost of his long dead friend, "Can't help you any longer, a man jes' gotta 'cept their lot."

Gust Coykendall headed out the door and didn't look back when he heard the sound of breaking glass and the muffled voices of men entering the doomed general store.

At the Shandaken Tunnel terrace, Sidney Clapp pointed toward the man leaving the Stinson & Bidwell General Store. "That's Coykendall; he's the last of them. The technicians are moving in. Lord, I hope we don't have to do this much longer." He turned his gaze to Daniel Mackey's Methodist Church further up the empty street. The gold crucifix on the steeple had caught the sun and flashed briefly at him before a cloud interfered. Not being much of a religious man himself, Clapp still appreciated that Merriman had put the church off limits to the backburners and allowed the church sexton to maintain the polish on the steeple's cross. But he knew it was only a gesture to the Reverend Mackey. *Burn 'em out or flood 'em out*...the church stood on the wrong side of the diversion dam; it would feel the rising water first.

He thought again of the night of the flooded cofferdam, the gathering in the church and of the Goldring woman; how quietly she'd sat as the shared fate of her ancient forest and the town of Gilboa was being decided.

Two years later, the 'cast' traces of the Gilboa Forest still lay under the mud and most of the fossils that had been saved had been trucked to Albany. There was an exhibition planned; not to celebrate the town, but to celebrate the time-bound layers of the earth beneath its abandoned foundations. Soon to become yet another of the earth's sedimentary layers, the "settling" of Gilboa was now on nature's time, not mankind's.

Clapp felt sorry that he had ever doubted the "woman" from the museum. She had taught both him and Mr. Hugh Nawn a good lesson, not the least of which was that the intertwined histories of the earth and humankind were embedded in the ground upon which a man – or a woman – only briefly walks.

∗   ∗

Fifty miles to the north and east of Gilboa, Winifred Goldring was at the museum, standing in front of a small group of teenage girls from The State Normal School. It was her students first visit to the museum and only eight girls had come. Winifred had anticipated a small showing but had hoped for a larger one. Still, she thought to herself, they were brave to have come at all. She imagined the teasing - the science of geology was still as unlady-like as when she and her sister Mattie had been students at the school. The "science" the school believed most valuable was in its mission statement: "*to train young women in the science of education and the art of teaching.*"

Mattie had followed the call in becoming a teacher like most of the girls who attended the School, even though she'd agreed with her younger sister that teaching children was not unlike bearing and raising them – it was important work, but always women's work. When Winifred left the school to study the natural sciences at Wellesley College, Mattie was in full support of her and had always remained so...doing the 'women's work' for both of them so Winifred could have the life Mattie had wanted, but feared, for herself.

"Rocks keep time," Winifred said, smiling at her students, "To think like a geologist is to focus your mind's eye not only on what you can see on the surface but also on what lies below it. Every outcrop is a portal to an earlier and future world. The past has directed its present form, and its present form will direct what and where it will be."

One of the girls raised her hand. "Will you use real rocks behind the glass?" she asked.

"Of course," Winifred answered, "the diorama must be as true to Life as possible."

"But how will you make the trees for the forest, the sperm...sperma..." the girl sighed with exasperation, "...the Gilboa tree!"

Two of the girls covered their mouths to stifle giggles.

"*Eo-sperma-topteris,*" Winifred said, "*Eospermatopteris erianus...*I know it's a mouthful, ladies. *Eospermatopteris* is the name I gave it; it's derived from Latin, and it means..."

"*You* named it?" one of the gigglers asked, interrupting her.

"Yes, I named its genus. You see, in a sense, I was the one who discovered the forest. Others had found the petrified stumps earlier but could not identify the *tree*. It was only after I found the fossilized branches of its canopy that we finally knew what a tree almost four million years ago had actually looked like. And I was given the honor of naming the Gilboa Tree in the traditional language of science – Latin." Winifred smiled again at the girls and added, "Of course, there is a bit of poetry in its translation. It means 'Dawn of the Seed Fern'. Does anyone know what makes a fern with seeds special?"

"Ferns don't have no seeds."

Winifred looked with surprise over at the girl who'd spoken. "That's exactly right. The leaves of the Gilboa Tree looked like large ferns, and ferns typically reproduce with spores, like mosses, while trees grow from seeds. That's why the traces of the seeds that we found with the branchlets were so special, A *fern* tree...So, what's your name, young lady?"

"It's Belle, ma'am," the girl said. She looked uncomfortable and

304

stepped closer to one of the other girls. She was younger than the other girls, early teens at best, and she was dressed differently, more poorly. Her black hair hung loose at her shoulders and her complexion was dark as if she'd spent a great deal of time in the sun.

"She came with me, Miss Goldring," The girl who spoke linked her arm with Belle's. "She's my cousin from Florida. She's visiting and I thought it would be alright if she came with me. She's real smart...about nature and things. She even knows who you are."

"Well, I'll be. You're the young girl Mr. Fuller wrote me about. You're from Princeton, is that right?"

"Not really, ma'am," Belle said looking down and scuffing one shoe on the other. "I live most of the time in Indiantown."

The two gigglers nudged each other but held their tongues as Winifred lowered her head at them. Turning back to Belle, she said, "You are more than welcome here, Belle." Then addressing all of the students, she added, "In fact, girls, Belle is not only correct about ferns, but she has already helped with the exhibit.

"One of you asked me how we'll make the trees in the diorama, how we can make them life-like without their being alive...would you like to tell them, Belle?"

"They're gonna be real," Belle answered, jutting out her chin, "Ferns...and some sawgrass palmetto and palm leaves." She was feeling more self-assured in the company of the older girls, but kept her arm linked with her cousin's.

"That's right," Winifred said, reaching over to a nearby table and picking up a notebook. She opened it and flipped through a few pages before turning it to face the girls.

"This is a drawing of the Gilboa Tree. It was done by a friend of mine who lives there...in Gilboa. Or who once lived there, I should say.

305

I'm sure you all have heard about the large Dam they're building. The town will be gone soon, under water, and, with it, the forest floor where this tree once grew. But notice the leaves in the drawing. They look like ferns and palm fronds, and that is exactly what we're going to use in the exhibit; special cuttings that will be coming from Florida and Belle here knows them well, I believe."

"I helped pick them out, me and my friend Saskia," Belle said, excitedly, "Her brother works on the plantation, and he let us help. Mister Fuller said he could."

"We've arranged for the plantation to send us their ferns every month or so, that way we'll be able to keep them fresh inside the diorama. It is important that they match and blend with the trees painted in the background. Science and art and real life, all coming together to tell the story about our most distant ancestor.

"Older than what we call the Cenozoic Era with its many types of mammals including, and only quite lately, all of us." Winifred said, waving her arms over the girls. "...Or the earlier Mesozoic Era with its great but doomed dinosaurs. No, our diorama goes further back in time to the Paleozoic Era with its murky coal-swamps, scuttling trilobites, and, most significantly, its Lungfish at the swamp's edge, gasping for air."

"Can we see it? Can we see the Lungfish?" Belle's cousin asked.

Winifred shook her head, "I'm afraid I can only show you a drawing of one of the Lungfish fossils here in the museum. The Lungfish for our diorama is being prepared by a taxidermist at the Museum of Natural History in New York City. It came to us from Australia a few weeks ago, and it's almost unchanged, anatomically, from the lobe-finned fish of the Devonian Period, millions of years ago. In a sense, this Australian Lungfish, *Neoceratodus forsteri*, is a *living* fossil. Next week, I'll be taking the train to the City to see it for its final mounting. Everyone here at the museum is very excited."

"Can people become fossils, too?...like animals and trees, after they die?" Belle asked.

Winifred smiled at the young girl. "Well, firstly, you *are* an animal. And secondly, you'd have to be very lucky. It takes millions of years to become a fossil, so you'd have to be buried very deep where your remains could survive the first hours, days, centuries, and thousands of years without being dug up or exposed to scavengers, including the scavengers we can't see like bacteria."

"Like if you're safe inside a coffin?"

"No, no...it's better *not* to be in a coffin so mineral-rich water can flow easily through your bones, filling the empty spaces with minerals like iron and calcium. It's called permineralization."

"But if you're buried so deep, how can you ever get discovered?"

Winifred tilted her head and raised her finger, "That's the other part of being lucky. To be discovered as a fossil, you would also need to survive the slow shifting continents that build mountains and lift your remains high enough where erosion can expose them, still in one piece, to the paleontologists.

"And you know, every fossil tells a story, about the environment you lived in, how you died...and even what you were doing at the moment you died," Winifred looked around at the girls, "...You understand?"

Most of her pupils were staring back at her, wide-eyed and mouths open but silent. Only Belle nodded her head with excitement.

Winifred turned back to the notebook in her hand. As she opened it again, it slipped from her grip and fell to the floor. Belle let go of her cousin's arm and ran forward to pick it up. She held it out with both hands to Winifred as if it was a holy book; her thumbs framing the gilded 'No. 8' on its black braided cover. As Winifred gratefully smiled at her and took back the book, Belle wondered, with marvel, at what might be in the other seven of Miss Goldring's books. Stepping back to her cousin, she felt her heart leap with the thought that she could someday become a woman like Miss Goldring.

Winifred, in turn, wondered what lay ahead for Belle. Her own life was a hard example.

After the girls had left the museum and were shepherded back to the Normal school, Winifred returned to her office and re-read Endurance Fuller's letter for the third time. Fuller had written about the precocious girl from Florida. She was a collector of rocks, soil samples, plant life, insects – alive and dead, animal skeletons, and even scat, if it was hard enough to sit on a shelf in the small makeshift museum she'd made out one of the plantation's run-down coops. Belle had tagged all her specimens and charmed just about everyone on the plantation along the way, including Fuller's new foreman, a young man named Rembrandt Stikkey.

Fuller's letter spoke of other matters as well – the logistics of sending up the ferns and palm fronds, delivery schedules, shipping invoices, storage needs in Albany. But he had also included a personal appeal to Winifred, expressing his hope that she might change her mind about the child. He understood the importance to her of her work, but it was a man's right to know, he wrote...particularly a *good* man, like Piedmont. She could trust him to do the right thing.

The right thing. Winifred fanned her face with the letter as if to shake off the words that she so much wanted to believe, as if to re-set them in an earlier time. Fuller did not know that Piedmont had been a father twice.

The sisters had had trouble talking about it. Mattie Goldring had made her separate peace, and too much time had passed for unsettling the world she'd chosen – her six-year-old daughter would not know her

308

father, that was clear to both of the sisters. But Winifred's heartbreak and disappointment on learning about Mattie's sweet little Mina had not taken root; she could not shake off Piedmont. Fuller's plea had not fallen on deaf ears. Tomorrow, she would return to Gilboa and explain everything to Piedmont – her distance, her absence, her willingness to forgive, and her need of two things: his unswerving love in the years ahead and his unwavering support for her embrace of epochs past. If both were possible, she would then go to the city and bring back their boy from Bathgate Avenue.

* 13 *

Shem's FingerBreak...

Gust Coykendall
1993, Conro's Flats NY
"...when things are past where do they go? Is there some secret place where they exist and, if so, are they past there, or present...they cannot be past there otherwise they would be somewhere else, but if present then nothing is truly past?"(St. Augustine)

I AM SITTING WITH my great-aunt Jenna in her kitchen, holding one of her hands in both of mine. I am gentle with it, as her hand is mostly bone and aged flesh, thin as dry parchment like the insentient Lungfish in the attic. But Jenna is in pain. Her jaw is clenched, and the good side of her face is tensed as she holds back tears. I have been talking with her, questions mostly, about the events described in Winifred's eighth notebook, and she is trying hard not to show the heaviness of her heart over events that occurred almost seventy years ago.

The lock of hair is on the kitchen table. Three strands of different colors and textures woven into a small talisman-like braid. One of the strands is clearly from a child.

"She must have meant that for you," Jenna says, looking wistfully at the braid, "It's your family; the outer strands are Piedmont's and Winifred's...and that soft one in the middle, that's your father."

"Before she gave him to Mattie," I say, pointedly. I can't help but think that if the braid is my family, Mattie is missing from it. Not because she raised my father, but because Piedmont sits on both sides of my family tree. And Belle, too, the woman who mothered me in Mina's place. And Mina...

"Who is Gust Coykendall?" I ask, changing the subject.

"Oh, he was a local boy, one of the grave diggers. I never much cared for him, even after he showed up at the museum."

"And the gun? It was Gianni's?"

Jenna nods, solemnly. "Winifred never told me that Mister Coykendall had given her Gianni's gun, just that he'd come forward to tell her what happened."

"Is he still living?...Coykendall?"

"I don't know. Last I heard, he was still back there, living in Conro's Flats...in that damned saloon, of all places. If he's alive, he won't be much longer; he's got to be near on to either side of my age."

"The FingerBreak?"

"Yes...where all the trouble started."

Jenna sits up and withdraws her hand from mine. "What have you told Delano and Trifina? Do they know about the gun...and the Senator's part in it?"

"Not yet" I answer, shaking my head, "I need to make sense of it first."

I have not yet been wholly forthcoming to Trifina or Del about my discovery in the attic for a number of reasons. I am still sorting out Winifred's account of 1924 and the year that followed.

Last night, I shared what I'd learned of our families – the patriarchs – with the two of them. There was closure for Del and Trifina, knowing where the bodies of our grandfathers could be found, knowing that what had been suspected had been confirmed. Each man had been as different from the other two as any man could be. Piedmont Kinsolver, Lincoln Lincoln, and Gianni DeAngelus – different origins, different lineages, different cultures, from different places in the world.

But, for a brief time, they had lived together, loved together, sired children together...and died together. It seemed only fitting that they be buried together...forever.

I say their bodies could be found, but they will not be. Not unless the Schoharie Dam is breached, and the Reservoir gives them up.

They are there, somewhere inside the Dam wall, but the human remains cited in the draft of the *Board of Water Resource Management Stakeholder's Report* that Waterhouse Hawkins had shared with us in the Gatehouse were not theirs. The femur found by the welder on the filter screen at the Shandaken Tunnel Intake turned out to be from an unidentified woman. It was not Mina Goldring,...they had found her at the time of her drowning. The bone was more recent. The New York State Police and the FBI believed the woman had probably been murdered elsewhere and dumped into the concealing depths of the Reservoir; just another grisly and unsolvable crime.

As far as the soft tissue found at the crack in the Dam wall at the Low Water Outlet, that proved to be only a bit of farm animal flesh snagged on an exposed re-bar in the fissure.

Nevertheless, in Winifred's notebook, she had written that the men were there, locked within the last thick walls of concrete that had been poured at the Intake Chamber.

Despite the sense of acceptance that both Del and Trifina expressed over this long past time, I wonder if their dreams last night had re-lived the event as much as my dream did.

Then again, I had left out the mention of the other items I discovered inside the Lungfish, and my troubled sense that the accounting was not over.

I understand the significance of the braid. It binds me tightly to Winifred, but the small handgun surprised me. According to Winifred – or more exactly, according to a man named Gust Coykendall – it was last fired in that year of 1924 by Elohim Gallagher's young son, the boy JayJay...the man who is known today as State Senator O'Graéghall Van Pelt.

The story behind the shooting was difficult to read. It is one thing to discover a man's true identity, it is another thing to learn what he did to make him hide from it.

Winifred had not witnessed the shooting or the fight that had preceded it. She had not been there. And the authorities investigating the death of Elohim Gallagher and the contemporaneous disappearance of Piedmont Kinsolver, Lincoln Lincoln, and Gianni DeAngelus, had come up empty on both counts. But there had been a witness. Gust Coykendall had been there, wishing he wasn't, just above the unfinished formwork of the Shandaken Intake Chamber. He saw the whole thing...and the whole thing, he intended to keep to himself.

But apparently some things just don't hold for men who are born with either a big conscience or a big mouth. Fifteen months later, Coykendall changed his mind and showed up at the State Museum in Albany asking for Winifred Goldring.

"It was the day that Trifina's granddad won the big horse race,... later,...that evening," Jenna says, "He and my Gianni should never have gone up there; they should have stayed home with Billie and me...home with their boys, and Piedmont would never have had to go after them. But they went to the FingerBreak to do their music and show off that damned gold coin," Jenna shakes her head and sighs, "Did you know that after the three of them went missing, the men from the Board came after Billie for that gold coin; they even came after me. That was one of the reasons Billie left for Florida. Get as far away from the trouble as she could.

"I had a mind to go with her, just to keep our little boys together. But Winifred was working so hard at the museum, and I knew she would want me to stay close to Mattie and your father...her boy. She needed her sisters."

Jenna lowers her head. "Didn't do much of a job with that, I guess," she says.

"Sure you did, Aunt Jenna. We're all here aren't we...Del, Trifina and I?"

I reach again for her hand, but she withholds it and leans back in her chair, cocking her head and eyeing me suspiciously. "You're not thinking of going there, are you? Up to Gilboa...up to the Flats?"

She has read my mind, but before I can fashion a proper answer, Trifina appears in the doorway of the kitchen.

"Of course he is, Jenna," Trifina says. There is exasperation in her voice. "Kinsolver believes he's doing this for the family, but he's doing it for himself. And he won't let it go until...god knows what."

She turns to address me directly. "I'm going back to the city with Delano," she says, "...to see his father."

"Yes, Trif," I say, softly, "I understand. It makes sense; I think Del needs you now."

I don't know how much of Jenna's and my conversation Trifina has overheard, but it doesn't matter. She is making her point, as she did last night when she did not sleep in my room. We must let each other go. I have prepared myself for it. It is a familiar task – preparing myself to let go,...to move on.

This time, however, it feels different.

In the past, it would be followed by a hiding – a form of self-abandonment, as if moving on and hiding could, somehow, leave *me* behind,

314

along with everyone and everything and every place that made me. No more; I am certain now that it is the "hiding" that binds me most to Van Pelt.

So yes, I indeed intend to go to The FingerBreak...if there is a living witness, there can be an ending. And, as Del suggests, I will be able to close the door on it, once and for all.

"We were going to keep Dante with us," Trifina says, "Do you think you could stay put for a few days and watch him?"

Jenna looks over at me. "I'd like that," she says, "He's a sweet boy; it will make me happy to have him with us."

Trifina looks for my approval. "You know that I've been given custody of him."

"Yes, Francesca Van Pelt explained everything to me."

"Delano helped her file the papers, but I still don't know what the Senator will do."

"He has no legal claim, Trif. Dante was adopted by Francesca, not him."

"I know, but he must know by now that Dante is here...and when he discovers that you got to the Australian Lungfish before him, who knows what he'll do. Keep Dante close, ok?"

"I will, I promise."

"Tell Xaviero that I love him," Jenna says, "If I could, I'd come with you, but I'm too old and would just be in the way. Tell my boy that I will wait for him here. As I always have. To come home."

If only...

If only everyone here had planned to leave Slingerlands the day before. If only death had waited down there an extra day. Here or there, two missed chances...if only.

Shortly after Del and Trifina drove off, Lincoln Gilboa called to say that Xaviero DeAngelus had passed away.

Lincoln had been with him at Mount Sinai Morningside the evening before, but it was an elderly communicant from Mount Savior on Poverty Hill who was at his side when Xaviero died in the morning. A woman named Dorothy Stinson.

"Well, I'm happy for that, at least," Jenna sighs, brusquely wiping at a tear on her slack cheek. "Dottie was always a good girl. And a sweet friend to Xaviero in the years after Mina passed."

For a moment, Jenna is silent, as if recounting those years to herself, then says, "She was there that day,...did you know that? When Mina went into the water."

"Xavi told me," I say, quietly.

Dante is on the floor nearby and I am aware that he can overhear us. But he seems focused elsewhere, lying on his stomach, drawing a picture of a Triceratops. A toy model of the Cretaceous dinosaur stands on the floor about twelve inches in front of his face, and Dante's eyes flit, bird-like, from creature to pencil.

"Maybe it's some kind of blessing that Dottie was with Xaviero when he crossed over as well...an angel to carry him over to Mina," says Jenna, "They would have grown up together, Xaviero and Dottie, all things bein' equal."

Jenna pauses,"...But they weren't; it seems things never get to be equal. A mother should never outlive her child. I keep waiting for someone to come for me, but the Good Lord is keeping me around for something, I guess."

Watching Dante trying to capture the likeness of a creature that went extinct – along with much of life on earth – from the massive impact of a celestial body, I can understand why the intention of Jenna's "Good Lord" gets called into question. Humankind has always had a way of shifting blame from both the Empyrean's and Nature's indifference to human affairs.

The next morning, I kept my promise to keep Dante close. I have taken him with me to Conro's Flats. It is only a short drive from Slingerlands and the Altar-Boy is riding shotgun, keeping me well-entertained, disarming me with his quirky and precocious observations about his surroundings. This has always been true about the boy, whether in the airy attentions of people and their doings, or in the indifferent thickness of the natural world, Dante has always had a keen sense for what lies behind. It is no wonder that he and Del are so fond of one another, and why, in our banter, I often treat him as an equal.

"Del says that people are like trees," Dante says, absent-mindedly staring out the car window at the woods and shaley ledges that flank the winding road up into the Catskills.

"Oh, did he tell you which tree you were," I tease, "You sure he didn't mean that people are *related* to trees...from way back?"

"Uh-uh," Dante says, correcting me, "He says they can talk to each other and have babies; they get sad sometimes, and sometimes they push each other around. Just like people."

"Or maybe that's simply the sound of the wind in their treetops," I say, "And their seeds on the ground, and they certainly look sad with broken limbs or lost leaves. As for pushing one another around, perhaps that's the struggle in the forest for sunlight as one tree grows over another and shades it; the smaller tree can never grow up properly after that."

"Uh-uh," Dante says again, holding on to the arm rest as he is rocked back and forth with the car's winding ascent. "They can breathe, just like us."

I laugh, having been bested again by the Altar-Boy, "I can't argue that one, Dante."

"Del thinks you're like one of the really old trees...the big ones that have tunnels through them."

"You mean a Sequoia?"

Dante shrugs, "I saw a picture of one. There was an old car driving right through it."

"Being an old and hollowed-out tree is not a good thing to be, Dante. I'd prefer to be something else."

The Altar-Boy returns to the window and grows quiet. But a moment later, he turns back to me and says, "I don't feel so good." His face has turned a yellowish gray. The curves and switchbacks have caught up to him and he is clearly carsick.

"Hold on, Dante, I'm going to open your window and pull the car over."

The shotgun window makes it only part way down, before the Altar-Boy's sick stream spills at the top edge of the glass. Some of his vomit makes it clear, the rest splashes back onto his shirt. Dante looks down at himself with his arms spread to avoid touching the remains of his breakfast. Fruit loops and banana.

I feel a wave of tenderness, as Dante looks up at me. His arms are still spread apart as if beseeching, his young face a display of pained feelings – shame, embarrassment, confusion,...need. I am reminded, forcefully, that he is just a child.

And also, in his face, I am reminded of the other one. *He*, too, was just a child. The same age as the boy next to me. Perhaps, all those years ago, young JayJay Gallagher looked at Coykendall the same way that Dante is looking at me, arms outstretched, eyes wide with the mistake he'd made, the small handgun dangling off his trigger finger like an abhorrent appendage.

"It's okay, Dante...even trees get sick from cars."

A mile or so on, I turn off on a small overlook to help Dante clean himself up. A small creek tumbles down a rocky rivulet on one side of the road, flows beneath it and the overlook into a still pool below us, then falls over the pool's far edge into the mountain air. A small yellow and blue cast-iron sign marks "Conro's Falls." We are close. The Flats will be upstream.

Jenna had only a vague memory of the exact location of Shem's FingerBreak. She'd gone there once to hear Gianni and Lincoln Lincoln sing, but didn't approve of most of the goings on, or the women that came and went; she'd seen too many of the Dam builders come into the camp clinic with pus in their pants.

"Look for the old cement silos,...unless they've torn them down," Jenna had said. "One of the logging roads behind them went up there. Everyone used to walk in or go by buckboard. Maybe there's a road now... if Gust is still living there."

I find the silos, what is left of them. The steel trestle that once carried in the lime and the cement out is also there, a rusted skeletal tongue emerging from the gray silos caved-in maw. Skirting the old cement works is a dirt road that heads up a shallow incline into the woods and disappears around a bend. It is rutted with dry mud, and I can see tire imprints. They are recent.

Stopping at the edge of the forest, I peer up the road wishing I could see more of it – how long it is, where it leads, wondering whether it will carry us. It is getting late in the summer. The trees are thick with leaves, but the bright green of early summer has faded with the subtle shortening of days, less light, less chlorophyll. The forest is between things now; more colors will soon come but the screen of oaks and

319

hickories is holding fast to dull gray-green leaves, hiding everything in the thickness behind.

I drive slowly. The rented car is one those ubiquitous low-slung sedans with bland forgettable names that occupy the cheap end of rental options. It rocks in and out of the ruts in the road, signaling its displeasure as its aggravated undercarriage scrapes along the ridges of hardened mud.

Dante is feeling better. He unbuckles his seatbelt and leans forward in his seat with his hands on the dashboard, his head at the front windshield. He peers up the dirt road as if he has been asked to stand watch.

Turning at the bend in the road, we are met by a half-open metal gate about fifty feet in. It is open just wide enough for the car to pass through and looks as if it has been this way for years; its top hinge has rusted off and the gate leans backward off the hinge post. A red cedar has grown up through its metal rails. The remains of a large wooden sign covered with lichen and moss is propped against the latch post on the other side of the road.

Shem's Fin.......k are the only visible letters on the rotted sign; someone has been keeping these particular letters clear of the lichen.

"There it is!" Dante shouts, pointing up ahead.

I had been focused on the old FingerBreak sign and had not noticed the side of a log building edging out of the woods ahead. Even if I'd been looking right at it, Shem's FingerBreak would be easy to miss; it blends into the trees as if it had roots along with the other forest hardwoods.

As we draw near, the old cabin swings into view. It is much larger than I expected, three or four times longer than its width...like a dance hall. A covered porch with two continuous steps up from the ground runs the full length of the cabin, deep enough for a rowdy gathering.

A run-down green pick-up truck without plates is in front of the cabin, and I park behind it. There is a man sitting in the driver's seat and, hearing our approach, he turns in his seat to the gun-rack at his rear window. I can see that he is quite elderly, as he takes down a double-barreled shotgun and pushes open the truck door with his foot.

"Christ, Dante, get down," I whisper, suddenly very much regretting that I followed Trifina's request to keep Dante close. I have also kept the snub-nose Bulldog .32 close – the one from the Lungfish. I now regret that as well; it is in my coat pocket, safety on, a single bullet in its chamber.

Getting out of my car, I step away from it with my hands raised. "Mister Coykendall?...I just want to ask you a couple questions...I have a boy with me."

Gust Coykendall remains by the truck door but lowers the shotgun. He eyes me for a moment, then looks furtively left and right as if sensing something hidden in the woods. "A boy, a boy...is he here?" he asks, "Who are you, how do you know me? I don't see no one with you...did he send you?"

"I'm sorry, Mister Coykendall, I don't know what you mean. Who would have a sent me? Who were you expecting?"

"The boy...are you here with the boy...JayJay?"

The boy...JJ? Coykendall is not making sense. I lower one of my arms and gesture toward the car. "His name is Dante,...he's in the car," I answer, warily.

"I don't see nothing...he hides from me sometimes. But he's due any time now; he's coming, he always comes...he gives things to me." Coykendall begins looking around again, muttering quietly to himself. He has jammed the barrels of the shotgun into the dirt and is putting his weight on it with both hands on the buttstock.

Other than having lost quite a few of his teeth, Gust Coykendall looks pretty good for his years. His eyes are clouded, probably by cataracts, but his face is fairly free of wrinkles, and he is clean shaven. He also has a bit of belly girth which one rarely sees on a nonagenarian. He wears a pair of clean denim coveralls and a simple plaid shirt that was pressed fairly recently. Yes, he looks fit enough, but not that fit...someone has been taking care of him.

And his shotgun? I see now it could not do much harm. The top lever and both hammers are missing.

"Mister Coykendall, my name is Piedmont Livingston Kinsolver. I believe you knew my family. I'm Winifred Goldring's grandson."

Coykendall's aspect changes, as if whatever had been scrambling his mind has taken its leave and allowed him to gather back up the pieces of himself that it had disturbed. He leans forward on the shotgun, squinting at me. "Come closer," he says.

Before I get within a few feet of him, his toothless mouth opens wide in a look of surprise. "Oh Lord," he says,"...if you ain't Bramlett's ghost."

"Yes, I'm *his* grandson as well; and I know him by the name he took when the Gilboa Dam was being built – Piedmont...'*at the foot of the mountains.*"

"Oh Lord," Gust says again, "that thing...at the foot of the mountains." This time his godly invocation sounds like a warning, something he knows that I don't.

"You visited my grandmother a long time ago at the Museum in Albany. Do you remember?"

"Some things I remember, some things I don't. Maybe I did, maybe I didn't. I come and go," he says, pointing at his head, "He says I got that old folk's disease...wisenheimer or some such thing."

So, there it is...Gust, able bodied, addled brain. He's Jenna's opposite, her sharp mind set to a failing body. If you live long enough, one or the other is going to let you down. I can only imagine who the '*he*' is that is inside Gust's head.

I step to the side to place myself between Gust and Dante's view from the car.

"You gave her something," I say, reaching into my coat pocket and feeling for the pistol, but Gust raises his hand as if to stay mine, as if he knows what I'm about to show him.

"Whoa there, fella," he says, looking over my shoulder. He quickly lifts the useless shotgun up out of the dirt, arming himself again with his muddled imagination. "Sweet Jesus," he mutters, "...that ain't the boy. Who the hell is that?... a white nigger boy. I don't like this, Mister, you're getting me clouded up again."

Dante has left the car and come to my side. I let go of the pistol in my pocket and take hold of Dante's small hand. "It's okay, Gust. This is Billie Kinsolver and Lincoln Lincoln's grandson. You remember them too, don't you?" I am telling a little white lie about Dante's parentage, hoping to jog Gust back in time again.

The look on Gust's face is indeed cloudy as if he is retreating into the protection that his senility provides from the ghosts of his past.

"Gust, who's the boy you're talking about? Who's coming?" I ask, "... Is it the Senator?"

Gust re-emerges and breaks into a big smile. "He's all grow'd up now...and he's a big deal. A big one. He takes care of things. Let's me stay here. Brings me things...anything I want. Sometimes I just see the boy. All over again, but that's just sometimes...when I get confused. 'Course sometimes I see all of them. Just like when they was last here at old Shem's place...the FingerBreak."

He pauses with his thoughts, then looks up at the graying sky. "Rain's comin'," he says, wrinkling his nose, testing the moisture in the air. "Tell you what. You two come on inside, clean that boy up. I know the smell of weather and I know that sick smell, too. *He* had it on him,...it weren't no carsick 'tho. Some doings make it hard to hold anything down. For a man or a boy."

Gust climbs the steps to the porch, using his shotgun as a cane, then turns to me.

"I know what you want to hear, and maybe I just don't mind telling you. You saw that sign out there by the gate?...That's me, I'm Shem's Fink...and too goddamned old to care much about it any longer."

14

The Taking Line...

Elohim Gallagher
1924, Shandaken Intake Tunnel Chamber
"You see a meadow rich in flower and foliage and your memory rests upon it as an image of peaceful beauty. It is a delusion...not a moment passes in that holocaust, in every hedge and copse...battle, murder and sudden death are the order of the day." (T. H. Huxley)

A YOUNG BABY-FACED DEPUTY from The Bureau, Franklin Curley, took a seat at Darryl Pott's desk as the Chief stood by The Bureau door, putting on his coat. Potts was going off-duty, hopefully for the night, and was leaving Curley in charge of overseeing things...particularly, at the FingerBreak. Earlier that afternoon, the Virginians and their mule team had claimed the gold coin once again, and there was likely to be a bit of a ruckus up at the Flat's. Last year, a couple of drunken fellows got it in their heads to climb the conveyor at the cement works in a test of their tight-rope skills. One of them fell and pulled the other down along with him. Couldn't even count the number of broken bones on the ground below; cement dust mixed with mud dries plenty hard and makes for an unforgiving landing.

"They say that Shem's got more last names than whiskers on his chin...is that so?" Curley asked.

"Wouldn't surprise me, Franklin, but I've never heard any of them. Maybe down in the city they could tell you, but up here, he's just Shem. You can guess all you want, but he isn't going to give you a last name. He's a sketchy one alright.

"You sure you got those cells cleaned up for possible company tonight?" Potts asked, for the third time, opening the door to leave.

"Yessir, Chief, they're ready and waiting...if need be."

"Ok then, Franklin. I'm going to swing by the FingerBreak on my way home just so the rowdies, if they're not already too drunk, know we're paying attention. You send a few of the boys up later, every hour or so."

"You can count on me, Chief."

As he stepped outside and closed the Bureau door, Potts was not so sure. He was giving the young deputy his first real test. It had to come sooner or later; the ranks of the Bureau were thinning. The waning days of the Dam construction had arrived, and the BWS was starting to lay off men, even from The Bureau.

Potts thought again about Shem...and his whiskers. The small man who set up and ran the FingerBreak had a thin face and a long sharp nose that jabbed from a salted black mutton chop beard under a head of hair combed forward on his forehead, roman style. He had a habit of constantly cracking his knuckles in one hand or the other, and most imagined that was where the name of his saloon came from. Potts knew better; Shem was not to be messed with. He'd originally come north clean-shaven, and Potts had seen the file on him. He'd worked for a rack-eteer named Arnold Rothstein in Manhattan's Tenderloin District – the same Rothstein that "fixed" the World Series back in 1919. Shem was an "enforcer" and had run one of Rothstein's saloons on 34th Street out of a tenement called 'Hell's Kitchen.' The file didn't say why he left for Gilboa, but Potts figured there were debts due, maybe even a bad bet on the Black Sox Scandal. And there were indeed a lot of aliases mentioned in Shem's file; the hair and thick beard disguising his face seemed to be trying to hide them all.

At the FingerBreak, Shem was always friendly enough...in his skittish way. But he usually stayed out of sight, running the hall and the women from a private room secured from the inside with a heavy oak drop bar and a back door that opened to the thick woods behind the speakeasy. From time to time, he'd appear to keep tabs on the other room at the opposite end of the main hall. There was no drop bar on its door, men came and went; there was always one of the FingerBreak women inside. They called it the "Love Nest."

Shem's going to have his hands full tonight, Potts thought. The BWS always gave the men a day off after the Olympics. There wasn't much point in doing otherwise since their work would be pretty useless in the light of the next day.

There were only a few more waxing gibbous days until the full moon, but the howling inside the FingerBreak was already at full pitch as the Chief tied up his horse and climbed the steps onto the long covered porch. A few men were strung along it in small groups, some laughing, some arguing, some bent over the porch rail clearing their guts for more hard drinking. The front door of the former hunting club had been retrofitted with batwing saloon doors which helped to ventilate the sweat, vomit, and beer spills inside. It also made it easier for Shem's bouncers to toss an unruly man outside. Most, including Potts, knew to approach the door carefully, a little off to the side.

"Well, hello there, Chief," Piedmont Kinsolver said. He was on his way out, but stopped at the swinging doors when he saw Potts heading in. Stepping back, Piedmont held one of the batwings open for Potts.

"Good evening to you, Kinsolver. You keeping things orderly, are you?" Potts teased. He could barely hear Piedmont's greeting with all the noise coming out of the FingerBreak.

"Not rightly...getting too hot in there for my blood."

"Where you off to then?"

"Ah, cool air, maybe a quiet smoke...You missed the big singalong with Lincoln and Johnny. *The Camptown Races*...funny as all hell," Piedmont added with a smile, "Lincoln changed the words, poking fun at all the camps, but he really had it in for some of the locals...it was all in good fun, but a few didn't like it. You can probably guess, never liked any of the black Virginians in the first place." Piedmont shook his head with a smile, then leaned toward Potts, still speaking in a loud voice, "And Lincoln put my sister front and center; she probably put him up to it, too. They're likely to sing again if you stick around long enough."

"Maybe," Potts said. He points at a BWS Model T Runabout pickup that is sitting on the side of the road about fifty yards away from the FingerBreak, "I see you've got the Quarry fossils loaded."

"That I do, Chief. The BWS put me in charge and I'm trying my best to please her. Got a big day tomorrow."

"Oh, and how that be?" Potts asked, "You still seeing that Goldring woman, Piedmont?"

"I'm hopin' so. Haven't seen her in quite a bit and feelin' somewhat nervous. She'll be here tomorrow to look over the crates, and I want her to look me over as well. I'm hoping she'll come with me when I drive those rocks to Albany, 'stead of taking the rail back."

"Well, good luck with it. She's an impressive one,...smart as a whip and fine to look at too, tempting even to the eyes of an old bachelor like me."

The two men took their leave from one another, passing in opposite directions. But Potts did not venture very far into the FingerBreak. He remained by the door, taking stock of the activity inside...and letting others take stock of him. That was usually enough to calm things down if need be. For a while at least.

The saloon was close to fifty feet long end to end, with log walls that had been parged with plaster to keep out the wind. Newspaper clippings, old tintypes, and mounted animal heads – black bear, deer, and a moose – adorned the logs. A drinking bar, centered below the moose, ran the full length of the back wall between Shem's office and the money-making "Love Nest" at the opposite end. The bar had been hammered up with oak planks painted red with a countertop of tin sheet metal puckered with oil-can dimples. The stools along the bar were fully occupied, as were a dozen large tables strung along the outer wall. Shem had considered round tables, but ended up cutting corners,...quite literally. Over time, the original square tables had become either pentagons, octagons – or something in between – to make more sitting space. Men had their favorites and the whittled names in the tabletops marked them.

Shem's pianola stood in the corner near his office on a small platform stage. The upright player-piano was well-worn, but prized. Shem had trained one of his bouncers to change out the perforated paper rolls and work the foot pedals. But the man's poor sense of music matched the heaviness of his footwork. The accent and tempo levers under the keyboard were a mystery as well, even to Shem. It was only after Lincoln Lincoln took a seat at the pianola that the instrument found a partner.

Lincoln had a nice touch with both the pedals and levers that gave the revolving rolls above the keyboard their true calling, but it was on the keyboard itself, with no mechanical paper rolls to interfere, that Lincoln could really give the pianola life. Sometimes, he'd even play along with the roll mechanism, layering in harmonies.

Once Lincoln learned that Johnny of the Angel had a similar musical touch, the two of them would often sit side by side, improvising over the pianola rolls. Johnny only had eight fingers from the garroting he'd suffered during the war, but when he played with Lincoln, the simple music of the rolls disappeared in a weave of contrapuntal melodies and antiphonal chord changes. Lincoln, with friendly teasing, referred to their sessions as Johnny of the Angel's 'Eighty-Eights,' despite the fact that the pianola had only sixty-five keys.

In a final touch, Johnny of the Angel had secured Winifred Goldring's permission to have some of the stone carvers bring two of the lesser stump fossils to the FingerBreak. Too often, one patron or another had been grabbing the piano stool and taken it to their table as an extra chair. Johnny had his men place the heavy fossils next to each other at Shem's pianola at a perfect distance for his and Lincoln's legs. Shem was fine with the arrangement. Hell, those dumb rocks were famous now, and they sure as hell weren't going anywhere far from the pianola. If that was what Lincoln Lincoln and Johnny of the Angel needed to keep packing his house with their music, well then, okay.

Potts did not stay long at the FingerBreak. It was noisy but calm enough. All the tables were filled with men playing cards or swapping boozy stories. He checked in with Shem and told him that Deputy Curley would be swinging by later. It was both a courtesy and a warning. Shem reached under his desk and pulled out a small unlabeled bottle.

"It's from the city, just got a case of it," he said, offering the bootleg liquor to Potts, "It beats the White Dog we sell to most of those poor bastards out there. I think you should have the Bureau analyze it." That was Shem's code – *analysis* – for both his illegal alcohol and his habit of graft. Potts took the bottle and put it in his pocket, without another word. No point, no harm done.

Lincoln and Gianni were starting to sit down on the fossil stump stools at the pianola when Potts came out of Shem's office. He nodded a greeting at Lincoln, who smiled back and lifted the gold coin hanging off a ribbon around his neck. The Chief lifted his thumb in acknowledgement but kept walking through the FingerBreak toward the door. He avoided meeting anyone else's gaze; he was on duty, and everyone knew why he was there and that they were all part of it.

Nevertheless, he couldn't help but notice the boy. It was the ragamuffin they called JayJay – Eli Gallagher's little bastard. He was sitting on the floor with his back to the wall next to one of the tables where his father and Gust Coykendall were sitting with a few other locals. The boy looked bored and sleepy, idly picking at the floor with a whittling knife.

Christ, thought Potts, the kid's not even ten years old with no where better to go than to that man's wherever. And Gust, hell, he's full-grown, but not much better in the company he keeps. Potts wondered if Gallagher knew that Gust had abandoned the general store earlier that day. Stinson & Bidwell would be a heap of ashes by now. They seemed peaceable enough with one another, Potts thought, as he pushed through the batwings into the night air.

Passing by the Flats' cement works, Potts could still hear the FingerBreak and the singing:

My Camptown lady sings to me
Doo-da, doo-dah
A long tailed filly to her black sweetie
Oh, de doo-da day.
Gonna run all night
Gonna run all day
Should'a bet his money on the big black mule
but the poor ass bet like a fool

Chief Potts chuckled to himself and leaned forward to pat his horse's neck. Two of Lincoln's mules, harnessed to his buckboard, had been tied up near his horse outside the FingerBreak. Piedmont had said it true – his sister Billie was more than likely the bet that the 'poor ass' lost, and there were probably a bunch of them, heart-broke, in Gilboa.

Inside the FingerBreak, Elohim Gallagher was restless in his chair, feeling the flushed heat in his face, as if *he* was the one and only ass...and everyone there was laughing at him behind his back. He was no longer paying attention to the men at his table...or the boy on the floor. His attention was on 'the big black mule' at Shem's pianola. He'd planned on a visit to the Love Nest, but his ardor had waned with all the drinking he'd been doing and was now completely drained by the rage that was filling him in its place.

"Gust, I can't take this shit any longer. I got an idea, but you gotta help me." Gallagher rose from the table, holding himself as steady as he could. He pushed out his chest as if trying to loom as large as possible over what he believed were the lesser men in the FingerBreak. He held his glare at Lincoln Lincoln's back. "JayJay," he said, without looking down at the boy, "...get up on your feet; we're going for a ride."

"Where we going, Eli?" Gust asked, getting up quickly from his chair. He wobbled backwards, then sideways; one of the other men at the table reached out to stop his fall.

Eli had drunk as much if not more than Coykendall, and a dark sense of resolve and purpose had further riled his mind. "Just shut your goddamned pie-hole, Gust, and follow me," he said, dismissively. He turned his back on the pianola and lurched toward the door, ushering JayJay along in front of him.

Outside, night clouds had covered the moon and the darkness made it easy enough for Gallagher to unhitch Lincoln Lincoln' mule team without being noticed. "Get in, both of you," he slurred at Gust and the boy.

JayJay did what he was told and climbed up into the buckboard, but Gust hesitated, placing his hand on one of the mules' rumps to steady himself.

"Get the fuck on up, Gust. I'm going to need you to help me with this," Eli opened his coat, and tapped on the butt of a gun that was tucked into his waistband next to a large, sheathed bone-handled hunting knife.

Shem's bootleg liquor started rising in Gust's gut, and he took a few steps back.

"C'mon now, Gust," Eli said with a heavy-lidded and cold grin, "Whadda you think I'm gonna do, huh? You got 'spicious turn of mind."

Gust's sudden fear began to sober him, he could feel his heart quicken. He looked up at JayJay, who seemed unsure and confused by his father's intentions. This is no good for the kid, Gust thought to himself, and hoisted himself into the back of the buckboard next to the boy. "JayJay, stay close to me," he whispered.

Eli climbed into the driver's spring-seat and took up the heavy harness reins like he'd seen Lincoln Lincoln do countless times at the graveyards. "Let's run these asses over to Pine Mountain," he said, pushing the large handle of the wheel brake free, "...see if they're really worth their weight in that gold coin."

At first, the mules wouldn't back up off the rail, then Eli remembered Lincoln's call. "Teeyo, t'yo!" he said, in a loud voice and pulled back on the reins, "...Teeyo, t'yo!"

Moments later the buckboard was underway at a good clip down the road, out of the woods, past the cement works and past two men walking in the dark in the opposite direction.

In hindsight, Gust wondered if Eli had seen the men, as he had. Pontrain and Dexter, the Twincoat brothers, were Virginians. They would have run fast to the FingerBreak to tell Lincoln Lincoln that his buckboard and prized mules had been stolen. And if any of the men on the porch had been listening to Gallagher as he unhitched the mules, they knew where they were headed.

The run to Pine Mountain in Gallagher's dark mind was actually the run to the Riverside Quarry by way of the Shandaken Tunnel Intake Chamber. But as he reined on the two mules, he was still pondering the logistics of his plan. The animals were strong and plenty heavy to pull or push around, alive or dead. He would have to get real close to their necks and they could be real ornery; he'd seen them take a bite out of a body. Gust would have to help; he could be the one to hold 'em.

Gallagher's original thinking was to just shoot the mules some-where off in the woods where no one would find them, but he figured the stink of the carcasses would likely draw folks as quickly as the coy-dogs and vultures. And then there was the report from the handgun to consider; it wouldn't go unheeded, especially at night. No, Eli had a better idea. He put the reins in his left hand and reached for the feel of his hunting knife at his side. He had sharpened it just that morning and smiled to himself thinking how funny it was – him, Elohim Gallagher, a 'muleskinner,' too.

He pictured Lincoln Lincoln and Johnny of the Angel sitting on the Goldring woman's beloved fossils at the pianola, none of them knowing what was coming. Gallagher was striking out at all of them – as if Lincoln was only the embodiment of all the forces that had conspired to thwart and mock him at every turn. In his twisted thinking, his life was constantly being pushed backwards not forward...and they were all in on it somehow.

Gilboa had become Gomorrah, and the flooding of the Schoharie

Valley that he had once fought so hard against, he now welcomed. Holding out at Stinson & Bidwell's General Store had nothing to do with trying to save the town. It was a way to make him feel as if he could still resist his backward fall, putting his shoulder, riven with inchoate spite and anger, against Creation while he stood watch for Noah's return on the flood waters. In his tangled mind, Gallagher's plan for the Riverside Quarry seemed fitting, a perfect circumstance of time and place – cutting the throats of Lincoln's Virginia mules at the quarry, the spilling of their blood on to the stones of the Veronese carver, and the blood's slow seeping into the Goldring woman's antediluvian forest floor.

However, if the transitory nature of Time and Place has any lesson to offer, it is that circumstances can change plans at a moment's notice at any point on Earth.

The buckboard never made it to the Quarry.

It was overtaken on the road just before the Shandaken Intake Chamber by one of Hugh Nawn's Model T Runabout pick ups. As the truck passed, Gust Coykendall could see that the flatbed was loaded with wooden crates; he recognized them from Riverside Quarry. A few days earlier, he'd been paid to help crate the last of the fossils selected by Miss Goldring for the museum. The truck was due in Albany tomorrow evening, but now it was coming for them. He knew who would be at the wheel.

The driver of the pickup cut in front of the mules and stopped, blocking the buckboard's way. Piedmont Kinsolver rolled down his window. "You going somewhere tonight, Eli?" he asked, propping his elbow on the window ledge and looking out with disgust at Gallagher. "First you and that boy go smashing up Miss Goldring's fossils, now this."

There was a man sitting next to Piedmont in the cab, but in the dark, Gallagher could only guess that it was Lincoln Lincoln. Jumping down to the ground from the spring-seat, Gallagher was defiant. "I'm done with it, Bramlett, Piedmont, or whatever the fuck you want to call yourself now. You poisoned me to your sister, never gave me a chance, and that bastard next to you laughs at me like I'm the nigger."

"Not true, Eli..." Piedmont said calmly, as he stepped out of the truck. "You did that poisoning yourself. Deputy Curley is coming along soon; you can't be screwing around with folk's livelihoods."

What happened next, happened fast, with violence and few words.

Piedmont's deliberate calm had only further provoked – and was no match for – Gallagher's focused fury. Gallagher ran around the front of the truck to the passenger side, reaching at his waist as the truck door began to open. The gun was no longer in his waistband. For a split second he wondered where the hell it had disappeared to, where he might have dropped it, but his hand was just as quickly on the bone-handle of his hunting knife. The trucks headlights had somewhat blinded him, but he could see well enough to push hard against the door, trapping the man inside, and then, through the open window, thrust his knife into the neck of Johnny of the Angel.

There was a gurgle from his larynx, as Johnny fell back on to the seat of the truck, but Gallagher had little time to register his mistake. Out of the corner of his eye, he saw Lincoln Lincoln appear from between one of the crates on the flatbed and start to climb down. Gallagher had his knife in the man's back before Lincoln's foot touched ground. Lincoln groaned with pain and fell off the pickup as Gallagher went to silence him for good. He was stopped by Piedmont who had gotten hold of him, hauling him backwards with one arm around his neck, and the other fighting to get hold of the knife hand. Both men went down, with Gallagher thrashing wildly, digging his heels into the dirt and pushing the two of them along on their backs into the truck headlights.

There was a sudden close-in sound of a gunshot, then another. Piedmont, momentarily startled, saw one of Lincoln's mules rise up on its hindquarters. It was a fatal distraction, as he felt Gallagher's knife bang hard on his femur bone, and then, at his ear, the searing heat and concussive report of a third gun shot.

The mules took off, thundering the ground with their hooves as the buckboard lurched past the truck. Piedmont did not witness the stampede. He was elsewhere, listening to the gunshot echoing back at him from somewhere off in the woods, then to a silence, deeper and more complete than any he'd ever heard. His grip on Gallagher loosened despite his desire to hold fast, his strength seeming to disappear into the strange quiet along with the echo of the last gunshot. He lay still, his arms now limp at his side and the clamorous sound of silence ringing in his ears. He could taste the iron in his mouth and felt confused, not scared, just confused. Gallagher was gone, but someone else was there, a small pair of legs standing before him, backlit by the truck headlights as if they belonged to an emerging little angel and, in his last thought, he wondered dreamily if the angel was tending to the burning on the side of his face, cleansing it for him, like the Angel of Bethesda. He could feel the warmth of the water. But he could not hold this thought and closed his eyes. On the side of his face, the flow of blood running from his ear pooled momentarily over his eyelids, then crossed the bridge of his nose to join the blood ushering from his mouth and, from there, into the larger pool that held his head and framed his dying like a dark crimson aura.

"Jesus Savior...you've killed them all! All three of them!"

Gust Coykendall stood frozen in the middle of the road with his hands on his head, staring at Gallagher and the bodies lying on the ground like rag dolls.

Gust had been thrown from the buckboard when the mules bucked and ran, but not before he'd seen JayJay crawl over to the gun under the spring-seat. He'd tried to stop the boy from giving it to his father. But JayJay seemed to have had something different in mind. He'd climbed down and, holding the gun in two hands, began walking toward the fighting. He fired, wildly at first, but the second shot joined the deep knife wound in Lincoln's back. The third shot had been fired inches from Piedmont Kinsolver's head. The flash had burned Piedmont's cheek as the bullet grazed his ear, smashed through his collar bone, and sliced his aorta before coming to rest in the left ventricle of his heart.

"Weren't just me,..." Gallagher said, rising from the ground and rubbing his neck. He was looking with uncertainty at the boy.

JayJay had dropped the small handgun to the ground. The gunmetal had become too hot from the shooting and, he stood in front of the truck with his hands in his armpits, shivering, as if he were cold.

The headlights on the truck were beginning to dim from the pickup's draining battery. Gust moved quickly over to the boy and took hold of JayJay's shoulder.

"This is a bad business,...and a man's business; you should'a stayed close like I asked, JayJay," he said. The boy looked up at Gust. His expression seemed vacant and unfocused, lifeless. But, in the fading light from the truck, Gust could see that there were tears.

Gallagher had walked around and opened the passenger's side door. He'd taken hold of Johnny of the Angel's legs and dragged him out of the truck, letting him fall to the ground near Lincoln Lincoln. He grumbled at the amount of blood in the cab, wiping clean his knife blade on the seat.

"Gust, you gotta wake up; start this truck up so we can see what we're doing," he yelled. He looked up and down the service road to see if there was anyone coming. "And with those mules off in the night somewhere, we're going to need it to drive us out of here."

"You stay put, JayJay, I mean it," Gust whispered, "You don't need to be a part of this anymore; don't need to see it neither." He squeezed the boy's shoulder and went to the truck, calling out to Gallagher, "This is no good, Eli, what you gonna do now? How you gonna get out of this... and JayJay, too?"

"I got a plan, Gust...it's a good one. Start that truck and get over here," Gallagher said, without looking up. He had Piedmont's legs now and was pulling him to the edge of the road where both Lincoln and Johnny lay.

By now, both Gallagher and Coykendall were fully sober. Gust started the truck, grimacing at the blood slick on the seat next to him. Looking out the passenger window, he suddenly realized the dark plan that Gallagher had for all of them, alive or dead.

Lincoln Lincoln's fall from the flatbed had taken him to the edge of the service road where one of his legs was dangling over the open top of the wooden formwork for the next morning's concrete pour. It gave Gallagher's plan its idea, and he'd dragged Johnny and Piedmont into position along with it.

Gust wanted out. He'd wanted out of Gallagher's meanness, his fight-picking, his blaming everyone and everything for every trouble he'd just brought down on himself...and the abuse to that boy. Gust took hold of the steering wheel, thinking he'd make a run for it, but JayJay was still standing in the middle of the road, crying to himself.

"C'mere, Gust, help me roll 'em in," Gallagher said. He was at the passenger side door with his hands on the open window ledge, looking suspiciously at Coykendall, "This ain't the time for cold feet; you're in it, too. Who's to say who fired that gun...maybe it was you." Gallagher let that thought sink into Gust's head for a moment, then added "Hell, maybe you was just acting in self-defense but, even so, the shooter had no cause to go so crazy." Gallagher slammed both palms on the window ledge and laughed coldly, "I got all kinds of fingers I could point, Gust."

Coykendall had never been a match for Eli Gallagher, too simple in the head, folks often said; had a good heart, taking care of his old mother like he did, but he was like Gallagher's little bastard boy, both of them following that bad actor around like a pair of trained hounds.

So, Gust did what he was told.

They moved the three dead men, placing them at intervals along the formwork where the vertical bars of reinforcing steel offered enough clearance in the wooden forms to allow each man to fall all the way to the bottom. The last to go was Lincoln Lincoln. As they began to roll him over the edge, Gust saw the gold coin. It was still tied to the ribbon that Lincoln had hung around his neck at Shem's pianola. He reached for it but was too late. Lincoln fell and took the gold with him into the afterlife.

"Least we gave 'em separate graves." Gallagher had brought a hand lantern from the truck and was aiming it into the formwork to make sure the bodies had not gotten hung up on the steel rods. "Can't even see 'em down there...guess that's dust to dust," he said, then turning to Gust, "Let's get gone. You go get the boy into the truck, while I scuff some dirt to hide the mess here. You can drive us, since that's been your thinking anyway, ain't that right, Gust."

The boy was sitting between Gust and Gallagher when they approached the Riverside Quarry. Gust had put his coat down on the truck seat so JayJay wouldn't have to sit in the blood, and he'd kept looking at the boy out of the corner of his eye to see how he was faring. JayJay had stopped crying and wasn't talking, his eyes straight ahead; but he wasn't looking out at the road, he was looking at the gun that Gallagher had placed on the dashboard in front of him.

Gust had reached to move the gun out of sight, but Gallagher, without a word, had stayed his hand, signaling to both Gust and the boy that there would be no dodging, no forgetting what had taken place. They were in his world now.

"Well, lookee there," Gallagher said, leaning forward in his seat. At the turnoff, down in the Quarry, Lincoln's mules were standing quietly, still harnessed to the empty buckboard. "Turn down there, Gust," he said, "Might as well go all the way, take the lot of them to hell."

Gallagher pulled the knife out from his waist and reached for the door handle. It was the last act of his life. Gust had been wrong when he'd cried out that Eli had killed three men; not all had died at his hand. But a man's thinking, that alone, can cause death,...even his own. It was four men that Elohim Gallagher killed that night, not three.

The following morning, four of Hugh Nawn's Barrymore mixers pulled up to the Shandaken Intake Tunnel Chamber. They had gotten an early start; the sun had not cleared Pine Mountain and the last of a thick morning fog hung in the valley. The men on the ground were sleepy and annoyed to be working in a dense fog. It was dangerous, and they were having to be extra careful guiding the trucks that were backing up to the formwork.

One of the men remarked on the dried blood that had mingled with the dirt from the road, figuring some hunter was putting away venison for his household. None of Nawn's men saw the blood at the bottom of the formwork. Nor did they see anything else down there as the slurry fell from the mixer chutes and spread out along the bottom.

Over at the Riverside Quarry, Deputy Franklin Curley was walking Darryl Potts through the crime scene for a second and third time. There was just no clear sense of what had happened. The truck that Hugh Nawn had entrusted to Piedmont Kinsolver was there but there was no sign of Piedmont. And Lincoln's mules were there, a bit jittery in tangled harness, but not a scratch on them. And where the hell was Lincoln? Gianni DeAngelus should have been there as well. His team of stone carvers were uncomfortable with his absence and pacing about as jittery as the mules.

Everyone was spooked by the dead man inside the truck.

Deputy Curley had not touched Eli Gallagher's body. It was hard up against the closed passenger door, head hanging out the window. The outside of the door was awash with blood, bits of bone and brain tissue. Potts had never seen anything like it. At first, he wondered if Gallagher had taken his own life; the gun that would have produced a mess like that would have been inches from his head. Not many men would let a weapon get that close without a fight. But along with the missing men was the missing gun.

And then there was the smeared blood inside the truck on the bench seat. It did not belong to Gallagher and looked as if someone had done a very poor job of wiping it up. There was also a small amount of dried vomit, as if someone had been made carsick. It was on the dashboard and had run down into the truck's open ashtray, and it, too, did not appear to have come from Gallagher. Potts checked for footprints in the Quarry dust around the truck, but there were too many to tell much about comings and goings.

Gust Coykendall, who'd been seen getting aboard Lincoln Lincoln's buckboard, was questioned at his mother's house later that day. He knew nothing; said he'd jumped free with the boy within minutes of leaving the FingerBreak; Gallagher had gone off on his own and that was the last he'd seen of him.

What had taken place would remain a mystery.

Years later, when Potts took a law-enforcement position in Miami-

Dade, he recalled that confusing morning at the Riverside Quarry. He was in Princeton Florida, leading a search for a kidnapped boy and, while investigating footprints in the red dirt near the Everglades, he'd found the ones that belonged to the doomed child. And he remembered the Quarry – the strangeness of seeing the inexplicable tread marks from the soles of small shoes in the white stone dust.

Back at the Shandaken Intake Chamber, the concrete slowly rose, like an oozing flow of magma from a rupture in the earth's mantle – past the 'Taking Line' that marked the reservoir's final surface, and upward to the top of the formwork.

In a brief time, the concrete would cure and harden, casting the flesh and bone sealed within it like the doomed citizens of Herculaneum and Pompei. And in a much longer time, the human fossils would be on the move again – like all fossils – thrown back up to higher ground in the tectonic shifts of continents, endlessly seeking their temporary places elsewhere on the earth's surface.

15

The Vale of Siddim

James Jules Gallagher
1993, The Catskill Watershed
"... The Child is father of the Man;
And I could wish my days to be bound each to each by natural piety."
(W. Wordsworth)

I AM UNCERTAIN HOW much of Gust's story Dante has understood or even listened to. He's been sitting at the dusty piano at the far end of what used to be the main room of the FingerBreak banging away on the keyboard. There is no sound other than the thump and clack of fingers on cracked ivory. According to Coykendall, Shem's pianola has been dead to music for years, foot pedals rotted off and broken piano wires tangled in the upright's sound box. Even the original floor under the piano bench has apparently rotted out. Someone, a while ago, nailed 2 x 12 planks to cover the hole. "Pry them boards up, you'll find a couple of Mizz Goldring's stone stumps down in the crawl space," Gust had said, "Fell right through the old floor back in '56, just after Shem took off and the place shut down...some kind of heavy, they was."

The remains of the FingerBreak had hidden its past well. Gust lives mostly in one room of the old speakeasy – the 'Love Nest' – and in an outhouse off the front porch. There is no plumbing; a wood stove and a propane space heater hanging in a corner of the main hall offers the only warmth. The palimpsest of the hall's long saloon bar is visible on the floor despite all the ground-in dirt; one would have to know the FingerBreak's history to see it for what it was. The bar itself has long ago been dismantled for firewood. Shem's office door now opens onto a collapsed roof and a fallen rear wall that is nestled into the encroaching forest, as if Shem had finally made his getaway into the woods and closed the door behind him.

The ramshackle appearance of the FingerBreak mirrors Gust Coykendall's rambling account of what would have been a sickening event in most men's lives. It was delivered as if he'd only heard about the killings, second or third hand. I could not tell if his distance was a result of the staleness of time, his wobbly mind, or just an indifference brought on by even worse things that a very long life might have encountered.

"JayJay got sick by it, threw up all over himself...just like your boy there," Coykendall says, gesturing toward Dante. "I got him out real fast; we left that quarry lickety-split. Kept him at my mother's place for a few days; told the sheriff we'd jumped from the buckboard and walked home from the FingerBreak."

Gust looks around the hall as if he is seeing his memories – sitting at tables, laughing at the bar, flirting with the women. His eyes rest on Dante at the pianola.

"Dorlene Stinson took him in. Her little girls liked JayJay, so she and her new fella, that shit inspector from the city, adopted him."

"Shit inspector?" I ask. I want to hear his name spoken out loud.

"Yeah, they were shutting down all the outhouses, said it was gonna ruin the water." Gust laughs to himself. "Folks just kept shitting in the woods anyhow. Pelt was his name. He was okay enough, but I never had much truck with him."

Gust rises from his thread-worn armchair and walks stiffly toward the window.

"He'll be here soon enough...or maybe just his man. He takes care of me. Whatever I need, he always says." Gust chuckles again."

I tell him all's I need is to get on with it. There's old age, and then there's somethin' even more past that; ain't natural to approach a century."

Gust turns and looks at me. His clouded eyes seem suddenly clear and focused. "'Course, I know JayJay's a big deal...big deal, big deal. And I know he's paying me to keep my mouth shut...or watching me to make sure I do." Gust gives me a toothless grin. "He don't know what I told that Goldring woman, and what I gave her...your grandma."

"Gust," I say gently, "I believe that he knows everything."

I turn my back to Dante at the far end of the hall. I don't want him to see me take the handgun from my coat pocket. I hold the Bulldog .32 out to Coykendall by its barrel so that he can see the carved initials on the grip. He steps forward and peers down at the gun. His face falls and what little color had been in it drains away, as if he is seeing Gallagher's ghost. For a moment, I worry that he might lose his balance and go down, but instead he turns away and sits heavily in his armchair, sending up a cloud of dust motes. He closes his eyes, "I don't want to see that thing,...like the devil himself, it just won't stay gone, no matter what goodness we do..." His words trail off in incoherent mutterings as if he's wrestling with Satan himself.

Dante is suddenly there, at the old man's side. He touches Coykendall's arm, and Gust slowly opens his eyes, then shuts them again as if his eyelids can no longer carry the weight of his world. "No JayJay," he says, flopping his arm about limply, "you can't be here, it weren't your fault; it was the flooding made him crazy. Ma sees it coming – The Vale of Siddim, the Vale of Siddim. Get to that woman she says...get to that Goldring woman from the museum. Tell her the truth, tell her she don't know that it was the flooded forests of Gomorrah what she found...Noah, Ham, Shem, Japeth... they're coming on the waters."

Gust closes his mouth and is still. Dante remains at his side, with his hand on Gust's arm, but he is looking with uncertainty at the gun in my hand.

"It belongs to Mister Coykendall, Dante," I lie, "I came here, so I could return it to him. It's very old and has no bullets." That part – the part about the bullets – is also a lie.

Gust slowly opens his mouth, and I brace for the truth of things. But, instead, he only emits a long slow rush of air from his lungs,...as if his soul is making its final escape. Unburdened, his chest flattens, and his body recedes further into his armchair, into what appears to be his passing.

"Dante, move away from him. Come here." I speak gently, not wanting to alarm the boy; he's too young to understand that standing witness to a man's dying always brings another kind of loss along with it.

But I am relieved to see that my concern about Coykendall's mortality is unwarranted. A drip of spittle begins to run down Gust's chin, his tongue flicks at it, and he begins snoring lightly through his nose.

Dante looks more closely at Gust, then walks over to me. "He's drooling," he says with a sheepish smile, embarrassed for the old man.

"Let's let him sleep, Dante. We can come back another time, and there's one more stop I want to make before we go home."

Back in the car, Dante asks again if he can see the gun. He wants to hold it; I put him off. Although the safety is on, and I have placed tape over the safety's latch for good measure, I do not want to show the gun to him, much less put it in his hand. I can only imagine how angry Trifina would be with me if she knew that I'd heedlessly brought the Altar-Boy into my selfish scheme...of revenge, or whatever it is that I am after with this handgun.

I had wanted to look into Coykendall's eyes, the eyes that had last seen the men – Jenna Goldring's husband; Lincoln Gilboa's father; my grandfather. It was as if, in his eyes, I might see the men as well. Not as something imagined, but as afterimages burned onto Coykendall's retina. But I saw nothing, and at the same time, I saw all that I needed to see – the fading brightness of years gone by, and the futility of trying to reclaim them. And even if I could get hold of them again, his years could never belong to me, or anyone else for that matter. Looking at Gust's dull clouded cataracts was like looking at a marble bust from Greek antiquity whose seemingly sightless eyes are more like the inward turn of their gaze, inward to the knowledge and privacy of a life as it was actually lived, not as others imagine.

Nevertheless, I have decided to make a last pilgrimage to the place where, in a sense, my own private life begins.

It had been raining while we were inside the FingerBreak, not one of those mountain storms, but a more gentle fall as sodden southwesterly clouds brushed the peaks of the Catskills. The sun has now broken through, and as we clear the woods to the open road along the Reservoir, I can see the sparkle of quartzite off the stone facade of the Shandaken Intake Tunnel Chamber ahead. It is slightly below the road by the water's edge and surrounded by a chain link fence with razor wire along its top edge. There is a turn-off and an open gate, but it is posted for no trespassing. The driveway to the Chamber runs down the slope and turns parallel to the water, then levels off before disappearing behind the building.

I slow down, considering the trespass, as Dante suddenly leans forward, straining against his seatbelt and pointing toward the windshield, "Look! It's so big!" he cries, excitedly, "...And there're two of 'em!"

Dante has been looking up at the sky while I have been looking down at the water. He points out the double rainbow. The lower one has completed its evanescent arc, rising out of the hills of the eastern bank high over the water and the distant Dam, before falling behind Pine Mountain. The smaller upper rainbow hovers above it like its offspring, less colorful, more translucent and partial in its arc, but it shimmers like a galvanized fledgling in the light.

"Go faster. I wanna drive through it...go faster," Dante says, rocking in his seat back and forth against his seatbelt.

I smile at the boy, remembering having that same feeling as a child. The 'pot of gold' was always less interesting to me than the thrilling thought of passing into the colors, wondering how thick they would be, what they would feel like, and whether I could stand within the shower of hues as if a rainbow might be a true thing, anchored to the ground, waiting to prove to me that the world was indeed magical...if only I could get there in time. And that was always the problem, getting there in time before the light disappeared. Like all illusions, I was disappointed to learn that *that* was the rainbow's true thing.

"It'll be gone before we can get there, Dante," I say, pulling over to the side of the road. "Let's just watch it instead. Before it leaves."

Dante and I get out and, leaving our jackets behind, we climb on to the warm hood of the car to watch the spectacle. The rainbow frames the wide Dam with remarkable precision. The smooth surface of the Reservoir disappears over the Dam's top as if the arched spectrum of light had been designed for it – as a portal, engineered by a playful back-room mystic at the Board of Water Supply in order to allow the Schoharie to flow into another world.

Rainbows are like that. Otherworldly, intangible and elusive, open to whatever meaning we find in them. Is it Wordsworth's rainbow, the one that caused the poet's heart to leap when he beheld it? Or the gruesome 'bow' in Genesis that Coykendall's mother foresaw, the one offered to Noah after the Lord's killing Flood – *to be the sign of the covenant between me and all living creatures on the earth. That never again will the waters become a flood to destroy all life.*

The reflections on the water remind me of my strolls around the water of Central Park with Trifina – the upside-down city skyline at its edge. Here too, the placid surface is like the sheet of glass on a diorama, offering a lens and a trick of the eye into the curved reflected bowl of blue sky and cotton clouds. And at its edges, the upside-down hills above Gilboa reach into the water with their wooded limbs as if to reclaim the lost depth of the valley and the small creek that for millennia had carved its way between their eroding slopes.

I wonder if Senator Van Pelt sees what I only imagine when looking into this water, into this diorama – the town below as it was before the Flood. He had come into the world there...Gilboa, a sleepy settlement on a shallow rocky stream. He would have been born in one of the simple, white-washed houses, too young to have known the lively shops and stores strewn haphazardly along the single winding main street, or to have dodged the horse-drawn wagons and carriages kicking up dust in the summer, the sledges carving the snowbound street in winter as the farmers, loggers, and merchants plied their trades. He might have had his baby chin chucked by a downstate guest taking the mountain air at the hotel or been given a sweet from the general store. Perhaps he'd been carried to the creek to watch the sparkling fall of fresh water from the plank wheels of the grist and sawmills, or to the services of the Methodist Church on the high ground at the end of the street, the gold cross on its steeple glinting in the sun above the tree line.

His fate was the promise of a simple life broken; first, by the arrival of pleasant visitors with their innocent-looking surveying instruments, then the more sullen men with ominous diamond drills, followed by the court agents, noses buried in notebooks as they appraised and condemned properties by due process of law.

When the light and understanding of himself in a world among others came to him as a six-year-old boy, he was already drowning in a rising tide of anger and despair.

As I watch the rainbow's slow evaporation, I am still trying to square the child with the man. Trying to imagine a young desperate mind that does not yet comprehend the arc of time, the refraction of light on droplets of water, or the consequences of a butterfly's wing. And that unwitting child – James Jules Gallagher – now the man, Senator O'Graéghall Van Pelt, who has no recourse to take back what he did as a boy, only to hide it. What becomes of a child with an absent mother and a heartless father, a child who grows into taking his turn as an adult, from being uncared for to becoming uncaring?

In the wake of Eli Gallagher's death, James Jules had been offered a home with Reasonable Pelt and Dorlene Stinson, but the damage was done. Now, in the Senator's troubled hiding of his troubled younger self and troubled parents, what chance was there for him to be any kind of a father to Dante.

And yet, more than ever, I feel our strange kinship, Van Pelt's and mine. It is the self-protective hiding from the cycles of time, the repetition of past things, past mistakes. For him, it is the memory of what he did; for me, it is the fear of what I might do.

I have an affectionate feeling for the boy with me, perhaps even love for Dante, but I know I could never be father to him either. Or to anyone else. Trifina never asked, but she had sensed that she didn't need to.

"She's gone, Dante. The sun has taken her away, I'm afraid," I say.

There is no longer anything but open sky over the Dam. Dante sits forward on the car hood and clasps his knees with his arms. He sighs happily, then turns to me and points at the open gate to the Intake Chamber. "Can we go down to the water?" he asks.

"I don't think we should, Dante, this is probably not the best place, they don't want trespassers."

"Why not?"

"This is where the water leaves the Reservoir and goes down to the city...to your home at the St. Urban."

Dante looks at me and frowns as if I'm teasing him...or if the thought of returning to his home at the St. Urban is making him uncomfortable. I can't help but smile, thinking what a pair of misfits we are.

"No, it's true, Dante," I say, "In fact, it used to go to Waterhouse's gatehouse in Central Park. It's hard to explain exactly how it works, but water always flows downhill; it's gravity. And if you don't block its path, a waterway, it will flow for miles and miles and won't stop until it reaches the ocean."

"Is it true that there are houses under the water?"

"Once upon a time, yes."

"And some people, too...that drowned?"

"No, everyone had left the valley when the water came."

"Del said there is a very old forest under the water, and the houses were built from the trees in it." Dante looks thoughtful, then says, "Gilboa trees, I think."

"Well, I suppose you could say that, but I don't think he really meant those actual trees. The Gilboa forest was even longer ago...and even harder to explain, Dante."

Del's conflation of Time for Dante does not surprise me, and I am glad to see this body of water through the eyes and imagination of the child, now in his and Trifina's care. It is as if they are both here, in Dante,

352

helping to pull me free of the gravesite of the men below, somewhere down in the Chamber's foundation walls.

But even as this thought occurs to me, I am pulled back.

A black sedan appears from behind the building and heads up the driveway toward us. Dante sees it as well, and I realize right away that I am not yet free.

"That's the car that was at the house," Dante says in a frightened voice, "...my father." He jumps off the hood and scrambles into the car, locking the car door and slumping out of sight in the front seat.

As the sedan draws along side, it slows and comes to a stop. The driver's door opens, and the Senator gets out. Van Pelt is alone and looks disheveled, older with heavy bags under his eyes, as if he has been sick or without sleep,...or left his body altogether in order to let James Jules "JayJay" Gallagher into the husk.

"Kinsolver."

He addresses me as he often does at the St. Urban; it is an acknowledgment that I am standing there in front of him, not an actual greeting. But, although I am still wearing my doorman grays, his tone is different, as if we both know, this time, we have real business with one another.

"Gallagher," I reply with a nod.

The Senator grimaces at the sound of his name. He draws a deep breath. "You found the fish."

"Yes."

"And I imagine you also found something inside it?"

"Yes."

He takes a step forward and points a finger in my face. "Listen, Kinsolver, you may think you know what is going on, but you don't. This is state business, I can have you arrested for stealing from the Museum."

I ignore his threat. "I don't think so,...I've also found Gust Coykendall."

For a moment, he glares with his hand still raised. I brace myself in the event he is thinking of taking a swing at me. "Be careful,..." I say, "I am not your wife, or your son...or anyone else you think you can fuck with."

But Van Pelt has been disarmed by the mention of Coykendall. He tries a different tack.

"I don't remember what happened, Kinsolver – what Coykendall says took place, I was just a young kid. And Coykendall...he's been senile for years, making up stories."

"Is that why you've been taking care of him? To help him with his memory or to make sure he loses it."

"I don't know what you're talking about, who do you think you are anyway?" He looks me up and down again, as if my wrinkled uniform says it all.

"You know who I am...Winifred Goldring's grandson. And the three men buried down there," I add, pointing at the Intake Chamber, "one of them was Piedmont Kinsolver. Maybe you were too young to remember that name...it's my name."

Van Pelt looks increasingly uncomfortable, cornered. It is dawning on him that I know a lot more than he suspected.

"And you're getting all this from that...*fish*?" he says, derisively. He is trying to be dismissive of both me and Winifred's taxidermy, as if I'd imagined that the Lungfish had used its respiratory bladder to tell me its story.

"*Neoceratodus forsteri*...Winton Conrad must have told you its proper name when Hanrahan carried its replacement to the trunk of your car. Winifred Goldring took the original from the diorama when it was being dismantled. It has held her secret...and yours."

"You're as crazy as Coykendall."

"Coykendall wasn't crazy when he gave her the gun. And I'm not so crazy that I can't read the initials on the grip...JayJay...the Gallagher family gun."

His shoulders slump and his arms hang heavily at his sides. He looks defeated, a far cry from the fit elderly Princeton Man, Board Trustee and Grandee of the St. Urban.

"You...you have the gun?" he asks.

"Yes. I have it with me."

"What do you plan to do with it?"

I do not answer and hold fast to his eyes. I watch them widen as his mouth slowly drops open in what appears to be fearful understanding. He steps toward me and raises his hand again, but now he seems to be beseeching me for forgiveness.

"You have to understand...I was scared," he says, plaintively, "...afraid of what he might do...of what he did, things he did to me. I just wanted to please him so he would stop."

"Why did you keep his name – O'Graéghall – and hide it at the same time?"

"I don't really know why, maybe it was atonement. Or to face down my father's ghost. That's why I'm here, that's why I have come here every year of my life; to offer myself and him back to the ghosts of the men down there. Each year, I think I will go into the water to join them. But I don't, I've never been man enough."

He straightens up and clenches his jaw, then says, "Go ahead, Kinsolver,...finish this. Get that goddamned gun and put an end to it."

"I'm going to do that, Gallagher. I'm going to put an end to it for all of us."

I let my words sink in.

But my plan has always been his reckoning, not his death, and there is something even more he can restore to the families.

"I'm going to give the gun back to you," I say carefully, "...in return for Dante."

He opens his mouth to speak, but I stop him.

"In return for your promise not to interfere with your wife's wishes, not to interfere with Delano DeAngelus or Trifina Lincoln. You wouldn't have known or remembered those names either, but their families are buried here, as well," I say, nodding at the water, "Dante wants to live with Del, and he deserves the chance to grow clear of the trouble that you'd only pass down to him. You as much as anyone should understand this.

"I believe that you *were* a lost boy and I believe that, even with the pain Winifred must have felt learning the truth, she was giving you a chance when she buried the handgun inside the Lungfish. She always had the long view...about time and change. The Gilboa Forest diorama told the story of man's fate, I'm not surprised that she placed your fate there as well. Now's your chance to pay her back."

"He's in there, isn't he?...Dante," Van Pelt speaks quietly. His expression has gone vacant, and he is looking at the car. "And it looks as if he has something else in mind for me."

Turning, I see Dante leaning forward into the windshield. He is holding the gun in both hands; the tape that I'd placed on the safety is gone.

My heart pounds and I feel a wave of dizziness, as if the wheeling of the earth has reversed itself, mocking the cycles of time and the burst of oxygen from the Gilboa Forest.

The Gallagher gun – once again – is aimed at the father.

I step in between, to meet the bullet.

* 16 *

The Gun-Man...

Belle Stikkey
2013, Seminole Hammock Home for Assisted Living, Indiantown, FL
"Man, in a word, has no nature; what he has is…history"
(Jose Ortega Y Gasset)

I WILL TRY TO find a proper ending.

Not my own. Like anyone, it is not for me to know my ending, it is for others. I may experience my dying when it draws near, but the end itself – Death – I'm pretty certain *that* moment eludes every sentient being. How could we experience the nothingness of it?

No,…one's death does not belong to the knowing self, it belongs to others, to those who are alive to witness it and say that it was so.

I'm now almost as old as Senator O'Graéghall Van Pelt was when his body was found floating in the reservoir. It was unexpected, but there was an uncanny logic to it just the same.

I had no hand in his death, nor did anyone else. It was just Van Pelt himself. He was sending a message and, although he would not be around for the reply, he knew there would be a few who would read it.

It was the late Waterhouse Hawkins who found him in the south basin of the Central Park Reservoir – wrong reservoir, same water – with a bullet hole in his heart. He'd left a note about "putting an end to it"and that an unidentified doorman by the name of James Jules Gallagher would be taking care of his affairs.

Of course, no doorman by that name showed up, nor any doorman for that matter. The superintendent of the St. Urban, Buckles Hanrahan, was questioned, but he had nothing to offer the authorities, except Winton Conrad.

Conrad was out of town, representing the Museum of Natural History at the opening of the re-furbished Gilboa Forest Diorama in Albany's State Museum. He had delivered the plaque that was attached on the wall next to the exhibition:

In Gratitude for his Generosity and Support
for the Gilboa Forest Diorama:
State Senator O'Graéghall Van Pelt

In his interview with the New York City police, Conrad apparently left it at that. The Lungfish in the diorama was a great sensation, but it didn't seem to get a mention to the NYPD.

A City detective even tracked down Van Pelt's former wife Francesca. She was living abroad on the Adriatic coast of Italy, the city of Rimini of all places. She'd remarried and was not helpful either, only suggesting that Van Pelt had been a complicated and private man. He had not tried to contest the second adoption papers of their son, Dante, but his affairs were always his, not hers, she maintained.

As for the gun, I imagine the police would have dredged the south basin and found it. I picture it in a ziploc bag at the bottom of a cardboard box, stacked behind other boxes, on a dusty metal shelf with peeling identification labels, somewhere in a far corner of a precinct basement.

It's life is over. And even if there is yet another resurrection to come, it is likely and fortunate that I'll not be around for it.

No one from the NYPD ever came for me, or Del...or Dante.

I would have been hard to find anyway since I was already here, a thousand miles away in Indiantown, Florida, living most of the time under the name of Livingston 'Skeegie' Stikkey.

The name is a compilation of the drifting identities that Belle Stikkey sees when she looks at me – my father, her first husband Rembrandt... and, well, her son. But, instead of calling me 'Cash,' she calls me by the name of his stuffed alligator, the ruined hand-puppet alligator that the Miccosukie scouts found abandoned in the Glades before Lincoln Gilboa and my father found the boy.

Belle will die soon. She can no longer take care of herself, but she is in good hands, and I am very nearby.

Saskia is here, living in Indiantown as well...with Belle. They're both at Seminole Hammock where I work now as the Pool-Man.

I'm actually the head groundskeeper at the assisted living community, but early on, when I was pulling a palmetto leaf from a drain, one of the old swags sitting poolside with a group of admiring elderly ladies referred to me as the Pool-Man...and it has stuck. Most of the residents wouldn't know the difference anyway.

Like Belle. She will never again know who I am, despite Saskia's cheery reminder whenever I come around.

I also don't think she knows any longer who the woman is in the photograph on her bedside table. It's a gelatin silver print from the 1920's. I remember it from my childhood and being told, back then, that it wasn't a family photograph; rather it was a picture of a woman that Belle had simply admired since she was a child. In the photograph, a tall woman in a broad-brimmed touring hat and jodhpurs is standing next to the sidecar of a motorcycle. She's holding a field rock hammer and is smiling at the camera. It's a loving smile, not meant for the photograph, but for the photographer.

I am glad to be here for Belle. For better or worse, she was a mother to me after accepting Mina's dark offer, and I owe her. I'm also glad that I could convince Saskia to come south after Linc died. I owe her as well, for stepping in the times when Belle slipped free from her mothering and fell into her own dark place.

Over the years, Lincoln Gilboa and Waterhouse Hawkins had made a point of attending the Civilian Conservation Corps reunions every five years or so. Initially, they were held at a dozen different camps across the country, but as the recruits died off, the reunions became a single reunion at a single camp. It was good fortune that the Highlands Camp was selected for the 75th Anniversary. Linc and Waterhouse got a last look. Linc joked about going to get back the missing piece of his tongue; I imagine Saskia gave him a quick scolding slap on the rump.

Neither of the men were alive to make it to the 80th at the 'bug camp' in the woods of Boiceville, New York. Perhaps it was just as well. The Boiceville site is only a few miles south of the end of the Shandaken Tunnel. Schoharie water runs right through it.

In the early morning hours of October 20th, 1927, the Schoharie water passed the 'Taking Line' and went over the top of the Dam. By then, the men of the camps were gone, along with most of the Gilboans. Hugh Nawn had sent his own crew back to Roxbury, but he himself stayed to witness the moment. Gone, too, were the construction managers and engineers from the Board of Water Supply. Only Thaddeus Merriman, Sidney Clapp, and Reasonable Pelt were on hand to join Nawn and the new mayor of New York City, Jimmie Walker. Walker had brought along family and some of his Tammany Hall pals to witness the completion of the last reservoir of the Catskill Water System, the City's crowning achievement.

It had been hard to predict exactly when the Schoharie water would fill to the basin brim; a lot depended on the rainfall, evaporative rates, and the tinkering with the lower outlet in the Dam itself. But Merriman assured the celebrants that it would be a daylight affair and had authorized the closing of the lower outlet the day before to make good on his promise.

But water seeks its own level, as it did millions of years before when the Catskill Sea rose to cover the ground of the Gilboa Forest and drown the feet of Winifred's beloved *Eospermatopteris*. This was only a second coming.

Perhaps Merriman miscalculated the fissures in the ground among the many fossils still buried in the reservoir floor as they took the water down to their mineralized roots. I like to think so. When night fell, with the Schoharie still lapping at the course of carved coping stones on the Dam lip, Merriman called for a convoy of trucks and had light poles hooked to their batteries. It was close to two in the morning when the first small spills went over at the random low points on the coping, then joined one another in what would be, at first, a quiet, seamless wash down the Dam's dry face into the severed bed of the original Schoharie Creek. Within minutes, the sleepy men and women would have had to stand back from the spray, barely able to hear one another over the thundering sound of the cascade echoing off the hills.

None of our family was there. Jenna was helping Winifred prepare for the opening of the Gilboa Forest Diorama later that same week. Hugh Nawn would attend that ceremony as well. Winifred had mentioned in one of her notebooks that the Dam builder from Roxbury Massachusetts had been pursuing her. He was a nice man, she said, respected her work and even took her side over the BWS and his own profit margin. But he returned to Roxbury with only one of her fossils, not with her broken and hardened heart.

Winifred and her sister Mattie had died relatively young, but Jenna crossed the century mark before passing in her sleep in Slingerlands. Dottie Stinson had been there in the family house caring for her, just as she'd been there in the hospital when Jenna's son Xaviero died in '93, and also at the Schoharie when Jenna's daughter-in-law died in '55.

Delano DeAngelus was grateful to Dottie, but I think he was just as happy when she moved to California to live with her twin sister Starling's family while he remained, alive and kicking, on the far side of the country.

Trifina comes south to Seminole Hammock every six months to visit her mother. Sometimes Del and Dante come with her, which is fun for Saskia and me. Even Belle seems to perk up in their company.

I turned over my penthouse on Museum Mile to Del and Trifina as a wedding present. They renovated the place and turned my old bedroom into a guest room with a view – leaving the Central Park Reservoir and what lies beyond to the thoughts of others. There is a painting on the wall next to the window – Jacob van Ruisdael's *Torrent in a Mountainous Landscape*; Del's final 'crazy fucker' touch,...with an assist from Trifina.

Del and Trifina have two teenage daughters now – twins, Queenie and Remmy. The two girls have a lively social life in the city and visit their grandmother less often. I hear that they idolize their adopted older brother.

And Dante? He followed in his adoptive parents' footsteps and works in The Department of Earth and Planetary Sciences at the Museum of Natural History. I like to think that with his doctorate in Environmental Studies, Dante completed my degree for me. But the earth has changed

and the sciences along with it. Global Warming is Dante's area of expertise – deforestation, melting glaciers and rising waters. When he visits,
he makes the point that Seminole Hammock will be one of the first
places to go under as the spreading sea finds its new shoreline. Perhaps
he's right, but Belle and Saskia aren't going anywhere. Nor am I, not
anymore. Seminole Hammock is as good a place as any to lay down my
bones. Dust to dust, Saskia says. Water to water makes more sense to me.

My only regret is that they will say of me: He did not obey the
Miccosukie Law of Seven Generations – to flourish at the center of
Family Time. What can I do? It is too late – my ancestors, always absent;
my descendants, never to be.

Dante and I rarely mention the last time we saw Van Pelt, or the rainbow, or the exploding windshield when the gun discharged. Dante had
been lucky he was not hurt, and I'm lucky not to have to live with that.
He's tried to let me off the hook for leaving the gun where he could get
at it, but I'm still ashamed when I think of what happened, what *could*
have happened.

Both Van Pelt and I had misread our fates that day; we were too far in
the stories of our lives to imagine Dante could be anyone other than the
boy Van Pelt had been. But Dante was only playing with the Gallagher
gun, feeling its heft, and studying the initials on the grip. He had already
turned away from us when the lone bullet shattered the rear window of
the rented car.

Speaking of laying down bones, I don't dream as much anymore.
Although there is one; one dream, that is. I am wearing my charcoal gray
gabardine coat with its white and maroon stripes, polished brass buttons,
and double fleur-de-lis at the end of each sleeve. My doorman's cap with
its two rows of braid and matching cord sits snugly on my head. I am
standing watch over Dante, the boy. He has a gun. Not the Bulldog .32,

but a different one. I am uncertain but have the sense that it is the Black Powder Frame Peacemaker that Winifred Goldring brought with her to Gilboa. Dante is looking at me with a cute mischievous smile on his face as he shoots at the glass of a Diorama. It is not a malicious act; he's offering me a gift. I don't recognize the Diorama – there is no Lungfish – but when the glass shatters, rather than falling in a heap of jagged shards, it bursts into tiny crystals that float upward, free, like small stars twinkling in the light. And in each star, I can see bits of the world reflected back at me – the mirror of nature – mountains, forests, streams, and river valleys, all the other places on earth where my life might have unfolded along the slow grinding fault lines of the ever-drifting ground beneath my feet.

Afterword

The Door-Man is based on actual events that took place in upstate New York at the beginning of the 20th century.

A large valley in the Catskill Mountains at the town of Gilboa was taken over by New York City through the power of eminent domain in order to construct a reservoir for the city's water system. Despite the attempts of the families and businesses of Gilboa to block the reservoir and resist forced re-location, construction on the half-mile long dam across the valley's Schoharie Creek began in 1917.

That same year, fossils were uncovered in one of the sandstone quarries supplying faceblock for the dam. A young paleontologist from The New York State Museum in Albany, Winifred Goldring (1888-1971), made the identification of an ancient forest, dated to a vast flood from the Devonian Period, 350-400 million years ago. The fossils drew international attention as the oldest trace, yet discovered, of the botanical explosion that opened the path for the evolution of humankind.

As the scientific community celebrated the significance of the fossils and urged a delay in construction to further explore the area, the citizens of Gilboa held out hope that their efforts to remain in their homes might be realized.

Nevertheless, most of the fossils were ultimately re-buried, and the doomed town of Gilboa now lies under the Schoharie Reservoir water.

Although *The Door*-Man is a fictionalized account of the fossil discovery and its aftermath, many of the events in the book actually took place, and many of the people from 1917 onward actually existed. Like Winifred Goldring's, their real names have been retained. Also, some of the dialogue has been drawn, with minor editing, from letters and files researched in the archives of the NY State Museum in Albany and elsewhere. Lastly, while the precise dates of certain events have been altered, their truth and chronological order have not been changed.

So it is with the mixing of fact and fiction.

In Walker Percy's last novel, *The Thanatos Syndrome,* his protagonist, Dr. Tom More, muses that "...small, disconnected facts, if you take note of them, have a way of becoming connected."

There is a lot in this simple remark, and it's exceptionally good advice for a writer. It suggests how wonderfully woven the world is – as if the world and its "facts" are *there* for the taking if one only takes the time and allows their imagination to do its work.

I am indebted to the environmental historian William Cronon, for his writings on the clash of nature and culture; to journalist Diane Galusha for her book, *Liquid Assets: A History of New York City's Water System*; and to architects Kevin Bone and Gina Pollara for their book, *Water-Works.* Also, to Linda Van Aller Hernick, former Paleontology Collections Manager at the NY State Museum, who provided access to Winifred Goldring's letters and the Gilboa Fossils. All of these people helped to provide the facts and provoke the fiction. I would also like to thank my editors at Fomite Press, Marc Estrin and Donna Bister, for their unwavering and good-natured support.

Finally, thanks to my intrepid readers, particularly the writer Andrea Barnet, whose fine book, *Visionary Women,* could easily have included Winifred Goldring.

Peter Matthiessen Wheelwright is a novelist, architect, and Emeritus Professor at The New School (Parsons School of Design) in New York City.

As It Is On Earth, his first novel, received a 2013 PEN/Hemingway Honorable Mention for Literary Excellence in Debut Fiction.

He comes from a family of writers with an abiding interest in the natural world. His uncle is three time National Book Award winner, Peter Matthiessen, and his brother, Jeff Wheelwright, is an earth-science journalist and author.

Fomite

More novels from Fomite...

Joshua Amses — *During This, Our Nadir*
Joshua Amses — *Ghatsr*
Joshua Amses — *Raven or Crow*
Joshua Amses — *The Moment Before an Injury*
Charles Bell — *The Married Land*
Charles Bell — *The Half Gods*
Jaysinh Birjepatel — *Nothing Beside Remains*
Jaysinh Birjepatel — *The Good Muslim of Jackson Heights*
David Brizer — *Victor Rand*
L. M Brown — *Hinterland*
Paula Closson Buck — *Summer on the Cold War Planet*
Dan Chodorkoff — *Loisaida*
Dan Chodorkoff — *Sugaring Down*
David Adams Cleveland — *Time's Betrayal*
Paul Cody— *Sphyxia*
Jaimee Wriston Colbert — *Vanishing Acts*
Roger Coleman — *Skywreck Afternoons*
Stephen Downes — *The Hands of Pianists*
Marc Estrin — *Hyde*
Marc Estrin — *Kafka's Roach*
Marc Estrin — *Speckled Vanities*
Marc Estrin — *The Annotated Nose*
Zdravka Evtimova — *In the Town of Joy and Peace*
Zdravka Evtimova — *Sinfonia Bulgarica*
Zdravka Evtimova — *You Can Smile on Wednesdays*
Daniel Forbes — *Derail This Train Wreck*
Peter Fortunato — *Carnevale*
Greg Guma — *Dons of Time*
Richard Hawley — *The Three Lives of Jonathan Force*
Lamar Herrin — *Father Figure*
Michael Horner — *Damage Control*
Ron Jacobs — *All the Sinners Saints*
Ron Jacobs — *Short Order Frame Up*
Ron Jacobs — *The Co-conspirator's Tale*
Scott Archer Jones — *And Throw Away the Skins*
Scott Archer Jones — *A Rising Tide of People Swept Away*
Julie Justicz — *Degrees of Difficulty*
Maggie Kast — *A Free Unsullied Land*
Darrell Kastin — *Shadowboxing with Bukowski*
Coleen Kearon — *#triggerwarning*
Coleen Kearon — *Feminist on Fire*
Jan English Leary — *Thicker Than Blood*
Diane Lefer — *Confessions of a Carnivore*

Fomite

Diane Lefer — *Out of Place*
Rob Lenihan — *Born Speaking Lies*
Colin McGinnis — *Roadman*
Douglas W. Milliken — *Our Shadows' Voice*
Ilan Mochari — *Zinsky the Obscure*
Peter Nash — *Parsimony*
Peter Nash — *The Least of It*
Peter Nash — *The Perfection of Things*
George Ovitt — *Stillpoint*
George Ovitt — *Tribunal*
Gregory Papadoyiannis — *The Baby Jazz*
Pelham — *The Walking Poor*
Andy Potok — *My Father's Keeper*
Frederick Ramey — *Comes A Time*
Joseph Rathgeber — *Mixedbloods*
Kathryn Roberts — *Companion Plants*
Robert Rosenberg — *Isles of the Blind*
Fred Russell — *Rafi's World*
Ron Savage — *Voyeur in Tangier*
David Schein — *The Adoption*
Lynn Sloan — *Principles of Navigation*
L.E. Smith — *The Consequence of Gesture*
L.E. Smith — *Travers' Inferno*
L.E. Smith — *Untimely RIPped*
Bob Sommer — *A Great Fullness*
Tom Walker — *A Day in the Life*
Susan V. Weiss —*My God, What Have We Done?*
Peter M. Wheelwright — *As It Is On Earth*
Suzie Wizowaty — *The Return of Jason Green*

Writing a review on social media sites for readers will help the progress of independent publishing. To submit a review, go to the book page on any of the sites and follow the links for reviews. Books from independent presses rely on reader-to-reader communications.

For more information or to order any of our books, visit:
http://www.fomitepress.com/our-books.html

CPSIA information can be obtained
at www.ICGtesting.com
Printed in the USA
LVHW111524210622
721681LV00006B/59